Kelly Elliott is a *New York Times* and *USA Today* bestselling contemporary romance author. Since finishing her bestselling Wanted series, Kelly continues to spread her wings while remaining true to her roots and giving readers stories rich with hot protective men, strong women and beautiful surroundings.

Kelly has been passionate about writing since she was fifteen. After years of filling journals with stories, she finally followed her dream and published her first novel, *Wanted*, in November of 2012.

Kelly lives in central Texas with her husband, daughter, and two pups. When she's not writing, Kelly enjoys reading and spending time with her family. She is down to earth and very in touch with her readers, both on social media and at signings.

Visit Kelly Elliott online:

www.kellyelliottauthor.com
www.twitter.com/author_kelly
www.facebook.com/KellyElliottAuthor/

THE LOVE WANTED IN TEXAS SERIES

Without You

Love Wanted in Texas
Book One

Kelly Elliott

piatkus

PIATKUS

First published in 2014 by K. Elliott Enterprises
First published in Great Britain in 2016 by Piatkus
This paperback edition published in 2016 by Piatkus

1 3 5 7 9 10 8 6 4 2

A CIP catalogue record for this book
is available from the British Library.

ISBN 978-0-349-41342-6

www.hachette.co.uk

www.piatkus.co.uk

WANTED
family tree

Ten Years Old

I stood there and listened to my younger brother, Colt, complain about the girls playing football. I was ten, and my brother was nine, but right now, he was acting like a two-year-old.

"He's just afraid we're going to kick your butts," my cousin Grace said as she folded her arms and stared my brother down.

Will walked up to me. "You can't play, Alex. You're a girl, and you could get hurt."

I tried not to smile at Will's sweet words. I rolled my eyes and turned away. I didn't want Will to know I liked him.

Daddy smiled at Colt. "Colt, the girls are gonna play."

Colt whined and then said to Grace, "Fine. But you're not kicking our butts!"

After playing for a while, it seemed like Grace was going to be right. We were kicking their butts—that was, until my cousin Luke, Grace's brother, tackled me and busted open my lip.

Will came running over and pushed Luke, causing him to fall. "You hurt her, you idiot!"

"William Hayes! You do not call people names. Say you're sorry right this second." Aunt Heather was standing there with her hands on her hips, looking down at Will, as she waited for him to apologize.

I quickly glanced between Aunt Heather and Uncle Josh. Will looked just like Uncle Josh. Both had wavy hair and the same smile—or at least, that was what my mom had said.

Aunt Heather and Uncle Josh—Libby and Will's parents—weren't really my aunt and uncle, but I called all my parents' friends aunt and uncle. Aunt Amanda and Uncle Brad were Maegan and Taylor's parents. Aunt Jessie and Uncle Scott were Lauren's parents. Luke and Grace were my cousins, and their parents were my Uncle Jeff—my mom's brother—and his wife, Aunt Ari. They were all really good friends, and someday, all us kids would be just as close and live in houses near each other just like our parents.

Will and I will be married, and we'll have lots of kids while we run the ranch.

"What are you smiling about?"

I looked up at my mother, and my smile instantly faded. "Nothing, Mama. I just thought of something funny."

She raised her eyebrow at me and then glanced at Will as he told Luke he was sorry. Both boys shook hands and then walked off toward Colt.

My mother looked back down at me and smiled as she squatted down. Making sure no one else could hear her, she whispered, "You have to admit, it was kind of cute how he came to your defense, wasn't it?"

I smiled bigger and nodded. "Someday, Mama, I'm gonna marry Will."

She made a funny face. "Is that right?"

I giggled. "He makes my tummy do funny things."

"Your daddy makes my tummy feel the same way. But let's keep our options open. After all, you are only ten."

I grinned and nodded my head. "Okay, Mama, but I'm telling ya, he's the one."

I turned and headed over to Grace as I heard my mother say, "Oh Lord."

I glanced over toward Will and smiled as I walked by. I couldn't help but notice Luke watching Will and me.

Luke grabbed Will and said, "Come on, let's go find a snake."

Will winked at me before he turned and started running behind Luke and Colt.

Yep, I'm gonna marry that boy someday.

Seventeen Years Old

"Daddy, he's the most beautiful thing I've ever seen!"

I ran my hands down the leg of my new horse. He was breathtaking. I'd always wanted a paint horse, and I couldn't believe my parents had gotten me one for my birthday.

Daddy smiled and shook his head. "Aunt Ari will train him with ground work and get him ready."

My mouth dropped open. "No, Daddy, no. I want to train him."

He let out a chuckle, and I placed my hands on my hips.

He lifted his hands. "Okay. If this is something you want to do, then by all means, you can do it but not alone. I want someone with you."

I glanced over and looked at Will. After helping Daddy get Banjo out of the trailer, he had been leaning against the barn, watching everything.

I smiled. "I won't be alone. Will can help me with the training."

Will pushed off the barn and smiled back at me. "I'd love to help."

Daddy nodded his head. "All right—as long as you only train when Will is with you." He turned and faced Will. "Will, you've broken in about three horses so far, correct?"

Will nodded his head. "Yes, sir. I've broken in two for Luke along with my own."

Daddy smiled. "Good. Keep my little girl safe at all times. That's my number one rule."

"Always, sir. I'd never let anything happen to Lex."

I felt the heat move through my cheeks as Will smiled at my father, and then he turned to me and smiled bigger.

Will and I had been working together and training my horse for the last few weeks. Today, he had me standing on a stool, grooming Banjo.

"Lean over his back, Lex. Then, let him turn to the right and reach for the carrot."

I did as he'd said. "What is this teaching him—with the carrot?"

"Teaches him to stay well positioned for mounting."

"Oh," I said as I smiled.

Will had been the one leaning over Banjo the last three days. My baby had bucked a few times, but Will would just slide off and land on his feet.

I loved this horse more than anything. He was proving to be a gentle giant. To bond us even closer, I'd been coming down and sitting in his stall with him at night. I'd fallen asleep in the stall a few times, and Will had carried me back up to the house four times already. Last night, Daddy had told Will that if I kept up at it, that would be all the exercise Will would need. I didn't want to admit it, but the last two times, I had done it on purpose just so Will would carry me in his arms.

"Lex?"

"Mmm?" I said as I daydreamed of being in Will's arms.

Will snapped his fingers in my face. "Earth to Lex."

"Sorry. I was lost in thought."

He let out a chuckle. "I'll say. Hop down, babe, and let me put on the bareback pad."

My cheeks instantly felt hot, and the lower pit of my stomach clenched. I slowly slid down and looked at Will as he walked around. I couldn't pull my eyes from him. I stepped off the stool, moved a bit forward, and leaned against my big guy. Banjo didn't even budge.

Will stopped in front of me and went to turn to put the pad on, but he stopped mid-movement. When our eyes met, I was pretty sure I felt the earth rumble. He smiled slightly, and I licked my lips in preparation for what I prayed would be our first kiss.

His eyes darted down to my lips before he quickly looked back into my eyes. "Lex?"

"Yeah?"

"I don't want to ruin our friendship, but…"

I smiled slightly and willed him to move closer to me. *Kiss me. Please, Will, just kiss me already.*

When he dropped the pad onto the floor, my heart began racing. He stepped closer and placed one hand on Banjo and the other hand on the side of my face. His thumb gently moved across my skin as he closed his eyes.

Oh God.

His touch did things to my body that made me want to get on my knees and beg him to satisfy me.

He opened his eyes and gently bit down on his lower lip.

"Will…please…"

He leaned down and barely touched his lips to mine. "Lex, you don't know how long I've wanted to kiss you."

I ran my hand up his chest and around to his neck. When my hand pushed into his soft, wavy hair, I let out a moan. He smiled against my lips, and then he kissed me.

Everything from this point on would change.

Everything.

alex

"Will, if my father catches us in here, he is going to be really upset." I nervously looked back at the barn door.

"Lex, we're both leaving for college in a few months. Don't you think you need to let your dad know what school you picked?" Will said as he reached for my hand.

My father had it all planned out. He wanted me to go to the University of Texas like he had and get my degree in marketing, but I had other dreams. Will was going to Texas A&M to get his degree in agribusiness so that he could help Jeff, Colt, and my father run the ranch. I'd been accepted into both schools, and my parents were just waiting on me to say yes to the University of Texas.

It was Luke, Colt, and Will's dream to take over the ranch someday. I had no doubt in my mind that they would all make great partners—if only Luke and Will would stop fighting…about me. Luke hated that Will and I had been sneaking around and seeing each other, and he'd threatened to tell my father on more than one occasion. The fights between Luke and Will would drive me insane. Each time, one or the other would end up with a black eye, and they would blame it on football.

It wasn't like my father didn't like Will. He loved Will…like a son.

Daddy had dreams for me though, and those dreams didn't include a boy who would be working on a ranch. His dreams were of me moving to the city and getting to experience all that city-living would offer. Then, if I wanted to, I could decide to come back to Mason.

I wanted what my mother had. I wanted to live on the ranch, wake up and work in the garden every day, and see my husband off to work with a kiss every single morning. I wanted the life my parents had. They were both so happy, and I couldn't figure out why my father didn't want me to have that life.

Will moved his lips to my neck, and his hot breath on my skin caused my stomach to drop.

God…just being around him makes my body do such crazy things.

Grace had said I was just horny and that Will and I needed to at least move on to a little bit more than kissing. As she'd said, we needed to cop feels here and there. Will was such a gentleman, and he'd never once pushed me into doing anything I didn't want to do.

I could hear Grace's voice in my head.

My God, you're eighteen. Stop piss-assing around about it, Alex. I swear y'all have liked each other since…what? Since you were ten years old?

I was eighteen now, and Will was seventeen. He would turn eighteen in August.

I had to smile though because Grace was all talk. She liked Michael Clark, but she had been too afraid to even talk to him up until this year.

"What are you smiling about, Lex?"

Since we were kids, Will was the only one who called me Lex, and I liked it that way. It was special—something just between the two of us, something only we shared together—and we could do it in front of everyone.

"Us."

He pulled away and looked at me. "Us? What about *us*?"

I felt my cheeks turning red, and I was almost positive Will could feel the heat coming from them.

"You're blushing, Lex? Why, honey?"

I looked down and away, but he brought his finger up to my chin and forced me to look at him.

"Alex? What about us?"

"I'm tired of hiding. I want to tell our parents that we've been dating. I want to tell my dad I've decided on A&M, and I want…I want…"

His smile was from ear to ear. "You want what, sweetheart?"

Oh God…his voice alone sends me over the edge.

"I want more…" *Damn it.* I couldn't bring myself to say it.

"More of what?" he said with that stupid smile of his.

When he tilted his head and gave me that dimple, I knew he was teasing me.

I took a deep breath and quickly let it out. "I want to make love."

Will's smile faded, and he took a step back.

Oh no. What if he doesn't feel the same? What if my feelings for him are stronger than his feelings for me? Oh. My. God. What if that's the reason he's never pushed me into anything more?

I instantly felt like a fool. I pushed past him and started to walk away.

"Wait, Lex…please just wait a second." He reached for my arm.

I felt the tears burning my eyes as I looked everywhere but at him. "I'm…I'm sorry. I should have just kept my mouth shut. Obviously, you don't feel the same way, so…"

I inwardly cursed Grace for even planting this in my head, and I hatched a plan to bitch her out the next time I saw her.

Before I knew what was happening, Will was backing me up until I came to a stop against the barn wall.

I looked up into his beautiful blue eyes. With his wavy light brown hair, he looked just like his father. I wanted to run my hands through his hair so badly. He was probably the sweetest guy I knew—besides Luke and Colt, who were both hopelessly romantic.

He ran the backs of his fingers down my face and smiled. My skin almost felt like it was burning where he touched. He bent down like he was going to kiss me, but he stopped just short of my lips. His eyes darted down to my lips and then back up to my eyes.

"Lex, I love you," he whispered.

I sucked in a breath of air and fought like hell to keep the tears from falling. It wasn't the first time he'd ever said it to me, but this time, it felt so…different. A tear fell, and he quickly brushed it away with his lips as he let out a low, soft moan.

"You have no idea how hard it is for me not to make love to you every time I'm with you. I want nothing more than to be with you, but I want it to be right. I want it to be perfect for you. I don't want us to sneak into a barn or do it in a car. You deserve so much more than that, sweetheart. I want to make you feel special the first time we make love."

Wow. Oh…just wow. My breaths were coming out faster. I looked at his lips as I licked mine.

He closed his eyes. "You drive me mad with desire, Alexandra. You have to know that."

Oh dear God…I think I might have an orgasm…right now…right here.

When he opened his eyes, they were filled with something I'd never seen before. The intense feeling of need I had for him grew about a hundred times.

I tried to talk, but only a whisper came out, "Will…"

When his lips touched mine, I let out a moan. I opened my mouth to him so that our tongues could explore each other like they had done a hundred times before. I brought my hands up and ran them through his hair. When he pushed himself into me, I felt his hard-on, and I wanted to wrap my legs around him so badly.

The kiss started to become passionate…until I heard someone clear his throat. I snapped my eyes open right as Will pulled back and scrunched up his face.

"Shit," he whispered so that only I could hear.

He took a few steps away from me as he ran his hand through his hair. *Lord, help me.*

I wanted this boy, and even though I knew we had just been caught making out in my father's barn, my desire for him was so intense that I wanted to cry. I never took my eyes off of him.

He winked at me before turning to the side. "Dad, Gunner, um…I mean, Mr. Mathews…um…I mean, sir…"

I closed my eyes and took in a deep breath. *Oh…holy…hell. My father just caught me making out in his barn.*

I tried to compose myself as I pushed off the wall and turned to face my father and Will's father, Josh. I wanted to giggle over Will struggling on how to address my father, but when I looked into my dad's eyes, I knew that wouldn't be the smartest thing to do.

"So…" Josh started to say as he shook his head and smiled at Will. "Damn, boy…you picked the wrong girl to get caught making out with in her daddy's barn."

I quickly glanced over at Will, who looked at my father and then back at his dad. He smiled slightly, but then he looked back at my father and swallowed hard.

Dragging in a deep breath, my father looked at us. "Alex, Will…I think y'all need to head on up to the house and wait for us on the back porch."

Will and I looked at each other, and at the same time, we said, "Yes, sir."

As we walked out of the barn, Will grabbed my hand right in front of my father.

Will looked at me, winked, and whispered, "I think that went well."

I just looked at him with my mouth hanging open. "You must have a death wish."

2
WILL

I didn't say another word to Lex as we walked back up to her house. Grams, Ellie—Alex's mom—and my mother were all sitting on the back porch. Grams and Ellie both looked down at Lex's hand joined with mine. Grams smiled.

My mother said, "Oh Lord, all hell is fixin' to break loose."

Ellie laughed as she shook her head. "By the look on your face, Alex, I'm going to guess your father knows?"

Alex stopped walking and stared at her mother. "What do you mean? Did you know?"

Ellie and my mother both started laughing.

"I have eyes, darling," her mother said.

I glanced over at my mother, who smiled sweetly at me. Last year, I'd told my mother how I felt about Lex, so I knew what was about to happen wouldn't surprise her.

Grams smiled as she looked at Lex. "Alexandra, I wish you had taken my advice and told your daddy."

Lex's face blushed.

Ellie snapped her head over to Grams. "Emma, you knew?"

Grams laughed. "Of course I knew. I walk with the girl every morning. I probably knew it before she did."

Lex giggled. "Grams…"

"Go into the kitchen, Alex and Will."

My skin crawled at the tone of Gunner's voice. I peeked over to my father.

He mouthed, *Good luck.*

I grinned slightly and dropped Lex's hand. I started to follow her and her father into the house.

Grams grabbed my hand. "William, you stand up for your feelings. Don't let Drew bully you. Do you hear me?"

I nodded my head. Grams always called Gunner by his real name, Drew. Everyone else would call him by his nickname that he'd gotten in high school football.

"But you be respectful of his feelings as well. That's his baby girl."

I smiled. "Yes, ma'am."

I opened the screen door as Lex sat down.

Gunner leaned against the counter. "How long have you been sneaking around behind my back?"

Lex stood up. "Daddy, we weren't purposely hiding it from you. We just didn't know how to tell you. I was scared."

His eyes filled with sadness. "Alex, why in the world would you be scared to tell me?"

I walked up and stood next to her. She reached for my hand, and Gunner stood up straighter. He gave me a look that I'd never seen before, and I wanted to drop Lex's hand, but I knew better.

"I'm going to ask again. How long have you two been dating?"

I swallowed hard and cleared my throat. "Over a year, sir. We, um…it started when I was helping Lex train Banjo."

He closed his eyes and slowly shook his head. When he opened them again, Lex dropped my hand and sat down. All I wanted to do was run and hide behind my own daddy. I didn't think I'd ever seen Gunner so mad in my life.

The screen door opened, and Ellie walked in. She walked up and smiled at Lex and me, and then she sat down on the other side of Lex.

Gunner looked at me and said, "I trusted you, Will."

My heart dropped.

He pushed his hand through his hair. "Have you…have you both…have things gone far?"

I began shaking my head. "No, sir. I would never do that to Lex—ever. Gunner…Mr. Mathews, um…" I paused and took a deep breath. *What in the hell do I call him now?* This was twice I'd stumbled over what to say to him. "I would never do anything to make you lose respect for me, sir. I love Lex too much."

His face softened a bit, and he nodded his head. "I appreciate that, Will. But that doesn't excuse the fact that you've been making out with my daughter in my own goddamn barn for over a year! I ought to kick your ass right here and now."

"Gunner!" Ellie yelled as she jumped up.

I looked down at the floor. I couldn't deny it, and I wasn't about to lie to him.

"Daddy, I'm eighteen years old. You can't tell me what to do anymore." *Oh shit.*

Gunner glared at me. "Since you seem to be interested in my daughter, cut the Gunner shit. It's sir or Mr. Mathews."

"Gunner," Ellie whispered, "stop being so mean to the boy."

He turned to Lex. "What happens in two months when you go to the University of Texas and Will goes to A&M?"

Oh hell, it keeps getting worse.

I turned and looked out the window. My father caught my eye, and I pleaded silently for him to come protect me. He laughed and shook his head.

Bastard.

Lex slowly stood up. "I've been meaning to talk to you and Mama about that. I've decided to go to A&M."

Gunner laughed and shook his head. "Excuse me?"

"Daddy, I really—"

"No. You're not going to A&M. You're going to UT." He pushed off the counter and began pacing back and forth. "We already have it all set, Alex. Just because Will is going to A&M doesn't mean you will change your whole life to follow him there."

Lex sucked in a breath of air. "What? Daddy, I'm not changing my whole life. I know what I want, but you seem hell-bent on making me do what you want."

"Oh, Alex, honey, tread easy," Ellie said.

Gunner stopped and pointed his finger at Lex. "Grace is going to UT, and you're going to UT. If this whole"—he looked at me and pointed his finger—"relationship thing is real, then the two of you can just wait for each other for four years."

Lex put her hands up to her mouth. I could see the tears in her eyes, and as she dropped her hands, I saw them ball up. I quickly looked outside and saw Grams. She walked into the kitchen and gave me a gentle smile. The way she was looking at me told me she knew exactly how Lex was feeling, and in that instant, I knew what I had to do.

I took a deep breath and stepped in between Lex and Gunner. I turned and looked at Lex. "Lex, don't do this."

She looked at me with a confused expression on her face. "What?"

I grabbed her hand and glanced back to Gunner. "Mr. Mathews, I have no doubt in my mind how I feel about Lex. I understand your concern, and if Lex going to UT puts your mind at ease, then that's what we'll do."

Lex dropped my hand. "What? Wait a minute, Will. I thought—"

I turned and placed my hands on the sides of her face. "Lex, I love you. I know our love is strong enough, and I don't want to start our relationship off like this with your parents. We'll see each other on weekends, breaks, and during summers, sweetheart. I promise you, it will be okay. I promise."

The tears forming in her eyes about made me sick.

She slowly shook her head. "I can't be without you, Will."

I longed to pull her to me, but if I wanted to live to see another day, I knew better. I used my thumbs to wipe her tears away. "I promise you, Lex, I'll love you forever."

She threw herself into my arms and began crying. I wasn't sure what to do at first, but after one look from Grams, I wrapped my arms around Lex. I looked over at Gunner, but I couldn't read his face. Ellie wiped a tear away as she walked up to us and took Lex from my arms. She began to walk Lex into the living room, but Lex stopped in front of her father.

She looked at him as she said, "I'll never forgive you for this—ever."

As she began walking away, Gunner closed his eyes. When he opened them and looked at me, I could see the hurt in his eyes, and I instantly felt like shit. The last thing I ever wanted to do was make him disappointed in me.

"Will, please go saddle up two horses. Let's go for a ride."

I swallowed hard and nodded my head.

As I walked past Grams on my way out, she took my arm and said, "I'm proud of you, son. Know what you feel in your heart is real. Love can weather any storm."

I gave her a weak smile and whispered, "Why does it feel like I just made the biggest mistake of my life then?"

She smiled and shook her head.

As I made my way out onto the porch, my mother and father stood up.

"I'm proud of you, Will," my father said as he slapped me on the back.

My mother walked up to me and gave me a hug. "Will, you did the right thing, honey. Don't overthink this."

I kissed my mother on the cheek and whispered, "I love you, Mama."

My father walked with me down to the barn. We began saddling up two horses, neither of us speaking.

"Dad?"

He looked up at me and said, "Yes?"

"Is Gunner gonna kill me now?"

My father threw his head back and laughed. "I'm not sure. If I saw Luke or Colt kissing Libby in my barn, I'm not sure what I would do." He let out a chuckle and then looked at me with a serious face. "I also know that I love those two boys like they were my own sons, and if I trusted anyone with my daughter, it would be one of them."

I laughed. "You'd better think twice about Luke."

My father winked at me. "That boy is so much like his father, it's unreal. They're both hotheaded and full of crazy ideas."

I let out a breath and said, "Dad, why does it feel like my heart just got ripped out, and I just let go of the best thing that ever happened to me?"

He walked up to me and pointed to a chair for me to sit down. He sat down in front of me and put his hands on his knees. "Will, I'm not going to sit here and fill your head with a bunch of bullshit. I don't know what the future holds for you and Alex. I know that when I see you look at her, I see a younger version of myself when I used to look at your mom."

"When did you know Mom was the one, Dad?"

The smile that spread across his face had me smiling along with him.

"It seems like it was just yesterday when I saw her walking into the room. Jeff and Gunner were throwing a party, and when your mother walked in, something happened. To this day, I can't even explain it. The only thing I knew was that I wanted to get to know her more. It was almost like I needed to be near her to breathe properly."

I smiled bigger. My father and mother were so in love, and everyone could see that. I wanted a love like theirs. As far as I could remember, my mother and father always showed how much they loved each other. I couldn't even count how many times Lib or I had walked into the kitchen to see our parents making out. At first, it had disgusted me…until I'd begun having stronger feelings for Lex. Then, I'd understood it—the need to always have the one you loved in your arms.

"Did you and Mom have problems in the beginning?"

My father laughed and shook his head. "Hell yeah, we did. Ask Jeff and Ari, or Brad and Amanda, or Scott and Jessie. Hell, son, you could even ask Gunner and Ellie. We all had problems, and we still do. Nothing in life comes easy, especially the good stuff. We all have troubles and obstacles we have to overcome. Will, I'm not going to tell you that it will be easy. It's gonna be hard to be away from her, but…" He looked down and then back up at me. "Neither of you have been anywhere but Mason. I know that you say you love her, and I don't doubt that. Just know, Will, that college is a whole other world. Gunner is right. If your love is strong and meant to be, then you'll be okay, son."

I blew out a breath. "I can't lose her, Dad. I can't. I love her more than I love anyone or anything."

Gunner cleared his throat, and I immediately jumped up. My father slowly stood up and walked over to Gunner. He whispered something into Gunner's ear. Gunner smiled and looked at my father as he nodded his head. When he glanced back at me, his smile faded some, but he was still smiling a little as he walked up to me. My knees felt like they were about to give out from under me.

"Um…Gunner…uh…I mean, Mr. Mathews, um…the horses are ready."

His grin grew bigger, and he let out a chuckle. He put his hand on my shoulder. "Will, just call me Gunner. I can't do the whole Mr. Mathews thing. I keep looking for my father."

I nodded my head. "Yes, sir. Gunner it is."

He squeezed my shoulder. "Let's go for a ride and talk, shall we?"

I swallowed hard and said a quick prayer that I would make it back alive after our *talk*.

We rode for a bit before Gunner started talking, "I love this ranch. I always have, and I always will."

I nodded my head. "I do as well, sir."

Maybe this won't be so bad.

Gunner seemed relaxed. He was always happy when he talked about the ranch. When he turned to look at me though, his smile faded. Something changed in his eyes, and I was trying desperately to think about something else on the ranch to talk about. He finally gave me a look that I knew I would never forget.

He tilted his head and asked, "So, Will, how long have you been in love with my daughter?"

alex

I kept looking down at my phone, waiting to hear something from Will.

"Stop staring at that thing and enjoy nature, Alex."

I smiled and pushed my cell into the pocket of my shorts. "Grams, may I ask you a question?"

Grams and I were on one of our daily walks. We'd been going on walks for as long as I could remember. We usually walked in the morning, but Grams had felt that we needed an evening walk since I'd kept pacing on the back porch while waiting for Daddy and Will to get back from their ride.

"Of course you can. You can ask me anything you want, Alex."

I took a deep breath and stopped walking. "Grams, this is kind of weird, but I know you'll be honest with me." I stood there, staring at her. I wasn't sure how to say what I wanted to ask.

The look in her eyes changed, and she nodded her head. "Well, are you gonna just stand there and stare at me? Or are you going to ask me if I saved myself for marriage?"

My mouth dropped open, and I couldn't even form words to speak. I'd overheard my mom and Aunt Ari talking about how Grams knew things. They had said it was like she knew what you were going to say or do before you even did. I'd always thought they were crazy, but as I looked at my great-grandmother, I knew they were so spot-on.

"Grams, how did you know what I was going to ask you?"

She let out a chuckle and started walking again. "Alex, I was seventeen years old when I met your gramps. I knew the moment I saw him that he was the one. I couldn't wait for him to make me his."

I smiled. I could just picture Grams and Gramps meeting for the first time. "So, you didn't wait for marriage?"

She shook her head. "No, honey, we didn't."

"How did you know?" I felt the blush hit my cheeks.

She shrugged her shoulders. "Anytime Garrett walked into a room, I used to get the strangest feelings. I once begged him to make me his, but he wouldn't. He said he wanted to make it special. I'm glad we didn't rush into anything because the first time should be special, Alex. It should be with someone you love. Now, your mama and daddy would want me to tell you to be a good little girl and wait. I'm not gonna preach something to you when I have no right to. Do I think it would be better to wait? Yes. Just be careful, baby girl. Don't rush into anything because y'all think you have to prove something. You don't. Love is more than sex."

"Daddy thinks what I feel for Will isn't love. He says I need to get out of Mason and see what else is out there for me. I know what I feel in my heart, Grams. I want to be with Will more than anything. The way my body feels when he is around me…I just don't understand it."

She stopped and turned to face me. She reached for my hands and smiled the same smile she had given me since I could remember. "Alex, don't rush into anything because you're afraid of what your daddy is going to make you do."

"Grams, I've been in love with Will for so long now. He's all I've ever known."

She raised her eyebrow. "Maybe that's why your daddy wants you to go to UT."

I placed my hand on my stomach and took a deep breath. I looked down, and for the first time in the last few years, I felt doubt. "Yeah. Maybe."

We continued on with our walk, and neither one of us said another word. By the time we returned to the house, Will was sitting on my back porch. I picked up my pace and then practically ran, so I could be in his arms. He stood up and gave me a funny look. I slowed down as I went up the steps. When my father came walking out, I stopped and tried to read his face.

"Alex, did you enjoy your walk with Grams?" Daddy asked with a slight smile. He looked at Grams as she made her way up the steps.

I nodded my head. "Yes, sir."

Grams stopped in front of Daddy. "Whew, I think I'm getting too old for two walks a day. Drew, will you take your grandmother back home now? I'd better check on Garrett and make sure he hasn't gotten himself into any kind of trouble."

My father smiled and nodded his head. He looked back at me and smiled. He appeared to be a lot calmer, and I couldn't help but wonder why.

Did he talk Will into breaking up with me? Did he threaten Will? Oh God, what if Daddy threatened him?

"Come on, Grams. Let's get you home." Daddy took Grams by the arm and led her back into the house.

I slowly turned and looked at Will. My eyes traveled up and down his body. He appeared to be unhurt. He slowly smiled and winked at me.

There goes my stomach.

"What did he say to you?" I held my breath.

Will glanced at the door and then turned back to me. He walked up to me and took my hand in his. We began walking to his truck.

"Wait—are you leaving?"

"I have to get back home, Lex. Are you still planning on going to the party tomorrow night?"

I nodded my head and barely said, "Yes. I thought we were going together."

He stopped and leaned against his truck as he smiled. "We are."

I rolled my eyes and looked away before glancing back at him. "What did my father say to you?"

He grabbed my hips and pulled me to him. I was shocked he was being so forward with his affections, especially knowing my father or mother could see him at any moment.

"He asked me how long I've been in love with you. Then, he asked again if we've had sex."

I slammed my hands up to my mouth. "What?"

He laughed. "That was about my reaction, too."

"He didn't!"

"Yeah, he did. I was just glad as hell that I could honestly tell him we haven't had sex...yet."

My heart dropped, and I felt sick. "Will, please don't let him change anything between us. If I have to go to another college...well, I want us to be together before we leave for school."

He closed his eyes and then opened them. "Lex, I don't want to have sex just because we're afraid."

"I'm not afraid, Will. I love you. I know what I want, and I want you. I'm tired of waiting."

Will licked his lips, and then he let out what sounded like a growl. "Fuck, Lex. I want you, too, but I want it to be special."

He looked my body up and down and pulled me closer to him, so I could feel just how much he wanted me.

"You have no idea how hard it is to wait," he said.

I leaned up and went to kiss him when something hit the back of my head. I quickly turned around to see Luke standing there.

"What the hell, Luke?" I picked up the Nerf football and threw it back at him.

"Gunner is going to kick your ass if he sees you pawing on her," Luke said.

"Shut up, Luke. Gunner knows about me and Lex," Will said.

Luke's face dropped. "No shit?"

I smiled and leaned back against Will as he wrapped his arms around me.

"He's okay with this?" Luke asked.

Will stiffened behind me, and then he relaxed a bit. "After he threatened to kill me if I ever hurt her, he gave me his blessing."

I spun around. "He threatened to kill you?"

Will laughed as he placed his finger on my chin and pulled my lips to his. "I love you, Lex," he whispered before kissing me gently. "I've got to go. I'll call you when I get home."

I smiled. "I love you, too. Be careful driving."

I took a step back and watched as Will got into his truck. He waved and took off down the driveway. When I couldn't see his truck anymore, I turned and glared at Luke.

He held his hands up. "What? You're like my little sister, Alex. I'm gonna protect you even if it means beating the shit out of my best friend."

I grinned. "You should be more concerned about Michael Clark and Grace."

Luke's smile faded, and he pushed his hand through his hair. "I hate that guy. I don't know what Grace sees in that ass."

"Me either."

Luke slowly grinned. "So, Uncle Gunner knows. You finally tell him?"

"Uh, no. He caught us kissing in the barn."

Luke started laughing. "Shit. I would have given my right arm to see Hayes's face."

I giggled as I walked up to him and pushed him in the chest. "You're so mean."

He threw his arm around me, and we headed back to my house.

"Alex, if he ever hurts you, I hope you know you're going to ruin a damn good friendship."

I punched him in the stomach. "He won't."

He dropped his arm as we walked into the house. "For his sake, I hope not," he whispered.

Grace, Maegan, Libby, and I all sat on Will's tailgate as we watched Colt, Will, and Luke load a trailer with square bales of hay. Luke stopped to pull his T-shirt off, and he threw it down on the ground.

Maegan and Libby both sighed.

"I swear, Grace, your brother has the body of a god. What I wouldn't do to have my legs wrapped around him," Maegan said as she fanned herself with a piece of paper.

Grace looked at Meg. "Gross, Meg. I just threw up in my mouth."

I giggled, but then I noticed how Libby shot her head over and looked at Meg. Both Libby and Meg had a thing for Luke. He was getting ready to head off to his second year at A&M, and from what Will and Colt had said, Luke had his fair share of girls falling over him. He was totally clueless when it came to Meg and Libby liking him.

I bumped my shoulder into Libby's. "You getting excited about heading to A&M?"

She smiled. "Yeah, I'm pretty excited about it."

Meg looked over and let out a sigh. "Crap, I really wish my parents weren't so hell-bent on me going to Baylor."

Grace started laughing. "Please, bitch. The only reason you want to go to A&M is because Luke is going there. Hence, the reason your daddy won't let you go to A&M."

We all started laughing.

"Right? I wonder if I have any chance of hooking up with Luke before the end of the summer," Meg said.

Grace jumped off the truck, and as she turned to look at Maegan, she put her hands on her hips. In that moment, I saw Aunt Ari all over Grace's face.

"Jesus H. Christ, stop with the talk about my brother. I can't take it. It's disgusting, Maegan."

I peeked over at Libby, and she was staring at Maegan. I glanced back out and noticed the guys were nearly done. I leaned over to Libby and said, "You should go offer them a drink of tea."

She quickly looked at me. "Yeah?"

I smiled as I nodded my head.

Libby wasn't shy by any means, but when it came to Luke, she was beyond shy. Last year, Luke had kissed her behind the bleachers before he headed off for college. After Will had found out about the kiss, he'd punched Luke, but then Luke had explained that he hated himself for kissing Libby. It wasn't because he hadn't wanted to kiss her. It had just made their friendship awkward. They used to spend a lot of time together, but Libby and Luke's friendship hadn't really been the same since.

While Grace and Maegan were busy going back and forth, Libby jumped down and grabbed three bottles of tea before making her way toward the guys.

"Where is she going?" Maegan jumped off the tailgate.

"Taking tea to the guys." I looked at Grace and winked.

Grace rolled her eyes and put her finger in her mouth like she was gagging herself. I chortled and jumped off the tailgate. I needed to distract Maegan for a bit to give Libby a chance. I wasn't playing sides by any means. I just knew that Maegan wanted to sleep with Luke only because she knew Libby liked Luke a lot.

"What are y'all wearing to the party tonight?" I asked.

Grace was the first to answer, "Oh my gosh, I found the cutest dress in my mom's closet. It's all vintage and shit. I'm totally wearing it."

"Jean shorts and a T-shirt," Maegan mumbled as she watched Libby.

I looked at her. "You of all people wearing just shorts and a T-shirt?"

Maegan glanced back at me and smiled. "Yep. I'm so sick of dressing up for these country bumpkins, only to have them talk about fences and cows. God, I can't wait to get out of Fredericksburg and Mason. I just want to be in the city."

My heart sank a little when Maegan talked about leaving. She and Grace wanted to leave Mason as fast as they could while Libby and I dreaded leaving. Mason was my comfort zone. It was where I felt happy, safe, and loved. I hated the few times I'd been to Austin, and I hated UT also. It was too big and had way too many people. Grace was over the moon about going to UT, especially after she'd found out that Michael Clark was going there.

I glanced back over and saw Luke talking to Libby. I turned back to distract Maegan, but I was too late.

"Oh, hell no. Libby is not moving in on my man," Meg said.

She was about to take off, but then Grace pushed her.

"Stop it, Meg. You know how much Libby likes Luke. Why are you going after him so hard? If you want to have sex with someone, plenty of guys are waiting in line here in Mason or in Fredericksburg."

Maegan's mouth dropped open. "Excuse me?"

Oh shit.

Grace said, "Tell me you aren't after Luke just for sex."

"Go to hell, Grace."

Maegan turned and started walking off, but then Grace grabbed her arm.

"Meg, I'm serious. All you ever talk about is wrapping your legs around him and how great he probably is in bed. Do you seriously think Luke is interested in screwing you?"

Maegan pushed Grace's hand off her arm and smirked. "You seriously think Michael is interested in screwing you?"

"Stop it. Now," I said. "Just stop this. Meg, Libby is just asking them if they want some tea. Stop being bitches to each other and make up. We have a party to get ready for."

Grace glared at Maegan.

Meg looked at Libby and Luke and then turned back to Grace. "Fine. Just so you know, Grace, I like Luke and not just because I want to sleep with him." She turned and started back toward the ranch Jeep.

I let out a sigh and looked at Grace. "Why did you say that?"

She shook her head and walked closer to me. "Alex, you know as well as I do that Meg only wants to sleep with Luke because she knows Libby likes him. Meg has been jealous of their friendship for years."

I knew she was right, but I didn't want to be pulled into this argument that had been going on for the last few years.

I let out a sigh and said, "I don't think Luke is going to sleep with or even go out with either one of them, so let's just drop it."

I turned and started making my way toward Will. He was covered in sweat, and my body ached for his touch. The closer I got, the more turned-on I got. I bit down on my lower lip, and I was pretty sure I let out a moan.

I looked over my shoulder to see Grace hadn't followed me. She pulled out her cell phone and started texting someone. I glanced back to see Will smiling at me.

When I walked up to him, he grabbed me and pulled me in for a kiss. I didn't even care that my brother and cousin were standing there. I wrapped my arms around Will, and as he picked me up, I wrapped my legs around him.

"Motherfucker, put my sister down now," Colt said.

I pulled my lips from Will's. I turned to Colt and smiled.

"Seriously, Alex, get the hell off of him."

The last thing I wanted to do was piss off my brother. He'd go running back to our father and tell him. I looked back at Will and pouted as he slowly let me down.

He put his lips to my ear and whispered, "I can't wait any longer. Tonight, baby."

Holy crap. I was sure my heart had stopped beating.

I had no idea what he'd meant by that, but I was sure hoping that he'd meant tonight would be the night he made me his.

"You going to the party tonight, Lib?"

I looked over at Luke, who was trying to act like he didn't really care what Libby's answer would be.

She shrugged her shoulders. "Not sure. Jason Stone asked me to meet him there."

Luke had been getting a drink of tea when he choked on it. "What? Jason Stone asked you out, and you said yes?"

I glanced at Will. He was smirking and nodding his head.

He grabbed my hand and said, "Come on, we're finally done. I need to get home and take a cold shower. It's hot as hell out here."

Colt was already walking ahead of all of us as he texted on his phone, and Will and I began following him.

"I didn't say he asked me out." Libby started walking next to me.

Oh, she is good. I tried to hide my smile, but all I could think about was how Maegan had no idea what she was up against.

"Um…yeah, ya did. You just said that Jason Stone asked you to meet him there."

I watched as Luke walked next to Libby while he frantically pulled his T-shirt back over his head.

Libby shrugged her shoulders. "So? That's not a date, Luke. What do you care if it is a date anyway? I heard you making plans to meet up with Hope Kirkland."

Luke started laughing. "Hope? Please." He rolled his eyes, and then he began walking backward as he looked at all of us. "Hey, I have an idea."

"No," Will, Libby, and Colt all said at the same time.

I began laughing. Luke was always coming up with these crazy plans. He had gotten us all in trouble more times than I could even remember.

"Come on, y'all. Let's all meet at the river first. We can hang out a bit before we go to the party. Are Lauren and Taylor going?"

"Yep," Libby said.

"Shit. No alcohol if they're going to be there," Luke said.

Since Lauren and Taylor were the youngest, Luke would insist on no alcohol anytime they were with us. It would drive Lauren mad, but Taylor couldn't care less. She'd never had the desire to even try a beer.

"How can you say that? Colt isn't that much older than them, and you don't care if he is there," Libby said.

Luke shrugged his shoulders. "Colt's a guy. He's different."

Libby stopped walking.

Will moaned, "Great. Here we go."

I giggled as I hit him lightly on the side.

"Luke Drew Johnson," Libby said.

Luke smiled that big ole smile of his that could melt all the girls' hearts. He stepped up to Libby and lifted his hand to her hair. "You have a piece of hay in your hair, Isabella Gemma Hayes. Don't call me by my full name, sweetheart. Only my mama can do that."

"You're such an ass," Libby said as she pushed him away.

Luke lost his balance and began falling back but not before he grabbed Libby and took her down with him. He fell right onto his back, and she landed right on top of him. The way Luke was looking at Libby had me blushing for her. He looked like he wanted to…kiss her.

Will must have noticed it, too, because he quickly picked Libby up. "Are you okay?"

She said, "Yes," and then she looked at me.

The flush on her cheeks caused me to smile at her. She quickly walked off and headed to the Jeep. I turned back, only to find Will had Luke by the shirt.

"Don't ever look at my sister like that again, Johnson. I'll fucking beat your ass, you hear me?"

"Will!" I walked up and pulled his hands from Luke's T-shirt. "Libby pushed Luke. It was just an accident. Will, stop it."

Luke seemed stunned, and I wasn't sure if it was because of what Will had said to him or if it was because it had finally hit him that he had feelings for Libby.

"This is going to be one interesting summer." Colt started laughing as he walked toward his truck.

4 WILL

I couldn't help but watch every move Lex made. The way she smiled drove me crazy. The sound of her voice warmed my body. I closed my eyes and tried not to think about how we would be going our separate ways in less than two months.

"Open your eyes, dude. It creeps me out."

I opened my eyes and saw Colt standing there. I smiled and laughed. "What are you gonna do when we all go to college?"

Colt let out a sigh. "Not sure. I guess I'll get bigger and stronger since I'll be working on the ranch more."

I glanced over toward Lauren and then back at Colt. "What's going on with you and Rachel?"

He rolled his eyes. "Hell if I know. She told me yesterday that I was too romantic and that she needs to be more independent. I don't even know why I'm dating her."

I smiled slightly. Colt had gotten trashed a few weeks back, and Luke and I had kept him in my barn until he sobered up. If Gunner had seen Colt like that, he would have killed his own son. Colt never really drank, but when he'd seen Lauren out on a date, he'd lost it. He'd admitted to Luke and me how much he liked her.

"Colt, can I ask you something?"

He nodded his head. "Always, Will."

"Why are you trying to avoid how you feel about Lauren?"

His face dropped. He quickly looked at Lauren and then turned back to me. "What are you talking about?"

"Colt, when you got shitfaced a few weeks ago, you told Luke and me that you had feelings for Lauren."

He dropped his head back and let out a sigh. "Fuck. You didn't tell Alex, did you?"

"No."

Colt ran his hand down his face. "Good."

"Why don't you want her to know?"

"Want who to know what?" Lauren asked as she came up.

She kissed Colt on the cheek, and his face instantly turned red.

"Um…" Colt looked at me as he struggled for something to say.

I smiled. "Colt likes a girl, and he won't tell her."

Lauren turned to Colt and tilted her head. "I thought you and Rachel were going out. Did y'all break up?"

Colt gave me a dirty look. "Will's just screwing around. You meeting anyone at the party, Lauren?"

Lauren stared at Colt for just a little too long before she looked toward the rest of the girls. "No. I've officially given up on guys."

Colt and I both laughed.

"Why?" Colt asked.

Lauren turned to Colt and then glanced at me. When the tears filled her eyes, I instantly got pissed.

Someone hurt her.

Colt lifted Lauren's chin up, so she would look at him. "What happened?"

Lauren sucked in her bottom lip and shook her head. "Nothing," she whispered.

"I swear to God, Lauren, if you don't tell me right now…"

Lauren quickly wiped a tear away. "Colt, it's okay. I'm sorry. I didn't mean to get all emotional. Just drop it. I'm going to head on over—"

Colt cut her off, "Lauren."

I walked up to her. "Lauren, please tell us what happened."

Lauren looked between us. "Do you both promise not to go all big-brother crazy?"

I nodded, but Colt remained silent.

Lauren sniffed. "Paul Hines…he, um…he tried, um…"

Oh, holy shit. I'm gonna kill that fucker.

I quickly glanced over to Colt, and he looked like he was about to get sick.

"Lauren, honey, take a deep breath. What did he do?" Colt said in a soft voice.

"I told him no, and he got upset with me. He said I was a tease. I swear, y'all, I never did anything to make him think I would have sex with him. When I got out of his truck, he jumped out, grabbed my arm, and pushed me against his truck. He said…he said I really did want it and that I was just scared. I told him that even if he was the last guy on earth, I'd still rather get myself off than sleep with him. He…he…" She looked down and then looked up into Colt's eyes. "He slapped me and called me a whore."

When I saw Colt's body shaking, I quickly grabbed Lauren in for a hug. I pointed to Colt and mouthed, *Calm down.*

Lauren started crying.

"Shh…it's okay, sweetie. Don't listen to that bastard. Lauren, you didn't do anything wrong, and if your dad ever found out that ass hit you, he would kill that guy."

Lauren pulled back and wiped her tears. "I know. It was just…scary, ya know? When he pinned me against his truck, I was really scared."

I looked up to see Luke, Grace, and Lex walking up.

Grace and Lex both dropped their smiles as they walked up to Lauren. "Why are you crying?" they both asked at the same time.

"What's wrong? What's going on?" Luke asked as he glanced at Colt and then me.

Lauren looked at Colt and me with pleading eyes. "Nothing. I twisted my ankle, and I'm just crying like a baby," she said.

Lex looked at me, and I knew she wasn't buying it.

"You okay, baby girl?" Luke asked.

Lauren nodded her head and attempted to smile.

Luke slapped his hands together and said, "Then, let's go."

"Where are Meg and Taylor?" Grace asked.

Luke shrugged his shoulders. "Not sure. Maybe they'll be at the party. Let's get going. Colt, you're driving, so nothing but soda."

Colt gave Luke a weak smile.

Lex and I were sitting on the back of my tailgate, watching everyone at the party.

She bumped me with her shoulder and smiled. "You're so quiet tonight. What are you thinking about?"

"I'm watching Colt."

She turned and scanned through everyone, looking for Colt. "Why?"

"'Cause Paul Hines just showed up."

She looked at me. "So? Does Colt have something against Paul?"

I raised my eyebrows. "You could say that he does."

"Will, what's going on? Lauren was upset earlier, and now, you're telling me that my brother is pissed at Paul. I know Lauren went out with Paul last week. So, what gives?"

I glanced over at my girl. *I love her so much. Nothing gets by her. I can't wait to make her mine.* I moved my hand and slid it across my front left pocket. *It's still there.*

"I promised Lauren I wouldn't say anything," I said.

Lex nodded her head. "Then, I trust you and Colt know what you're doing."

I grabbed her hand and jumped off the tailgate as Gloriana's song "Best Night Ever" began playing. "Dance with me, Lex."

She smiled, and the next thing I knew, she was in my arms. I walked her out to where everyone was dancing. As I pulled her to me, her scent filled my senses and caused my dick to jump.

I moved my lips up her neck and gently bit down on her earlobe. "Lex, I want you."

She sucked in a breath of air and whispered, "Yes, Will. I want you, too."

I pulled back and placed my hands on the sides of her face. I leaned down and kissed her. We both let out low moans as our tongues moved against each other. When we both pulled back for air, I smiled as I leaned my forehead against hers.

"Lex, my parents are out of town. I want to make you mine…tonight."

Her eyes lit up with a fire I'd never seen before. "What about Libby?"

The song changed, and Thomas Rhett's "Get Me Some of That" began playing. I looked up and began searching for my sister. When I saw her dancing in the arms of Luke, I instantly got pissed.

"That bastard," I whispered.

Lex turned to where I was looking. As Luke spun Libby around on the dance floor, I noticed the look on her face. I hadn't seen my sister smile like that in a long time.

Lex squeezed my arm and caused me to look down at her. "Will, it's okay."

I chuckled and looked back at them. "That's my sister…and Luke. Lex, it's *Luke*."

She placed her hand on the side of my face. "All the more reason to trust them. He's your best friend. We all grew up together, Will. Luke would be the last person to hurt Lib. They're just dancing."

I nodded my head as I glanced back at Luke and Libby. I looked down into Lex's beautiful blue eyes and gave her the sexiest smile I could manage. "When can we leave?"

Lex bit down on her lower lip and then ran her tongue across it. I let out a whimper. I needed to adjust myself to accommodate my shrinking pants.

"Now?"

That was all I needed to hear. I grabbed her hand and began making our way back to my truck.

"Should we tell the others that we're leaving?" Lex asked.

I held the passenger door open and helped her up into my truck. I shook my head. "No. They'll just want to leave with us." The flush that moved across her cheeks caused me to smile. I leaned in and kissed her nose. "Anytime it gets to be too much, Lex, just say stop, and we will."

She opened her mouth slightly. "I'm not going to want to stop, Will. I can promise you that."

Holy shit.

I smiled and stepped back to shut the door. I walked around the back of the truck, so Lex couldn't see me panicking.

I'm actually going to make love to her.

I knew I didn't want to wait until the end of summer. I wanted to show Lex how much I loved her. I wanted her to know that what we shared was real, and even though we were going to be a few hundred miles apart, nothing would come between us.

Opening the truck door, I was just about to get inside when I heard Lauren yell out. I quickly turned and saw Paul Hines trying to pull Lauren out onto the dance floor. She kept yelling for him to let her go.

"Ah fuck." I looked back at Lex. "Stay in the truck, Lex."

"Wait! What's going on?" Lex called out.

I shut my door.

It didn't take me long to find Colt. He was already heading toward Paul. I gave Luke one look, and he nodded. We both started running, but we didn't make it there fast enough. Colt grabbed Paul and knocked the shit out of him. Lauren screamed and jumped back as Paul stood up and went after Colt.

Luke grabbed my arm and shook his head. "It's his battle. Let him go for a second."

Paul swung and missed as Colt landed another hit. Paul stumbled backward and fell to the ground.

Colt walked up to him and said, "You ever lay a finger on her again, and I swear I'll break every bone in your damn body. You hear me?"

Paul wiped blood from his mouth and nodded his head. "Yeah, I got it."

Colt turned and walked up to Lauren. He grabbed her hand before leading her back to his truck, and he helped her in. He walked around, jumped in, and took off.

I looked at Luke, and he was smiling.

When Paul walked by us, Luke stepped in front of him. "Dude, what in the hell made you think you could touch her? Between Colt, Will, and me, you should have known better."

Paul looked at Luke and then at me. Then, he pushed Luke out of the way before leaving.

Maegan came running up and threw herself into Luke's arms as she let out a little scream. "Dance with me, cowboy."

Luke smiled at Meg before looking at me.

I gave him a look and shook my head. "I need to talk to you, Luke."

He smiled and gave Meg a slight push back. "Not now, Meg. Maybe later, okay?"

Her face dropped before her smile returned. "Okay. Later it is."

I turned and headed over toward my truck. Lex had gotten out, and she was standing next to it, but then she quickly got back in and shut the door.

"What's up?" Luke asked.

"What's going on with you and my sister?"

Luke laughed. "Nothing. Why?"

"Luke, cut the shit with me. I see the way you look at her, and I also see the lust in your eyes when you look at Meg. Don't do this. You're gonna end up hurting one, if not both, of them. I don't want to see my sister get hurt by you again."

He opened his mouth like he was going to argue with me, but then he turned and scanned the area before stopping and staring at someone. I followed his eyes, and he was looking at Libby.

"I promise you, I have no intentions of hurting either one of them."

He looked back at me, and his eyes were filled with something I'd never seen there before—sadness.

He slapped me on the side of the arm. "I'm going to pretend I don't see my cousin sitting in your truck, like y'all are getting ready to leave. I just happen to know your parents are out of town. I'm going to take Libby out for breakfast after the party, so she doesn't walk in on anything. I don't know how I really feel about this, Will, but I know you love Alex, so I'm gonna tell you the same thing. I don't want to see her get hurt, so make sure this is something you both want." He held out his hand.

I shook it and said, "I will, Luke."

I watched as he walked back to Libby. I didn't like the way she smiled at Luke when she saw him walking up. He leaned down and whispered something in her ear. She smiled bigger as she looked around him and at me.

I pushed the uneasy feeling I had deep down inside as I made my way back to the driver's side before climbing in.

Lex looked at me. "Do I want to know?"

I let out a breath of air. "Ask Lauren."

She nodded her head. "Where do you think Colt took Lauren?"

I shrugged my shoulders. "I'm guessing home."

She turned in her seat, facing me, and gave me a sexy smile. "Will?"

"Yeah, babe?"

"I can't wait for you to make love to me."

I swallowed hard as Gunner popped into my head. "I'm scared, Lex."

Her smile faded a bit before she smiled bigger. "My daddy?"

I laughed. "Yes!"

She reached for my hand and then looked down. "Is this going to be your, um…I mean, will I be…"

I squeezed her hand and let out a chuckle. "Lex, I knew when I was ten years old that you were the one. I grew up dreaming of what it would be like to be with you. There was no way in hell I was going to sleep with any other girl. You're it for me."

The tear sliding down her face caught the moonlight, and I reached up and brushed it away.

"Will…"

She leaned over and began kissing me. Our kiss was quickly turning more passionate, and I needed to stop.

I pulled back. "Lex, I don't want to do this in my truck."

She giggled as she sat back in her seat and pulled her seat belt on. I began to drive, and we headed the short distance to my house. My hands were sweating, and a million things were running through my head. I brushed my hand across the ring in my pocket and then had a brief moment of panic.

Did I buy condoms?

"Do we have to use one?"

I snapped my head over and looked at Lex. "Huh? Do we have to use one what?"

She tilted her head, and her cheeks turned a beautiful pink. "A condom. You just asked if you bought condoms."

"Did I say that out loud?"

She nodded her head and laughed. "Yes, you did."

I looked back at the road and gripped the steering wheel tighter.

Motherfucker. I can't believe she asked if we have to use a condom.

Yes!

No.

Yes!

Oh fuck.

We drove in silence as everything raced through my head. As I pulled down the driveway, I glanced over at Lex. She was staring out the window and rubbing her hands up and down her legs. She was just as nervous as I was.

After I pulled up and parked, she turned to me and smiled. My heart dropped, and I knew what we were about to do was exactly what we both wanted—and needed.

alex

5

The way Will was staring at me caused me to smile bigger. I was nervous as hell, but I had no doubt in my mind what we were about to do was going to be perfect. And it was long overdue.

Damn it. My hands wouldn't stop sweating, and I had to keep rubbing them on my pants.

Will turned his body to face me, so I did the same.

He reached for my hands. "Lex, are you on the pill?"

Oh God. This is getting real. I nodded my head. "Yes. I've been on it for the last year."

His face dropped. "Does your father know?"

I laughed and shook my head. "No. My mother and I talked about it, and even though I told her that I wasn't sexually active, we both agreed it would be best if I started it."

Will's face turned white.

"What's wrong?" I asked.

"Nothing. I just keep thinking back to your dad telling me he would break both my hands if I ever touched you the wrong way."

I giggled and rolled my eyes. I brought his hand up to my lips and kissed the back of it. "Well, my dad isn't here, is he?"

Will slowly licked his lips and whispered, "No."

"So, are we going to sit in the truck? Or are we going in?"

"Um…Lex, I don't think I have any condoms."

I frowned at the idea of having a barrier between us. "I'm on the pill. It's okay."

He leaned back and dropped his head on the headrest. "I can't, Lex."

I instantly felt sick. I turned and faced forward. "Why don't you want me, Will?"

He sat up and looked at me. "What?"

I quickly wiped the tear away and whispered, "Can you just take me home?"

Will grabbed my hand. "Lex, look at me."

I slowly turned and looked at him.

"Lex, I want you so damn much that I can hardly breathe. What I can't do is make love to you without a condom. I won't do that to you or me or our future. I promised your dad that I would never hurt you and that I would always keep your best interests first."

He closed his eyes and then opened them again. I let out a small sigh as his eyes pierced mine.

"Lex, I don't want anything between us either, but I won't be reckless about this."

I nodded my head and whispered, "Okay. I love you, Will. I just want to be with you." I leaned over and kissed him gently on the lips. Then, I went to turn and get out of the truck.

"Um, Lex?"

I stopped and looked back at him. "Yeah?"

"I think I left the condoms in Colt's truck."

My mouth dropped open, and I felt like I couldn't breathe. "You bought condoms when you were with my brother? Oh my God! Will, how could you?"

"We were in Austin, and we all bought them at the same time. Colt threw them in his toolbox, and I'm pretty sure they're all still there."

His face turned to terror, and he pulled out his cell phone. He sent off a quick text and then looked back at me.

"What? What's wrong?"

"Libby is with Luke."

"So?" I tried to figure out where his panic was coming from.

"Libby. Is. With. Luke. What if he tries…oh God."

He pushed his hand through his hair, and I instantly wished his hands were on my body.

His phone went off, and he read the text message. Then, he looked at me and smiled. "They're all heading to Luke's house to watch movies. Colt and Lauren are going there, too."

I smiled and raised my eyebrows. "See? Nothing to worry about. Luke is not going to try anything with Libby. Will, we're wasting time."

I turned and got out of his truck. I began walking around the front, only to see Will still sitting in the truck.

I laughed and opened his door. "Now what?"

He looked down at me. "We have to go buy condoms."

My smile vanished. *Oh, holy hell.*

Will parked in front of the Script Shoppe Pharmacy. He looked at me as I looked at him.

"Now what?" he asked as he glanced back at the pharmacy.

"Well, you just walk in and buy some."

Will snapped his head over at me. "*Me?* Why do I have to be the one who buys them?"

I glared at him. "You're a guy. Guys buy condoms."

"A guy who wants to see the next day's sunrise doesn't buy condoms in his small-ass town where his girlfriend's father has already threatened him in more than one way."

I laughed. "Will, what do you think is going to happen? They're gonna call my dad and tell him you bought condoms? They probably don't even know we are dating." I moved my head down to look into the store's window. "Look, Katy Polk is working. She isn't going to say anything."

"Then, you go buy them if you are so confident."

I shook my head. "Fine. I'm gonna do my thing then."

"What? What does that mean, Lex? You're gonna do your thing?"

I smiled as I opened the truck door and jumped out. "Piece of cake." I walked up to the entrance and pushed the door open.

Katy looked up and smiled. "Hey, Alex!"

I waved and said, "Hey, Katy!"

I started to make my way to where the condoms were displayed. I walked up and looked at them. "Holy crap," I whispered. "Why are there so many? What the heck?"

"Why, hello there, Alex. Do you need some help this evening?"

I closed my eyes and silently prayed to God that I was not hearing Mr. Bell's voice. I opened them and turned to see the pharmacist standing next to me.

"Um…Mr. Bell…well, I, um…" I turned to look back at the wall of condoms. I didn't mean to say it out loud, but I couldn't stop it once it came out of my mouth. "There are so many. What's the purpose of each?"

Then, Mr. Bell kicked into his pharmacist talk. It was like he was talking to me about cold medicine, for Christ's sake. I just stood there, frozen, unable to move as he pitched condoms to me.

Where is the closest rock?

"Now, most of these are about the same. It depends on what you and your partner are looking for." He picked up a box labeled *Magnum Ribbed*. "These, for instance, have a spiral effect for extra stimulation."

Dying. I'm slowly dying.

He set that box down and picked up the one next to it. "The Trojan Ecstasy is all about comfort. The shape gives you a more natural experience."

I quickly looked around and saw Katy laughing her ass off behind the counter at the front of the store. My mouth dropped open, and she laughed even harder.

"The Trojan Bareskin is forty percent thinner. Again, it's for a more natural experience." He set that box down and picked up another one. "The Magnum Fire and Ice is probably more popular among the younger folks."

What did I do in my life to deserve this? Really, what?

"The Fire and Ice has a dual action that provides a warm and tingling sensation to both partners."

Oh. My. God. He didn't just say that.

I quickly reached out and grabbed the Trojan Ecstasy condoms. "These are fine, Mr. Bell. They're for Grace anyway. She's a natural kind of girl." The moment it came out of my mouth, I knew I would be in deep shit with Grace.

Mr. Bell smiled and nodded his head. "How are your parents?"

Awkward. I swallowed hard. "They're doing great." I looked down and whispered, "My father though…if he knew what I was doing, he might have a heart attack."

When I glanced back up, Mr. Bell smiled and nodded his head. "Tell everyone I said hello. Be safe, Alex. That goes for, uh…Grace, too."

I tried my best to smile. "Yes, sir."

I watched as he walked through the door. The pharmacy was closed.

Why in the hell was he even here?

I closed my eyes and shook my head. I quickly turned and made my way up to Katy, who was still giggling. I put the condoms down, and when I looked out the window, Will was gone. His truck was there, but he was gone.

What in the hell?

I looked back at Katy, who shrugged her shoulders. She looked out the window and then quickly rang up the condoms. She then grabbed a few bags of chips, put them all in a bag, and threw in some flyers.

"Oh, Katy, I didn't want the chips, and—"

"Alex?"

No. No, no, no, no!

I gave Katy a look of horror as I heard my father's voice coming from behind me. I smiled and turned around. "Daddy! Oh, hey."

He smiled and tilted his head. "Where's Will?"

I looked back out the window, and Will was crawling over his seat and getting into the backseat.

"Um…"

"Didn't you say he was still at the party, Alex?" Katy said.

I looked back at my father. I'd never lied to him before. "Grace was craving potato chips, so—"

"She borrowed Will's truck. How are you, Mr. Mathews?"

My father glanced down at the bag in my hand. I was shocked my hand wasn't shaking as I stood there and tried to seem normal.

He looked up at Katy. "I'm doing good, Katy. How are your parents?"

"They're good. What can I help you with tonight?"

He looked back at me. "I've had a terrible headache the last two days. I need more Advil."

My heart hurt, knowing that my father wasn't one hundred percent happy about Will and me. I looked down and then back up at him. He smiled and winked at me.

"I'm sorry, Daddy."

He walked up to me and placed his hand on the side of my face. "Go have fun, Alex. Be safe, baby girl. Don't be out too late."

Oh God, the guilt. "Yes, sir. I'll see you tomorrow morning." I turned and looked at Katy.

She winked at me and motioned for me to go.

I walked out of the drugstore and almost went to the passenger side of Will's truck. Instead, I opened the driver's door and climbed up. I threw the bag into the backseat.

Will cried out, "Shit. Ouch! What in the hell is in the bag?"

"I don't want to talk to you right now, William Gregory Hayes. Not right now."

I started the truck and began backing out. I looked over and saw my father leaving and heading to his truck. I silently thanked God that Mr. Bell hadn't come out to talk to him.

"It's safe to come out now," I said as I shook my head.

Will crawled over the seat and started laughing. "When I saw your dad's truck, I just ducked down. Can you imagine if he had walked in while I was in there, buying condoms?"

I slammed on the brakes.

Will shouted, "Shit! Lex, what are you doing?"

"Seriously, Will? Mr. Bell stood there and gave me a rundown on the different types of condoms. If my father had walked in two minutes earlier, I would have been the one getting caught buying condoms, and then my father would have killed both of us!"

Will looked at me and then busted out laughing. I rolled my eyes and floored the gas. The more he laughed, the more I attempted to hold my laughter in.

By the time we drove up to Will's house, he had been laughing hysterically for a while, especially after I'd told him how Mr. Bell described each condom.

Will jumped out of the truck, opened the back door, and grabbed the bag. We met in the front of his truck, and his smile faded as he searched my face.

He placed his hand on my face and whispered, "I love you, Lex. I don't want to do anything you're not ready for."

My heart slammed in my chest, and I realized I'd been holding my breath. I slowly let it out and smiled. "I love you, too, Will. I'm not going to lie and say I'm not scared 'cause I am, but I know in my heart that I want this more than anything."

Will smiled again as he leaned down and gently kissed me. He took my hand in his and slowly led me to his house. The moment we walked inside, my heart began racing, and my head was spinning.

Will walked us upstairs and stopped outside his bedroom. He turned and leaned back against his door. "Tell me what you want, Lex."

I looked into his eyes, and my heart instantly began to speed up. I knew what I wanted. I knew what I needed. "You. I want you, Will."

WILL

6

I never thought I'd experience the feelings I had at this moment. The moment Lex said she wanted me, my heart ramped up into overdrive.

I need to make this special for her.

Lex looked calm, too calm.

She walked up to me and pushed her body into mine. "Please don't make me beg, Will."

Oh. Dear. God.

She brushed her lips against mine, and it didn't take long before I was lost in her kiss. What started out as soft and gentle turned passionate and hungry. I reached for the doorknob and opened the door to my bedroom. Before I knew it, I had Lex on the bed, and we were kissing like we'd never kissed before.

"Jesus, Lex. I've never felt this way before," I whispered when I finally broke our kiss.

She closed her eyes and then opened them again. She had the most beautiful blue eyes I'd ever seen. Her brown hair was lying against my pillow, and she looked sexy as hell.

"Will, my body is aching for you."

I swallowed hard and sat up. She looked at me, confused, as she sat up, too.

"Lex, before we do this, I want to do something. I mean, I want to give you something."

She smiled that sweet smile of hers, and my heart melted. There wasn't anything I wouldn't do for her. Leaning back, I reached into my pocket and pulled out the ring box. I took a deep breath and looked at her. She was staring at the box. She slowly looked up into my eyes. She seemed scared. I knew she was probably thinking it was an engagement ring, but we weren't ready for that right now.

I smiled as I opened the box, revealing the promise ring my mother had helped me design. The ring meant the world to me because not only did my mother help design it, but my grandfather had made it. He had taken up making jewelry after he retired, and he had made a successful business out of it.

"Lex, I want to give you this promise ring as a symbol of my love and my commitment to our future together. I want you to know that when we make love tonight, when I take you as mine, I intend on making you mine forever."

Lex let out a small sob and quickly wiped away the tears rolling down her face. She looked into my eyes and whispered, "It's beyond beautiful."

I reached for her hand and slipped the ring onto her finger. The ring was white gold with four small round diamonds framing the center diamond. The band consisted of two rows of diamonds that formed an infinity symbol on each side.

Lex started crying harder as I pulled her hand up. I kissed the back of it and then the ring.

"My mother helped design it, and my grandfather made it. This ring was made especially for you, sweetheart. I hope you like it."

"Will, it's the most beautiful ring. I love it!" She threw herself into my arms and held on to me tightly.

My heart was soaring, and I knew I had set the tone for what I hoped would be the most amazing night of her life.

I pulled back and looked into her baby-blue eyes. "I love you, Lex."

The left side of her mouth moved up into a smile. She pulled her T-shirt up and over her head, and it felt like all the breath had been knocked from my body.

"I love you, too, Will."

I stood up and dropped the box onto the floor. I reached for her hands and pulled her up into a standing position. When I reached down and touched her stomach, she jumped slightly. I moved my hand down and began to unbutton her jeans. My heart was pounding so hard in my chest that it echoed in my ears. I was sure Lex could hear it.

I dropped to my knees. She held on to my shoulder while I pulled her shoes off. I reached up and began removing her jeans. I looked back up at her body and let out a moan. She was wearing black lace panties that matched her bra.

"Your body is so beautiful, Lex." I placed my hands on her hips, and I watched goose bumps cover her entire body.

When I gently kissed her stomach, she let out a long, soft moan. Her hands went to my hair, and I had to force myself not to push her panties down and bury myself in her.

A few weeks ago, the guys had been sitting around, and Luke had talked about his sexual encounters and orgasms. He'd said a girl needed to have a few orgasms before her first time. Luke's words popped into my head.

If given the chance, give her the first one through oral sex.

I wanted to taste Lex, but I wasn't sure how she would feel about it. I slowly began pulling her panties off as she moved one hand and began touching her breast through her bra.

Holy shit. I'm gonna come before I even get inside her.

"Oh God, Will…yes," she whispered.

If I'd thought my heart was beating hard a minute ago, it was about to pound the fuck out of my chest. She stepped out of her panties, and I just stared at her.

I closed my eyes and then looked up at her. "Lex, I want to taste you."

She snapped her head down and looked into my eyes. When she smiled and nodded her head, I was pretty sure all the blood rushed straight to my dick. It was so hard that it hurt, and I was almost positive I was about to pass out. I stood up and reached behind her to unclasp her bra. I gently pushed it off her shoulders and looked at her amazing breasts.

"Lex…I'm about to die."

She giggled. "Please don't. You've got me so worked up, Will. Please…"

"Lie down on the bed, Lex. I want you to be comfortable."

She bit down on her lower lip and quickly moved onto the bed. When she lay down on my bed, I had to close my eyes. I'd been dreaming of being with her for so long, and now, my dreams were coming true. I moved onto the bed and got between her legs. When I placed my hands on her upper legs, she jumped.

"Lex?"

She shook her head. "Please don't stop. It's just…your touch, Will. It always makes my body feel like electricity is running through it."

I swallowed hard. I didn't want to mess this up for her. "Lex, I've never…I mean…you're the first person I've ever done anything like this with. Baby, I just want it to feel good."

She lifted herself up and rested her body on her elbows. I saw the tears building in her eyes, and I wasn't sure if they were happy tears or what-in-the-fuck-am-I-doing tears.

She smiled sweetly and said, "Will, it's all going to be perfect because it's you. I've dreamed of this for so long."

I smiled at her and then moved between her legs. She was still watching me as I gently began kissing her inner thigh. When I looked up at her, she was chewing on her bottom lip. I used my tongue and ran it up her thigh, and she dropped her head back and let out a whimper.

I started kissing her again, all around her sweetness. Lex's breathing was increasing as I got closer and closer to the spot I'd dreamed about for years. I pulled back and closed my eyes as my dick throbbed in my pants. I took a deep breath and quickly swiped my tongue up and across her lips and clit.

"Oh my God!" Lex cried out.

Fuck. This is and will always be the hottest moment of my life.

One taste of her, and I needed more. I repeated my action, but this time, I moved my tongue around her clit. Lex pushed her hands into my hair and pulled my face closer to her. I couldn't help but smile. I began playing with her clit as I moved my finger up and slipped it inside her.

"Will…feels…oh God. Yes."

Holy shit.

I moved my fingers in and out of her body as she began to rock her hips.

"Yes. More. Will, please more."

More? More what? Shit, shit, shit.

I pushed another finger in and began sucking on her clit. She jumped as she began moaning and repeating how good it felt. Thank God I'd kept my damn pants on because I wanted so badly to release this crazy buildup. I moved my fingers apart some to stretch her, and she hissed in a breath of air. I stopped all movement.

"No! Don't stop. I'm so close, Will."

I pulled my fingers out and moved my tongue down to get a better taste of her. When I moaned, she bucked her hips into me even more.

"Will…" she whispered.

I moved back to her clit as I pushed three fingers into her this time. I began moving in and out, gently stretching her open more. She was so tight, and I couldn't wait to be inside her. I began sucking on her again, and she lost it.

"Yes. Oh God, yes. Will…I'm going to come. I'm coming! Yes!"

In this one moment, knowing that I was doing this to Lex for the first time, I knew I would never be the same. She was it for me. I never wanted to touch another woman.

I could feel her squeezing down on my fingers, and I had to do everything I could to stop myself from coming in my own damn pants. I looked up, and she was moving her head back and forth, calling out my name. When she finally started coming down from her orgasm, I quickly got up and pulled my T-shirt off.

"No, wait," Lex panted.

I stopped and watched her get up. Her face was covered in a beautiful flush, and I grabbed her and pulled her to me.

"Lex, can I kiss you after what I just did?"

She slammed her lips to mine, and I let out a moan as she ran her hands through my hair. She placed her hands on my chest, and it was now my turn for my breathing to increase. Her touch drove me mad with desire. She slid her hands down to my jeans, and she began unbuttoning them. I said a silent prayer that God would give me at least five minutes.

She pulled back and looked into my eyes. "I want you, Will. I want you so much that it hurts."

I quickly removed my pants and kicked them to the side. She glanced down and smiled when she saw my boxer briefs.

"I've waited so long for this," she whispered as she hooked her thumbs on my boxers and began pulling them down.

When my rock-hard dick sprang free, she let out a gasp. She snapped her eyes up to mine, and for the first time ever, I saw fear in her eyes. She swallowed hard and looked back down. I put my finger on her chin and pulled her face up until I was looking into her eyes.

"Lex...I'm scared, too, sweetheart. Let's just go slow, okay? I need to give you another orgasm, baby."

She glanced down and looked back up at me. "What about you?"

I smiled and pushed her hair behind her ear. "Honestly, Lex, if you were to just blow on it right now, I'd come."

Lex laughed and shook her head.

"Lie back down, baby."

She ran her tongue along her bottom lip and nodded.

I've died and gone to heaven.

alex

My body felt like it was in overdrive as I moved back onto Will's bed. The moment I had seen his hard-on, I'd panicked. He was huge.

How did I not notice how big he is?

I'd felt him before, and he had felt me, but it was never anything like this—with us so completely open to each other. He always made me stop before he came, and he'd say he'd take care of himself later.

I lay back on the bed and watched Will move next to me. As soon as he touched me, I jumped.

Shit. His touch makes my core just clench with need.

He moved his hand down between my legs, and I closed my eyes. He slipped two fingers in and began moving them in and out. I didn't want to come again. I wanted to orgasm with him inside me, and I wasn't sure if I was going to or not. Maegan had said she had yet to orgasm while having sex. She'd also failed to tell me how amazing oral sex was.

"Lex...baby, you're so damn wet." Will leaned down and began sucking on my nipple.

Oh God. Oh God. That feels...so...amazing. How does he know what to do to make me—

"Will...Oh my God...oh God, I'm going to come again. Will!"

I couldn't believe how I was calling out his name over and over, but I couldn't help it. I would forever be addicted to this feeling. The most amazing orgasm hit me so hard and so fast that I almost couldn't take it. It felt like it was going on forever. I squeezed down on Will's fingers as he moved them in and out while he continued to suck on my nipple. When he gently bit down on it, I lost it.

"Fuck, Lex. I can't wait any longer."

I shook my head quickly to clear my thoughts. I'd never in my life felt so amazing. I looked at Will as he moved between my legs. He kissed my stomach, and then he moved up to one nipple and then the next. I tried to talk, but I couldn't. I was lost in ecstasy.

When his lips reached my neck, he said, "I love you, Lex."

"I...love...you."

"I want you so badly, sweetheart."

"Will, I want you, too."

Then, I felt him at my entrance, and I tensed up.

Will moved his lips up to my ear. His hot breath on my body was pushing me back to the edge of another orgasm.

How? How does he do this to me?

"Lex…baby…relax."

I closed my eyes and completely relaxed. I knew Will would never do anything to hurt me. I opened my eyes, and Will stopped moving at the same time. He pulled back and looked into my eyes.

"Fuck! The condom!" He jumped up, quickly grabbed the box, and ripped it open.

I couldn't help but giggle at how fast he was moving. I smiled, knowing that we had realized it at the same time. I watched his shaking hands as he rolled the condom onto his shaft. I licked my lips and dreamed of the day I could take him with my mouth.

Will quickly moved back to where he was and smiled at me. He barely pushed against my entrance as he leaned down and kissed me. The kiss was utterly romantic and sweet.

"Lex…I'll love you forever."

My eyes were burning from the tears I was attempting to hold back as he began moving into me. I wasn't sure if it was from the sweet words he'd whispered to me or from the pain of him stretching my body to fit him.

"I'm going to make you mine forever, Lex. Mine. Forever."

"Yes…" A sob escaped my throat.

Will stopped moving, but I opened my legs more and grabbed him to pull him closer.

"Don't…please don't stop."

Will pulled back and looked at me. "I don't want to hurt you."

"Will…I need to feel you inside me. Please."

He buried his face in my neck as he began pushing in. I wasn't sure if him going so slow was making it worse or not. He pushed in and then pulled out some. He moved in more and let out a long, soft moan.

"Oh…God, you feel so good," he whispered against my neck.

I wrapped my legs around him and pulled him to me. It was hurting like a bitch, and I closed my eyes tightly. "How much more?"

"I'm almost all the way in."

"Will…just do it…please," I said as I let out a whimper.

When he pulled out and pushed in again, something happened. It felt like heaven and hell at the same time.

"Ah…shit…Lex. I'm all the way in."

When he looked at me, he sucked in a breath of air. He reached up with his thumb and gently wiped my tears away. "Lex, you'll never know how much this moment means to me."

I started crying more.

Will stopped moving. "Talk to me, Lex. Please tell me I'm not hurting you."

I shook my head. "Will…I love you so much. Please don't stop."

He slowly pulled out some and began moving. At first, the pain was almost too much, but the more he moved, the more incredible it felt.

I arched my back. I needed him deeper in me. I needed more of him. I squeezed my legs around him, and he let out a moan.

"It feels so amazing…Will…I love you. Oh God. Will…don't stop."

I couldn't believe it. I swore I could feel the buildup in my toes, and as it traveled up my body, it hit my core so hard that I let out a scream.

"I'm coming, Will! Jesus…oh God, I'm coming."

I could feel him getting bigger inside me, and I squeezed down around him.

"Lex…baby, I'm gonna come. Lex."

Will pushed in deep and hard as he began kissing me, and we both came together for the first time as one.

Will had his arms wrapped around me as he held me while our breathing slowed down. "Are you okay, Lex?"

I smiled. "I'm more than okay. I've never felt so wonderful in my life." I rolled over and faced him.

He was smiling as he ran his finger down the side of my face. "I hope it was special for you."

My heart slammed in my chest, and I had such an urge to crawl on top of him. "I don't think you could have possibly made it any more special, Will. It was perfect, beyond perfect."

"Did I hurt you at all?"

My heart melted at how much Will cared about me. "No." I ran my tongue across my top teeth as I pushed him onto his back. I crawled on top of him. "Matter of fact, I think I'm ready for some more."

My core clenched when I felt his hard on growing beneath me. I loved that I could turn him on so easily.

"Lex…" Will whispered as he placed his hands on my hips to stop me from grinding against him. "Condom, baby."

I leaned over and reached for the box of condoms on the floor. I grabbed one, and then I grinned as a naughty thought entered my head. I moved off of him some and began stroking him.

"Jesus, Lex."

I was hugging myself internally. I knew I had it in me. I just needed to be a bit more open to things. There were so many things I wanted to try with Will, and I was already wondering when and where we were going to make love after tonight.

Will had his eyes closed, and I looked down at him. He was more than ready to go again. I ripped open the wrapper, and I was about to pull the condom out of it when I suddenly became very brave. Before he could stop me, I leaned over and quickly took him in my mouth. I began moving up and down his shaft with my hand following my movements.

Will jumped and yelled out, "Holy fuck!"

I smiled and then moaned. Will sat up, grabbed me, and pulled me off of him. He was breathing heavily, and I couldn't help but smile.

"My God, Lex…you can't…you can't do that. I almost came right on the spot in your mouth!"

The idea made my insides tighten, and I instantly felt wetness between my legs. "I would have been okay with that."

Will's face dropped, and he shook his head. "Wha-what?"

I began chewing on my lower lip. *What if Will doesn't like the idea of me giving him a blow job?* I quickly looked away. "I'm sorry I even tried."

I went to move away from him, but he grabbed my arm.

"Lex, wait. I mean…I want you to do that." He ran his hand through his hair and smiled at me. "I've woken up from dreams of you doing that. I just…I never want you to think you have to do something to make me happy."

"I know that, Will. I know you would never ask me to do something I didn't want to do."

Will's eyes lit up with something I'd never seen before. "Lex, do you want to be on top? Or do you want to do that?"

Oh God. The idea of being on top of Will and being in control turned me on in more ways than I could count, but giving him something he'd dreamed of also turned me on.

"What do you want me to do?" I asked.

The crooked smile that spread across his face made my stomach take a hard dive south.

"Honestly?"

I nodded my head.

"I want you to ride me."

Oh. My. God. If I'd thought I was turned-on before, his words had pushed me to the edge of an orgasm, and all he had done was say something to me.

I slowly grinned as I placed my hands on his chest and pushed him back. When he lay back, I took out the condom and began to put it on.

"How do I know if I'm putting it on right?" I intently watched what I was doing as I rolled the condom down his shaft. The whole time, my core was pulsing. "Will, am I doing it right?"

I had it almost all the way on when I looked at Will. His mouth was slightly open, and his chest was heaving up and down. I smiled bigger and gave myself an internal fist pump.

I looked down at it again and tried to think back to health class when we had practiced putting condoms on fake dicks. I was pretty sure I had put it on right. I moved and positioned myself above him. He had his eyes closed, but he placed his hands on my hips. When I moved down, his tip barely pushed in.

He stopped me and opened his eyes. "Lex, this is gonna feel different. It might stretch you open more."

My sex was throbbing so badly, and I needed relief. I sank down on him and let out a gasp as I felt him filling me completely. Will sucked in a breath of air as I sat there and tried to get used to this new feeling. I threw my head back, and I wasn't sure what had come over me, but I moved my hands up my body and began feeling my breasts.

"Jesus…my God, Lex. I've never seen anything so damn sexy in my entire life."

I slowly began moving myself up and down just a bit. It felt so good. Something was hitting on the inside, and I swore I could feel another orgasm building already. I began to move faster. I moved my body up and down more as Will let out a long moan.

He gripped my hips harder. "Lex…baby, that feels…I'm not going to last long, Lex."

Once I got past the stinging of being stretched out more, something inside me switched on. I needed it harder. I needed more. I placed my hands on his chest and began moving up and down, faster and harder.

"Yeah…this feels…so good," I said as I looked into Will's eyes.

"Lex…are you going to come? 'Cause I can't hold off."

I could feel it. *Oh God.* I was so close. "Will…yeah…so…close!" I called out.

Will reached down, and the moment he touched my clit, I began calling out his name. He sat up and wrapped his arms around me. I was hit by another orgasm before the first one even stopped. This one was much more intense, and I screamed out his name as he called out my name.

"Lex…oh, Lex. I'm coming. Don't stop."

I moved my body against him, rubbing that spot that was driving me so insane that I could hardly think. I'd never in my life had such an intense orgasm. I felt like I had left my body, and I was looking down at myself. The way I was calling out his name surprised myself, but it felt so amazing.

When my orgasm finally subsided, I just sat there in Will's arms with him still inside me. I didn't want to move. I loved the feeling of being one with him. He held on to me tightly, and I could feel him twitching inside me. I wondered how many times he would be able to do this.

"Lex…I never imagined it would be like this."

I pulled back and smiled. "Me either."

I glanced at the clock. I pushed Will back and jumped out of the bed. "Oh my God, it's after midnight. What if Colt gets home before me? He has no idea where I am, and everyone is at Luke's."

I quickly ran into Will's bathroom and began cleaning myself off. When I ran back into his room, he was already dressed in his jeans, and he was pulling his T-shirt on. He had the goofiest grin on his face, and my heart swelled up, knowing that he was happy because of what we had just shared.

I grabbed my panties and pulled them on. Then, I dropped to the floor to find my bra. "There you are!" I put my bra on, and then I slid on my shirt and jeans. I pulled on my boots and looked at myself in the mirror.

Do I still look like a virgin? Will anyone be able to tell? I placed my hands on my face. I was flush, but maybe that was from running around.

In the mirror, I saw Will pulling the sheets off his bed, and I turned around. "What are you doing? We have to go!"

Will looked at me and then down to the sheets.

When I saw the blood, my hand slapped over my mouth. "Oh no. What's your mom gonna think? Will! Oh no!"

He shook his head and gave me the sweetest smile. "Don't worry, Lex. A few weeks back, I bought more sheets when I found out they were going out of town. Just in case we…well, you know."

I tilted my head and gave him a questioning look. "You bought extra sheets?"

He shrugged his shoulders. "Yeah. I mean, I knew I could wash these, but I wasn't sure, so I thought it would be better to just throw them out and put new sheets on."

I put my finger up to my mouth and gently bit down on it. Grace had said nothing turned a guy on more than biting on your finger or licking your lips. There went that look in Will's eyes.

Yep. There went that pulsing in my core.

Will shook his head quickly. "No. We can't, Lex. Come on. Help me with these, so I can get you home."

I helped Will put the new sheets on. He balled up the old ones and carried them down into the kitchen. He pulled out a garbage bag and placed the sheets in it.

Then, he put it in the trash compactor. "I'll take this out now."

I sat down at the kitchen island and texted Colt.

Me: Where are you?

Colt: Watching TV at Luke's. Where the fuck are you?

Me: At Will's.

Colt: Are you okay?

Me: Of course I am. When are you going home? If Dad or Mom ask, I've been with y'all.

Colt: Alex, please tell me you wanted this.

Me: Colt, I love him, and yes, I wanted it more than anything.

Colt: You know I want to pound his ass right now.

Me: I love you for that.

Colt: Luke is gonna freak, Alex.

Me: It's none of his business.

I glanced up and noticed Will watching me. "Colt knows."

Will closed his eyes and pushed his hands through his hair. "Ah hell."

I let out a giggle and then quickly looked at the back door when I heard it opening. I snapped my head back at Will, who was looking at the door in horror.

When the door opened, Josh and Heather walked in.

Heather stopped and looked at me. She smiled. "Alex, darling."

Josh stopped and glanced over to Will before turning and looking at me. He tilted his head a bit as he looked at me, then back at Will, and then back to me again. He smiled sweetly, but then he slowly turned to face Will. "Will, it's pretty late, and I'm sure Alex needs to be heading home."

Will nodded his head and grabbed his keys from the island. I jumped off the stool and instantly felt sore. I was pretty sure I'd played it off, but with the way Heather was staring at me, I knew I had done a piss-poor job of it.

I started to walk by when Heather reached for my hand. I stopped and turned to face her.

Her eyes softened, and she smiled at me. "Will, wait for Alex out by your truck, please."

Oh shit. Oh shit. Oh shit.

8
WILL

I glanced at Lex and gave her a small smile. Then, I headed out the door, and my father followed me. I walked up to my truck and opened the door, only to have him push it shut.

"You want to tell me what in the hell you were thinking?"

I'd never lied to my father, not once, and I wasn't about to start now.

I slowly turned and leaned up against my truck. I looked him in the eyes. "I love her, Dad. It was something we both wanted."

His whole body slumped, and he let out a sigh as he shook his head. "Her father would break you in two if he knew what happened tonight."

I pushed off my truck. "You're not going to tell him, Dad, are you?"

He just looked at me. "I ought to. In my house, Will? My. House."

"Dad, I didn't want her first time to be in my truck or some damn barn. I wanted to at least make it special and have her feel comfortable."

I saw a small smile play across his face.

He quickly looked away. "At least we taught you something right."

I knew what I was about to do was a low blow, but I was going for it anyway. "Did you and Mom wait, Dad?"

He spun around and glared at me. "Excuse me?"

"Did you wait, Dad? I'm just asking a simple question. Did you wait until you were married or until you found Mom? I love Lex. I saved myself for her, Dad. We both wanted this."

His mouth opened slightly. "You…you've never had sex before?"

I shook my head. "No. I told you, I love her and wanted my first time to be with her. I gave her the promise ring Granddad made. I gave it to her before we even did anything."

My father slowly nodded his head and let out a long breath. "To answer your question, no, I didn't wait. As a matter of fact, I was a bit of a player before I met your mother."

I pulled my head back. "Really?"

He let out a gruff laugh. "Yeah. I have many regrets, Will. I was foolish and disrespectful to many women. I don't want you to follow in my footsteps."

I stood there in shock as I took in what my father had said. He always pushed me to be a gentleman and to treat women with the highest respect. I guessed he'd learned from his mistakes, and he didn't want me to make the same.

"I'm sorry if I disrespected you and Mom by bringing Lex here tonight."

My father walked up to me and put his hand on my shoulder. "William, I'm not going to say I'm happy about this, but there is one thing I'm happy about."

"What's that?" I asked.

"I'm happy and damn proud of you for taking Alex's feelings into consideration in all of this. I'm not going to share this with Gunner because, honestly, I'd like to see you have a go at this life."

I let out a chuckle.

My father raised his eyebrow at me. "I'm being serious."

I nodded my head. "I know you are, sir. Nervous laugh, I guess."

"Did you use protection?"

"Yes, sir. I would never do that to Lex."

His face relaxed, and he nodded his head. "Always, and I mean *always*, use protection in some form. Please."

"I will, Dad. I promise you."

The door opened, and my mother and Lex came walking out. Lex turned and hugged my mom, and my mother whispered something to her while pushing a piece of hair behind her ear.

When Lex turned and started toward me, I couldn't really read her face. She walked up to me, and I smiled as I took her hand before leading her to the passenger side of my truck. I opened the door, and she quickly jumped in. As I walked back around, I glanced up and saw my mom and dad just standing on the porch.

"Will, please be careful driving."

I nodded my head. "I will, Mom. I love you."

"I love you, too, darling."

When I got in the truck and started it, Lex grabbed my hand. I backed up, turned my truck, and headed down the driveway.

I looked at her and smiled. "Are you okay, sweetheart?"

She nodded her head. "Yeah. Your mom knows."

I let out a laugh. "So does my dad."

"She promised not to say anything to my parents." Lex turned and looked at me. "Did your dad say if he was gonna tell my father?"

I could hear the panic in her voice. "No, he's not going to say anything. What did my mom say to you?"

"She asked me if you made sure I was ready and if you were gentle with me."

I rolled my eyes. "Oh God. My mother knows I had sex." I wanted to throw up.

Lex giggled and squeezed my hand. "She told me to soak in a hot bath if I was able to."

I looked at her, and my heart began to hurt. "Are you sore?"

She nodded her head. "Yes, but it's a good sore."

Lex pulled out her phone and began texting someone.

"Who are you texting?"

"Colt. I'm seeing if he is still at Luke's house."

About a minute later, her phone beeped. "Can you take me to Luke's? I'll ride home with Colt."

"Um...sure."

I was almost to Luke's driveway. I put on my signal and turned in. I punched in the gate code and started down the long driveway. When I pulled up and parked, I shut the truck off. I turned to see Lex staring at me.

"You don't regret it, do you?" she asked.

My mouth dropped open, and I pulled her over to me. She crawled onto my lap. I put my hand behind her neck and brought her lips to mine. I poured nothing but love into the kiss. It was slow, sweet, and meaningful.

I barely broke our kiss when I whispered, "I'll never forget this night for as long as I live, Lex. You have stolen my heart forever."

A tear moved down her cheek.

"Baby, please don't cry. I hate to see you cry."

She was about to say something when someone banged on the window. I turned to see Luke.

He opened the door and grabbed Lex. "Get the fuck out of his truck, Lex."

"What? Luke! Let go of me!"

Lex pulled her arm back, but Luke pulled her out.

"Luke, stop it right now!" Grace yelled.

I took a deep breath in and let it out as I got out of the truck. I had to put myself in Luke's and Colt's shoes.

How would I feel if I found out one of them had slept with Libby?

I shut the door and turned to face Luke. Colt was walking out.

Lex stepped in front of him. "Colt! Stop this right now! Grace, stop your brother."

Luke walked up and pushed me. "You motherfucker. You went forward with it? You slept with her?"

"Luke, I'm not doing this with you. You knew—"

That was when it happened. He punched me square in the jaw. Lex, Grace, and Lauren all screamed.

Libby came running up to me. "Will! Oh my gosh, are you okay?"

"I'm fine, Lib. Just step back, honey."

Luke hadn't hit me nearly as hard as he could have.

Libby turned around and walked over to Luke. She pushed him on the chest. Luke just stood there, staring at her.

"You asshole! He loves her, and she loves him. It's none of your goddamn business what they do!"

Luke looked stunned as he stared at Libby.

She pushed him again and then began hitting him. "He loves her! Alex is lucky to have someone love and worship her like Will does. You wouldn't know what that is like…to love and respect someone, you prick."

Luke grabbed Libby by her arms to get her to stop. She took a step back and looked at him.

"Libby…I…" Luke looked away as Libby began sobbing.

I walked up and took her in my arms. I had no idea if Libby was more upset by what Luke had done to me or if he had done something to her.

"Lib, it's okay, honey. He didn't even hit me that hard." I glanced over to Lex, who was still holding Colt back.

"You want a shot, too?" I asked him.

He walked up to me and looked me in the eyes. "I need to talk to you…alone."

I nodded my head and kissed Libby on the forehead. "I'll be right back, honey. Please don't worry. I'm okay."

Libby nodded her head and stood there as Colt and I walked away from everyone. We headed to the barn. When we stopped, I turned to face him. He stood there and stared at me.

"If you're gonna hit me, Colt, just do it."

He shook his head. "I'm not hotheaded like Luke. I just want to know one thing. Do you truly love her, Will?"

I smiled and nodded my head. "I love her more than anything, Colt. She's my reason for breathing."

He slowly nodded. "Did you make it special for her?"

"Yes. At least, I hope I did."

"All right. I just want you to know, I love you like a brother. You're my best friend, Will. But if you ever hurt her, I'll hurt you."

"I won't, Colt. I promise you, I'll never hurt her."

Colt stuck out his hand, and we shook. He went to turn, and I grabbed his arm.

"Hey, I have something to say to you."

He gave me a crooked-ass grin. "What's that?"

"You hurt Lauren, I'll hurt you."

His smile faded. He turned and walked back toward everyone.

Libby and Lex both walked up to me.

Lex went right into my arms and whispered, "What did he say?"

"He told me that if I ever hurt you, he'd hurt me."

She giggled. "I'm so sorry about Luke."

I gently pushed her back from me, so I could look her in the face. "I would have done the same thing."

I held out my arm for Libby, and she walked up next to Lex. I hugged them both. When I looked up at Luke, I could see the pain in his eyes. I wasn't sure if it had more to do with Lex and him hitting me or with Libby breaking down and crying. If he cared at all about Libby like I did Lex, I knew that Libby's tears had probably caused him pain.

Libby reached up and kissed my cheek. "I love you, Will."

I smiled as I kissed her back on her cheek. "I love you, too, Lib."

She turned and started to head to the house. Luke looked like he was going to say something to her, but he stopped. She walked right by him and followed Grace and Lauren into the house.

Luke ran his hands down his face and glanced back at me. "I'm going to bed. You working on the fence tomorrow?"

I nodded my head. "Yeah."

"Fine. Be here at six in the morning, or we're leaving without you." He turned and stormed off into the house.

Lex let out a sigh as she watched him. She turned to me and said, "I'm so sorry. He had no right—"

I pulled her to me and kissed her. She wrapped her arms around my neck and let out a sweet moan.

"Thank you for tonight, Lex."

She grinned from ear to ear. "Thank you. Thank you for my promise ring and for your promise. Thank you for making it the most amazing night of my life."

"Let's just hope your dad never finds out!"

We both started laughing.

Colt walked back out. "Alex, you ready to go home?"

Lex looked up at me and gave me a weak smile. "I love you, Will."

I leaned down and kissed her gently. "I love you, too, Lex."

Lex turned and made her way over to Colt's truck. She paused for a second to turn back and look at me. She waved and blew me a kiss, and I smiled and waved back. I watched as Colt's truck drove down the driveway.

"Are you okay?"

I nodded my head and turned to face my sister. "Yeah. You ready to go home, Lib? Mom and Dad decided to come home early."

The look on Libby's face turned to horror. She slowly moved her hands up and covered her mouth. "They didn't..."

I laughed. "Nah, but they knew. Lex and I were in the kitchen when they walked in."

Libby closed her eyes. "Shit, Will. Mom texted me earlier and asked what we were doing. I said we were all watching movies at Luke's. She asked if you were here, and I said yes. Will, I'm so sorry. We're both going to get in trouble now."

I shrugged my shoulders as I walked up to her. I threw my arm around her and began walking her to my truck. "Nah, I don't think so. Besides, nothing will ever be worse than both my parents knowing I just had sex for the first time with my girlfriend."

I chuckled, but Libby stopped walking.

I stopped and looked at her. "What's wrong?"

A huge grin spread across her face. "Will, did you…oh my gosh. Did you wait for Alex?"

I felt my face turn fifty shades of red. I smiled slightly and whispered, "Yeah."

She slowly shook her head. "William Hayes, you are the most romantic man I'll ever know, and it really sucks you're my brother."

We both busted out laughing as I opened the passenger side door for her.

Before she got in, I took a hold of her arm. "Hey, Lib?"

"Yeah?"

I looked down and kicked the dirt. I wasn't sure how to even ask her or if I even wanted to know. "Lib, do you, um…well…do you have feelings for Luke?"

Her smile instantly dropped. "It doesn't really matter if I do."

I tilted my head and stared at her. It was dark, but I swore I saw tears in her eyes.

"Sure it does, Libby. I know Luke had feelings for you at one time, and—"

She held up her hand and quickly shook her head. "No, he doesn't. He made that perfectly clear this evening when he made out with Claire at the party."

I instantly felt the heat move up into my head. "What?"

"Will, I don't want to talk about it. Can we just go home? Please."

I nodded my head. "Sure, Libby."

As I shut the door and walked around my truck, I glanced back toward the house and saw Luke standing on the porch. I raised my hand.

He nodded as he stared into the truck. "Libby going home with you?"

"Uh…yeah. I thought you were going to bed?" I asked as I opened my door.

Luke started down toward the truck, and I had to admit, I tensed up, expecting him to throw another punch at me.

He walked up to me. Then, he looked around me and into the truck. "Y'all going to the river on Saturday night?"

I wasn't sure if he was really asking both of us or just Libby.

Libby remained silent in the truck.

"Yeah. I mean, as far as I know, we'll be there," I said.

Luke nodded his head, never taking his eyes from Libby. "Night, Lib."

She turned slightly and looked out the passenger side window. "Good night, Luke."

Luke frowned and ran his hand through his hair as he looked at me. He gave me a weak smile. "Sorry for hitting you, bro."

He stuck his hand out, and I shook it.

"I would have done the same thing, dude. No worries."

"See ya in the morning," Luke said before walking back to his house.

I jumped in and looked at Libby. It only took me a few seconds to realize my sister was crying.

I knew the reason why she was crying.

Luke.

I started the truck and began driving off. I looked over toward Luke and gripped my steeling wheel harder.

The next time my sister cries over him, I'm going to be the one throwing the first punch.

9

"Good morning, my handsome man."

I walked into Banjo's stall and gave him a handful of oats while he bobbed his head up and down. I ran my hand along his back, and my heart broke. I was going to miss him so much.

Banjo and I would go for a ride at least once a day. He was my everything—next to my parents, Colt, and Will.

"You want to go for a ride, big boy?"

"May I join you?"

I quickly turned to see my father leaning against the wall. I smiled and nodded my head. He winked at me and turned to saddle up a horse. I watched him as he got my saddle and his saddle. My father was so handsome, and Colt certainly inherited Daddy's good looks. Colt and I both got our parents' blue eyes and brown hair. Colt favored my father, and I favored my mother. I had to admit, when people told me I looked like my mother, it would make me feel good. To me, she was breathtaking, a natural beauty. My parents made such a cute couple.

"Alex, why are you staring at me with a goofy grin?"

I laughed and began to bring Banjo out of his stall. "I was thinking about how you and Mama make a cute couple with your handsome good looks and Mama's natural beauty."

My father grinned and then tilted his head. "What do you want?"

I hit him on the arm and said, "Nothing, Daddy. I was just thinking about how happy you both are. I want that, too. I want it with Will."

His smile faded a bit, and he turned and grabbed his saddle. He began getting his horse ready. Neither one of us said anything as we saddled up the horses, got on them, and headed out.

I couldn't take the silence anymore. "Daddy, why don't you like Will?"

He snapped his head over and looked at me. "What? I love Will like a son. I just don't like the idea of him dating my daughter."

"I would think you'd like it better than some strange guy I might meet at UT. Will loves me, Daddy, and he treats me so good, like how you treat Mom."

Daddy smiled and nodded his head. "I don't doubt that, sweetheart." He let out a sigh. "Alex, it's just that the two of you only know each other and your close circle of friends. You've always been a part of the ranch and Mason. I want you both to have the chance to explore other things, other ideas. I know you say you want to come back and live on the ranch with

Will, but you haven't even begun to experience life outside of Mason, Alex."

I looked down and frowned. "Daddy, why is it so hard for you to believe that I want to have a life like you and Mom? I love the ranch just as much as you, Mom, Colt, Will, and Luke. It just seems unfair."

He nodded his head and looked ahead. "Alex, you're going to college, and things will be so different. I know you love the ranch, sweetheart. I just want you to keep an open mind. You might go to Austin and decide that you love Austin. I want you to be happy, Alex. I never want you to settle. I want you to have every opportunity possible, and I don't want this relationship with Will to cloud any of that."

I bit down on my lower lip. We stayed silent as our horses walked along for a bit more.

"Daddy, I love Will. I can't see my future without him."

"Alex, I'm not doubting your love for him. Just know that it is possible that you will meet someone else in college who will—"

I looked at him. "Who will what?"

He stopped his horse, and I brought Banjo to a stop.

"Who will make you doubt your feelings for Will."

My mouth dropped open. I looked down at my promise ring and then back into my father's eyes. "That will never happen—*ever*."

He gave me a weak smile and nodded his head. "Come on, let's see what Banjo has against Apache. Let's race down to the river."

I giggled as I kicked Banjo, and we took off racing toward the water.

I ran down the stairs as soon as Will had sent me a text saying he was pulling down the driveway.

"Stop!"

I turned and looked at my father.

"Where are y'all going?"

My mother walked into the living room and smiled.

Colt came down the stairs and walked right past me. "Later."

My mouth dropped open as he walked right out the door without my parents saying a word to him.

I used my hands and gestured toward where Colt had just left. "Um…hello? He just walked right by, and you didn't ask him where he was going! I'm older and out of high school, and you're going to stop and ask me?"

My father gave me a smirk that just made me all the madder. Ever since our ride the other day, he'd kept planting it in my head that I should take a break from Will when I headed to college. He'd said that if our love was true and strong, it shouldn't matter.

My father walked toward me. "Your brother already told us he was going to a party down on the river at Claire Montgomery's place."

I slowly shook my head. "Daddy, surely you know I'm going to the same party."

He chuckled. "I figured. Will there be alcohol, Alex?"

I raised my eyebrow at him and tilted my head. "Really, Dad? We're in the country. There is nothing else to do but have river parties, field parties, and barn dances."

"That doesn't answer my question, does it?"

I never lied to my father—well, with the exception of the night when I'd bought the condoms.

"Yes, Daddy. There will be alcohol. Yes, I will watch everyone. No, I won't let Will or Colt drink since they are driving. There is a plan already set up. Whoever drove and ends up drinking will stay the night at Claire's. Plus, her brother, Duke, is home from college, and he will be keeping an eye on things, too."

My father nodded his head. My parents weren't very strict, but then again, they were. As long as we were always truthful with them, they would be okay with things. Colt and I always knew we could call our parents if needed.

I had gone to a party in Fredericksburg with Maegan, and I'd ended up drinking. I'd called my father, and my parents had come to pick me up. I'd gotten a nice long lecture the next day, but they always told us that we could call anytime with no punishments. If we didn't call and we got caught, then the wrath of my father would fall upon us. Neither Colt nor I would want that.

"Watch Lauren and Taylor if they go, okay? They're younger."

I nodded my head as I leaned up and kissed my father on the cheek. Then, the doorbell rang. I smiled as I bolted to the door and threw it open. Will was standing there, looking hot as hell in his Wranglers, boots, and light-blue T-shirt. His hair was peeking out from under his cowboy hat before he took it off. I was instantly turned-on. We hadn't been together again since our first night. I was hoping he would take care of that tonight.

Will walked in and shook my father's hand. Then, he said, "Hello," to my mother.

"Don't keep her out too late, Will. If y'all decide to stay, you call me, Alex."

"Yes, sir. Night, Mama! I love you."

"I love you, too. Will, please be careful driving."

Will placed his hat back on his head and nodded. "Yes, ma'am. Always."

Will grabbed my hand, and we made our way to his truck. He opened the passenger door and held my hand until I sat down.

He leaned in and kissed me gently on the lips. "I love you."

I smiled and placed my hand on his face. "I love you, too."

"I'm going to take you again tonight, Lex."

My mouth barely opened, and I instantly felt the wetness between my legs. I whispered, "Will…"

He gave me another look that had me sucking in a breath of air before he stepped away and shut the door. He walked around the front of the truck and then jumped in.

"Do we have to go to the party?" I asked when he shut the door.

He threw his head back and laughed. "Yes! This is our last summer before we head to college."

I sighed. "We'll be home every summer, and I'm sure Claire will throw a party each summer. Besides, I don't even like Claire."

Will looked over at me, shocked. "What? Since when?"

I shook my head and thought back to a few days ago when Libby, Grace, Lauren, and I had all gone for a ride at Lauren's place.

Grace brought her horse alongside Libby's. Grace had told me something had happened between Libby and Luke the night Will and I slept together. Luke had been pouting since Libby left with Will.

"Libby, spill it. You got upset with Luke the other night when Alex and Will came back. What gives? Y'all seemed to be having fun at the party, and then the next thing I knew, Luke was in the corner, feeling up Claire Montgomery," Grace said.

Libby looked at Grace, who stared straight ahead. "I guess I was just upset to see Luke and Will fighting. I hate when they fight. You know that, Grace."

I glanced over to Lauren, and she was frowning.

Grace was not about to let it go. "Bullshit, Libby. You and my brother used to be so damn close. Then, he pulled the whole kissing-you shit before he left for college, and things haven't been the same. The other night, y'all seemed to be back to your old selves, having fun and dancing. How did Claire come into the picture?"

Libby turned away from us, and I could tell she was upset. I stopped my horse, and Lauren and Grace stopped as well. Libby turned her horse around to face us. When I saw the tear moving down her face, my heart broke.

"Oh, Lib, what did my asshole brother do to you? I'm going to kick his ass," Grace said.

Libby attempted to laugh but failed. "He didn't do anything. That's the problem, Grace. We were having fun, dancing and all. He even asked if I wanted to go to the diner for something to eat. Then, a slow song came on, and he pulled me closer to him as we danced. I really thought…"

A sob escaped her throat, and Lauren sniffled. I glanced over and looked at Lauren. I saw she was attempting to hold back her tears. We all knew how much Libby liked Luke. With Maegan always talking about wanting to sleep with him and Luke's player ways, we knew it bothered Libby to even be around him.

Grace jumped off her horse and walked over to Libby as she began getting down. Lauren and I quickly followed.

"You really thought what, Lib?" Grace asked.

Libby swallowed hard. "I thought he might have feelings for me. He looked like he wanted to kiss me, so I figured I'd just go for it."

I put my hand up to my mouth and let out a gasp.

"Did you kiss him?" Lauren asked.

Libby shook her head. "No. I told him that I missed him, I missed us, and I wanted him to kiss me again."

"What did he say?" all three of us asked at once.

Libby's eyes filled with tears. "He leaned down, and he was about to kiss me, but then he stopped right before our lips touched. He looked into my eyes and said…"

I noticed Grace's hands balling into fists.

Libby sobbed. "He said…he said that kissing me was a mistake, and he never thought there was an us outside of being friends."

I closed my eyes.

Grace whispered, "Bastard."

"He stepped back, and I swear his eyes looked so sad, but he began looking around. Claire had been trying to flirt and dance with Luke from the moment he got there. He must have seen her. I don't know. He looked back at me and smiled. Then, he thanked me for dancing with him. He told me we were all going back to his house to watch movies and that if I needed a ride, he'd take me. A few minutes later, I saw him with Claire."

Lauren walked up to Libby and pulled her into her arms. "I'm so sorry, Libby. He's just a stupid, scared ass."

I looked at Grace.

She mouthed to me, I'm going to kill him.

I nodded my head.

Libby began laughing and pulled away from Lauren. "It's okay, really. I was stupid to think Luke ever really had any feelings for me. I mean, he probably wants to sleep with Maegan, and I'm just in the way."

"No, he doesn't," Lauren said.

I wasn't so sure about that. Maegan had a way of flirting with Luke, and I knew he had mentioned more than once to Colt that if Maegan kept pushing, he was going to give her what she wanted.

We all sat down and talked for a bit more.

"Lib, you're going to A&M. Are you going to be able to go to the same school as Luke? What if you, you know, see him on dates?" Grace asked.

My heart sank at the idea of Will being at a different school than me, especially knowing he would be rooming with Luke. I didn't think Luke was a man-whore, but I knew he had already slept with his fair share of girls.

Libby shook her head and stood up. "I'll be fine. I guess it's my fault for letting my feelings for Luke get in the way of our friendship. I'm going to be fine. I'll meet someone at A&M and forget all about Luke Johnson." She turned and climbed back onto her horse. She looked down at us and smiled. "You always forget about your first love after high school anyway, right?"

Grace laughed and nodded her head. We all started talking about Lauren's last year of high school.

I couldn't help myself, but I kept thinking of Libby's comment.

You always forget about your first love…

"Lex? Hello? Are you still with me?" Will asked.

I smiled weakly. "Sorry, I was thinking about the other day. Libby told us that Claire and Luke were making out, and she was bothered by it. I just think Claire is out to get Luke before she heads off to college. I just don't like her."

Will gripped the steering wheel and shook his head. "I swear, if Luke hurts my sister again…"

I placed my hand on his arm, and he looked at me.

"Let's just enjoy our evening, okay?"

He smiled and winked at me. "Deal."

Will pulled up and parked next to Colt's truck. I waited for Will to open my door, and we began walking down toward the river. I could already hear people screaming and laughing. I saw Colt talking to Rachel. She didn't look happy at all. I knew he was breaking it off with her for good.

"Has Colt ever mentioned anything about Lauren to you?" I asked Will.

Will looked over toward Colt and then quickly back to me. "Um…well, um…"

I smiled and slowly nodded my head. "I won't make you share a secret. Come on, let's go find everyone."

Will took my hand in his, and we made our way over to Grace and Libby.

"Hey, y'all!" Grace said as she jumped up. She hugged me and then Will.

Libby gave me a hug and then looked at Will. They exchanged looks, and Will smiled from ear to ear. I looked between them with a questioning look, but Will quickly kissed me before sitting down on the giant log and pulling me onto his lap.

"What was that about?" I asked with a smirk.

He winked and turned to Grace. "So, is Mike here?"

Grace's smile faded for a quick second. "Um…yeah, he is somewhere."

I looked around and saw him over on the rope swing with his hands all over that bitch, Claire.

Ugh. What a slut.

"Grace, why do you even bother with him? He's such an ass. He flirts with everyone and treats you like—"

"Alex, please, not again." Grace looked at me with pleading eyes.

I knew she didn't want Will to know how Mike had been treating her.

"Treats you like what? Has that jerk ever laid his hands on you, Grace? I'll kick his damn ass."

Grace laughed. "No, Will. He has never touched me. Alex and Libby just don't like Mike, that's all."

Grace looked around. She must have found the bastard because when she turned back around, I swore I saw her eyes filling with tears.

We spent the rest of the afternoon swimming, playing horseshoes, potato-sack races, and tug of war. You named it, and we did it. I was exhausted by the time the sun went down. I looked over and saw Lauren leaning against a tree. She was talking to some guy I'd never seen before. Colt was standing nearby, and I noticed he kept looking over.

I nudged Will. "You need to go tell Colt that he'd better make his move if he's interested in Lauren. I have no clue who the new guy is."

Will looked up and nodded. "That's Claire's cousin, Brax. He just moved here from Montana or something like that."

"Huh. Well, Brax sure seems to have his eyes on Lauren."

"Yeah, he does." Will leaned over and kissed me on the cheek. "I'll be right back."

He got up and walked over to Colt. He leaned in and said something to him. Colt nodded and pushed off the tree, and then they started making their way over to Lauren and Brax.

"Oh shit," I whispered.

Libby sat down across from me and asked, "Oh shit what?"

I didn't look at her as I kept watching Will and Colt. "Colt…I think he likes Lauren. The new guy, Brax, is giving Lauren a lot of one-on-one attention. I told Will to tell Colt that he'd better make his move now if he was interested before this Brax guy gets too much into her head."

"Oh shit. They're walking over there, Alex!"

I looked at Libby. "I know, Lib! That's why I said, oh shit. The overprotective big-brother syndrome is playing out before our eyes."

"What's going on?"

Libby closed her eyes at the sound of Luke's voice. I turned and looked up at Luke staring down at Libby and me.

I smiled at my handsome cousin. "Oh, um…nothing. I think Colt likes Lauren, and some new guy named Brax has been talking to her. Will and Colt are walking up to them. You know how y'all get with each of us, all protective and stuff."

Luke smiled weakly and then looked over at Lauren. "Yeah, Colt likes Lauren."

Libby snapped her head to look up at Luke.

Speaking at the same time, we both said, "He does?"

Luke took a drink of his beer and sat down next to me. He was sitting directly across from Libby and staring right at her. "Yep. He got drunk and told us how much he liked her."

Libby looked away, but Luke kept staring at her.

Libby was watching what was happening with Colt and Lauren as she said, "Why doesn't he just tell her he likes her instead of playing games?"

Somehow, I didn't think Libby was talking about Colt and Lauren anymore.

"I don't know. Maybe he's afraid."

Libby turned her head and looked at Luke. "Of what?"

He shrugged his shoulders. "Don't know. Maybe he's never felt the way he feels when Lauren's around him. Maybe it freaks him out."

Libby just stared at him before she smiled slightly. "Maybe he should stop being such a pussy about it then. Seems to me that Lauren isn't going to wait around for him, is she?"

I saw the muscles in Luke's neck tighten, and I knew neither one of them were talking about Colt and Lauren.

"Colt, knock it off!" Lauren shouted.

I looked back at Lauren, and Colt had Brax pushed up against a tree while Will was trying to get him to stop.

"Great," I said. I jumped up and walked over there. "Colt Mathews, stop it right now."

Colt looked at me and then gave Brax a good push that caused him to stumble.

Lauren ran over to Brax. "Are you okay?" She looked at Colt with a confused look. "What is wrong with you?"

Just by looking at Colt, I could tell he'd had too much to drink. "Colt, why don't you go lie down in the back of your truck for a bit?" I tried to pull him away.

Colt laughed. "If you want another guy to treat you like a whore again, then by all means, Lauren, have at it."

Lauren's mouth dropped open.

Will and I said, "Colt!"

"You want to be treated like that again?" Colt asked.

Will grabbed Colt and began pulling him away. "You're just making it worse, you ass. You want to push her to him?"

Colt shook his head. "No."

"Then, shut the fuck up."

Lauren was looking at Colt and Will with a confused look. "What is going on?" she asked as she walked up to Colt. "Why are you so angry?"

Colt wouldn't look at her.

Lauren frowned. "Colt, please talk to me. We're friends."

He turned and grabbed Lauren by the shoulders. "That's just it, Lauren. I don't want to be friends with you. I want more."

Lauren sucked in a breath of air. "What?"

"I want more, Lauren. Why can't you see that?" Colt let go of Lauren. He pushed his hands through his hair and let out a groan before turning and walking toward his truck.

Lauren just stood there and watched him walk away. Why she didn't go after him I had no clue.

She slowly turned and looked at us and then Brax. "Um…Brax, do you want to head down to the fire?"

"What? Lauren, Colt just—"

Lauren looked at me and smiled. "I know, Alex. Thanks. I'll take care of it later."

My mouth dropped open as I looked at Will, and he shrugged his shoulders. I turned and watched as Lauren walked away with Brax.

WILL

Libby threw her hands on her hips and said, "Where is she going? She's going with Brax? What about what Colt just told her?"

"I have no clue," Lex said as she looked over to me.

Luke let out a gruff laugh. "Stupid bastard shouldn't have told her how he feels. Look at him now—alone and drunk in the back of his truck."

Libby spun around and glared at him. "What do you think he should be doing, Luke? Maybe sneaking off with someone and fucking her?"

The left corner of Luke's mouth raised in a smile. "Maybe. That's what I'd do."

Libby swallowed hard and slowly shook her head. "Well, you're in luck, Luke. With the way Claire is walking around with nothing on, you might just find yourself getting lucky tonight." Libby looked at me and Will as she squared her shoulders off. "Excuse me, y'all. Jason wanted a dance earlier. I think I'll go find him."

Libby started walking away.

Luke grabbed her arm. "Libby, wait. Don't…"

Libby bit down on her lower lip as she looked at Luke. "Don't what?"

Luke looked like he was struggling with something before he smirked. "Don't be sneaking off to fuck Jason."

Right as I was about to grab Luke and knock the hell out of him for saying that, Libby reached back and punched Luke in the jaw.

Lex let out a small scream as Luke shook his head and looked back at Libby.

Libby quickly wiped a tear away as she said, "You're right, Luke. There never was an us, and there never will be."

She turned and walked away as Luke stood there, speechless.

I stepped in front of him. "You ever talk to my sister like that again, and you're gonna regret it."

Luke nodded his head and downed the rest of his beer. "I'm sorry, Will. I'll apologize to her."

I put my hand on Luke's chest. "No. You're gonna leave her alone. Stay away from her, Luke."

Luke nodded his head and barely said, "Right."

My heart was racing a mile a minute as I tried to keep my anger down. I hated that he had just said that to my sister, but Libby had handled it. I was pretty sure her hit was far more impactful than mine would have been. I stepped to the side and let Luke walk by. I let out a sigh as Lex wrapped her arms around me.

"Will, what's happening? It feels like everything is starting to fall apart."

I placed my finger on her chin and lifted her eyes to mine. "As long as we don't fall apart, I don't care. Come on, baby. I have something to show you."

She smiled that beautiful smile as I began walking her back to my truck.

"Are we leaving?" Lex looked over her shoulder at everyone dancing on the makeshift dance area.

I stopped and looked down at Lex. "Do you want to stay?"

She shrugged her shoulders. "I wouldn't mind a dance or two."

I smiled and began leading her over. I pulled her into my arms and gently kissed her lips as "Still Fallin'" by Hunter Hayes began playing. I brought her in closer to me and held her as we danced.

She wrapped her arms around my neck and looked into my eyes. "I love you, Will."

My heart slammed against my chest as I looked into her beautiful blue eyes. "I love you, too, Lex, more than you will ever know."

Lex buried her face in my chest as we finished out the song. I looked over and saw Libby dancing with Jason. I quickly looked around, and I couldn't believe my eyes when I saw Luke. He was away from everyone, and he was holding Claire up against a tree as she had her legs wrapped around him. They were going to town, making out. I looked back toward my sister, and she was talking to Jason. I hated what was happening with everyone. I closed my eyes and said a silent prayer that Libby wouldn't look over there.

"What do you think happened between Lib and Luke?" I asked Lex.

She pulled back, and her eyes filled with sadness. "I think two friends fell in love with each other, and one of them is terrified of his feelings."

Lex looked around and must have seen Luke. She closed her eyes and shook her head.

"Lex, I want to make love to you so damn bad. Please, can we leave?"

She looked at me and smiled. "Where are we going?"

I grinned and said, "It's a surprise."

"Let's go," she whispered. She turned and began walking away.

I glanced over toward Libby. She was staring at Luke and Claire.

Shit.

She turned and said something to Jason, and they began walking to his truck.

What in the hell does she think she's doing?

I followed Lex to my truck, but I never took my eyes off my sister. Libby leaned against Jason's truck, and he began kissing her.

That motherfucker.

His hands started moving all over her body.

"Lex, hold on."

Lex turned and glanced over to where I was looking. "Will, no. She is a grown woman, and you can't keep interfering in what she is doing."

I looked back at Lex. "He's got his paws all over my sister."

Lex put her hands on her hips. "Will, let her be. She knows what she is doing and what she wants. Y'all don't have to keep jumping in every time. It's no wonder no one asks Taylor and Lauren out. Other boys are scared to death of you, Luke, and Colt."

I smiled. "Good. They should be." I turned back to see my sister was making out with Jason. My fists balled up, and I let out a sigh. "Lex, she's only doing it because she saw Luke. She doesn't want this."

I started to walk over there.

Lex grabbed my arm. "William Hayes, stop right now."

I turned back to see where Luke was. He was staring at Libby and Jason as he downed a beer. Things were not going to turn out good.

"Lex, I think we should take Luke home."

Lex stepped in front of me and followed my eyes to where I was looking. "Oh shit. Will, go get him before he goes after Jason."

I quickly began walking toward Luke. I looked over toward my sister, who was still kissing Jason. I stepped in front of Luke and smiled. "Dude, I think you've been drinking way too much. You don't want to stay here, so let me drive your truck home, and Lex will follow me."

Luke never took his eyes off Libby. "Claire wanted me to fuck her. I couldn't do it, Will. I have no desire to be with her—none."

I put my hand on his shoulder and said, "Good. Dude, you don't need to be with someone like Claire. She's slept with half the guys in my class. Come on, let's get you home."

Luke looked me in the eyes, and I couldn't believe how sad he looked. "Yeah. This party sucks."

He started walking over to his truck, which unfortunately was parked next to Jason's. As he got closer, I began walking in between Luke and Jason and Libby.

Right before Luke got into his truck, he turned and looked at Libby and Jason. They were now just talking.

"Have fun tonight, Libby," Luke called out before he got in and slammed the hell out of his truck door.

I turned and looked at Libby and then Jason. As much as I wanted to go over there and threaten that bastard, I followed Lex's advice. "I sure hope you know what you're doing, Lib."

Libby just stared at me. She stepped away from Jason, said something to him, and began walking over to where Grace and Lauren were sitting.

I let out the breath I had been holding and glanced over to Lex. She smiled weakly, and we both got into the trucks and headed to Luke's house.

Luke didn't say a word to me the whole way back to his house. I parked his truck, and he got out and started walking to the barn.

"Luke, I'll leave the keys in the truck."

He raised his hand and called out, "Thanks, Will. I appreciate it."

I shook my head and made my way to my truck. Lex had jumped out and moved to the passenger side.

Once I got in, I looked at her and sighed. "Jesus, our friends are like a damn soap opera."

Lex giggled and grabbed my hand. "I'm just glad Libby came to her senses."

I ran my hand down my face. "God, so am I."

"So, what's this surprise?"

I put the truck in drive. I smiled at her, and then I headed toward my house.

"Will, where are we going? We're not even on the road anymore!"

I laughed. I had come through our property's back gate so that my parents wouldn't know we were back. I was driving on one of the old trails that Libby and I had made with our horses years ago when we would go to our secret fort. We'd spent three years building it. My father had helped us with a few of the things, but we'd mostly built it ourselves. It was our secret place that none of our friends even knew about. Libby and I had camped out there so many times that my parents had ended up buying us twin beds for it. Looking back now, I couldn't believe that we hadn't been afraid to stay there alone.

"Just a little bit more, and then we'll be there." As I pulled up, I could see the faint outline of the building.

"What is that?" Lex asked.

I put the truck in park. "Hold on, babe." I jumped out and opened the back door. I grabbed the two duffel bags that I had packed earlier today and a flashlight. I walked around and opened Lex's door. Then, I turned on the flashlight.

We made our way up, and Lex let out a gasp.

"Will, is this your and Lib's secret house?"

I stopped and looked at her. "What? How do you know about it? It's supposed to be a secret!" I felt betrayed by my own sister.

Lex giggled. "Libby accidentally let it slip about two years ago. She made Grace and me swear that we would never let you know that we knew. Oh my word…y'all built this, Will?"

I looked back at the tiny hideaway. "Yep. My dad helped put the windows and door in, and he built us a few things inside, but Lib and I did most of it. We would spend hours down here, just me and her talking."

Lex bit down on her lip. "I love the bond that you and Libby share. It's amazing."

I nodded my head. "Libby had the idea to use this place for you and me. Kind of like our own little cabin in the woods." I grabbed her hand and led her up to the door. "Let me just make sure no snakes or anything got in here. My dad made sure we were doing things right along the way, but ya never know."

She giggled and nodded her head. "Okay."

I unlocked the door and walked in. I dropped the bags onto the small round table and started digging through one of them. I pulled out the bigger flashlight and turned it on.

"Oh, damn, Lib. I freaking owe you big time," I said to myself.

The room was filled with unlit candles. A bouquet of flowers was sitting on the little table that separated the two twin beds. I shined the light over and saw the two beanbag chairs. An image of Lex on top of me in one of those chairs filled my mind, and I had to adjust my growing dick.

I quickly reached in a bag for the lighter and began lighting a candle. "Hold on, Lex!" I shouted.

She laughed. "You either found a snake, or you're up to something! Is that light I'm seeing?"

"Patience, baby. I promise, it will be worth it."

"You do know you left me outside…in the dark…with no flashlight."

I closed my eyes and silently cussed as I ran back over to the second bag and unzipped it. I pulled out a gift box and set it down on my bed. I swallowed hard, thinking about the gift I had bought for Lex when Luke, Grace, and I went into Austin last week. Grace had helped me pick it out.

I walked over and lit the candle by the beanbags. Then, I put the lighter and big flashlight back into one duffel bag and threw it down on the floor. Next, I pulled out a box of chocolates and a few bottles of water from the other bag. I set them on the small table before putting that bag on top of the other. I walked over to the door and slowly opened it, but Lex was gone.

"Lex? Baby, where are you?"

The light in my truck came on as Lex opened the passenger door. "I kind of got spooked, so I ran back to the truck."

I wanted to laugh, but I quickly walked over to her. "I'm so sorry, sweetheart."

I picked her up, and she let out a small scream as I carried her back over to the secret clubhouse. I pushed the door open more, so we could walk in, and Lex let out a gasp.

"Oh my goodness, Will."

I slowly put her down and watched as she looked everywhere.

"Did you…did you just do all of this?"

"With Libby's help. She came by earlier today and put out all the candles and cleaned it up a bit since we haven't been here in so long. She brought down clean sheets and…"

I felt my face grow hot as Lex looked over at the beds.

Then, she glanced back at me and bit down on her lip. "Oh, Will…" she whispered as she threw herself into my arms.

I wasn't sure what happened, but what I'd thought would be a sweet and tender moment turned into a moment of pure passion and lust.

Lex began taking my T-shirt off, and I did the same to her. We both began fumbling with each other's pants before we finally gave up and started taking our own clothes off.

When I saw her standing in front of me with nothing but her bra and panties on, I let out a moan. "Jesus…I want you so much."

She reached behind her back, and in one movement, her bra fell to the ground. My dick jumped.

She slid her panties off and then moved to the bed. Lying down on it, she said, "I want you so much, too, Will, more than you know. I've been dreaming of being with you again. It's been killing me."

I slowly moved onto the bed and began kissing her as I moved my hand down her stomach.

"Yes," she whispered.

I pulled my lips from hers. I slid my hand further down as Lex spread her legs open for me.

"Will…I need you so much."

I slipped two fingers in, and I let out a moan. "Fuck…Lex, you're so wet."

I moved my mouth down and began sucking on her nipple as I moved my fingers in and out of her.

"More. Will, I want more."

As I sucked and pulled on the nipple in my mouth, I reached my free hand up and began playing with her other nipple. I slipped another finger in and then began rubbing her clit with my thumb as she squeezed down on my fingers. She was getting close. With one bite of her nipple and more pressure on her clit, Lex was calling out my name. It took everything out of me to ride out her orgasm.

When Lex finally came down from her orgasm and smiled at me, I got up and reached down to my jeans. I grabbed a condom and ripped it open.

I rolled the condom on as Lex watched me. When I crawled back onto the bed, I couldn't help but notice her eyes sparkling in the candlelight. Placing my hands on the sides of her face, I gently kissed her. I sucked her bottom lip into my mouth, and she let out a long, soft moan.

"You're so beautiful, Lex. You take my breath away."

She arched her body up and whispered, "Will, please make love to me."

Lex spread her legs open more, and I began teasing her entrance with my tip.

"Oh God…I'm so ready, Will. I need you."

I began pushing in, and my eyes about rolled into the back of my head. She was so wet, so warm. I didn't move for at least a minute. I moved my lips to her neck and then up to her ear where I gently bit down on her earlobe.

"Will…please move. Do something."

Smiling, I whispered, "I'm going to make love to you now, Lex."

"Will…oh God, I can't believe how amazing it feels."

Will let out a moan as he began moving faster. I wanted to tell him not to be so gentle, but I wasn't sure what he would think.

"Lex…baby…nothing feels better than being inside you."

Oh God. I need him to move faster. I need it harder.

"I…won't…break…"

He pulled back and looked at me. "What?"

My heart was pounding. *I can do this. I know I can do this.*

"I want it faster…harder, Will. Please don't be so gentle."

"Ah…Jesus, Lex. I just about came."

I let out a giggle as he smiled at me and raised his eyebrow.

"Talk to me, Lex. You have to tell me if I hurt you."

I nodded my head quickly. "I promise, I'll tell you."

Then, he began moving faster. He leaned back and grabbed my hips. He bit down on his lip as he pulled my hips and slammed himself into me. I let out a moan, and I knew it wasn't going to take long before I came.

"Yes! Will, yes! That feels…so good."

"Lex…baby, come."

"I'm so close. Faster, Will…I'm so close."

He began to thrust into me harder, and then something happened. He was hitting a spot that was causing my toes to start tingling.

"Oh God…stay right there. It's hitting a spot. Will, I'm going to come!" I screamed out.

I began calling out Will's name over and over as my orgasm raced through my whole body. I could feel my sex pulsing over and over as Will moved in and out.

"Yes. Right there, Lex. Oh God, baby…I'm coming."

Will began slowing down as he dropped his body over mine and began kissing my neck. He slowly moved to my lips and gently kissed me. "I love you, Lex. I love you so much."

I squeezed my eyes together to hold back my tears. I'd never felt so loved before in my life. I could practically feel the love pouring from his body to mine.

"I love you, too, Will, more than the air I breathe."

"Jesus H. Christ. It is hot as hell out here."

I grinned and peeked over at Grace. She was so much like Aunt Ari that it was unreal.

"I think it is hotter than hell, truth be told," Taylor said while she attempted to fan herself with a makeshift fan.

I sat up and looked around. The guys were all working on repairing a fence, and Grace had suggested the great idea of tagging along and then heading to the river.

"Why didn't we just meet them down at the river? This is insane." Lauren opened a bottle of water and began splashing some water on herself.

I giggled. "Just think how the boys feel. They're working in this heat, and it's only ten in the morning."

Maegan stood up and cursed. "You're just happy because you're having hot sex, Alex. I haven't had any sex in over a month. I need to be fucked."

"Nice," Libby said as she looked back over at Will, Luke, Colt, and Jason.

Every one of them still had their shirts on, and Maegan wouldn't stop bitching about the heat.

Luke had been livid when my father hired Jason to help out around the ranch this summer. Luke had tried telling his daddy and mine that they didn't need extra help, but Daddy wasn't going to listen to any of it.

I glanced over at Libby to see if I could figure out who she was staring at—Luke or Jason.

Maegan walked right in front of Libby, blocking her view of the guys. "You still dating Jason, Lib?"

Libby looked up at Maegan and smiled. "I was never dating Jason, Maegan."

Maegan smiled and looked down at Libby. "That's not what Luke said. He told me you and Jason were getting it on pretty hot and heavy at Claire's party."

Libby looked away and glanced over to me. I shook my head. Maegan was egging Libby on, and we all knew it.

Libby stood up and looked directly at Maegan. "You know what, Maegan? Why don't you just go find some guy to fuck, so you can get out of the bitch mood you've been in for the last few months? You said yourself that you wanted a good fuck, so go find it."

Maegan's mouth dropped open as she stared at Libby.

"Who needs a good fuck?"

Oh great.

Luke came walking up, and the Cheshire Cat grin spreading across Maegan's face turned my stomach. I loved Meagan like a sister, but this thing with Luke and Libby was starting to drive a wedge between all of us.

I was expecting Maegan to make a smart-ass remark to Luke, so when it was Libby who opened her mouth, I about fainted.

"Maegan does. You're so good at it, Luke. Why don't you help her out?"

"Libby!" Taylor and Grace said at the same time.

Maegan began laughing. Lauren and I looked at each other and then jumped up. Maegan walked up to Luke and wrapped her arms around his neck. Libby turned and started heading toward Will's truck.

"Libby, hold up," Lauren called out as she ran after Libby.

I began to follow them.

"Get your paws off my brother, Maegan, and stop acting like a tramp. This is not you, so stop acting like it is," Grace said.

"Grace! Oh my gosh. Y'all just stop this now," Taylor said.

I turned back to see Luke pulling Maegan's arms off of him. He started following us, and I quickly picked up my pace to warn Libby that Luke was coming. I was sure he was pissed at her comment.

"Uh…Lib? Libby!" I shouted.

"Not now, Alex. I don't feel like talking."

Luke jogged by me and stopped next to Libby. He grabbed her arm. "We need to talk—now."

I walked right into the back of Lauren as I watched Luke pulling Libby away from us.

"Shit. You don't think he'll do anything, do you?" Lauren asked.

"No! Gesh, Lauren, you know better than that."

"I know, but the last couple of months, the two of them have been at each other nonstop. Now, they're pretty much avoiding each other, and with Libby going off and saying what she just said…"

I shook my head. "I think they need to talk. Things need to go back to normal."

Luke stopped and let go of Libby, and she turned her back to him.

Lauren let out a gruff laugh. "Things will never be normal again, Alex."

I turned and looked at her. "What do you mean?"

"Alex, come on. I know you and Will are happy and all, but you have to see how the rest of us are all drifting apart. Luke never does anything if he thinks Libby will be there—or worse yet, if Jason and Libby are both there. Colt hasn't talked to me in over a month."

"That was your doing, Lauren."

She shrugged her shoulders. "I guess so, but still. We all used to be so close, Alex. Maegan is acting like some sex-craved nutcase. Grace is dating the biggest dick on the planet, and somehow, she is the only one who doesn't see it. Taylor is burying herself in schoolwork and has no life whatsoever. Things are not the same. Y'all are leaving in a few weeks for college, and well…"

I saw the tears building in her eyes, and my heart broke.

"I just want us to be…us. I want us to have fun without everyone fighting. I'm going to miss y'all, and if you leave with our group being broken, I'm just afraid it will never be fixed."

I pulled Lauren into my arms as she began crying. "Shh…it's okay, Lauren. I promise you, I'll fix this. I promise you."

I looked over and saw Colt staring at us. I knew he had been hurt so badly the night he admitted to Lauren that he liked her, and she'd walked away. He had begun dating Rachel again, and I knew he was so unhappy. Every time I tried talking to him, he would just tell me that he was fine.

Colt looked directly at me and mouthed, *Is she okay?*

I smiled and nodded my head slightly.

Lauren pulled back and wiped her eyes. "I'm sorry. What a baby I am. I think I'm just sad that y'all are leaving for college, and it's just going to be me, Taylor, and Colt left."

"I know, honey. I'm sad, too."

Libby came walking by with Luke following closely behind her.

I grabbed his arm and stopped him. "What did you say to her?" I asked as I looked at Libby walking over to everyone else.

Luke smiled weakly. "I called a truce."

"Oh," I mumbled.

"Let's go to the river and cool off, y'all!" Luke yelled.

Everyone began walking over to their cars.

Will came up and wrapped his arm around my waist. "Is Lauren okay?"

I shook my head. "I need to talk to you, Grace, Libby, Luke, and Maegan. I need to talk to y'all sometime today."

Will nodded his head. "Okay. Yeah, I'll make it happen."

When we got to the river, Will told me to head over into the open field behind the large oak. I began walking over there.

Maegan walked up right after me. "Hey, what's going on? Will said we all had to meet here. Something about Lauren?"

I heard Luke, Will, Grace, and Libby all talking. They stopped and all stared at me.

"What's up?" Grace asked.

I took a deep breath and just went for it. "We need to get our shit together, all of us. Lauren broke down today because Luke and Libby are fighting. And, Maegan, you've turned into a sex-craved bitch."

"Hey!" Maegan said, putting her hands on her hips while giving me a dirty look.

"Grace, you're so wrapped up in your boyfriend that we never see you anymore, and Will and I have been so wrapped up in us that we've forgotten about Lauren, Taylor, and Colt."

Everyone began looking at each other. We all knew things hadn't been the same within our tight little group.

"So, here is what we're going to do. We only have a few weeks before we leave for college, and we are going to make the most of it, starting today. Luke and Libby, either admit how you feel for each other or move the hell on. It's getting old."

Libby's mouth dropped open as she stared at me.

"Maegan, for Christ's sake, stop throwing yourself at Luke." I faced Luke and raised my eyebrow at him. "Luke? Are you ever going to sleep with Maegan?"

His face instantly turned bright red. Maegan and Libby both snapped their heads over and waited for his answer.

"Um…well, um—"

"Luke!" I shouted.

"No! Jesus, Alex. No, I'm not ever going to sleep with Maegan," he shouted back at me.

Maegan's face dropped, and I knew Libby was attempting to hold back a smile.

"I'm sorry, Meg. Honey, you're like my little sister, and I-I don't think of you like that." Luke pushed his hands through his hair and rolled his eyes. "Thanks, Alex, for putting me on the damn spot."

I put my hand on my hip and sighed. "Well, it's out now. We all knew you never had any intention of sleeping with Maegan." I turned and looked at Maegan.

She smiled weakly and nodded her head. She turned to Libby. "I'm sorry, Lib."

Libby looked shocked as she looked at Maegan. "Uh…sorry for what?" she asked Maegan.

"I knew you liked Luke, and I don't know what came over me. I just got jealous and all. I knew my flirting with Luke drove you nuts."

Libby quickly glanced at Luke before looking back at Maegan. Luke stared at Libby, but he didn't say anything.

I cleared my throat. "Grace, I think we all just want to know. What in the hell do you see in Mike?"

Luke stepped in front of Grace and put his hands on her shoulders. "I swear to God, Grace, if I ever catch him talking to you like he was the other night, I'll kick his damn ass."

"What? What happened?" Will asked as he pulled me into his arms.

Grace stepped back and away from Luke. "He was drunk, Luke. He isn't normally like that."

"Grace…" I whispered.

I hated that she was making excuses for that ass. I had heard him belittle her on more than one occasion. Why Grace put up with him I didn't know, but she didn't put up with anyone's shit. She looked at me and smiled weakly.

"I promise. He really isn't a dick like y'all think. Once we leave Mason, things are going to change," Grace said.

I had a terrible feeling in my stomach. Things were for sure going to change, but I didn't think it would be how Grace thought.

Will slapped his hands together. "All right, y'all. Let's make the next few weeks like the last eighteen years of our lives. Let's have fun and get crazy!"

"Hell yeah!" Luke said as he and Will slapped their hands together.

We all laughed, and Will grabbed my hand as we began walking down to the river. Taylor and Lauren were standing on the edge of the river while Colt tried to talk them into using the rope swing.

"It's freaking cold, Colt!" Taylor said in a whiny voice.

Will dropped my hand and pulled his T-shirt up. Then, he looked over at Luke.

"Oh no, y'all! Don't!" I said as they both took off running.

They ran up, and Luke grabbed Taylor. She screamed when he threw her into the water. Lauren attempted to run away from Will, but he got her and threw her over his shoulder. He ran up to the rope swing while Lauren called him every name she could think of.

"William Gregory Hayes, if you even think about—" Lauren yelled.

Will grabbed the rope swing, and Lauren screamed the entire time. She was even screaming when she finally popped up out of the water.

Grace and Libby took off running and jumped into the water while Colt did a flip off the deck.

I stood back and watched my best friends laughing and having fun. My heart grew heavy, knowing that this would probably be one of the last times we all did this together.

12
WILL

"You're sure quiet today," Luke said as he continued to work on the fence.

"Just thinking."

He stopped and let out a sigh. "Come on, let's sit for a bit and take a second to relax under a tree. It's so damn hot out here."

I reached into the cooler and pulled out two bottles of water. I gave one to Luke, and we made our way over to the large elm. Luke sat and leaned against the tree. Closing his eyes, he let out a long, drawn-out sigh.

I sat down and looked at him. "You like being single and going from girl to girl?"

He opened his eyes, and I saw sadness even though he was smiling.

"Hell yeah, I do. I don't have time for a relationship. I figure when I meet the right girl, it will all change." He took a long drink of water and looked away.

I nodded my head and took a drink.

"Are you worried about you and Alex?"

I knew Luke would just cut to the chase.

"Yeah. A part of me is worried, but another part of me isn't worried, if that makes sense. I love her, Luke. I mean, I'm pretty damn sure I fell in love with her when I was ten years old."

He started laughing. "That's a long time, dude." He shook his head and looked at me. "Will, I love Alex. I mean, she's more like my sister than my cousin. I want to see her happy just like I want to see you happy, but…"

"But what?"

He pushed his hand through his hair and let out a quick breath. "Will, what if you meet someone else? What if Alex meets someone else? The only thing y'all have ever known is each other. I mean, did you even date anyone else before Alex?"

I looked down at the ground before glancing back up at Luke. "I don't know how to explain it, Luke. When I see her, she steals my breath. When I'm near her, I can feel the attraction between us. I feel the love. I've never in my life felt like that around another girl."

"Dude, there are a lot of girls in college. A lot."

"Not interested."

Luke threw his head back and laughed. "You're a better guy than me."

I stared at him. "How many girls did you hook up with last year while you were at school?"

He shrugged his shoulders. "Two. One is just a fuck buddy. She doesn't want anything from me, and I don't want anything from her."

"The other one?" I asked.

"Just a girl I dated for a bit. She wanted more, but I wasn't ready to give it to her."

I nodded. "So, there has never been a girl who made you want more?"

He looked off over the pasture. He turned back to me and said barely above a whisper, "No. Never."

But his eyes were giving me a different answer. I knew Luke cared for Libby. How much he cared about her was what I didn't know. I wondered how Libby would react to seeing Luke at school with another girl. I pushed it aside and finished off my water.

"She loves you, Will."

I smiled and nodded my head. "I know she does. I also know Gunner has been filling her head with you-need-to-experience-more-in-life bullshit."

Luke laughed. "Sounds like Uncle Gunner. He just wants to make sure she's happy, Will. You'd be the same way if it were your daughter, and you know it."

I stood up and let out a moan. "Fuck, I know. I just feel like Lex is…"

Luke stood up. "Is what?"

"I don't know. Never mind. I'm letting my imagination run wild, and all it's going to do is eat me alive this year."

Luke slapped my back. "Ain't that the truth? Dude, you can't worry about Alex and what she's doing. Trust her, Will. She loves you."

Nodding my head, I agreed. "We still throwing the field party tomorrow night?"

He looked over at me and gave me a funny face. "What the hell is wrong with you? Hell yes, we are still throwing it, and I plan on getting drunk off my ass."

I let out a gruff laugh. "Why?"

"I just need to forget shit for a bit."

"Dude, that doesn't help."

His eyes grew sad, and he smiled weakly. "It will for a little bit."

I watched as Libby talked to Lauren, Lex, and Grace. I was so glad my sister was coming to A&M with me. Jason had been hanging around a little too close to Libby all night, and my patience was running thin with him. He had asked Libby to dance twice, and she'd turned him down both times.

I glanced over to Colt while he was dancing with Rachel. The bastard looked miserable. When my eyes caught Mike, I balled my fists. The fucker was whispering something to a girl I'd never seen before. I quickly looked back at Grace, who noticed Mike, too. Her smile faded, and she just stood there, watching.

This wasn't the Grace I knew. The Grace I knew would walk up to the bastard and kick him in the balls. The girl handed Mike a piece of paper, and he stuck it in his back pocket. I looked back at Grace as she downed her beer.

I walked over to where the girls were standing. I made my way to Grace and smiled weakly. "Grace, tell me you're not letting him get away with cheating on you."

"What?"

I shook my head as I took her by the arm and pulled her off to the side. "Grace, I know you saw that girl give Mike her number. Why are you putting up with his shit?"

"I know what I'm doing, Will. For once in your life, will you please keep your nose out of my damn business?"

Taking a step back, I held up my hands. "Fine. You know what? If you want to be treated like that, have at it, Grace. It's your choice."

I turned and walked up to Lex. I kissed her on the cheek and asked, "Wanna dance?"

She nodded her head quickly. "I sure do, cowboy!"

Lex and I danced and laughed for most of the night. I knew we were both just trying to hide the fact that we would be leaving for college in two weeks.

She pulled me closer to her as she whispered, "Make love to me."

Smiling, I asked, "Where?"

She looked around and bit down on her lower lip. "The river. Right now."

My mouth dropped open. "Are you nuts?"

She started laughing, and then she began running to the river. I quickly followed after her, but there was no way I would have sex with her in front of all these people—dark river or not.

Lex stripped out of her T-shirt and then pulled her boots off. Next came her jean shorts. Two seconds later, she was jumping into the river in her two-piece suit.

Right before coming to the party, we had all jumped off the rope swing into the river—well, mostly Colt and Luke had jumped off it, trying to outdo the other—so we still had on our swimsuits from earlier.

I pulled my T-shirt over my head and took off my sneakers. I'd opted to just wear my swim trunks here and not sweat my ass off in jeans. I glanced around. No one else was in the water.

I turned back around and looked at most everyone dancing. Taylor and Lauren were dancing with their friends, and Maegan was making out with some guy she had brought from Fredericksburg. Some people were standing by the fire we'd started in the fire pit. I saw Luke talking to Libby. He was already drunk, so I just prayed he wouldn't say anything to hurt her.

I looked back at Lex, and she was holding up the bottoms to her swimming suit.

Motherfucker. She's gonna kill me.

I quickly checked my pocket for a condom and ran toward the river. I jumped in, and she let out a small scream. I made my way to her and pulled her to me. My dick was already hard as a rock, knowing she was half-naked in the water.

She wrapped her legs around me, shoved her swimsuit bottoms into my pocket, and stuck her hand down my shorts. She slowly began stroking me.

"Damn it, Lex. If your brother sees us…"

She began kissing me. "He won't."

"Luke…" I whispered against her lips.

"He's so damn drunk that he has no idea what's going on."

When she pulled her hand out of my shorts, she began pushing them down until my dick sprang free. She jumped off me, and I ripped the condom open as I moved to shallow water. I quickly rolled it on before moving back to where Lex was.

She quickly positioned herself over me and sank down.

I let out a groan.

She whispered, "Yes, that feels good. I've been wanting you all day."

"Lex…"

She began grinding against me as she brought her lips back to mine. "Will…oh God, this turns me on so much."

I began walking a little ways down so that we were somewhat away from everyone. I stopped and looked around, making sure I didn't see any snakes. One quick look back at the party, and I was satisfied no one could see us.

I turned back to Lex and decided to give her a little taste of something different. "I'm gonna fuck you now, Lex."

Her mouth dropped open as she slowly sucked in a breath of air and then whispered, "Yes."

I grabbed her hips and began moving in and out of her body, hard and fast.

She wrapped her arms around my neck and dropped her head back. "Yes! Will, yes!"

I could feel her tightening up.

She snapped her head forward and looked into my eyes. "I'm gonna come."

I stopped moving.

"No! No, no, no, Will. Why did you stop? I was about to come."

I could hear the frustration in her voice.

"I don't want you to come yet, baby."

Her eyes grew bigger. "Will, I want to come!"

After looking back again, I slowly made my way farther down the river, still buried deep inside Lex. I wasn't sure what in the hell I was thinking. We could be seen at any moment, and there could be snakes around us. At this point though, the only thing thinking was my dick. I saw the rock I was looking for, and I made my way to it. By the time I reached it, Lex was panting with need.

"Will, I don't want to go swimming. I want you to do what you said."

I looked back and couldn't see anyone.

When I turned back to Lex, I smiled. "Tell me what you want, Lex."

"What?" she barely said.

"I want to hear you say it, Lex, from your sweet, innocent lips. I want to hear you say it."

She closed her eyes, and when they opened again, I could see the moon in her eyes, and they were sparkling with lust.

"Fuck me, Will. I want you to fuck me."

I pulled out of her and spun her around. We were in waist-deep water now, so it was easier to stand. I pushed her bathing suit top up, exposing her breasts.

I kissed her neck and said, "Touch yourself, Lex."

She quickly brought both hands up and began playing with her nipples.

"Shit…that is sexy as hell."

She dropped her head back and moaned.

I couldn't wait another second. "Spread your legs some, Lex, and promise me, you'll tell me if I hurt you."

Her breathing became heavier, and she looked over her shoulder at me. "I-I promise."

"Put your hands on the rock, baby. I'm gonna fuck you from behind. I've been dreaming about this for weeks."

"Oh God, Will…yes…please now…"

I pushed myself into her, hard and fast, and she let out a gasp.

"Are you okay?"

"Move! Will, move!"

I grabbed her hips and began doing just what I'd said I was going to do. The sound of our bodies hitting in the water and Lex moaning had my dick growing harder. It was so damn hard that it almost hurt.

"Jesus, Lex. You look so damn sexy. Does it feel good?"

"Yes! Will, I'm going to come. Harder! Please…harder."

I grabbed her hips and began fucking her harder. The friction of our bodies and the sounds of splashing water were soon replaced by us calling out each other's names at the same time.

"I'm coming! Oh God, Will…it feels…so…good. Will…oh, Will!"

"Yeah…right there it is…ah…Lex, I'm coming. Oh God, Lex."

I'd never had an orgasm like that before. It was more than intense. It was unbelievable, and it lasted for what seemed like forever. It had never felt so damn good, and for the first time, I wished I wasn't wearing a condom, so I could just spill myself into her.

Lex collapsed over the rock as she gasped for air. "My. God. That. Was. Incredible."

I quickly looked, and no one was around. I pulled off the condom and gave it a toss.

"Lex…I've never felt something so…amazing." I was trying to take in slow deep breaths.

She turned and pulled her swim top down, covering her breasts. She walked up to me and smiled as she wrapped first her arms and then her legs around me.

"It just keeps getting better and better, Will. I wanted to just scream out because it felt so good."

I gently kissed her lips. "Yes, it did. We're gonna have to fuck more often."

She giggled and nodded her head. "Yeah, we are."

"I love you, Lex."

"I love you, too, Will. I always will."

I gently sucked her bottom lip into my mouth as she let out a small moan. I began moving us back up the river, and we drifted back to where everyone was.

"What are y'all doing alone down here in the river at night?"

My lips pulled away from Lex's, and she had a look of horror on her face. We both turned to see Gunner and Jeff standing on the edge of the river.

Fuck. Fuck. Fuck. Where did I throw the condom? In the river? On the bank? Oh, holy shit, Lex doesn't have her bottoms on.

"Swimming, Daddy. What does it look like?"

I swallowed hard.

"Get off of him, Lex. Will, you know better. There could be snakes. Both of y'all get the hell out," Gunner said.

Lex got off of me, and she stuck her hand in the pocket of my swim trunks. I jumped back, but she glared at me. She pushed her hand in again and pulled something out.

Her bottoms.

As we moved farther up the stream, Gunner and Jeff walked along the edge. I pulled up my trunks and attempted to act normal.

"What are y'all doing down here?"

Jeff looked at me and then back at Lex, who was attempting to put her bottoms on while making it seem like she wasn't putting her bottoms on.

I stood up and began walking out of the river.

Gunner looked back at the party and then back at me. "Where did y'all get the beer? And who is drinking?"

I silently said a prayer that Colt wasn't drinking. He had football practice the next day, and he wouldn't want to get sick from drinking.

"Um…Luke, me…" I turned back and looked at Lex.

She was still trying to get dressed, but she just looked like she was sitting there. She nodded her head, and I looked back at Gunner.

"Um…Lex had one, and Libby had one."

Gunner tilted his head. "Taylor here?"

I nodded my head. "Yes, sir, but both Lauren and Taylor know they aren't allowed to drink."

Jeff and Gunner both nodded their heads.

Gunner looked back out at Lex. "Alex, what in the hell is wrong with you? Get out of the water right now."

I was just about to say something when she popped up out of the water…with her bottoms on.

She got out and walked by, making her way over to her T-shirt and shorts. I watched her every move and got a slap on the back of the head…and then another slap.

"Hey!" I shouted.

Gunner gave me a look that honestly scared me. "Put your damn eyes back in your head."

Jeff laughed and shook his head. "Will, is Luke drinking?"

I nodded my head. "Yes, sir, a lot, but I'm planning on keeping my eye on him."

Jeff nodded his head. "I'll kick his ass if he tries to drive."

I shook my head. "No, sir. No one will be driving if they've had anything to drink. We took the keys, and Taylor put them in a safe place."

Both Gunner and Jeff nodded their heads.

"Y'all have fun, and don't get too crazy. No more swimming, you two."

Lex gave an awkward laugh and just stood there, not saying a word. I watched as Gunner and Jeff began walking back down the river trail. They both got on their horses and started to ride away.

I let out the breath I had been holding.

Lex grabbed my arm and said, "Oh my God! Will, we almost got caught!"

I slowly nodded my head and whispered, "I know. I think I just saw my whole life flash before my eyes."

Thank you, God. I owe you so big for this one.

Lex giggled and began skipping toward everyone. She turned around and threw her hands up in the air. "I feel amazing!"

I laughed as I watched her run up to Grace and Libby. She said something, and Libby put her hands up to her mouth as Grace started laughing.

When I walked up, Libby turned to me. "My ears! Oh my God, I need to wash out my ears!" She walked off as Grace and Lex started laughing.

Grace looked at me and winked. "Fuckin' in the river. That should be a title to a song."

Lex hit her. "Grace! Oh my God!"

I smiled as I looked at Lex. She was beautiful and happy.

She's all mine.

If only I could shake the uneasy feeling I had about that last statement...

alex

"Alex, just relax. Everything is going to be fine."

I paced back and forth in our kitchen as I glanced up and looked at my mother. *Relax? Relax! I can't relax.*

I was leaving for college in a little over a week. I was leaving Will.

"I don't know if I can do this, Mom. I don't know if I want to do this."

My mother frowned and shook her head. "Nonsense. Of course you can do it, and you will do it. You're getting your degree if I have to go and sit with you in each class for the next four years."

I sat down and put my head in my hands. Tears were threatening to spill at any moment. I heard the screen door open, and I instantly relaxed when I smelled my great-grandmother's perfume.

"Are you ready to go for our walk, Alexandra?"

I looked up at her, and she smiled her beautiful, bright smile. I stood up and walked up to her. "Yes, Grams, I'm ready."

We walked for what seemed like forever before she broke the silence. "What are you afraid of?"

I shrugged my shoulders, but I instantly thought back to the other day when Daddy and I had gone for a ride.

I saddled up Banjo and Pinto and walked both horses out of the barn. I smiled when I saw my father walking up to me. It had become a weekly thing for us to go for our father-daughter ride. I would ride Banjo nearly every day, and my heart was breaking that I was leaving him. Besides Will and my father, Banjo was the only other man in my life. He was my comfort zone. Being with my horse relaxed me, and I felt at peace.

I had fallen asleep last night in Banjo's stall, and I had woken up to Will whispering in my ear how much he loved me. He'd carried me all the way back up to the house and kissed me good night so tenderly.

"You ready to go for our ride, Little Bear?"

I smiled and nodded my head. "Yes, sir."

We rode for a bit in silence before Daddy started talking about how much I was going to love UT.

"There are so many places to eat in Austin that it is unreal."

I giggled and looked at him. "Places to eat, Dad? That's what you want to talk about?"

He winked at me and looked straight ahead. "Are you getting nervous?"

I swallowed hard. "Yes. I'm scared, nervous, angry."

He quickly looked back at me. "Angry?"

I looked at him and gave him a weak smile. "I'm going to miss him, Daddy, more than you will ever know."

He gave me a weak smile in return. "I know you will, Alex. You just have to trust me. I know it will be hard to be away from Will, but if you're truly meant to be together, it will work out."

I shook my head and let out a sigh. As Banjo rode along, I closed my eyes and listened to the birds chirping. The hot sun felt so good on my face.

I love it here.

My father's voice pulled me back to reality.

"Alex, the only thing you've known your whole life is Mason, this ranch, and your friends. Have you ever wondered what else could be out there?"

"No! Why is it so hard for you to accept that I want this life, Daddy? You don't question Colt when he says he wants to take over the ranch someday."

My father looked away. "Colt is different."

My mouth dropped open. "How? How are his wants any different than mine?"

"Alex, I want the world for you. I want you to experience life outside of Mason, outside of Will."

I sucked in a breath of air. "You want me to meet someone else? Daddy, I love Will, and I'll always love Will."

"Okay. Well then, why are you so angry, Alex?"

I went to say something back, but I stopped.

I'd had the same dream over and over again the last few weeks. It was me…kissing someone other than Will. What had scared me the most was…I was enjoying it.

"I just want you to keep an open mind, Alex. I'm not asking you to forget about Will. Hell, visit each other on weekends. I don't care. Just keep an open mind. That's all I ask."

I nodded my head and quickly tried to push all my doubts and fears from my mind. "Want to race?" I asked before kicking Banjo and taking off.

Grams stopped and looked at me. She grabbed my hand and made me stop to face her. "What are you afraid of?"

"What if Will meets someone else?"

She raised her eyebrow at me and gave me that all-knowing look. "You're worried about *Will* meeting someone else?"

I looked down and away as I whispered, "No."

"I'm sorry. What was that?"

I looked back up at her with tears in my eyes. "I'm worried I'll meet someone else. Grams, I don't know what is wrong with me. I keep having this dream where I'm kissing someone else, and Daddy keeps filling my mind with how I need to experience more outside of Mason. I'm…I'm…"

I started crying as she pulled me into her arms.

"I'm so confused, Grams. I love Will. I love him so much."

"Shh…don't cry, baby girl. Come on, let's walk while we talk about it."

"What was it like for you when you had to leave Gramps?" I asked as we started walking again.

She chuckled. "It was very hard. Remember though, Alex, you have ways of keeping in touch, unlike what Garrett and I had."

"Did you ever doubt your feelings for him?"

She thought about her answer. "No and yes. I remember there was a boy...oh, what was his name? I don't even remember." She chuckled.

"Did you like him?"

She looked at me and smiled. "I liked the attention he gave me. It was different. He looked at me in a different way than Garrett did, and a small part of me enjoyed it. Would I have ever done anything with him? No. Never."

I looked down and smiled. My grandparents had such a strong marriage. The fact that Gramps still held Grams's hand, kissed her on the lips, and told her how beautiful she was warmed my heart.

"Your love with Gramps is so different, Grams."

She stopped walking and put her hands on her hips. "Is that so? Are your other grandparents different? What about your parents? Their love must be different, too."

I bit down on my lower lip. "Well...I, um..."

She shook her head and started walking again. "Let me tell you something, Alex, and you listen closely to me. Garrett and I are no different than any other couple in love. The same goes with your other grandparents and your mother and father. It's true love, Alex. True love is a forever love. It is tested and tried all the time. It's sometimes broken, but it always, always heals itself. It stands strong during storms, even when it feels like it is about to fall apart. Love's roots grow stronger and deeper after the storm. That's true love. There are ups, and there are downs. You just weather them."

I nodded my head. "Did you and Gramps have a lot of downs?"

She laughed. "We had a few. Nothing big, but yes, we had a few. There were times I wanted to knock that man senseless, but I always took a deep breath and stared at him. All he had to do was look at me with those beautiful blue eyes of his or play Nat King Cole's 'Send for Me,' and I would be butter in his hands."

I giggled. "I remember Daddy playing that song once, and he and Mama danced in the kitchen to it. I walked in and saw how Mama looked at Daddy. I knew then, in that moment, that I wanted what they had. I want a love like that."

Grams laughed. "Oh, Gramps must have told your daddy about that song."

"What about it?"

"Your grandfather only plays it when he's done something to upset or anger me or when he's feeling…romantic."

She winked, and I could feel the blush hit my cheeks.

"How romantic," I whispered.

She nodded her head and began walking again. "Yes. Yes, it is."

We continued to walk in silence as I tried to figure out why I was feeling like I was.

"Grams? Do you think I'm feeling this way because I'm just worried that Will and I will grow apart?"

She didn't look at me as she kept walking. "When I had to move back to Austin and leave Garrett, my whole world felt like it was over. We went for months without seeing each other, and we could only talk on the phone a few times. I'm not going to lie. It was hard, Alex, but nowadays, you kids have those phones, and you can talk to each other over video. You're only going to be a few hours away from each other. You can visit him, and he can visit you. I will agree with your daddy on one thing. If your love is strong enough and is meant to be, you will be okay."

I smiled and nodded my head. "Grams, only you can make me feel so sure about things."

She laughed. "No, darling. You feel sure about things when you finally learn to listen to your heart and not your brain."

I chuckled and then felt sad. "I'm going to miss our walks."

"So will I."

"I'm taking Emma to school."

Grams looked at me and laughed. "The doll I made you when you were little? Why?"

"Yes! I love that doll. Emma and Banjo are the two things that make me feel happy—well, besides, Will and family. Oh! And our walks together make me feel the happiest of all."

"Well, I'm glad to see I came before the horse at least."

Grams and I both laughed as we turned around and started back for home.

Grace and I were in the barn, taking care of Banjo when Luke walked in humming a song.

Luke walked up and smiled at us. "Are we ready to party?"

Grace rolled her eyes. "We've had way too many parties this summer, Luke."

"Come on, baby sister. You're heading off to college. You're going to the big city. Lord knows what will happen to you."

I laughed and shook my head. "Luke, if I remember right, you got pretty drunk last week, and Uncle Jeff and Aunt Ari had you training horses the whole next day as punishment."

"Hey, I don't mind working on the land I was raised on. Shit, that reminds me of the song by Sam Hunt, 'Raised on It.' I was raised on it! Worked hard and played on it. Hell yeah, ladies, it's time to play on it."

"Whose place? And who are we inviting?" Grace asked.

I instantly knew where I wanted to have our last field party.

"Will and Lib's? How about if we make it just us and a few of our closest friends?" Luke said as he took the piece of watermelon from Grace.

I quickly agreed and pulled out my phone. "Let me see if Maegan and Taylor can come. They just got back from Baylor."

"What are y'all doing in the barn anyway?" Luke asked.

"Ugh…Alex wanted to spend some time with Banjo," Grace said.

"Alex, you know you can bring him to A&M. Oh, wait, you're going to UT."

I gave Luke a dirty look. "Funny, asswipe."

My phone pinged, and I looked down at Maegan's message. "Maegan and Taylor are down for a little get-together. She wants to know who we're inviting."

Luke laughed. "Tell her we are limiting it, so she can't invite anyone from Fredericksburg."

"Libby said it's not a problem to have it at their place," Grace said as she read her text message from Libby.

I smiled, knowing that Will and I could sneak off to the clubhouse.

Luke smiled and then pointed to Grace and me. "We can have alcohol, but don't let Lauren or Taylor drink."

Grace and I each rolled our eyes.

"Taylor doesn't drink, Luke. Anyway, they are going to be seniors, and you let Colt drink."

"Colt is different." Luke shrugged his shoulders.

Grace placed her hands on her hips. "No, he isn't, Luke."

"Doesn't matter. They're not drinking." Luke turned and began walking out of the barn. "Will and I will take care of everything. See y'all later."

I giggled as I watched Luke walk out of the barn. I turned and looked up at my baby boy. "I'm going to miss you so much, Banjo."

Banjo jerked his head up and down and whinnied a bit.

Grace laughed. "That damn horse loves you so much."

I looked over at Grace and smiled weakly. "Grace, you're really not going to miss all of this?"

Her smile faded. "I don't know. I think I'll miss it. I'll for sure miss working with the horses." She looked away. "Mike wants to live in downtown Austin and become a lawyer like his dad."

I hated even hearing his name. "Well, what does Grace want?"

She snapped her head back at me and then sat down on a hay bale. "I just want to go to college and get the next four years over with. I'm thinking I can come back here and visit anytime. With all the shopping, I'll probably love living in Austin."

She attempted to smile, but I could see sadness in her eyes. She'd said she wanted to leave Mason, but her eyes were saying something else.

"Grace, may I ask you something?"

She pulled her knees up and rested her chin on them. "Sure you can."

"Why are you going out with Mike? You have to know that he is not the right guy for you. Grace, you're so beautiful. You could get any guy you wanted."

She closed her eyes and then opened them. "You don't understand, Alex."

"No, I don't, Grace. He treats you like shit. I hear him and how he talks to you. Why do you put up with it? He tells you what to wear, for Christ's sake. He never lets you talk, and he answers for you. I can't stand that."

She stood up and brushed the hay from her pants. "You don't see how he treats me when we're alone, Alex."

I stood up and grabbed her arm. "No, I don't, and I can't imagine it is any better. Grace, why are you staying with him? Why? He is cheating on you!"

The tears began rolling down her face. "I have to, Alex."

I shook my head. "What do you mean, you have to?"

She sat down and began crying.

I sat next to her and put my arm around her. "Grace, talk to me."

She began crying harder as she turned toward me and buried her face in my chest. I sat there and let her cry.

When she finally settled down, she pulled back and wiped her face quickly. "Mike wasn't always a dick. At first, he was so sweet. I mean, he really knew how to talk me into things. One night, he talked me into…finally having sex with him."

I let out a gasp. I had no idea that Grace wasn't a virgin anymore. "Grace, did you want to do that with him?"

She nodded her head. "Yes, I thought he was the one. The whole time though, I had this feeling that I was making the biggest mistake of my life. Every time we were together, it felt…wrong. I guess it felt wrong for him, too, because that was when he started acting different. He's never hit me or even raised his hand to me, but he…"

She attempted not to cry again. "He just treats me different, and it got worse after his parents told him how much they liked me. With my grandparents having so much pull at UT, they thought him dating me would help him there. His mom and dad love me, and so do his grandparents. He told me one night that he couldn't break up with me now because his parents said I was his ticket to UT, so he couldn't screw this up, like he does everything else. Plus, if we keep dating, he thinks they'll stay off his back about shit."

I pulled back and said, "What? Grace, my God. Why do you stay?"

She wiped a tear away. "I told him I didn't give a shit about what he wanted. I was done. He, um…he said I would do what he wanted because he has…oh God."

"What? What? He has what?"

She looked at me, and the sadness in her eyes about killed me. "He has a video of us having sex in his barn. He said he would show my mom and dad if I broke up with him."

My mouth dropped open as I stared at her. I shook my head to clear my thoughts. "Are you sure he has a video?"

She nodded her head. "I've seen it. He had his brother record us. He set me up."

"Wait—I don't understand. Grace, there has to be another reason he wants to keep dating you, not just to keep his parents off his back. And what do your grandparents, Sue and Mark, have to do with anything?"

She looked down and slowly nodded her head. "My grandfather works for the biggest law firm in Austin, Alex. He sits on some board at UT, and he is pretty powerful. He's already talked to Mike about interning at his law firm. Mike's parents were beyond happy, and so was Mike. He's just using me, Alex. If I break up with him, he doesn't get to intern at Grandpa's law firm."

She stood up and started pacing. "It's all so messed up. I have to stay with him because the bastard recorded us fucking. I hate him so much, Alex. I can't even stand to be around him, and I'm not sure I can keep pretending like this. It's slowly killing me."

"I thought you were going to UT just because he was going. You always talked about going to A&M, Grace, but then everything changed."

She turned and looked at me with tears rolling down her face. "I never want my father to see that video, Alex. It would kill him. I can't do that to my parents."

"So, you'll give up what you want to help this bastard?"

She shrugged her shoulders. "I have no other options."

An idea popped into my head. A few weeks ago, I'd seen Mike flirting with Maegan when she was a bit tipsy.

"The hell we don't." I pulled out my phone and hit a number. "Maegan? I need you to dress slutty tonight. Yep. Show the girls like you've never shown them before. Make sure your phone battery is fully charged, too. I'll explain when you get to Libby and Will's."

I hit End and looked at Grace. She looked confused.

"Tonight, you get your damn life back. Nobody messes with my best friend."

WILL

I sat on the back of my tailgate, watching the girls all dance.

Colt walked over, jumped up, and sat down next to me. "Um…why is Maegan sluttin' it up tonight?"

I let out a laugh as I tipped my water back. I wasn't planning on drinking even though we were at my place. I was going to take Lex back to the clubhouse later.

"I have no clue. Lex said they were all on a mission tonight. Something to do with Mike Clark."

Colt made a grunt sound. "I really don't like that guy."

He went to take a drink but stopped. He was staring off to the side, so I followed his eyes.

Lauren was standing there, talking to Luke and Bryan Wilson.

"Why's Lauren talking to Bryan Wilson?"

I shrugged my shoulders. "How do you know she's not talking to Luke, and Bryan's just standing there?"

Colt slowly looked at me. "Because she's looking right at Bryan and smiling at him. That leads me to believe she's talking to him."

I just stared at him. "Why don't you go find out?"

He looked away and took a drink. "Nah, I don't care that much."

I raised one eyebrow and stared at him. He wasn't paying attention to me, so I just sighed and brought my attention back to Lex and the girls.

Luke came walking up and yelled out, "William Fuckin' Hayes! Dude, this year, we are gonna be at fuckin' A&M together. You and me as roommates! We're gonna raise hell."

I smiled as I watched a drunk Luke make an ass out of himself yet again. "Luke, you probably need to slow down."

He waved his hand at me and made a face. "Bushshit. I'm fine."

Colt started laughing. "Bushshit? Luke, watch out. That drop-off goes right to the river."

Luke grinned at Colt and pointed to him. "Colt, my dad said you play football like your daddy. Said colleges are gonna be watching you this year, so don't fuck it up, Colt. Don't be partying and screwing around with girls. You study, little buddy." He grabbed Colt and began hugging him. He rubbed his hand on top of Colt's head. "Dude, you're good-looking. I gets it. Girls throw themselves at you. Don't do it…look at me."

Luke was attempting to force Colt to look him in the eyes while Colt was attempting to push Luke away.

"Jesus, Luke. You make a terrible drunk. Your ass is going to fall in the water if you don't watch it. I'm not gonna mess anything up. I know what I want, and I want to play football for A&M. End of story."

Luke dropped his hands. "Yes, that's what I'm talking 'bout. A guy who knows what the hell he wants."

That was when it happened. I saw Libby walking up. She went to move around Luke to avoid him, and he quickly turned to look over the small bank. In the process of doing that, he ran right into Libby, who took a few steps back and began losing her balance.

I quickly jumped down to try to grab her before she fell over the edge, but Luke was in between us. Instead of helping her, he pushed her more by mistake. Libby screamed and grabbed on to Luke's T-shirt, pulling him right into the river with her.

"Shit." I looked at both of them in the water.

Libby was screaming as Luke was laughing his ass off.

"Lib, here, take my hand," I said.

Colt attempted to help Luke up.

"Nice going, you drunken fool," Libby said. "I have to go back now and change." She glared at Luke.

"I have a change of clothes in the clubhouse, Lib, if you want to go there," Lex said.

"Luke, I've got a pair of jeans and a T-shirt there, too," I said.

Colt started laughing. "Libby, you can take my truck, so y'all can change."

Libby looked at Luke and shook her head. "Fine."

Colt handed her the keys, and she began walking to his truck.

Luke followed behind her. "Libby...Libby...shit, don't run so fast. Everything is spinning."

Libby stopped and looked back at Luke. "Oh my gosh." She walked up to him and took him by the arm to lead him to Colt's truck. She opened the passenger door and pushed him in, causing him to hit his head.

"Who the hell just hit me on the head?" Luke called out.

I looked at Colt, and we both started laughing.

"Maybe you should go help her." I looked back at Libby getting into Colt's truck.

"Hell no. Those two need to get their shit together. The more time they spend alone, the better." Colt turned and walked away.

I watched my sister drive off with my drunk best friend. "I'll kill him if he tries something," I mumbled.

Lex walked up to me and tapped my shoulder. "I need your help."

I smiled. "Okay."

I followed Lex as we moved farther away from everyone. "Lex, where are we—"

"Shh!"

I closed my mouth and followed in silence. After Lex pushed our way through some brush, I saw an opening.

"Okay. She hasn't brought him here yet."

Lex began peeking through the trees and brush.

"Who? What are you talking about?" I asked as I tried to see what she was looking at.

"Maegan. I need you to record what happens between Maegan and Mike."

"Wait—what?"

She turned and looked at me. "Will, aren't you listening?"

"Um…I thought I was."

She knocked her hip out some as she put her hand on it, and my dick jumped. She was so damn cute when she was frustrated.

"Maegan and Mike. Record them when they get here."

"Why?"

She sighed. "We are trying to get him to admit something, and we need it on video."

"Again, why?"

"So, Grace can be rid of this asshole."

"Does Grace want to break up with Mike?"

"Yes!"

I stood there, confused as hell. "Why doesn't she then?"

Lex began shaking her head. "William Hayes, if you stop talking and just film, I'll give you a blow job tonight."

Instantly, my dick was painfully rock-hard. "Officially shutting up."

She smiled and nodded her head. "Now, what I'm about to do means nothing. Please remember that, okay?"

"Okay. What are you going to do?"

Lex looked at me and raised an eyebrow. "Will, blow job, remember?"

"Right."

"I love you. Here's Maegan's phone. It's fully charged. As soon as they get here, hit record. "

I let out a laugh. "Okay, got it."

I watched as Lex pushed her way back through the brush.

I stood there, just looking around. "What in the hell is going on?"

Then, I heard voices. I tapped Maegan's phone and got the video ready.

Maegan came rushing through the trees and stopped close to where I was. I was hidden, but if she stood too close, she or Mike might see me. Then, she did something unexpected. She pulled her shirt and bra down, exposing her breasts.

Yeah, no way Mike will see me now.

What are these girls up to?

"Get ready, Will," Maegan whispered in my direction.

I heard Mike calling out for her.

"I'm here, baby," Maegan slurred her words, like she had drunk a little too much.

I hit record right when Mike came into the opening.

"Maegan, what in the hell is going on?"

"Mike, Mike, Mike, please. I've seen the way you eye-fuck me. I know you want a piece of this. I'm leaving for Baylor in a few days. I want a good, hard fucking, and I've been told you're the guy."

Oh. My. God. I'm not filming Maegan fucking Mike. Grace is gonna kill her!

Mike smiled and tilted his head. "Is this a joke? Grace is like your sister."

Maegan laughed. "Please, dicks before chicks."

Mike moved closer to Maegan. "Is that so?"

"Mike, be honest with me. Are you exclusive with Grace? If you are, I won't put you in a weird spot."

He laughed. "Fuck no, I'm not. I probably get more pussy than any guy in our class."

I felt the heat moving up my body. *Luke is gonna kill this fucker.*

Maegan chuckled. "Why are you with Grace then?"

"Less talking, baby, and let's get to playing." Mike began unbuttoning his pants, but he stopped when he heard someone coming.

"Meg? Oh, Meg! I saw you sneaking—oh, hey there, Mike." Lex came walking over as she slipped her finger into her mouth.

She's flirting with him!

"Hey, Lex. You been drinking?" Mike asked.

She nodded her head. "I have. I'm super horny right now and in the mood to experiment."

She looked over to Maegan, who laughed.

Mike smiled. "You and Maegan?"

Lex nodded her head. "You want to watch us make out, Mike?"

Holy shit, Lex. Don't.

"Can I join you both when you're done with each other?" he asked.

Lex threw her head back and laughed. "Hell yeah. Oh, wait. What about Grace? She's my best friend."

"Fuck Grace. I'm only with her because of her grandparents' status at UT and to keep my fucking parents happy. Hell, I'm even fucking my father's secretary when he isn't. I couldn't care less about Grace."

Holy hell.

"Is that so?" Lex asked.

"Yeah, baby. You want a piece of me?"

I'm gonna kill this asshole.

Lex walked up to him, and I was ready to bolt.

She smiled. "You know what I want, Mike?"

"Anything, baby."

"I want the video you have of Grace and you fucking."

What?

"What?" he asked.

"If you want to fuck me and Maegan, I want that video."

"Hell no. That's the only thing keeping Grace with me. No way."

Maegan laughed. "Where is it?"

Mike smiled. "Why?"

"I want to watch it. I like porn," Maegan said.

Mike pulled his phone out. "I had my brother record us with my phone."

"You keep a video like that on your phone?" Lex asked. "Do you have it backed up?"

Maegan must have been playing with her breasts because Mike was staring at her. Thank God her back was facing me.

"Um…no. I don't need to back it up. Grace is so fucking scared that I have it. She'll do anything I say. I never felt the need to back it up."

Maegan let out a moan.

"Jesus, Maegan," Mike said. He hit Play and handed the phone to Maegan.

"Oh, wow. Look at y'all go."

Lex looked next and smiled. "You sure you don't have it anywhere else? We could all watch it together and FaceTime when we leave for college."

Mike moaned. "Fuck. I don't, but I can upload it somewhere, I'm sure."

Lex did something while Mike looked back at Maegan.

Lex took a couple steps back. "Done."

Maegan quickly pulled her shirt and bra up, covering her breasts again.

"Wait—what the hell? What are you doing?" he asked.

Lex held up Mike's phone. "Teaching your sorry ass a lesson." She dropped the phone and stepped on it.

Mike yelled out, "What the fuck? You fucking bitch!"

That's it.

I pushed through the brush and walked past Maegan. I put my hand on Mike's shoulder, pulled him around, and punched the shit out of him. He fell backward as Lex, Maegan, and Grace all screamed.

I looked at Grace. "Grace? Where did you come from?"

She looked down at Mike and then up at me. "I, um…I was on the other side of them, recording with my phone."

Mike looked up at Grace. "What in the hell are you doing here?"

Grace walked up to Mike and kicked the shit out of his stomach. Then, she bent down as he moaned over and over. "I got you on video, you piece of shit. You just admitted on video that you had someone record us, that you're only with me to gain something from my grandparents, and that you pretty much were blackmailing me with that video. Not to mention, you admitted that little bonus of you screwing your dad's secretary. The table is turned, asshole."

"You bitches tricked me?" he yelled out.

I reached down, picked his ass up, and pushed him against a tree. "You'd better be thanking them. If they weren't standing here, I would beat your ass to a pulp."

"Listen, Will, I was just…I wasn't gonna show anyone the video."

I got right in his face. "You were about to upload it, you ass."

Mike looked at Grace and then me. "What are you going to do with the video, Grace?"

She smiled. "Well, the first thing I'm gonna do is save it somewhere other than my phone. If you so much as ever look my way or attempt to contact my grandfather, I'll be sending the little video home to your parents and maybe to my grandfather as well, so he can see what a lowlife you are. You'll never get into the law program. *Ever.* I suggest you let my grandfather know you won't be interning for his law firm."

Mike moaned. "Grace, my father is going to kill me if I pull out of that for no reason."

Grace walked up to him and tilted her head as she looked him up and down. "Not my problem."

She turned and began walking away as I let go of him with a push.

Lex and Maegan followed her. Mike put his face in his hands and began mumbling how his father was going to kill him.

"If I find out that you've even looked at Grace ever again, you will regret it. Am I making myself clear?" I said.

Mike dropped his hands and looked at me. "Very."

"Good. Get the fuck off my property."

Mike turned and began walking back through the brush. I followed, walked him to his car, and watched as he drove off.

I felt a hand on my arm. I turned to see Grace.

"Thank you. I know how hard that must have been for you to watch Lex flirting with Mike."

"Grace, why didn't you tell Luke or me about the video? We would have handled it."

She swallowed hard and wiped a tear away. "I couldn't risk my father or mother ever seeing it, Will. I wanted to tell Luke so many times, but I knew if I did, he would beat the shit out of Mike."

I nodded. "Yeah, he would have."

"Please, Will. Please don't say anything to Luke."

I pulled her into my arms when she broke down crying. "I promise, Grace. I promise."

Grace and I walked over and sat down on one of the logs surrounding the fire pit. I would start a fire soon once the sun started to go down.

Lex sat down next to me and smiled weakly. "I'm sorry I couldn't tell you. If I had, you would have talked us out of it and gone after him yourself. I knew we would be okay with you there."

I shook my head. "Lex, that was dangerous. What if he had tried—"

She put her finger up to my lips. "He didn't, and you were there."

"Which one of you came up with this plan?" I asked as Maegan sat down opposite of me and Lex.

Maegan pointed to Lex. "The brains of Operation Take Down Mike."

Lex and Grace laughed.

I pulled Lex closer to me. "I love you. I have to admit, the whole you making out with Maegan almost threw me into a bit of shock."

Lex hit me in the stomach as Maegan laughed.

"Hey, what's going on?"

I looked up to see Libby standing there.

"Hey, sis. You all changed?"

She nodded her head. She seemed flustered and confused.

"Where's Luke?" Grace asked.

"Um…he's kind of passed out in Colt's truck. He managed to, um…change into dry clothes, but he's really drunk. I had to help him back into the truck."

Grace laughed. "What is with him getting so shitfaced lately?"

Libby sat down and glanced over to me. Something wasn't right.

I mouthed, *Are you all right?*

She nodded and smiled weakly.

"Libby, can I talk to you in private?" I asked as I stood up. I always knew when something wasn't right with my sister. It was almost like I could feel when she was upset or sad or just not right.

She stood up and began walking to my truck. She stopped and turned around with a fake-ass smile on her face. "What's up?"

I raised my eyebrow at her. "Libby, I know you well enough to know that something is off. You look flustered and confused as hell."

She laughed. "Will, I promise, everything is okay."

Then, I felt the heat moving up my body. "Did Luke try anything with you? I'll hurt that bastard if he did."

She shook her head. "Will, no. Everything is fine."

Sam Hunt's "Raised on It" began playing, and the girls all screamed.

Libby smiled at me and kissed me on the cheek. "I promise, I'm okay, Will."

"I love you, Lib."

"I love you, too."

Libby turned and walked over to the girls, and they started dancing. Out of the corner of my eye, I saw Luke walking up. He was for sure drunk and acting like a fool.

I pulled out my phone and started recording everyone. I couldn't help but think about how most of us would soon be leaving for college. I smiled as I watched Lex dancing. I tried to push away the uneasy feeling I got in the pit of my stomach. It was that same uneasy feeling that told me things were going to change soon, very soon.

I sat on my bed, holding Emma to my chest. Tears threatened to come again. I had cried so much the last two days that I was sure I had no more tears left.

I heard the door open and felt my bed move. The moment he entered my room, I knew it was Will.

"Hey," he whispered.

I couldn't talk. If I talked, I'd cry again. I shook my head and clutched Emma harder.

"Lex, I promise you, everything is going to be okay."

I turned and looked at him. His eyes were bloodshot.

Has he been crying?

Libby had told me that Will hadn't been sleeping well at all the last few nights.

"I-I can't leave you." I broke down crying again.

Will moved closer to me and took me in his arms. "Baby, I swear to you, we're gonna make this work. Our love is too strong, Lex. You have to believe in our love."

I sniffled and whispered, "I do, Will. I do believe in our love, but it doesn't make it any easier."

He ran his hand up and down my back. "I know it doesn't. I'm not taking classes on Fridays, so I can always drive to Austin for the weekends. I won't even be two hours away from you, Lex."

I pulled back and looked into his heavenly blue eyes. "Promise me."

"I swear to you, I'll come visit you at least twice a month."

I threw my arms around him and began kissing him. If I thought I could, I'd strip down naked and have him make love to me.

My father cleared his throat, and Will pulled back.

"Will, how are you today?"

Will stood up and winked at me before turning to shake Daddy's hand. "I'm doing fine, sir. How are you?"

"I've been better. Not too sure I'm ready to send my girl off to college."

I smiled as Will let out a small chuckle.

"You all packed and ready to go, son?"

Will nodded his head. "Yes, sir, I am."

"Good to hear. You have any regrets about not playing football?"

I rolled my eyes. Daddy couldn't understand how football was not a huge part of Luke's and Will's lives. They liked playing, and both had played in high school, but they each had turned down the chance to play in college. Colt, on the other hand, had every intention of playing football for A&M.

"No, sir. My goal is to focus on studying and possibly graduate early."

Daddy raised his eyebrow and nodded. "You want on this ranch that bad, huh?"

Will chortled. "Yes, sir, I do. I believe Luke and I will be valued assets to both the cattle side of the business and the breeding side as well."

Daddy hit Will on the back and shook his hand again. "I know you will. Y'all have already made Jeff and me proud as hell."

"Thank you, sir."

I smiled as I watched my father and the love of my life share a moment together.

Daddy glanced at me and winked. "I'll let y'all visit for a while. You taking Alex out tonight, Will?"

"Yes, sir. We are all going to dinner and then back to my place to watch a movie."

"Sounds low-key. I like it." Daddy turned and walked out of my room.

I slowly stood up and walked over to my suitcase. I was finished packing, but I couldn't bring myself to close and zip it up. I laid Emma on top and turned to face Will.

"You're bringing Emma?"

I felt my cheeks heat as I slowly nodded. "Yeah. If I thought I could bring Banjo, he would be ready to go in the trailer."

Will walked up to me and pulled me into his arms. He leaned down and kissed my lips tenderly. "You ready for dinner? I'm sure everyone is probably almost there by now."

I nodded my head and reached for his hand.

The entire way to the restaurant, neither of us spoke. It was as if we were simply enjoying the presence of each other.

Will pulled up and put his truck in park. He took a deep breath, sighed, and got out before walking to my side. I began to wonder why he'd sighed.

What is he thinking about?

He'd seemed so distracted over the last week, like something had been weighing on his mind, and he couldn't share it.

He reached for my hand and smiled the smile that melted my panties every single time.

When we walked into the restaurant, I saw everyone sitting at a giant round table. Colt and Luke were lost in conversation. Maegan and Lauren were laughing while looking at something on Lauren's phone. Grace, who seemed like a new person, was talking to Libby and Taylor.

Our little group...

We were only friends because our parents were all best friends, and somehow, we'd managed to become a tight group. My mother had said that we might even be tighter than their group. I had laughed because all our parents were tight, very tight. They never fought with each other—at least, not that I knew of. They loved each other unconditionally, and I'd seen my mother leave in the dead of night just to be with one of them.

Yeah, our little group is just the same. There wasn't anything I wouldn't do for any of them, and I knew they felt the same way.

Will started walking toward the table, and Luke looked up and smiled. He and Colt both stood up. I loved how my brother, Luke, and Will always stood up when a girl either walked up to a table or got up to leave. They had for sure been raised the right way.

"Alex, you look beautiful," Luke said with a smile.

I grinned. "Liar."

He chuckled and kissed me on the cheek. Then, he whispered, "It will be okay, darlin', I promise."

I looked at him as tears filled my eyes. "I know."

Will pulled out my chair, and I sat down. Colt, Luke, and Will followed and took their seats.

Grace got me caught up on the Mike scandal. Apparently, he'd talked his father into letting him take a year off to travel around Europe. After Grace had broken up with him, he'd claimed to be having a breakdown, and he needed to find himself.

"What a class-act jerk." I took a bite of pasta.

Grace nodded. "Tell me about it. I'm so glad to be rid of him. I feel free."

"Maybe you'll meet someone at UT," Lauren said.

Grace laughed. "No, I'm not interested, and I won't be looking either. I'm focusing on school, and that's it. No men."

Luke glanced at Grace and smiled. "Good, but if I have to drive to Austin every damn weekend to check up on you, I will, baby sister."

She rolled her eyes and gave Luke the finger.

He gasped. "Why, sister, that hurts me so that you don't love me."

Grace moaned.

"I just care about you. I want to protect you from all harm and evil."

"That's why you put the scorpion in my bathroom sink last night?"

"Yes. I want to make sure you stay on guard. Be prepared for anything and everything."

"Fuck off, Luke."

Everyone started laughing, and my heart grew heavier. I glanced around to each of my friends. Grace and I would be at UT. Libby, Luke, and Will would be at A&M. Maegan was heading off to Baylor all by herself. My heart hurt for her, but she seemed happy.

Then, there were those who were staying behind in Mason. Lauren, sweet Lauren, had feelings for Colt, but she refused to admit it. Taylor, innocent Taylor, was a wild child deep down inside, just waiting to burst out. Colt, my baby brother…I'd hardly spent any time with him this summer. Between him working on the ranch with Daddy, football camp and practice, and that stupid girlfriend of his, he was never home. I was always with Will though.

Colt looked at me and smiled. He mouthed, *I love you, Alex.*

I felt a tear slip from my eye and make its way down my cheek. Colt quickly looked away.

Luke was my crazy cousin, who—

Oh my God. What is he wearing?

My mouth dropped open as I read his T-shirt.

Fur trade is not cool. Shave your beaver.

I looked at Luke as he was talking to Will about some program at A&M.

"Luke, are you really wearing that T-shirt?" I asked.

Luke stopped talking as he looked down at his shirt and then back up at me. "No, Alex. I'm actually sitting here naked, but I've put a force field around me to make y'all think I'm dressed."

He looked over at Libby, who quickly blushed and looked away. Luke seemed surprised by Libby's reaction.

"You're such an ass. I can't believe Aunt Ari would let you wear that," I said.

Luke let out a gruff laugh. "Please. My mommy doesn't tell me what I can and can't wear." Leaning his chair back, he folded his arms behind him and rested his head against his hands.

Colt looked to the right and started laughing.

"Luke Drew Johnson…"

Luke looked over to Aunt Ari, who was standing there with Uncle Jeff. He was attempting to hold in his laughter, but he was doing a terrible job of it.

Luke lost his balance and fell backward.

Libby jumped up and ran over to him. "Are you okay?"

Luke looked at her and frowned. "Yes."

Libby went to help him up, but he pulled away from her.

"I'm fine, Lib," he said as he jumped up on his own.

Her face fell as she got up and sat back down. My heart broke for her. She hadn't been acting right ever since our last field party, and it was driving both Will and me crazy that she wouldn't tell us what had happened.

"Good Lord, the apple doesn't fall far from the tree, I swear. Jeff, take off your T-shirt and give it to Luke."

"What?" Luke and Uncle Jeff said at the same time.

Aunt Ari gave Luke a look, and he quickly went to the men's bathroom with Uncle Jeff following him.

When he came back out, Colt busted out laughing as he shook his head.

Luke smacked Colt on the back of the head. "Shut up, you little bastard, or I'll kick your ass."

Aunt Ari walked up and smacked Luke on the back of the head. "Knock it off." She turned and smiled. "Y'all have fun tonight, but don't stay out too late."

We all said good-bye to Aunt Ari and Uncle Jeff. After dinner, we decided to head on over to Will and Libby's.

Taylor rode with us, and she told Will and me all about the trip she was planning to take to Italy next summer. She had been taking Italian for three years, and she had rapidly picked it up.

I was going to miss her so much. I was going to miss everyone so much. I looked at Will as he smiled and asked Taylor another question about Italy.

I had to quickly look away. *I can't do this. I can't leave him.*

I began to think back to orientation week at UT.

Grace smiled at me as we both sat down and looked around. "I can't believe how freakin' huge this campus is. I really wish I was going to A&M."

My mouth dropped open as I stared at her. "Now, you want to go to A&M? Grace, if you had said that months ago, my dad would have probably let me go!"

Grace rolled her eyes. "Please, Alex, we both know our dads wanted us here at UT, but I already hate it."

I glanced around again, and I had to admit, I hated it already, too.

My eyes stopped on the dark-haired hot guy who had opened the door for Grace and me. When he'd said hello to us, Grace had said his voice sounded like a Greek god. He was helping with the tour, and he'd mentioned he was a sophomore at UT.

He smiled when he saw me staring at him. I smiled back and then quickly looked away.

What in the hell, Alex? You have a boyfriend whom you love more than anything. Why are you staring at this guy?

I peeked back over to the Greek god, and he was watching me. My father's voice popped into my head.

Alex, I want you to experience other things, other people.

The hot guy chuckled and winked. Then, he turned and headed over to talk to the other tour guide. I felt the heat move across my cheeks.

I love Will. I only want Will.

My stomach dropped as Will took my hand in his. I looked at him, and he smiled. Somehow, he always knew when I needed his touch.

He squeezed my hand. "I love you."

"I love you, too."

Taylor made a noise as she said, "Oh God, gag me."

16 WILL

Everyone was down in my dad's workshop, watching a movie. My dad had put in a projector a few years back for all of us to watch movies on a big screen when we hung out.

I had asked Lex if she wanted to go take a quick drive and see the stars while everyone was engrossed in the horror film.

"It's so peaceful and beautiful out here," Lex said.

We were lying in the back of my truck bed, looking up at the night sky. "Yeah, it is."

"I'm going to miss this." She turned and faced me.

I did the same. "Miss what? The stars?"

She giggled and nodded her head. "That's one thing I'm going to miss. Will, I'm afraid. What if we meet other people and—"

I put my finger to her lips to stop her from talking. Ever since Lex had gone to UT for a week, she had been acting different. She was unsure of everything, including us.

"Lex, I love you. I'm not going to lie and say it's not going to be hard to be away from you, your touch, your heavenly smell, and your amazing smile."

She grinned and looked down. I placed my finger under her chin and lifted her face until her eyes met mine.

"Lex, do you love me?"

She sucked in a breath of air. "Yes! More than anything, Will."

"Then, have faith in our love."

Her eyes began to fill up with tears. "Promise me you won't meet anyone, Will. Promise me."

I leaned her back and crawled on top of her. I pushed my body against hers. "Lex, no one will ever make me feel the way you do. No one. I promise you, it will always be just you and me."

"Always you and me, Will. Always."

I nodded my head and gently kissed her lips. "Always."

"Make love to me, Will."

Sitting up, I began taking off my T-shirt and unbuttoning my pants as Lex watched me. She was biting on her lower lip the entire time, and I couldn't wait to make love to her, to show her how much I loved her.

I got up and started taking off my pants as Lex sat up and began undressing. I had laid a few blankets down in the back of my truck, knowing I was going to be with her tonight. There was no way I would leave tomorrow without giving her another piece of me.

She lay back down, and I took her body in. She was breathtaking. Her body was beyond perfect. She wasn't stick thin at all. She had beautiful curves and toned muscles that drove me crazy mad.

When I reached down and placed my fingers inside her, I found she was soaking wet. I closed my eyes and whispered, "Damn, Lex. You are always so wet." I opened my eyes and looked into hers. "Do you want me, Lex?"

She arched her back and let out a low, soft moan. "Yes. Will, I want you so much."

I moved my lips to her neck and then down to her breast where I sucked on one nipple before moving to the next one. I ran my tongue down her stomach to right above her clit.

"Oh God, yes, Will."

I gently blew on her clit as I slipped two fingers into her and began moving in and out.

"More…" Lex panted.

I smiled as I leaned in closer and began sucking on her clit. It didn't take Lex long before she was calling out my name. She bucked her hips and cried out. I pulled my fingers out and tasted my girl. I reached for a condom, quickly put it on, and positioned myself at her entrance. I slowly began to push myself into her, and we both let out a moan.

I dropped my head and began kissing her neck. "You feel so good. God, you feel so good."

Her hands lightly began to move up and down my back as she whispered over and over how good it felt.

"Will, please go slow. I don't want this night to end."

My heart broke as I made love to Lex in the back of my truck under the stars where we had grown up and fallen in love.

She will always be mine. Always.

I felt her bearing down on my dick.

She let out a gasp and whispered, "Will, I'm coming."

I leaned down and captured her moans with my lips as I began coming. I stayed inside her for a few minutes as I let my breathing and heart rate come back down.

"I'm going to miss you so much, Will."

I felt the tears building in my eyes. "I'm going to miss you, too, Lex. I promise to come visit all the time, baby."

"Promise me, Will. Promise me."

"I swear, baby. I swear, I'll come and visit as much as I can."

I moved and pulled myself out of her warm body.

She whimpered and said, "I wish you hadn't used a condom. I just want to feel you once."

I shook my head. "Lex, that is playing a very dangerous game, and I won't do that to you or our future."

She smiled and placed her hand on the side of my face. "I love you, William Gregory Hayes."

I smiled. "I love you, Alexandra Eryn Mathews, more than you will ever know."

I leaned back against my truck and watched as Lex talked to Grams and Gramps. She was telling them good-bye, and her tears were causing me more pain than I'd ever thought imaginable.

"Are you okay, Will?"

I turned to see Ellie standing there. My eyes burned from attempting to hold back my tears all morning.

"Honestly? No."

She smiled sweetly and leaned on the truck next to me. "It's all going to be okay, Will."

I shook my head. "My brain is trying to tell me that, but my heart is putting up one hell of a fight."

I glanced over and saw a tear rolling down Ellie's face. As she wiped it away, she pushed off the truck and turned to face me.

"If it's meant to be, it will be." She barely smiled, and then she reached up and kissed me on the cheek.

I nodded my head and watched as she turned and walked away.

My mother and father had said the very same thing to me this morning before I'd left to come over here.

I watched as Grace and Lex said their good-byes to everyone. Luke was hugging Grace for so long that Ari finally had to pull him away. I smiled as I watched Lex say good-bye to Colt. He tried to seem unaffected, but I knew he was going to miss her so much.

When Lex turned and looked at me, she smiled that beautiful smile.

Lex and I had spent much of the morning with Banjo. We had gone for a ride early this morning, and then we'd sat in his stall and just talked. We'd agreed that the best thing to do would be for me to see her off with everyone else.

She walked up to me, and I held out my arms as she walked into them and began sobbing.

"Promise me, Will."

I held on to her tightly as I let my own tears fall. "I promise you, Lex. I promise."

She pulled back and gently wiped my tears from my face. "I love you."

I tried my best to smile as I wiped her tears away. "I love you more than that."

She giggled and shook her head. "I'll miss you."

I looked away and then back at her. "God, Lex, I'm gonna miss you, too, baby."

She reached up and kissed me. I placed my hands on her face and deepened the kiss. I didn't care that Gunner was standing right there. I wanted to make sure that she could feel how much I loved her. When we pulled our lips from each other, she began crying again.

"I'll see you…soon," Lex said in between sobs.

I nodded my head. I could hardly talk. "Yes. I'll see you soon."

She turned, walked away from me, and quickly got into her father's truck. When Gunner looked at me, he smiled weakly. I nodded my head and got into my truck. Then, I quickly took off.

I drove around the countryside for a little bit before finally pulling into my driveway. I just sat there. My heart grew heavier as each passing minute meant that Lex was just that much farther away from me.

I dropped my head back against the seat. "I swear to God, Lex…I promise you, you and me always."

77

I read the text message from Will, and I couldn't help but smile as the heat moved across my cheeks.

> *Will: I can't wait to see you this weekend. I'm going to bury my face between your legs first. Then, I'll bury myself so deep inside you that you'll feel me for days.*

The moment my body slammed into someone else, I felt like an idiot. Upon impact, I dropped the books I had been carrying, and I quickly bent down to pick them up while I shoved my phone in my back pocket.

"Shit! I'm so sorry!" I reached for my books at the same time another hand reached out as well. I quickly looked up. "It's you."

"Hey, Alex. How are you?"

I swallowed hard. "You know my name?"

Dark-haired hot guy laughed as he quickly scooped up my books and stood up.

I stood up and rolled my eyes. *Good God, Alex. Really?*

"Of course I do. How could I forget the most beautiful freshman on campus?"

I bit down on my lip and shook my head as I let out a small laugh. "I don't remember us ever exchanging names. I'm sorry. I don't know your name."

His eyes were a beautiful green. The light from the sun was almost making them sparkle.

"We didn't exchange names. I asked Rod, the other tour guide, what your name was, and he gave it to me."

My stomach dropped. "Oh."

"Are you coming to eat or just to study?" He lifted up my books and smiled.

I couldn't talk. All I heard was my father's voice over and over in my head.

Meet new people, Alex. Make new friends. Have fun and experience new things.

"Both. I have a huge test in calculus and another in chemistry."

When he smiled, I found myself smiling back. He opened the door to the Littlefield Patio Café and motioned for me to go inside. I did, and he followed behind me.

"You're in luck. I aced both classes last year, *and* I'm hungry."

I laughed. "Well, would you like to join me for lunch then?"

He winked. "I thought you'd never ask."

We made our way over to a corner table.

I went to sit down. "Wait—I still don't even know your name."

The way his eyes moved across my body made me both nervous and excited. He set my books down and held out his hand. I reached for it, and he shook it.

"Blake Turner."

"It's a pleasure to meet you, Blake Turner. Alex Mathews."

He pulled my hand up and kissed the back of it. "The pleasure is all mine."

His eyes danced with passion, and I knew I should immediately tell him about Will. Instead, I pulled my hand away and sat down.

The waitress came over and glared at me before she turned to Blake. "Hey, Blake. How are you?"

Blake looked up and smiled. "Hey, Chrissie. I'm doing good. How are you?"

She glanced over to me quickly before looking back at Blake. "Just got here for my shift and already looking forward to getting off."

Blake smiled and nodded his head. "Alex, you know what you'd like?"

I grinned and said, "I'll take a grilled chicken salad and Diet Coke, please."

"I'll have a grilled chicken wrap and iced tea, Chrissie."

Chrissie winked at Blake. "Sure thing. I'll go get your drinks."

He looked back at me. "How are you liking UT?"

I shrugged. "It's okay. Kind of big for this small-town country girl."

"Where are you from?"

"Mason."

I smiled up at Chrissie as she set my Diet Coke and Blake's tea down. "You need anything else, Blake?" she asked.

The way she was eye-fucking him was unreal. I smiled and looked at Blake.

He smiled at her and said, "No, thanks."

I bit down on my lower lip as I looked at his lips. They looked so soft. *I bet he's a good kisser.*

Oh. My. God. Alexandra, stop this now!

"You, um…free this evening, Blake?" Chrissie asked.

I snapped my head at her.

How does she know we aren't on a date or something? How rude.

Blake looked at me and then back to her. "Sorry, Chrissie, I'm not free."

She nodded her head and turned to leave. Blake watched her walk away and then looked back at me.

I busted out laughing. "Wow."

"I'm sorry. We went out a few times last year."

I held up my hands. "Please, you don't owe me any explanations. If she had done that to my boyfriend though, I would have been pissed."

Blake's smile faded some. "You have a boyfriend, huh?"

Well, I guess I just took care of letting Blake know about Will.

I smiled. "I do. His name is Will. He goes to A&M."

Blake smiled slightly. "Why did you not go to A&M with him?"

I began chewing on my bottom lip. "Well, um…"

He reached across the table and pulled my lower lip from my teeth. My body instantly came to attention. His touch didn't affect me like Will's, but it certainly did something.

"That is a bad habit, Alex. Now, what were you saying?"

Shit. What was I saying?

He smiled bigger. He knew he had just flustered me with his touch, and he was enjoying watching me struggle. I didn't know if I should be pissed off or not. The only thing I knew was that I was incredibly turned-on right now.

I shook my head and felt my phone go off.

Will's text. I'm just all hot and bothered by it, and that's why I'm behaving like this.

"My father went to UT. He wanted me to follow in his footsteps, experience life in the big city, meet new people, blah, blah, blah."

Blake started laughing, and I smiled. I pulled out my phone and saw that I had a new text from Will. I couldn't help but let a smile grow across my face. I missed him so much.

"Excuse me just one moment. I have to answer this text."

Blake nodded. "Have at it."

> *Will: Hey, did you get my last text? You went MIA on me.*
>
> *Me: Sorry. I ran into someone I met at freshman orientation. Eating a quick lunch while studying for calculus.*
>
> *Will: Okay, baby. I'll let you go. I have to meet Luke for a workout anyway. I'll see you Friday. I made hotel reservations for us.*
>
> *Me: Counting down the days. Have a good workout.*
>
> *Will: I will. Have fun studying. I love you, Lex.*

I was instantly filled with guilt. I stared at my phone. An uneasy feeling moved through my body. I hated that Will hung out with Luke, especially with Luke's player ways.

Stop being so jealous of nothing, Alex.

Should I tell Will I'm with a guy?
What good would that do? He'd just worry.

Me: It won't be fun. I love you, too, Will.

I put my phone into my back pocket again and looked at Blake. He was reading something on his phone and smiling. I didn't want to like his smile, but I did.

I pushed my thoughts aside. "Sorry. Will is making plans to come visit this weekend."

Blake nodded his head and looked down at my books. "So, calculus, huh?"

I moaned and rolled my eyes. I opened the book, and before I knew it, we were neck high in all things calculus and chemistry.

Three hours later, I was taking a sip of coffee as Blake helped explain the last problem to me.

"Gosh, Blake, I don't know how to thank you enough. You've really helped me a ton."

He smiled as he reached across the table and pushed a piece of hair behind my ear. "You, um…you had a piece of hair fall out of your ponytail."

I smiled and nodded my head. "Well, I guess I'd better get back to my room. Grace is probably wondering where I am." I started gathering up all my books and then stood up. I reached across the table and shook Blake's hand.

"Should we exchange numbers?" Blake asked as he stood up.

My stomach took a fast dive. "Why?"

He laughed. "I'm in a study group. We meet a few times a week. If you need help again, you're more than welcome to join us. Grace, too, if she wants."

It seemed innocent enough, and he'd even invited Grace.

"Okay, sure."

I gave him my cell number, and he immediately sent me a text.

"Now, you have mine. Good luck on the tests, Alex."

I smiled. "Thank you, Blake. I really appreciate all your help."

He placed his hand on the small of my back and led me to the door.

Once we got outside, he leaned down and put his mouth to my ear. "The pleasure was all mine, Alex."

He turned and began walking away, leaving me standing there. I felt utterly confused and in desperate need of…something. I just didn't know what that something was.

WILL

"Motherfucker, this is not happening." I pushed my hands through my hair and stared down at my truck's engine. I pulled out my cell phone again and texted Luke.

> *Me: Dude, where in the hell are you? My truck broke down, and I'm supposed to be in Austin in an hour.*

I didn't get a response, so I hit Libby's number.

"Hello?"

"Lib, do you have any idea where Luke is?"

"No. Why would I?" Her voice was laced with anger.

"Um…I just thought you might have talked to him. Damn it, Lib, why didn't you bring your car?"

She laughed. "'Cause you and Luke both have trucks, and I knew I wouldn't be going anywhere this semester. Why? What's up?"

I let out a sigh. "I made plans to spend the weekend in Austin with Lex. My truck won't start, and Luke isn't texting me back." My phone pinged, and I pulled it away to see a text from Luke. "Hold on. Luke just texted me."

> *Luke: I'm with Abigail.*

> *Me: My truck broke down. I need to get to Austin.*

> *Luke: Sorry, dude. We are in Port Aransas at her parents' condo.*

> *Me: Isn't Abigail just your fuck buddy? Why are you out of town with her?*

> *Luke: I needed to forget about some shit and just relax and have a good time this weekend. Abigail asked if I wanted to go, and I said yes.*

> *Me: Okay. I'll just have to let Lex know that I can't make it.*

> *Luke: Sorry, dude. I'm coming back tomorrow. I'm only staying one night. That's all I can take of Abigail. She's an awesome fuck, but damn, she gets on my nerves.*

"Will? Are you still there?"

I sighed. "Sorry, Lib. Luke texted me to say he was with Abigail at the coast for the night."

"Who's Abigail?"

"His fuck buddy."

Libby sucked in a breath of air, and I cursed inside.

Shit.

Luke hadn't wanted Libby to know about Abigail, and I'd just fucked up.

"What?"

Great. Now, what am I going to say?

"Lib, sweetheart, I'd better call Lex and let her know I can't make it."

Silence.

"Lib? Libby?" I swore I could hear her crying. "Honey, are you okay?"

"I'm fine. Tell Alex I said hey." Libby hung up without so much as a good-bye.

Ah shit.

I pulled up my last text message from Lex and read it.

Damn, I wanted to see her so bad.

> *Lex: My body is aching for you.*

> *Me: Hey, baby. I have bad news. My truck broke down, and Luke is out of town this weekend.*

She instantly responded.

> *Lex: No! No. No. No. Will, I haven't seen you in over a month. I was looking forward to this weekend.*

> *Me: I know, Lex. Believe me, I'm just as disappointed. Can you FaceTime?*

> *Lex: Yep. Grace isn't here, and she won't be back for another hour. I think she is going to some party tonight.*

> *Me: Give me a minute.*

> *Lex: Hurry!*

I quickly ran back up to my dorm room. I grabbed my iPad and called her. The moment I saw her beautiful face, my dick was harder than a rock.

Fuck, I want her. I reached down and adjusted myself.

"Hey." She giggled.

"Hey."

"So, I take it since Luke is gone, we can...play."

Oh, Jesus. I'd never seen Lex get herself off, and I knew I would come the moment she did.

"I'm game if you're sure Grace won't be back soon."

She nodded her head. "Will, I'm so horny that I have to, and I won't do it unless you're with me. If this is what we have to do, then this is what we have to do. Hold on though. Let me lock the door."

She jumped up, locked the door, and then sat back down on her bed. She bit down on her lower lip, and I let out a moan.

"Get undressed, Lex."

I could see her chest heaving up and down. She somehow propped up her iPad and began getting undressed. When she took her bra off, I sucked in a breath of air.

She pushed her panties down and said, "I'm naked. Now, you."

I jumped up and stripped naked in ten seconds flat. "Touch your breast, Lex."

She used her right hand and began playing with her nipple. "Oh God, Will, I need to feel you. I'm going insane."

I reached down and began stroking my dick. I needed to go slow, or I would come before I wanted to.

"Jesus, Lex. Touch yourself, baby. Tell me how it feels."

Lex moved her hand down and let out a gasp as she began touching herself. "Will, I'm so worked up. It's not going to take long."

I began stroking my dick faster. "Lex...talk to me, baby."

I watched as she took herself to the edge. It was the sexiest thing I'd ever seen.

"I'm...so...close. It feels...so...good," she moaned.

She began making noises, and I was fighting like hell not to come as I watched her body arch back in pleasure.

"Lex, baby, I'm dying over here, watching you make yourself feel good."

She shook her head. Her eyes were closed, and she began saying my name. "Will...oh God. Will, move faster."

I swallowed hard. "Baby, I'm not the one touching you."

She jerked her head forward and looked at the screen. "No. I want to see you stroking yourself faster, Will."

Fuck me.

I moved, so she could see me while I watched her.

"Yes. Oh God, yes," she said.

"Lex, are you close?"

"Faster, Will."

I began stroking my dick faster. *Fuck.* I was about to come.

"Shit," I hissed through my teeth.

"Oh yeah, I'm about to come, Will. I want to see you come."

That was when I lost control. Trying to hold the fucking iPad and jerk off was not an easy task. I felt it building, and I finally had to let it go and come.

"Oh, Lex…I'm gonna come, baby."

I looked down and saw my cum exploding out as I looked at the screen.

Lex yelled out, "Will…oh my God. Yes…yes, I'm coming. Don't move your hand!"

I kept it still, so she could see me, and I watched as she rode out her orgasm. I could hear her panting as she slowly came back down from her high.

"Lex, I have to go clean up. Give me a second."

"Okay. Need to get dressed…really…quick."

I jumped up, headed to our bathroom, and cleaned off my dick. I ran back into the room and got dressed. I picked up my iPad and waited for Lex. She flopped down on the bed and picked up the iPad.

She had a huge smile on her face. "That was awesome."

I laughed and nodded my head. "Yeah, it was."

"I think we are going to have to FaceTime more often." She raised her eyebrows.

"I miss you, Lex."

She closed her eyes and whispered, "I miss you, too, Will. When can you try to come to Austin again?"

"After tonight? Next weekend!"

Lex giggled and looked away. I heard the door open and saw Lex smile at someone.

"Hey, Grace."

"Hey, bitch. Who are you talking to?"

Lex looked back at me. "Will."

Grace dropped down on the bed next to Lex. "Hey, William. Um…why aren't you here?"

"Truck broke down."

Grace's smile disappeared. "Where is Luke?"

I let out a sigh. "Port Aransas with Abigail."

Grace made a funny face. "Who is Abigail?"

I shook my head. "A friend of his."

Grace raised her eyebrows. "Huh. So, is she a friend-friend or a *friend-friend*?"

Shit. Luke is gonna kill me. "A friend with benefits."

"Bastard," Lex and Grace said at the same time.

"Does Libby know about her?" Lex asked.

"Uh…she does now since I slipped tonight and said something about Luke being with Abigail."

Grace shook her head. "Damn men." She got up and walked away.

I heard Grace say in the background, "Lex, you can go to the party with me, if you want."

Lex frowned and then attempted to smile.

"I'm so sorry, Lex. I'll come next weekend, I swear."

"Promise?"

I smiled softly. "I promise, baby. Why don't you go with Grace to the party? Go have fun. Isn't this what your dad wanted? For you to experience life at UT?"

She rolled her eyes and sighed. "Grace and I both hate it here and wish our parents hadn't talked us into not bringing at least one car this semester." She shook her head. "I don't like it, Will. I want to be with you."

My heart physically hurt from hearing her say that she hated UT. "We'll be together next weekend, Lex. Now, go get ready and have fun tonight. Call me when you get back to your dorm, okay?"

She nodded her head. "The party is here in the building, so it shouldn't be that bad. It's someone's birthday, and his friends are having it in the commons area."

"Perfect! That is the kind of party I don't have to worry about."

Lex giggled. "Are you sure? You don't mind?"

"Lex, of course I don't mind. I love you. Have fun."

"Will, please try to come next weekend. My heart is hurting from not seeing you. Promise me, you'll try to come."

I smiled. "I promise, I'll be there next weekend even if I have to rent a car to get there."

She smiled that beautiful smile of hers. Then, it faded. I wished I knew what she was thinking. The soft features of her face seemed to be tense, and her blue eyes didn't have the same normal sparkle. It was almost like she was nervous.

"Lex, it's going to be okay. We're going to be okay."

She began chewing on her lower lip. "Have you…I mean…is there anyone there you might be—"

"Lex, stop this. There is no one, and there will never be anyone besides you."

"What if Abigail has a friend and…"

I let out a sigh. "Lex, please don't do this again. I'm not interested in anyone but you."

She smiled and tilted her head. "Promise me?"

I laughed. "I promise you. Now, go have fun. Don't take any drinks from anyone."

"Yes, *Dad*! I'll call you when we get back up to the room."

"Sounds good. Bye, Lex. I love you."

"Bye, Will. I love you more!"

I closed out of FaceTime and fell back onto the bed as I let out a long sigh. I made a note in my phone to make sure my truck was fixed by Thursday and to make hotel reservations for next weekend. I was going to skip my class on Thursday and head to Austin early. I couldn't wait any longer. I had to see Lex.

A strange feeling washed over my body, and I sat up. I opened up my text messages. I was about to text Lex and ask her not to go to the party, but I decided I was being a jealous fool. I stripped out of my clothes and made my way to the bathroom where I took a hot shower.

I got dressed in boxers and a T-shirt and made my way over to my bed. I sat down and looked at the clock. I set the alarm on my phone for one in the morning. If I didn't hear from Lex by then, I would call her.

I lay down and shut my eyes. "Lex…" I whispered before letting sleep take over. I felt myself quickly drifting off into a dream. All I could see was blue eyes staring into mine.

alex

Grace and I walked into the commons area and looked around. We knew no one. I had met a few people, and Grace had actually gone out on a date with one guy. She had come home four hours later and professed she was giving up on all men.

"So, who is the birthday boy?" I shouted over the music.

Grace shrugged her shoulders. "Beats me. Want something to drink?"

I looked around to see what everyone was drinking.

Beer. How in the world are they allowed to serve beer?

"If the R.A. catches us, we can get into a lot of trouble, Grace," I said.

She shrugged her shoulders and looked around. "No one else seems to be worried about it. I heard someone say he was gone for the weekend, so that's why they threw the party here."

I glanced around again. "I guess I'll have a beer. Seems to be what everyone is drinking. Make sure no one touches it!" I shouted.

Grace laughed and walked toward the other side of the room. I stood there and looked around. The French doors were open, and a group of people were dancing outside.

A bit later, Grace tapped my shoulder and handed me a beer. "Let's go outside. I feel like dancing."

I followed Grace outside. She instantly began moving her hips, and about ten guys focused on her. Three came up, one right after another, and asked her to dance, but she turned each one down.

"You weren't kidding when you said you've given up on men."

She shook her head. "Nope. I'm done. D.O.N.E."

Then, "Turn Down for What" by DJ Snake and Lil Jon started playing, and Grace really started dancing.

"Will you dance with me?" someone asked while I was watching Grace dance.

I didn't even bother to look at the person. I shook my head and turned it a bit as I shouted, "No, thanks."

"I can't believe you won't even dance with the birthday boy."

Then, I recognized Blake's voice. I spun around to see him standing there, wearing a silly birthday hat.

I smiled and shook my head. "It's your birthday? This is your party?" I let out a laugh.

"Yes, ma'am. It's my birthday, and I have to warn you. I'm feeling a bit tipsy."

Grace walked up and looked at Blake. "Hey, it's the hot guy from our tour!"

I instantly felt my cheeks warming up.

Blake looked at her and then at me. "Hot guy, huh?"

Grace laughed. "Yeah. You got a name?"

"Grace, this is Blake Turner. Blake, this is my best friend and roommate, Grace Johnson."

Grace stared at me.

"I ran into him at the café the other day."

She smiled and looked back at Blake. "Happy birthday, birthday boy!"

Blake smiled big and pointed to Grace. "Dance with me?"

Grace laughed. "Sure. Why the hell not?"

I watched as Blake grabbed Grace's hand and pulled her to where everyone was dancing. "Wiggle" by Jason Derulo began playing, and I watched as Grace and Blake danced close to each other. He was moving his hands all over Grace's body, and for some reason, it was starting to irritate me. Grace turned and pushed her ass into Blake. As they moved together, he said something into her ear, and she began laughing.

I looked away and pulled out my phone. *Nothing from Will.*

Looking back out, Grace was facing Blake. They weren't as close as they had been before, but talk about dirty dancing. I'd never in my life been jealous of Grace—with the exception of this very moment. I shook my head. I decided I was just missing Will, and I was mad and upset that I didn't get to see him.

I glanced around at everyone dancing, and my father's voice popped in my head.

Have fun, Alex. Just enjoy being young and experiencing new things.

I downed my beer and walked back inside for another one. I ran into Chrissie, who was in my calculus class, and I hadn't even known it until this last week. We talked for a bit while I finished my second beer. Then, Chrissie got us three Fireball shots each. I was starting to feel pretty good. I asked for another beer and decided I should go check on Grace.

She's probably making out with Blake.

For some reason, that thought made my stomach upset.

I stepped outside and took in a deep breath. I looked around and saw Grace talking to a girl and two guys, and neither guy was Blake.

"Stupid Love" by Jason Derulo started playing.

Someone must like this guy because they keep playing his songs.

A hand was suddenly on my lower back, and it began guiding me to the middle of the dance floor. Somehow, I knew it was Blake. I turned to face him and smiled when I saw him.

"You have to dance with me. It's my birthday."

I pulled out my phone. It was twelve thirty. "I do believe your birthday was yesterday, Mr. Turner."

He tilted his head and raised his eyebrow at me. He put his hands on my waist and pulled me closer to him.

Just have fun, Alex. Discover what's out in the world besides Mason.

I wasn't sure if it was the alcohol or my slight attraction to Blake, but I wrapped my arms around him and began moving my hips against his. He smiled as he dug his fingers into me a bit more. We slowly moved to the beats of the song, and I closed my eyes as I wished I were dancing with Will.

I felt a warm breath on my neck.

"Are you thinking of your boyfriend, Alex?"

I opened my eyes and looked at Blake's lips. I instantly licked my lips, and Blake let out a moan.

"If you are, he is one lucky son of a bitch."

I couldn't even think of anything to say, so I smiled. "I should probably head back up to my room. I think I drank too much."

Blake pulled me closer to him, and I felt his hard dick. He moved his lips to my ear. His hot breath was making me feel light-headed, and I was so confused by what I was feeling. I wanted Will so much, but being in Blake's arms aroused me.

"I want you to know what you do to me."

He moved his lips across my neck, not kissing me but just barely brushing them against my skin. My head was spinning, and when he stepped away, he was smiling. He knew what he had done to me. I was a weak and stupid idiot for letting him get to me like he had.

I shook my head and walked away to find Grace.

"Grace, I'm not feeling very well. I think I had too much to drink. I had three Fireballs."

"You had shots? With who, Alex?"

"Um...a few girls from my calculus class. Grace, I'm not feeling well."

Grace pulled me to her side, and we made our way back into the commons area. Then, we headed to the elevator. Once we got into our room, I made a run for the bathroom. I hit the floor and began throwing up into the toilet.

"Jesus H. Christ, Alex. How much did you drink?"

I began crying as Grace handed me a warm washcloth. "Too much I guess."

Grace sat down on the side of the tub and sighed. "I'd say so, Alex. I knew the moment I saw you dancing all up on Blake that you must have had too much to drink."

I looked up at Grace. "What? I wasn't all up on him."

Grace gave me a dirty look. "Please, Alex. I saw the way y'all were dancing. I almost walked over and pulled you away from him."

"Grace, I wasn't doing anything. Blake respects the fact that I have a boyfriend."

"Uh-huh. That's why he was pushing himself into you and running his lips along your neck."

I fell back onto my ass. "What the fuck, Grace? Should I dissect your dance with him when you had your ass all up on his dick?"

Grace stood up and looked down at me. "The difference with that, Lex, is I'm not dating anyone."

She turned, walked out of the bathroom, and slammed the door shut. I sat there on the cold tile floor, trying to make sense out of everything. I got up and brushed my teeth. I decided I would think about it all in the morning when my head wasn't fuzzy from alcohol.

After making my way back into our room, I stripped out of my clothes, grabbed a shirt, and pulled it over my head. Grace was already in bed. I walked over to my bed, pulled the covers back, and crawled in bed.

I'm so tired. I just need to sleep.

"Alex. Alex!"

I pulled the pillow over my head. "Grace, leave me alone. I have a hangover."

"Alex, damn it! Get the hell up. Will has been blowing up your phone!"

I sat up faster than I should have. I put my hand up to my mouth, jumped out of bed, and ran into the bathroom. I no sooner got in the bathroom before I was throwing up. I sat down and leaned against the wall.

"Oh my God, I've never felt so terrible before in my life."

I looked up to see Grace staring down at me, holding my phone.

"You left it in here last night. It looks like he has been trying to call you since one in the morning."

I reached for the phone. I had twenty-five missed calls and ten text messages. The last call was ten minutes ago.

"Oh shit."

I pulled up and read the messages. They were all pretty much the same.

> *Will: Lex, call me.*

> *Will: Lex, I'm starting to worry.*

> *Will: Fuck, Lex, you're scaring me.*

The last one really caught my attention.

Will: I'm heading to Austin. Borrowing a friend's car.

I snapped my head up and looked at Grace. Then, I let out a moan and held my throbbing head. "Oh my God, Will is on his way here."

Grace turned and walked away.

What in the hell is wrong with her?

I stood up and quickly brushed my teeth. I took a few Tylenol and headed back into the room.

"I need to get dressed."

"You need to take a shower. All I smell is alcohol and the remnants of Blake Turner."

I stopped dead in my tracks. I turned slowly to look at her. "Excuse me?"

"Smell your hair. You smell like his cologne."

I shook my head and went back into the bathroom. Turning on the hot water, I tried to remember what had happened last night.

Why is Grace so mad?

Oh God, did I do something with Blake?

No, I would never do that to Will, drunk or not.

I jumped in the shower and began washing my hair. I moved on to my body and scrubbed it with soap. After drying off, I brushed my teeth again and then made my way out to the room. I picked up my phone and hit Will's number.

"Alex?"

My heart dropped. He never called me Alex.

"Will, I'm so sorry."

"What in the hell? I've been worried sick. I even tried to call Grace, but she didn't answer."

I looked at Grace and gave her a funny look. "Um…I'm not sure why she wasn't answering her phone."

Grace smirked at me. "I wasn't answering because after I went running this morning, I stopped at Starbucks, and I left my phone there. They're holding it for me."

"Grace left her phone at Starbucks this morning. Will, I'm so sorry. I left my phone in the bathroom last night, and I just woke up a little bit ago."

"It's almost one in the afternoon, Lex."

I closed my eyes and felt the tears building. "I had too much to drink last night."

Silence.

I swallowed hard. "Will? Are you still there?"

"Yeah. I'm turning around and heading back to A&M."

"Wait! Where are you? I can meet you!"

Silence again.

"Will? I'm really sorry. I didn't even realize I had drunk so much, and…well, I just wanted to have fun."

"Sounds like you did, Lex."

I closed my eyes. "Where are you? I can meet you."

"I'm tired, Lex. I have a test on Monday, so I'm just going to head back to A&M. I'm glad you're okay. I was really freaking out."

My heart was literally hurting. I opened my eyes and felt a tear rolling down my face. "I'm so sorry. I didn't mean to worry you. Will you please tell me where you're at?"

"I'm in Austin."

I jumped up. "Will, why would you leave? You've already come all this way. Please…I need to see you."

"I'm sitting outside your dorm, Lex. I was just talking to your friend Blake."

My whole world stopped. *Oh God. What did I do last night?* I looked at Grace. "How in the world did you meet Blake?"

Grace's eyes widened in surprise.

"He asked who I was looking for. After I mentioned your name, he said you were in his study group."

My heart began pounding. Blake had lied to him. I had never gone to the study group before.

"I'm on my way. Let me throw on some clothes. Please, Will, please don't leave."

"I won't," he whispered.

"Be right there! Bye."

The phone went dead.

I looked at Grace and busted out into tears. "Oh my God, Grace. Did I do something wrong last night? I don't remember anything. Grace! What did I do?"

She got up, picked up a pair of jeans, and handed them to me. I pulled them on quickly and grabbed a T-shirt.

"Alex, you didn't do anything but drink too much. You danced a little too close to Blake, that's all."

I stopped moving. "What do you mean, danced a little too close?"

"You were all up on him, and his lips were getting a little too friendly with your neck."

I felt sick to my stomach. "Did I…did I…"

"You didn't do anything."

I let out a breath. "Oh, thank God."

I made my way to the door and quickly ran to the elevator.

Why would Will leave if he's right here? He's mad. He must be so mad at me.

I pushed open the doors and quickly started scanning the area outside. When I saw Will, my heart began pounding in my chest. Smiling, I made my way over to him. When his eyes met mine, I started running. He smiled, and I began crying. I jumped into his arms and wrapped my legs around his waist.

"Oh God. Oh God, I've missed you so much!" I cried as I buried my face into his neck.

"Lex, baby, I've missed you, too."

"Please don't be mad at me. I'm so, so sorry. I swear I'll never drink like that again. I swear." I pulled back and searched his eyes. "I love you, Will."

He reached up and placed his hand behind my neck. He pulled me in for a kiss. I wasn't sure how long we were kissing for, but it was turning more passionate by the second.

Then, I heard a male clear his throat. I pulled back some and smiled at Will. He smiled back and winked at me as he slowly put me down.

Will turned and looked at someone. "Thanks, Blake."

Blake? My stomach knotted up as I slowly looked over at Blake.

He smiled at Will. "Sure, no problem. I've never seen you here before, and you looked like you were lost." He glanced over to me. "Good morning, Alex. I heard you had a little too much to drink last night."

Bastard.

He was playing a game with me, and I wasn't about to participate.

"You would know, Blake. You were there."

Will looked between Blake and me with a confused look on his face.

Blake laughed. "Yeah, I was. It was my party after all." He slapped Will on the back. "It was a pleasure meeting you, Will. Hope to see you around soon. Take care of her. She's a special girl."

Wait—what? What in the hell?

Will attempted to smile as he shook Blake's hand. "Yeah, nice meeting you, too."

Blake turned and walked away. I quickly looked back at Will.

I grabbed his hand and smiled. "Come on, let me show you our room!"

He chuckled and quickly kissed me on the lips. "Sounds good."

I opened the door.

Grace screamed and ran into Will's arms. "It's so good to see a familiar face! I've missed you, William Hayes."

Will laughed. "Same here, Grace."

Grace and I showed Will all around our dorm room, the building, the café, and a few other places around campus.

Finally, Grace said, "Well, I think I'll go get my phone and hang out at Starbucks for a couple of hours or so. I have a book I've been dying to read."

Will grabbed my hand. Then, he leaned down and kissed Grace on the cheek. "Happy reading. Love ya, girl."

He quickly turned and began pulling me back toward our dorm.

I looked back at Grace and yelled, "Thank you! Love you!"

She lifted her hand. "Yeah, yeah. See ya soon. Have fun!"

Will opened the door to my room and shut it before pushing me against the other side of the door. He began stripping me out of my clothes.

"Oh God…Will…" I was panting heavily.

I quickly began unbuttoning his pants. He grabbed a condom before I pushed them down, and his dick sprang free. I grabbed it and began stroking him.

"Jesus, Lex, I want to make love to you. I want you so bad."

I dropped my head back against the door. "Take me, Will. I need to feel you."

Will reached down for a condom and quickly put it on before he ripped my lace panties off and picked me up. The moment I felt him inside me, I felt whole again. It was like something had been missing this whole time.

"Yes! Oh God, yes!"

"Lex, I can't stop myself."

He pounded in and out of me, fast and hard, and I loved every second of it.

"Harder. Will, I'm so close."

"Lex, baby, hurry."

He pulled out and then slammed back into me, causing me to slam against the door. I was sure anyone walking by would know what was going on.

"That's it! Yes! Yes! Yes!"

He pressed his lips against mine and let out a moan. He moved in and out of me a few more times before he stopped. He stopped kissing me long enough to pull out, take off the condom, and toss it into the trash. He kicked off his pants, picked me up, and carried me to my bed. He laid me down and crawled on top of me where he began teasing my entrance with his semi-hard dick. The way he was kissing me was both tender and passionate. I couldn't get enough of him.

"I'm. So. Sorry," he whispered between kisses.

I pulled back and looked into his eyes. "For what?"

He shook his head, and his eyes looked so sad. "For fucking you when all I really wanted to do was make love to you."

My stomach did a crazy flip, and my heart felt like it had dropped to my stomach. I placed my hands on the sides of his face. "I loved every second of it. It was hot as hell, and I'd love to do that more often."

He smiled bigger. "It was pretty hot, wasn't it?"

I bit my lower lip and nodded my head. He leaned down and kissed me as he began pushing himself into me, a little bit more each time. It felt amazing.

He moved his head back and closed his eyes. "Motherfucker. That feels so good, Lex, but I don't have a condom on."

No wonder it felt so good. "Just a couple more times, Will. Please, I just want to feel you."

He pushed all the way in, and we both let out a moan.

"Don't move, Will."

I wanted to feel him inside me with nothing between us.

"Lex…" he whispered as he moved just a little bit.

He quickly pulled out of me and jumped up from the bed. He went to his pants on the floor. When I saw him grab a condom, I felt disappointed. I was on birth control, so why he insisted on a condom was beyond me.

He rolled it on and climbed back over me.

When I felt his fingers inside me, I let out a sigh of relief. "Feels so good," I whispered.

Then, he moved and slowly pushed himself in so deep that I let out a gasp. He continued to move in and out. He was being so gentle. His lips came to my ear where he began telling me how much he loved me.

That was when last night decided to rear its ugly head. Blake's voice invaded my thoughts.

I want you to know what you do to me.

I squeezed my eyes shut as I pushed last night and Blake from my mind. I whispered, "I love you, Will. I love you so much."

WILL

Two Months Later

I sat in the small café, trying to study. I had only seen Lex one time in the last two months because of our crazy schedules at school. It seemed like both of us had taken on schedules tougher than we had anticipated. Then, Lex had a huge project she had been working on with a few classmates the last two weekends in a row.

I was going insane, and I knew she was, too. Our last two attempts to FaceTime each other hadn't worked out, and I had heard the frustration in her voice. Weeks of texting and not being able to release our sexual frustrations were getting to the both of us. After Thanksgiving vacation, Lex was going to bring her car to school, so we could at least attempt to see each other more often.

I let out a sigh and picked up my phone.

Me: Thinking about you.

Lex: Thinking about you. What are you doing?

Me: Studying. You?

Lex: Heading to a study group. Big chemistry test before vacation.

I knew Lex had been hanging around that Blake guy more and more. They were in a study group together, and she had brought him up a few times. I didn't like the guy. The first time I'd met him, I'd mentioned I was Lex's boyfriend, and he'd rubbed me wrong. The way he'd looked at her pissed me off.

Me: Who all is going to be there?

Lex: I guess the normal people. Grace was supposed to go, but she backed out. She's not feeling well.

Me: How late will you be there?

Lex: I don't think too late. I can't wait to see you! I can't wait to go home for Thanksgiving and see everyone!

Me: I can't wait to fuck you against another door.

Lex: God, Will. I'm so horny all the time, and you don't make it easier when you talk to me like that.

Me: Can you FaceTime? I'll go to my truck.

Lex: I can't. I'm here. I love you! I'll call you when I'm done. Bye!

Me: K. I love you, too, Lex. Later.

"Fuck," I whispered as I gathered up my books.

I headed back to the dorm. I pulled up and saw Callie Morgan talking to her fiancé, Joe Michaels. They were both in my English Lit class. Callie was a cute girl with blonde hair and green eyes, and she was shorter than Lex. She was probably one of the most outgoing girls I'd ever met. Joe was tall and built, and he had no problem telling you how it was. They made a cute couple, and where one was, the other was surely nearby.

"Hayes! How's it going?" Joe said.

I smiled and reached out to shake Joe's hand.

Callie smiled. "How are you?"

"Frustrated that my girlfriend is at another school, but other than that, I'm doing good. What are y'all up to?"

"We're planning our next mission trip. We're heading to Oklahoma to help rebuild some places that were destroyed by the latest round of tornados that moved through that area."

Callie and Joe were probably two of the kindest people I'd ever met.

"You want to go with us, Hayes?" Joe asked. "It's over Thanksgiving and Christmas breaks."

I smiled. "I wish I could, but I miss my family. Miss my girl, ya know? When is the next one?"

"Spring break! We're going home for a couple of days and then heading to Florida to help a church build a new schoolhouse."

I shook my head. "Y'all are good people. I'll keep it in mind."

"That's better than a no!" Joe said.

I laughed as I shook Joe's hand again and said good-bye. I headed to my room, and I spent the rest of the afternoon waiting to hear back from Lex.

"Alex is going to be so surprised that you're showing up a day early to pick her up," Libby said with a giggle.

I smiled and nodded my head. "I hope so. Hey, are you sure you want to drive home with Luke? You seemed uncertain the other day."

"Nah, it'll be fine. I'm going to bring back my car, I think. That way I don't have to depend on you two." Libby looked around. "Where is Luke?"

"At the gym. He's been going a lot lately. Something has been weighing heavily on his mind. He hasn't even gone out in the last month. He's been here every night."

I sighed and shook my head. Lex and I hadn't been able to have our FaceTime fun because both Luke and Grace were always in our dorm rooms whenever Lex and I could fit in a chat.

"Give Alex a big hug for me, and tell her I'll see her tomorrow night."

It was Sunday, and I wasn't supposed to be in Austin until tomorrow. The plan was to pick up Lex and Grace and head to Mason on Monday. I'd booked a hotel room in Austin for Lex and me for tonight to surprise her.

I walked out to my truck and turned to face Libby. "Lib, what's going on with you and Luke? Y'all used to be the best of friends."

Libby's eyes glossed over, and she looked away as she shrugged. "I don't know, Will. I guess Luke doesn't want to be friends with me. I think he likes his fuck buddies better."

I closed my eyes and sighed. "Lib, he hasn't even mentioned Abigail in so long. I don't think he's seen her since that weekend on the coast."

Libby sucked in a deep breath and let it out. "Doesn't matter. I've tried to figure it out, and I'm done with it. I just have to get through the drive home. Then, I'll have my own car, and I can see less and less of Luke."

My heart hurt for my sister. I knew she cared about Luke. She might even be in love with him. I'd also seen the way Luke looked at her. He had strong feelings for her, and he was fighting them. I needed to make sure it wasn't because of me.

"Have a safe drive. Let me know when you get there."

"Will do. Love you, Lib."

She smiled. "I love you, too, Will."

An hour and a half later, I was in Austin. I pulled over and parked my car in the parking lot, and then I sent Lex a text.

Me: Hey, baby. What are you up to?

Lex: Hey, handsome. Nothing. Just finishing up lunch with a few people. What about you?

Me: Not much. Where are y'all eating?

Lex: Just across the street from my dorm at the Littlefield Patio Café.

Me: Text me when you head back to your room.

Lex: Okay. We are finishing up and leaving now.

I smiled and jumped out of my truck as I made my way to Duren Hall, Lex and Grace's dorm. I knew where the café was, so I sat down on a bench where I could see when Lex would be walking up. The moment I saw her walking and laughing with Blake, it felt like someone had punched me in the stomach.

I sat there and watched them. Two other people were walking behind them. Lex turned and said something to one girl, and then everyone started laughing. They all stopped and talked for a bit.

I pulled out my phone.

Me: Are you back at your room?

I watched as Lex pulled her phone out of her back pocket before reading my text message.

Lex: Nope, not yet. Just saying good-bye.

Me: Who are you with?

Lex: Couple people from the study group.

Me: That study group is really starting to become a regular thing, isn't it?

Lex: What does that mean, Will?

Me: Blake with you?

Lex: Are you angry with me?

She avoided my question about Blake.

I didn't text her back. I watched as she looked down at her phone every few seconds. She pushed it back into her pocket and turned to say something to Blake. His smile dropped, and he motioned for them to head inside Duren Hall. I watched them walk through the door to the building.

I waited a few seconds and followed, but then an older woman at the front desk stopped me.

"Who are you here to see?"

"Grace. Grace Johnson."

"Is she expecting you?"

I nodded my head.

She picked up the phone and hit a number. "Miss Johnson, are you expecting a—"

"Will Hayes."

"Will Hayes? Okay, very well." She hung up the phone and smiled. "Do you know how to get up there?"

I smiled. "Yes, ma'am, I do."

I made my way over to the elevator. I hit the button for Lex's floor and took in a few deep breaths. When I stepped off the elevator, I heard Lex's and Blake's voices.

"Doesn't seem like he really makes an effort to come visit you, Alex."

"Blake, you don't know Will. He would be here every weekend if he could."

"Can you trust him? I mean, what if he's seeing someone else?"

"No, he wouldn't do that. He made me a promise. Why are you trying to plant doubt in my head, Blake?"

"What about us, Alex?"

What. The. Fuck?

"What do you mean, Blake? There is no *us*. We're friends, and that's it."

"That night at my birthday party, you didn't dance with me like you wanted to be just my friend, Alex."

My knees about gave out on me, and I felt sick to my stomach.

"From the way you look at me sometimes, I can see you're confused about your feelings. I want to be more than friends, Alex."

I looked around the corner to see Lex leaning against the wall with that fucker practically on top of her.

"Blake, I love Will. I love him more than anything. I'm not going to lie and say that I'm not confused about a few things. I keep hearing my father's voice in my head, telling me to experience new things and new people, but…"

I moved and leaned against the wall. *Lex, why?*

"Then, experience them, Alex. Just because he was your first love—"

"Blake…please."

"You're gonna see him tomorrow, Alex, and all will be good for a few weeks. Maybe you need a break from Will."

I waited to hear her response, but all I heard was silence. I pushed off the wall and made my way around the corner. I began walking up to them. When I saw Alex put her hand on Blake's chest, I balled up my fists, but I kept walking.

"Blake, I can't do this right now. I have to call—"

"Lex?" I called out.

She dropped her hand, and Blake took a step away from her. She looked at me, and her mouth dropped open.

"I guess I showed up at the wrong time...or maybe it was the right time," I said.

She shook her head. "Will, what are you doing here?"

She let a smile move across her face as she began walking up to me. She went to hug me, but I put my hands up and took a step back.

"You made *me* promise you, Lex."

She looked confused. "What?"

"How long have you had feelings for him?"

Blake walked up and went to say something to me.

I pointed to him. "You stay the fuck away from me, asshole. I heard everything you two just said to each other. If you value your life, you'll leave right now."

Blake held up his hands and took a few steps back.

"Wait, Will. Let me explain what you heard."

I looked down at Lex. She looked scared, panicked almost. Of course she did. She'd just been caught with another guy.

"I don't need you to explain it, Alex."

She let a sob escape her mouth. "Will, please don't call me Alex. Please just let me talk to you alone. *Please*."

"I heard it all. You're confused. Daddy's telling you to experience other people. That's what you want. That night of the party, you were wasted, weren't you? You said you'd passed the fuck out. What happened between you two?" I looked at Blake and then back at Lex.

She began shaking her head faster as she wiped away her tears. "Nothing! My God, Will, I'd never do that to you."

I took a step closer to her and leaned down. "I just heard him say how the two of you were dancing, Alex. I heard it with my own ears."

"No, it's not like that."

"How often do you see him, especially with all these study groups you go to?" I looked up at Blake. "Are you there every time?"

The fucker smiled and said, "Yes, I am. Always."

"No. Will, please let's just go somewhere and talk. It's not like that," Lex pleaded.

I took a few steps back as Lex began crying harder.

"You made me promise you that everything would be okay, that *we* would be okay. You made me promise you that *I* wouldn't meet anyone, Alex."

A loud sob escaped Lex's throat as a door opened.

Grace stepped out. "Will?" She looked back and forth between Blake and me. "What's going on?"

I glanced back at Lex. I took a deep breath and blew it out as I closed my eyes.

"Will, I love you. Please just—"

I opened my eyes. "No. No, Alex."

I turned to walk away, but Lex grabbed my arm.

"Will, please!"

I turned and looked into her beautiful blue eyes as I felt the tears building in mine. "I guess I should have asked you to make the same promise to me, Alex."

She sucked in a breath of air as I pushed her hand away. As I began walking off, I closed my eyes.

She screamed out, "Will! Will!" Then, I heard her yell, "Blake, let me go! Let me go!"

Grace told Blake to let Alex go as the elevator door opened. Before I got on, I saw Lex running toward the elevator, but I stepped inside with the doors shutting behind me before she got there. The sounds of her yelling for me almost had me rushing back to her, but the image of her hand on his chest while she'd looked into his eyes was now forever etched in my brain.

I heard a knock on my bedroom door, and I flew up out of bed. I threw open the door, hoping to see Will.

"Libby…" I walked back to my bed and sat down. The tears began falling again. "Please tell me where he is."

Will hadn't come home for Thanksgiving break, and no one knew where he was, not even Luke.

She walked up to me and dropped to sit on the floor. "I swear to you, Alex, I don't know. We've all been trying to call him. My parents are so worried about him."

"He wouldn't let me explain." I cried harder as I put my hands up to my face.

"Alex, I have to ask you something, and you have to be honest with me. I talked to Grace."

I dropped my hands and looked her in the face. "What did Grace tell you?"

"The truth—that you've been spending a lot of time with this Blake guy. Do you have feelings for him, Alex?"

"No! Well, yes…I mean, no. Damn it!" I shouted as I stood up. Spinning around, I looked at Libby. "I don't know. I don't have feelings for him like I have for Will, but something is there. I just keep hearing these voices in my head. I don't know what to do, Libby. I love Will. I want Will, but when I'm around Blake, I…I want…"

"Him?"

The tears were pouring down my face. "I don't think so. Sometimes, Will sends me these text messages. They drive me insane with lust, and then I'll see Blake, and I get these weird feelings. I'm not sure if I'm just missing Will, or if I…if I…"

"If you have feelings for Blake."

"Alex?"

I looked up and saw my father standing there. This was his fault. It was his damn voice in my head that I'd kept listening to.

"This is your fault," I said.

My father looked shocked. "Excuse me?"

"You made me go to UT when you knew I wanted to go to A&M. I hate UT! I hate it! If I had been with Will at A&M, none of this would have happened. I hate you!" I pushed past my father and ran down the stairs.

"Alexandra Eryn! You stop right now!" my mother called out.

I ran past Colt and out the back door. I needed to find Will. I needed to get fresh air.

I ran into the barn, and Banjo poked his head out of his stall. I grabbed a lead rope, and then I walked into his stall, clipped it on, and led him out. I jumped up on him and began riding him bareback. I let Banjo lead the way as I sobbed and fought to catch my breath.

I wasn't sure how long I had been out riding Banjo. I just sat on him, feeling numb. When he made his way to the river, I jumped off and stood there. I watched him graze on the grass. I dropped his lead, and I walked over to a tree. I slowly slid down it and stared out at the river. I had no tears left.

I leaned my head back and replayed the whole thing over again in my head. I thought of every single thing Will had heard and how it must have sounded to him.

I closed my eyes and whispered, "Will, please come back to me. Please."

I felt something hitting my boot, and I opened my eyes to see Banjo. I smiled and looked up at my giant beauty. "I can always count on you, boy. Isn't that right?"

He began bobbing his head up and down, and I let out a giggle.

I stood up and began running my hands along his side and back. "Oh, Banjo, I really messed things up." I buried my face into my horse and softly cried.

"Alex? You feel like company?"

I looked up and saw my father. I walked over to him, and he pulled me into his arms. I completely fell apart. My legs gave out on me, and we both slowly hit the ground. He pulled me onto his lap and held me while I cried.

"Alex, please don't cry, baby."

"Daddy, he's gone. He left me."

He began rocking me while I attempted to settle down.

"Shh…baby girl. Please, please don't be upset."

I pulled back and looked into my father's eyes. "I didn't…I didn't mean it when I said…when I said I hated you. Daddy, I didn't mean it."

He pulled me back into him. "I know, Alex. I know."

"I love him, Daddy. I love him so much, and I hurt him so bad."

He pulled back and placed his finger under my chin. "Alex, from what I understand, Will didn't give you a chance to explain. Just give him time to cool down, sweetheart."

I tried to smile. "Daddy, I kept hearing your voice over and over in my head. I tried liking UT, Daddy. I have to be honest with you though. I hate it. I hate it with a passion."

Daddy laughed and nodded his head. "Jeff told me that Grace told him the same thing."

"I don't want you to hate me, but this is not what I want."

My father swallowed hard. "Let's get back on the horses and ride."

We stood, and he helped me up onto Banjo. He got up on Crazy Eight. We began walking, and for the first few minutes, we rode along in silence.

"Alex, I had so many dreams for you. Since you were little, I think I had your whole life planned out. Your mother used to tell me that it was your life and not mine, but I knew you would do what I said, and that's how I always thought. Seeing you this weekend, seeing how unhappy you are, makes me realize that it's not my life to plan. It's your life. We only learn lessons in life by making mistakes. I was trying too hard to keep you from making any, but I made the biggest one of all. I tried to tell you how and why you should live your life the way I wanted you to."

I looked straight ahead and let what my father was saying soak in.

"Alex, I'm no longer going to tell you what I think you should do. I'm going to leave it up to you to decide what to do. It's your life, your future, your dreams—not mine."

I glanced back at him and smiled. "Grace and I talked about it. We were going to wait and talk to you and Uncle Jeff together, but I'm thinking now is a good time."

He smiled and winked at me. "I do believe Grace has already talked to her daddy."

I laughed. "I'm not surprised. She utterly hates UT."

I took a deep breath and got ready to lay out the plans I had made for my own future. "We both decided that we would stay at UT and finish out our freshman year. It's really hard being away from Luke, Libby, and especially Will, but I think it will be best for Grace and me to finish what we started this year. Next year, I'd like to transfer to A&M and get a bachelor of science in horticulture."

Daddy smiled. "Horticulture?"

I smiled. "Yep. I loved working every day in the garden with Mama and Grams when I was growing up. I find myself daydreaming about working in Mama's garden. I've always wanted to have my own nursery and teach other people the things Mama and Grams taught me."

I watched as my father's eyes filled with tears.

"I think that sounds like an amazing plan, baby girl. It makes me very proud of you."

"Yeah?"

He stopped his horse. "Very much so, Alex. I just want you to be happy. If that is what will make you happy, then it'll make me happy."

I instantly felt a weight lifting off my shoulders. "I guess we should have had this talk months ago."

He chuckled. "I guess so. I'm sorry I made you feel like you couldn't share your dreams with me, Alex. I wanted you to follow in my footsteps, but I never stopped to think about your own footsteps."

"Daddy, I love you so much."

"Darlin', I love you, and I'm so damn thankful you're my daughter. Come on, let's get home. You leave tomorrow, and I know your mother wants to spend some time with you."

We made our way back to the house as we talked about everything and anything.

"Daddy, what should I do about Will?"

"Alex, I suggest you go to A&M and talk to Will face-to-face. I also think you should take your car to school with you, so you don't feel stuck in Austin."

I loved Will, and I would do whatever I needed to prove that to him.

22
WILL

Two weeks had passed since Thanksgiving break, and we were getting closer to winter break. I'd finally broken down and called my parents the Monday after Thanksgiving. I'd never heard my mother so angry before in my life. She hadn't even cared that I had gone to Oklahoma to help rebuild houses. After both my father and mother had lit into me, they had told me to call Lex.

I wasn't ready to talk to Lex yet. She had been calling and texting me at least ten times a day. When I'd sent her a text back, saying I needed time to think, she had begged me to take her call. I just couldn't get what she'd said out of my head. If she was confused about us, then she also needed to take the time to figure things out.

"I talked to Grace earlier," Luke said.

"Oh, yeah? How's she doing?" I asked as I continued to act like I was studying.

"She's good. She said Alex is a mess. She told that Blake guy to take a hike when he kept coming by. Grace said Blake seemed to be stalking Alex, but she thinks he got the hint when Alex told him that she loved you and only you."

I glanced up and looked at Luke. "Is that so? She should have told him that before."

Luke let out a sigh. "Listen, I agree with you on that one. At the same time, Will, I can't say I blame Alex for being confused. I think she was mixing up her emotions of missing you and wanting you, and she was using this guy as a type of replacement."

I shut my book. "Really? So, in other words, when I get horny, I should just go find a study buddy, dance all close to her, and spend my free time with her. Don't fuck her, but just lead her on. Do I have that right?"

"Um…well, shit, when you say it like that, dude…"

I stood up. "If she was so fucking lonely and horny, she shouldn't have run to some guy. It should have been me she wanted and waited for."

"Jesus, Will, she didn't cheat on you."

"No, but she thought about it, Luke."

"You don't know that."

I slammed my hand down on the table. "I heard her! I heard her tell that fucker that she had feelings for him. I. Heard. Her." I turned and grabbed my wallet and phone.

"Will, wait. Where are you going?"

"Out. I need to forget about Alex for a while."

I opened the door and slammed it behind me. I made my way out of our building. I had no idea where I was going. All I knew was I wanted to get as far away from anything or anyone who reminded me of Lex.

I found myself wandering around before I heard Joe calling my name. I turned to see him running up.

"Hayes! Why in the hell are you walking around outside? It's freezing!"

"Trying to clear my head."

He grinned and nodded his head. "You need a drink, my boy."

"Hell yes."

"Come on, I'm heading to my friend's house. Let's knock a few back, shall we?"

I spent the next three hours downing beer after beer as some girl named Lucy flirted with me. I had zero interest in her even though she was hot as hell, but she couldn't hold a candle to Lex.

No one will ever compare to Lex.

When Lucy moved and made her way next to me, I knew it was time for me to head back to my room. When I stood up, I could feel the effects of the alcohol. I wasn't drunk, but I was feeling good.

Lucy stood up and grabbed my arm. "You interested in heading back to my apartment?"

I looked her up and down. *Nothing.* As much as I wanted to have sex, I didn't want to have sex with Lucy.

I shook my head. "Sorry, not interested."

She sat back down and pouted.

I walked around and thanked everyone for letting me join in on the fun. I'd found out that most of these people would go on mission trips with Joe and Callie. I would be spending more time with them soon. I hadn't told Joe or Callie that I was planning on spending my winter break with them in Oklahoma.

Joe slapped my back, scaring the shit out of me. "Come on, I'll walk you back to your dorm. I sent Callie a text and told her to meet me there."

"Sounds good!" I said with a laugh. The beer was starting to get to me.

Joe and I started making our way toward my place, and the whole way, he kept talking about how wonderful Callie was. I could see how much the two of them loved each other just by the way they would look at each other.

"When are y'all getting married?" I asked.

"After school. Our parents insist on it, and since they're paying for school and the wedding, I wasn't about to argue."

I laughed. "I see your point."

"Shit, I see Roger. I need to tell him something. Let me run and catch him. I'll meet you and Callie outside your dorm."

"Sounds good." I watched as he took off, calling for Roger.

I started toward my dorm and smiled when I saw Callie.

"Hey you! Where is Joe?"

"Took off after some Roger guy to ask him something. Said he would be right here."

"Okay. Were you able to enjoy yourself and relax for a bit?"

I laughed. "Does it show that bad?"

She nodded her head. "Yeah, kind of. Listen, Will, I'm really sorry about you and your girlfriend. I hope that y'all can work it out."

I tried to smile, but it came off as a poor attempt. "Yeah, I'm thinking when she calls me again, I'm going to talk to her."

"Good. You need to give her a chance to explain. Is she still calling every day?"

I nodded and felt my stomach knotting up. "Yep."

"Answer her when she calls. I'd hate to hear that she stopped calling because you kept blowing her off."

I needed to change the subject. "I have some news for you."

"Good or bad?" She laughed.

I reached over and pulled out a stick from her hair. "Jesus, where have you been? You have sticks and leaves in your hair."

"I was helping an older lady trim trees this afternoon. I've never been hit with so many branches in my life, but I had fun. So, what's the news?"

I raised my eyebrows at her and smiled. "I've decided to join y'all in Oklahoma over winter break."

She threw her hands up to her mouth. "Oh my God. Are you serious?"

I nodded my head as she jumped into my arms. I laughed at how happy she was. She loosened her grip, and I set her down.

"I'm going to peck you on the lips!"

She quickly did what she'd said, and I laughed.

"Wait until Joe finds out!" she said.

"It'd better be good!" Joe said, walking up to us.

"Will's going with us to Oklahoma, Joe!" she said.

Joe reached for my hand and shook it. "Damn, Hayes. You have no idea how much you're helping us out. We really could use the extra help, and with your background, dude, you just saved us. I'm gonna kiss you now!"

I pulled back and held up my hand. "Uh…let's not!"

Joe and Callie both laughed.

"Listen, give me all the details later, and count me in. I'm gonna head inside. It's getting colder out, and it's starting to rain."

Joe shook my hand one more time, and we said our good-byes.

I made my way inside, but then I stopped and looked around. For some reason, I had the strangest feeling that someone was watching me. I shook it off and decided I would lay off the beer for a while.

"Alex! Jesus H. Christ! Slow down!" Grace called from behind me.

My heart was pounding, and I was fighting like hell to keep my tears at bay. I was so stupid for coming here. I should have known he had moved on. He hadn't answered any of my calls or text messages. He was done with me.

It was starting to drizzle, and I began walking faster. That was when I heard Grace let out a small scream. I turned to see her on the ground, and a guy was practically on top of her.

"Oh my goodness! Grace, are you all right?" I asked.

I ran over to help her up, but the guy was already helping her.

"Are you okay? I didn't see you. I'm so very sorry. Are you hurt?" the guy asked.

I looked at Grace and smiled. She was awestruck. I peeked over at the guy, and I could see why. He was handsome, tall, and he had dark brown hair and caramel-colored eyes.

"Grace? Are you okay? Did I hurt you? I swear I didn't see you," he said.

Grace's mouth dropped open. "How do you know my name?"

He attempted not to smile. He turned to me, pointed, and looked back at Grace. "Well, your...friend?"

I nodded and smiled.

"Your friend here said Grace, so I just assumed it was your name."

Grace quickly responded, "Yep, it is, and yes, I'm totally fine. It was my fault. I was rushing, and I didn't see you coming out of the door."

"So, it's kind of both our faults then really."

Grace giggled.

Oh. My. God. Grace giggled.

"I guess so. Uh...well, we have to...we need to get going," she stammered.

He looked at me, and I reached my hand out.

"Alex Mathews. Thanks for knocking her down and helping her up."

Grace glared at me.

Oh hell...I just made myself sound stupid.

"Hi, Alex. Noah Ewing."

He turned and stuck his hand out toward Grace.

"Grace Johnson. Again, I'm really sorry," she said.

The way Noah smiled at Grace caused her to blush, and Grace didn't normally blush.

"Right…well, it was nice meeting you, Noah." Grace began walking off.

I stood there and watched Noah staring at her.

"Bye, Noah," I said before following after Grace.

"Um…bye, Alex. See ya around, Grace."

Grace threw up her hand and waved it quickly. She didn't stop walking until we finally reached my car. I walked around to the driver's side and unlocked the door.

When we got inside, she turned her whole body toward me as she glared at me. "We drove all this way, and you're just leaving?"

My heart dropped to my stomach. For a few brief minutes, I had forgotten what I had just seen. "He was with another girl. Did you not see them together, Grace?"

"I saw him talking to a girl. I saw the girl hug him and quickly peck him on the lips. That's all I saw."

I shook my head and laughed. "I saw him reach for her face, and then he talked to her like they were in a deep conversation. Then, she hugged him and kissed him. Doesn't matter if the kiss was quick or not. She kissed him on the lips, and they hugged. He's moved on."

Grace turned and stared out the front window. "If my memory is right, I remember Will walking up on something that wasn't what it seemed."

I glanced at Grace before I turned on the car and pulled out onto the street. "It doesn't matter. He hasn't returned a single text or call. Clearly, he wants nothing to do with me right now. Maybe it's for the best. Maybe we both just need time to think."

Grace let out a gruff laugh. "Okay, sure. You without Will though…is going to be pure hell for both of us."

Grace put her headphones on, and she didn't utter a word to me the whole drive back to Austin. I glanced down at my phone and tried to decide if I should send Will one more text.

Two hours later, I sat on my bed, staring at my phone. I jumped when it pinged.

Daddy: How are you, darling?

Me: Good.

Daddy: Have you talked to Will yet?

Me: No. Maybe you were right. I think I need to spend some time learning who I am.

Daddy: Alex, you need to listen to your heart, not my words.

Me: I know. It's just…I went to A&M, Daddy. Will was with a girl.

Daddy: Situations like that can be deceiving, Alexandra. You should know this better than anyone.

Me: I know. Grace said the same thing. I just need some time to think.

Daddy: I love you, baby girl. Call us this week, okay?

Me: I will. I love you, too, Daddy. Bye.

I decided to change and go for a run. I slipped on my sneakers and turned on my music. I was feeling so homesick after going home for Thanksgiving and not having Will to talk to. Plus, Grace was clearly pissed off at me for leaving and not talking to Will. I felt like I was totally alone. I pulled up a picture of Banjo and made it my screensaver.

Maybe a good run in the cold air will help clear my head.

I sat on the window seat and stared out the window while Grace went on and on about going home for Christmas.

Every now and then, I'd throw in an, "Oh, I know," or, "I'm so excited, too," and, "I can't wait to see everyone."

Grace put her hand on my shoulder. "Have you talked to Libby?"

I nodded my head and felt the tears burning in my eyes. "She said Will won't let her even mention my name. If she tries to talk about me, he just gets up and leaves."

Grace let out a sigh. "Yeah, Luke said the same thing. He also told me that he didn't think Will was dating anyone, Alex. He said he goes to class, comes back to the room, and pretty much just studies and runs. I told Luke you've taken up running, too."

I peeked over to Grace and tried to smile. "He's running?"

She smiled and nodded her head. "Luke said Will runs twice a day—every morning and every night."

My smile faded a bit. "What if he's going to see someone and just doesn't want Luke to know?"

Grace's smile turned to a frown. "Well, the only damn way to find out is if the two of you would stop being so damn stubborn and call one another. This is insane! You can't avoid each other over break. You're going to see each other."

I looked back out the window. I didn't want to admit to Grace how excited I was to be going home. I knew the moment I saw Will, I'd probably break down, but I also knew being home in neutral territory would be what we needed to work things out. I just prayed that what I had seen with that girl wasn't what I thought it was.

"Come on, Alex. Get packed, so we can get out of here tomorrow. I'm ready to get home to my damn horse!"

I giggled as I stood up and walked over to my closet. "I'm glad I'm not the only one excited to see my horse."

We both laughed and started making plans to go riding the moment we got home.

WILL

"What in the hell do you mean you're not going home?" Luke pushed my truck door shut.

I let out the breath I had been holding. "Just that, Luke. I'm not going home."

He stood there and stared at me like I was crazy. "What about your parents, Will? You haven't seen your mom or dad since August. Why are you doing this to them? It's Christmas, Will."

I looked down at the ground. I couldn't find my voice to talk. I missed my parents so damn much.

"Fuck, Will. From what Grace has told me, Alex is a walking ghost. She's devastated."

I shook my head. "She stopped calling. She doesn't even text anymore."

"Do you? Do you call or text her? Grace said they came here to A&M."

I snapped my head up and looked at Luke. "What? When?"

He ran his hand through his hair. "Right after Thanksgiving. Grace said Alex wanted to talk to you in person. I guess when they walked up, you were hugging some girl, and y'all kissed. That's what Grace told me."

I gave Luke a funny look. "What?"

He shrugged and leaned against my truck. "Dude, it was that day you went out and got hammered. You came back, and I didn't want to say anything, but you smelled like you had been all over some girl. The perfume was strong."

I shook my head, trying to think back to that day. I had drunk a lot at the party Joe took me to, but I didn't think I had been drunk. I tried to remember what had happened.

"Shit. I don't even remember that whole night. I was at the party, and some girl kept flirting with me, but I know I didn't hook up with anyone. I remember talking to Joe and walking back here with him. I think Callie might have been with us. Yeah, she was."

"Did you hug her?"

I pushed my hands through my hair. "Fuck, I don't know. Why in the hell would I hug Callie?"

Luke pushed off my truck and turned to face me. "Dude, just come home and talk to Alex."

I swallowed hard. "I can't see her right now. I know the moment I see her, I'll just want to take her in my arms, but I can't erase what my eyes saw and what my ears heard that day."

Luke closed his eyes. "Let her explain it, Will. Just give her a chance. She's not even seeing the guy. She hasn't seen him since she told him she loved you and asked him to leave her alone. Grace said he pretty much stalked Alex for a bit before finally leaving her be."

I smiled and shook my head. "Gunner wanted her to experience life away from Mason. Maybe this is what we both need. Maybe we need a break from the familiar. If our love is truly meant to be, then…it will be."

"Can't be if you won't let it."

I didn't say a word. Luke turned and walked toward his truck. Libby walked up, and Luke said something to her. She looked at me with such sadness on her face as she began walking over to me.

"Where are you going?"

I looked at my beautiful sister and smiled. "Oklahoma."

"You're really going to go there and not be home with your family? Mom is going to be devastated. Alex is going to be devastated."

"I need to do this. I'm sorry, Lib. I need time to think."

"'Cause you haven't had enough time in the last month?"

I stepped away from my truck. I leaned down and kissed her on the cheek. "I love you, Lib. Give Mom and Dad a hug and kiss for me."

"What about Alex? What am I supposed to tell her?"

"Tell her I love her."

I walked over to the driver's side, opened the door, and climbed up into my truck. I started it and began backing up. I looked at Luke standing behind Libby as they both watched me drive away.

I need this. I need time away from everyone. I need to learn to breathe again.

I sat down on the bed of my truck and began eating my turkey sandwich. I couldn't help but notice Allison, Callie's cousin, walking over to me. I sighed inwardly and wished like hell that she would get the hint that I wasn't interested in her.

"Hey, Will. How are you today?"

I shrugged my shoulders and took another bite. I looked her up and down. I couldn't figure out how in the hell she was wearing short-ass shorts and a tight T-shirt when it was forty-two degrees outside.

"Aren't you cold?" I asked.

She giggled and jumped up next to me. "A little, but you could warm me up."

"I have a girlfriend, Allison."

She frowned. "You do?"

My heart instantly began to hurt. I shook my head and looked at her. "I, um…well, we broke up…I guess."

She laughed. "You either broke up, or you didn't. If you did, then I have a hotel room key here for you. I'm pretty sure you want to know that I'm not wearing any panties right now, and my pussy is dripping wet for you."

My mouth dropped open. "Uh…"

She began moving her tongue along her upper lip as she raised her eyebrows. "Will, tell me you don't want to fuck me, and I'll walk away, but I'm pretty sure if I were to touch your dick right now, you'd be rock-hard."

What the hell?

I couldn't help it, but I started laughing. "You're kidding with me right now, right?"

She smiled and shook her head.

"What type of guy would actually go back to your hotel room after you just said all of that?"

Her smile instantly faded. "Excuse me?"

I jumped off the tailgate of my truck. "No, Allison. Excuse me. I need to be somewhere, and it certainly is *not* in your hotel room."

She jumped down and glared at me. "Fuck off, douche bag. You have no idea what you're missing."

I watched as she began walking over to a group of guys who had driven in this morning from Arkansas.

Good Lord, I feel sorry for those boys.

I looked around for Callie or Joe. I found Joe talking to an older gentleman. I took in a deep breath and slowly let it out. The sooner I did this, the better.

The temperature had warmed up some, so I took advantage of it. I went down to the barn to get Banjo and go for a ride. It was Christmas morning, but it didn't feel like it. Everyone was planning on coming to our house this evening for dinner. It was a tradition among all my parents' friends to spend Christmas day together in some way. They had been doing it since I could remember.

I walked into Banjo's stall, and he greeted me with his low rumbling nicker, like he always did.

I smiled and hugged his massive neck. "Please don't ever leave me, boy. I don't think I could bear the thought of losing you and Will."

Banjo rested his head on my shoulder, causing me to giggle.

"Boy, do you realize how big you are?" I turned and started getting his saddle ready for a ride.

Once I was up and on him, we slowly made our way outside the barn. We walked along the trail for a good two miles before I stopped in an open field. I jumped down, and I just let him graze for a while. I walked over to a fallen tree, sat down on it, and closed my eyes.

"Will…"

I wasn't sure how long I'd been sitting there, thinking about Will and all the times we had been together. I thought about the first time I'd known I wanted to kiss him, the first time I'd known I loved him, and the first time he'd held me in his arms, making me feel so safe.

Now, all I feel is emptiness.

Banjo made a noise, and I opened my eyes to see my mother.

I smiled at her and stood up. "How did you find me?"

She laughed. "Mary Lou here has a thing for Banjo. I just told her to find him, and she did."

I smiled bigger and started walking toward her when I felt something stinging me on the ass. "Ouch! Oh, holy hell! Motherfucking son of a bitch!"

"Alexandra Eryn Mathews!"

"Mom! Something is stinging me!" I turned around and tried to look at my behind.

I was just about to run my hand across my ass when my mother screamed.

"Oh God! Don't put your hand back there. Oh shit…oh…I might actually faint!"

"What? Mother! What in the hell is it?"

"Take off your pants. Oh my! Now, Alex!"

I stripped out of my boots and began taking off my riding pants. "Ouch. Fucker! Oh…oh!" I screamed over and over as I pulled my pants down.

My mother began stomping on something. "Get away, and watch where you step! Put your boots back on."

I grabbed my boots and ran over to Banjo. My ass and the top of my leg were stinging like a bitch. I looked back at my mother, who was screaming like a mad person while stomping on something. I walked over and saw a scorpion that was dead on the ground from her stomping on it. I instantly felt sick to my stomach. Then, I saw another one.

"Mom, how many were on me?"

She turned and looked at me. " Three," she whispered.

Three? Did she say three?

I swallowed hard and looked over at the log I had been sitting on. Scorpions were all over it.

"Mom…Mom…I'm gonna throw up. I'm gonna faint."

"Okay, well, which one are you going to do, so I can prepare myself?"

I had to turn away. The sight of all those scorpions was making it worse.

"Throw up!" I shouted.

She ran over and grabbed my hair. "Go for it, baby."

"No, I'm dizzy. I'm gonna faint."

"Okay, I'm ready." She positioned herself in front of me and dug her feet in as she held out her hands.

I heard someone riding up on a horse, and I looked up to see Colt and Luke.

Colt looked down at my bare legs and said, "What in the hell?"

That was when I knew for sure what I was going to do next. I looked at my mom and went to tell her to move, but instead, I threw up all over her.

"Gross! That was nasty!" Colt shouted.

Luke jumped off his horse and started throwing up.

Colt started laughing as he pointed at Luke.

"Mom…oh, Mom, I didn't mean—"

My mother held up her hand for me to stop talking. "Colt, give me your T-shirt."

Colt jumped off his horse and ripped his shirt off before handing it to her. She began cleaning off the puke. Luke turned and looked, and then he turned back around and started throwing up again.

"Colt, get your sister back right away. She's been stung a few times by scorpions."

Colt looked at me and then over to my pants. That was when he must have seen the log.

"Holy crap. Did you sit on that, Alex?" He turned back to me. "Um, Mom? Alex doesn't look so good."

"Get her home, Colt."

Colt picked me up, and I started having trouble breathing.

"Luke, text Gunner and let him know that Alex has been stung by scorpions. Hurry!"

"Yes, ma'am."

I was starting to feel really bad as Colt handed me to Luke, so he could jump up on his horse. Luke lifted me up to Colt, and Colt took me and placed me in front of him. He took off toward the house in a full-on run.

"Hang on, Alex. Please, just hang on. I'll get you home. Dad will fix it."

I started to close my eyes, so I could focus on pulling in air.

In that moment, I remembered that I was allergic to scorpions.

"Daddy...hurts. It hurts...can't breathe." I was gasping for air, and I knew it was more my nerves than anything. I could feel tingling in my ass and leg, but the pain was unreal.

I watched as my father pulled out an EpiPen, and he gave me a shot. Grams was on the phone with the doctor, and I could hear her talking.

"Yes, I remember. She was sixteen. Yes, he just gave her the shot. Okay. Will do, Doctor. Of course. Thank you."

"What did he say, Emma?" my mother asked as she stood there, watching me closely.

Grams looked at me and smiled. "Watch her closely and the shot should work here pretty quick. Keep her calm, and that will help her breathing return to normal."

Everyone stood there and stared at me for a few minutes. I wanted to laugh, but then I caught a glimpse of my mother's shirt.

"Mom..." I whispered.

"Yes, baby. I'm here."

"Please go shower. That is so gross, knowing my puke is on you."

Luke made a gagging noise. "Oh God!" He quickly ran by and went into the bathroom.

Colt busted out laughing, and so did my dad.

Daddy turned to my mother. "Ells, baby, go take a shower. She's already breathing better. Grams, will you get some ice? It looks like she's been stung three times, and that's it."

I looked at my father. "That's it? Like three times wasn't enough?"

"I know, baby. Let's get you some ibuprofen, and I think once you lie down for a bit, you'll feel better."

I nodded my head and glanced over to Colt. He had been so worried, but now, the little bastard was laughing his ass off.

"Colt, get out of here, you ass!" I barely shouted.

He held up his hands and made his way into the kitchen.

An hour later, after my parents had made sure I wasn't going to stop breathing, I made my way upstairs to my room with my mom following behind me.

Some Christmas this is turning out to be.

"Don't let me sleep for long. I want to be up when everyone starts getting here," I said.

My mother helped me get comfortable enough to rest, and then she put the ice under my ass and leg.

I shook my head. "I can't believe it. My ass. Why my ass?"

My mother giggled, but then she quickly stopped when I shot her a dirty look.

"I'll wake you up in a bit, Alex. Just rest."

As I lay there in bed, I tried to relax, but all I could think of was the pain. I was almost positive the pain in my heart outweighed the pain in my ass. I giggled at my thoughts. I closed my eyes and pictured Will. I made myself believe that when I woke up, he would be here just in time for Christmas. I opened my eyes and felt my tears running down my face.

Worst. Christmas. Ever.

I opened my eyes and stretched at the same time. I reached behind me and felt the cold bag of water. I pulled it away and sat up. At least my ass wasn't in so much pain. I stood up and walked to the mirror. My face looked normal, except for the dried streaks on my cheeks from where I'd cried myself to sleep. I walked into my bathroom and splashed my face with water.

That was when I heard Libby yell out something.

I walked back into my room and looked at the clock on my nightstand next to my bed.

"Damn it, Mom! I didn't want to miss everyone getting here," I said to myself.

I started making my way down the steps, and I could hear everyone going on and on about something. I rounded the landing, and Grace was about to start running up the stairs.

"Hey, Merry Christmas," I said with a smile.

Her smile grew bigger on her face as she looked at me. Then, she looked into the living room, and I followed her eyes. That was when I saw him. Heather was hugging him while Libby stood next to him. He was smiling. When he looked up, our eyes met, and his smile faded.

"Will?" I whispered.

He smiled slightly and looked back down at his mother when she pulled away.

"You're so lucky you came home, young man. Do you have any idea how much I've missed you?"

Will chuckled as his dad gave him a quick hug. Everyone else stood up and hugged him or shook his hand.

My father was last. "You missed all the action earlier, Will. Alex was stung three times by some scorpions."

Will's head snapped around, and he looked at me. "Are you okay?"

I smiled and nodded my head. "Yes," I barely said above a whisper.

My mother looked between Will and me. She slapped her hands together and said, "It's time to eat now that Alex is up and moving around. Shall we all head into the dining room?"

I started to make my way down the stairs and over to Will. He looked like he wanted to turn and walk away, but he didn't.

I stopped right in front of him and smiled. "Hi," I whispered.

He smiled back as his eyes moved everywhere on my face. "Are you okay, Lex?"

The moment he called me Lex, I felt like I could breathe again. "I am now."

He closed his eyes and then opened them to look me in the eyes. He went to say something, but my mother called for us.

"Alex, Will, dinner is being served."

I looked into the dining room and then quickly back at Will. "Can we talk later?"

He nodded his head and reached his hand around me. He placed it on the small of my back. My heart started racing as he led me into our dining room. He walked me up to my chair and pulled it out for me. This wasn't anything new. Will did it all the time, and so did Luke and Colt. Our fathers had raised them to be gentlemen, and that they were.

Everyone laughed and talked during dinner. Maegan talked about how much she loved Baylor. Grace whispered to me that Maegan loved it so much because she had a new fleet of men to sleep with. I wasn't so sure Maegan was as sexually active as she'd claimed to be. Libby talked about loving A&M, and Grace talked about hating UT. Luke didn't speak much at all. Something was going on with him, and I was bound and determined to find out what in the hell was bothering him. I did notice that every time Libby wasn't looking, Luke was staring at her.

I glanced over to Will, who was talking to his father. I watched his mouth move, the way he talked with his hands, and how he chewed his food. I smiled when he laughed after someone had said something funny. I was feeling so guilty that he hadn't come home until now, and I feared his parents resented me because of it.

My mother leaned over and whispered, "Alex, you're staring at Will, sweetheart."

I nodded my head. "I've missed him."

"I know, but you're really staring."

I giggled and looked at her. "We can blame it on the scorpions."

She let out a small laugh and shook her head. I peeked over to my daddy.

He mouthed to me, *Talk to him.*

I will, I mouthed back.

I glanced around the huge table.

Daddy and Uncle Jeff had put together two huge tables, so everyone would be able to sit together. When we were younger, all of us kids had sat at the kids' table. That had been until Will and Libby started having food fights and getting the rest of us in trouble.

I turned back to look at Will. Now, he was staring at me. We both smiled, and the butterflies in my stomach began to fly around.

I love him. I will always love him.

In that moment, it hit me harder than anything ever had before. I needed to let him know how I felt. I wasn't going to let this evening end without telling him.

WILL

Luke, Colt, and I all carried the extra table down to the barn and up to the loft.

I looked around and smiled when I saw the bed. "You think your parents still sneak out here, Colt?"

Colt made a disgusted face, but then he smiled slightly and shook his head. "Yeah, I'm sure they do. I want a love like that someday."

Luke and I both let out a long breath and looked at each other.

Luke busted out laughing and said, "Damn girls."

"Hell, you got that right," Colt said. "They drive you crazy. They don't tell you what's really on their minds, and when they do, they don't give you any damn warning."

I shook my head. "What's going on with you and Lauren?"

Colt grunted. "After she blew me off that night, I ended up getting back together with Rachel, who I can barely stand. Now, Lauren is pissed at me because I'm dating Rachel." He shook his head. "Makes me just want to give up on women altogether."

"No! Don't ever talk that way, dude. A man needs a vagina to function." Luke sat down in a chair and leaned back, balancing it on the back legs.

I looked at him. "Really? You just said that?"

"Hey, I could have said pussy, but I kept it clean. It's true though. A man does need pussy to survive in this world."

Colt started laughing. "Damn, Luke. What is wrong with you?"

Luke held up his hands and laughed. "Keeping it real. Just keeping it real."

"That's why he has his fuck buddy. No strings. Just a fun way to *survive in this world*. Isn't that right, Luke?"

I closed my eyes when I heard Libby's voice. *Shit.*

I turned and looked at Libby, Grace, Lauren, Taylor, and Lex all standing there.

"What?" Luke lost his balance on the chair and dropped backward to the floor.

Libby smiled and shook her head. "I'm heading out for a while to meet someone. I don't have my car. Can I borrow your truck, Will?"

"Uh…"

Luke jumped up. "You're going out? On Christmas night? Where in the hell are you going?"

Libby glared at Luke. "Jason's in town, and he asked if I wanted to meet him for dessert."

Luke laughed. "What kind of dessert, Lib?"

"Watch it, Luke," I said through gritted teeth.

"The kind you'll never get from me, Luke."

I snapped my head over and looked at Libby. She walked up to me and held her hand out for my truck keys.

"Wait. What did you just say?" I asked.

"Can I borrow your truck or not, Will?"

I looked at Lex and then back at Libby. I reached in, pulled out my truck keys, and handed them to her. I watched her walk away, and then I glanced at Luke. His hands were balled into fists.

Lauren walked up and waited a few seconds. "She isn't going to meet anyone. You pissed her off with your comment, Luke."

"How long were y'all in here?" Colt asked.

Lauren smiled and sat down. "Long enough."

I rolled my eyes. *I'm so tired of games.*

I glanced over to Lex, who was standing at the edge of the stairs. She gave me a look and then headed back down. I quickly followed.

She stopped at Banjo's stall and smiled at me. "You feel like a nighttime ride? It's still pretty warm out."

I grinned and nodded my head. "Sure. You want me to saddle up two horses?"

She shook her head. "Nah, I've been riding Banjo bareback. Do you mind riding him with me?"

My heart slammed against my chest at the thought of being so close to her. "That sounds good to me," I said as my voice cracked.

Lex attached the reins to Banjo's bridle and led him out of the barn. She looked over her shoulder at me. "Can you help me up?"

I knew damn well she could get up on him by herself, but I played along. The moment my hands touched her body, I felt it. It was the same sensation that always ran through my body whenever I touched her.

She adjusted herself and winked at me. I grabbed her hand and jumped up behind her. Banjo was a big paint horse—sixteen hands and built like a machine. I'd never seen a horse love a person as much as Banjo loved Lex.

She rode out of the barn and down the trail leading to the river. We rode along in silence. I took in every single detail of her—her smell, what she was wearing, how her hair was pulled up, the way she rode her horse in perfect form. I loved everything about her, and I always would.

Lex brought Banjo to a stop and stared out over the river. "I love it here so much."

I followed her gaze. "Yeah, so do I."

I slid off the side of Banjo and helped Lex down. Having her in my arms was bringing out so many emotions.

"I'd ask if you wanted to sit down on a log, but—"

She hit the side of my arm and smiled. "Colt or Luke?"

I laughed. "Both filled me in. I'm so sorry, baby, um…Lex."

She closed her eyes, and when she opened them, her tears about dropped me to my knees.

"I've never been confused about my love for you, Will—not once. I won't stand here and make excuses because I know my actions hurt you, but you have to believe me when I say nothing, absolutely nothing, happened between Blake and me. Would I change things if I could go back? Yes…and no."

I tilted my head and looked at her.

"I learned something through all of this. I need to start thinking for myself. I need to stop listening to my father's voice in my head and start listening to my own voice. And us being apart helped me find that voice within. The last few weeks have been hell, but the time apart has opened my eyes as well."

I swallowed hard. *She's moving on without me.*

"I'm glad you found yourself, Lex. I'm really happy for you." I turned and started walking toward the river. My heart felt like it had just been ripped from my chest and stomped on.

"Do you know what it's been like?" she asked from behind me.

I let out a sigh. "What has what been like?"

"My life without you."

I shook my head and closed my eyes.

"It's been empty, completely empty."

I turned slowly and looked at her. "What? You just said—"

"I said, I learned to hear my own voice, Will. I learned to stand up and make my own decisions. One of those decisions is to leave UT at the end of this school year. I'm transferring schools."

My head was spinning, and my knees felt weak. "Where are you going?"

She smiled as she walked up to me and placed her hands on my chest. "Where I belong. With you."

I looked at her with a confused expression on my face. "Lex, are you saying…"

She giggled and nodded her head. "Yes, both Grace and I are going to A&M next year."

I just stood there, stunned. "Lex, I don't…I don't…you're coming to A&M?"

She smiled bigger. "Being without you, Will, is no longer an option. I love you. I want to be with you. When I'm not with you, a part of myself is missing."

"Lex…" I pulled her closer to me and placed my hands on the sides of her face. "I love you so much. I've been so lost, completely and utterly lost, without you."

I pressed my lips to hers, and we both let out soft, low moans. I picked her up, and she wrapped her legs around me as our kiss began turning more passionate.

"I need to feel you, Will. Please, please make love to me."

I bumped into Banjo, who just turned his head and looked at me. I set Lex down and began unbuttoning my pants. Then, it dawned on me.

I shook my head. "We can't. I don't have a condom."

Lex's face dropped, and she slowly shook her head. Then, she suddenly said, "I have an idea. Help me back up on Banjo."

A short while later, we were riding up to the barn.

Lex slid off Banjo and yelled, "Hold on!"

I watched her run up the stairs. I looked around to see if any of our friends were still here, but they had all left the barn.

Lex came running back down the stairs. She began looking around and then looked back at me. "Want to be daring?"

"Uh…how daring?"

She bit down on her lower lip. "Really daring."

I shook my head. "No. I want to live, Lex. My life is really just beginning, and you want to end it prematurely. No, thanks."

She laughed. "Come on, all our parents are up at the house, and God knows where everyone else is."

I slid off Banjo and began walking him back to his stall. "Lex, listen to yourself. You want to have sex in your barn—the barn that is close to your house…where your daddy is…with his guns nearby. I want you, Lex. I want you real bad, but I'd like to marry you someday and have kids and—"

I realized what I'd said when her expression changed. I swallowed hard as I turned and gave Banjo some hay and checked his water before I shut the gate to his stall. I turned around, and Lex slammed her body to mine.

"I need you, Will. Now. I have to have you inside me. Please."

"Shit."

She ran her hand through my hair and tugged on it hard. I let out a moan and cursed my betraying body.

She pulled away and began climbing the stairs. She glanced over her shoulder and looked back at me. "Luke has a stash of condoms hidden up here."

Oh good God.

"Lex, maybe we should finish talking."

She disappeared as I walked back over to the barn entrance and looked out. I didn't see anyone outside, but I could see people in the house through the kitchen window. I spun around, made my way back to the stairs, and then took them two at a time. I stopped when I saw Lex standing there, naked.

"Fuck," I whispered.

"I'll take that, thank you."

"Lex, we were talking. Don't you want to finish talking?"

She shook her head and placed her finger in her mouth. I looked her body up and down. I wanted her so damn bad.

She began trailing her finger down her neck, between her breasts, to her stomach. She finally stopped short of where I wanted to bury my face. She lifted her leg and set it down on a nearby bucket. Then, she slowly pushed her fingers inside of herself while she held up a condom in her other hand.

"Fuck it." I quickly stripped out of my pants and boxers before walking up to her. I grabbed the condom.

She hissed, "Yes," through her teeth.

I rolled it on and grabbed her leg. I pushed myself into her, and she let out a moan. I stopped moving, so I could just feel her warmth.

Her head dropped back as she whispered, "Finally."

I began moving in and out, and we both moaned.

I need more.

"Will, I need more."

I smiled, knowing we both wanted the same thing. I picked her up, and she wrapped her legs around me. I walked her up to the wall and pushed her against it.

"Yes, Will. I'm so sorry. I love you so much, and I never, ever want to be apart from each other."

I pulled out and pushed into her. "Lex, you're my everything."

"Yes, oh God, yes."

"I love you, Lex. Don't ever leave me. Don't ever leave me."

She shook her head as she began thrusting her hips. "Never, Will. Faster. Will, please do it harder and faster."

I closed my eyes and prayed to God I lasted long enough for her to come. I began pounding into her over and over as she let out one quiet moan after another. There was no way I would take her to that bed.

Hell no.

"Will! I'm going to come. Kiss me! Oh God, kiss me!"

When I slammed my lips to hers, she began pulsing around my dick and moaning into my mouth. She dug her fingers into my shoulders, and I was glad I had a T-shirt on still.

Then, I felt my buildup.

God, how I've missed her.

I pulled out and pushed in deeper, and then I exploded inside her as one of the most powerful orgasms ripped through my body.

I pulled my lips back as I panted, "Jesus…feels so damn good…Lex."

By the time I was done, my legs and arms were shaking. Lex started kissing me again like she'd never kissed me before.

That was when I heard his voice.

"Banjo's here, so they must have come back."

Gunner!

My eyes and Lex's eyes grew bigger as I quietly put her down. I took off the condom, tied it, grabbed my pants, and slipped them on. I looked around for a place to hide the condom, and I ended up sticking it in my pocket. Lex opened her mouth, and she made a funny face by scrunching up her nose. I shrugged and put my sneakers on as I listened to Gunner, Jeff, and my father all talking.

"I'll text Will," my dad said.

I stopped moving and reached for my phone as Lex began jumping up and down ever so quietly. I slid the volume button down just in time. Lex and I both let out a breath.

Then, she threw her hands up to her mouth. She began pointing down.

I looked at her and mouthed, *What?*

She was about to say something when her phone went off, and we both stopped and stood perfectly still.

"Well, here is Alex's phone in the tack room. She must have left it," Gunner said.

Lex quickly began getting dressed as I stood there, thinking of my last moments alive on earth.

They were good moments. I'm with Lex, and that's all that matters.

"Let me see if they are with Luke and the others," Jeff said.

I closed my eyes and prayed that fucker came through for me.

"Luke, it's Dad. Are Will and Alex with y'all? Banjo is here in the barn. We found Alex's phone here, too, and Will isn't answering his phone."

I held my breath, waiting and praying. I watched Lex slipping on her boots. She slowly stood up, and we stared at each other.

"Oh, okay. Well, let Alex know her dad has her phone, will you? Y'all don't stay out too late. Okay, have fun, and be careful."

I slowly looked toward the stairs and then around the loft. *Where could we hide if they decide to come up here?*

"Luke said Will and Alex are with them in town. Guess they all decided to go play miniature golf."

"Will's truck is gone, so it makes sense," my father said.

I quickly pulled out my phone and sent Libby a text.

> Me: *Libby, I need you to pick me and Lex up, but take the old dirt road and meet us behind the barn at Grams and Gramps's place.*

Libby: Why? I'm busy.

Me: Bullshit, you aren't busy. If you want me to live another day and not die at the hands of Gunner, you will come get us.

Libby: OMG! Y'all made up! I'm so happy. Okay, I'm not too far away. I'm at our thinking place. I'll be there soon.

Me: Give us time to get out there. We're at Lex's main barn by her house.

Libby: I'm so laughing out loud right now. Y'all had sex in the loft, didn't you? Who's there?

Me: I hate you. Gunner, Jeff, and Dad!

Libby: You totally owe me.

Me: Anything.

Libby: I'll think about it. On my way.

I looked at Lex and gave her a thumbs-up. She nodded and smiled. We stood there and listened to Gunner, Jeff, and my dad talk about some stuff around the ranch. Finally, they started heading out of the barn.

As they left the barn, I heard Gunner say, "All right, well, let's head on back and let Ellie and Heather know that Alex and Will are with the rest of the kids."

I walked over to the edge of the stairs and listened to their voices as they retreated away. When I turned around, Lex slammed her body into mine and started kissing me. I was instantly turned-on again.

"One more time. We can be fast," she whispered after pulling her lips from mine.

I laughed. "No. Come on, we need to get to Libby."

She pouted. "For a minute, I thought your life was in serious danger."

I frowned. "So did I."

She chuckled, and we made our way down the stairs. I peeked my head out and didn't see anyone. I grabbed Lex's hand, and we began running toward the ranch's main barn. It was the original barn near Lex's great-grandparents' house, so it was a good couple of miles away from Lex's house.

By the time we got to where Libby was waiting, I was exhausted.

"I swear, I saw a mountain lion." Lex panted and tried to get her breathing under control.

I rolled my eyes and laughed. "It was a fox, Lex."

Libby stood there, smiling from ear to ear. "Are we good?"

I looked at Lex, and we both smiled.

"We still have some stuff to talk about, but we're better than good," I said.

Libby did a little jump and let out a small scream. Lex ran up to her, and they hugged.

"Come on, ladies, let's go play some miniature golf."

"Huh?" Libby asked as she jumped into the backseat of my truck.

Lex let out a laugh.

"You don't want to know," I said.

Will grabbed my hand as we walked up to the Pirates Miniature Golf. I could hear Colt and Luke arguing about something. When Grace looked over and saw us, she smiled from ear to ear. Grace and I hadn't told anyone that we were going to be heading to A&M next year. Only our parents and now Will knew.

Libby walked by Luke, who stopped and watched her. He looked like he wanted to say something.

Instead, he turned back to Colt. "You cheat, Colt."

"I do not, you asswipe. I got that hole in three swings. Lauren, did I not get that in three shots?"

Lauren smiled. "Hate to say it, Luke, but he got it in three swings."

Luke mumbled something under his breath and walked over toward the counter. "I need a Coke."

Taylor walked up to Will and me as she smiled. "I take it y'all worked things out?"

I grinned and nodded my head.

"Good, 'cause you two being apart really sucked. I've never seen two people so in love in my life. You're both really lucky."

Will dropped my hand and pulled Taylor in for a hug. "Tay, don't rush it. It'll happen when it's meant to happen."

She pulled back and nodded. "I know. I guess I'm just waiting for that one guy who makes a difference. I sure haven't found him in Fredericksburg or Mason, that's for sure."

I let out a chortle. "Taylor, you have plenty of time."

She smiled weakly. "Yeah, I guess so."

We spent the rest of the evening just hanging out and having fun. It felt normal yet different. Will and I still needed to talk about me going back to UT and him going to A&M.

I glanced over to Libby. She was listening to something Grace was saying, but she looked a million miles away. I decided I would talk to her tomorrow.

I turned to look at Luke. He was texting someone.

Probably his damn fuck buddy. I rolled my eyes and continued to watch him.

He seemed upset by something he had just read on his phone. He looked directly up at me. I smiled, and he returned my smile. His eyes seemed so lost and confused.

Tilting my head, I mouthed, *Are you okay?*

He nodded his head.

Liar.

I was going to talk to Will about Luke.

Libby let out a small scream at something Grace had just said to her, and Luke quickly looked at her as he jumped up. When he saw her smiling, he sat down.

Libby glanced up at me. "Y'all are coming to A&M next year?"

"What?" Maegan yelled out. "So not fair!"

I giggled as Will pulled me closer to him.

"Yep, Grace and I are both transferring to A&M," I said.

"Ugh!" Maegan sat down and pouted.

"I thought you loved Baylor, Meg," I said.

She let out a long sigh. "I do. It's just...I miss y'all."

"Think how we feel. We still have half a year in high school," Lauren said.

Colt cleared his throat and looked around. "We need to make each other a promise right now."

"What kind of promise?" Taylor asked.

Colt looked at each of us with the smile that I knew drove all the girls mad. He looked so much like Daddy with his dark brown hair, breathtaking blue eyes, and killer smile, and Daddy was so handsome. I would dare say that Colt was probably the one who all the girls really flocked to. His Southern charm was both a strength and a weakness for him.

"That we never lose touch with each other. I mean, I know the odds of all of us ending up in Mason like our parents are probably not too good."

Maegan laughed. "Yeah...no, thank you. I have no desire to live in Hicksville anymore."

Colt chuckled. "Let's promise we all get together for a week once a year. No matter where we end up—near, far, kids, no kids—we all plan to meet for a week and just hang out."

I smiled as tears began to fill my eyes. I looked around.

Grace had originally said she wanted out of Mason. After one semester in Austin, she'd realized her heart would always be home in Mason. When we'd discovered we had a mutual dream of owning our own nursery, we'd decided that we wanted to make that dream a reality, and Mason was the only place to do that.

Colt, Luke, and Will were destined to run the ranch. It was in their blood, and they would talk about it all the time.

I glanced over to Lauren. She loved Mason and helping her father with his breeding company. Since I could remember, she'd talked about taking over and making it even better. Scott and Jessie, Lauren's parents, would love that.

Lord knew where Meg was going to end up. Her spitfire personality matched her red hair. She would never live in Mason or Fredericksburg, not even if someone paid her.

Taylor was the baby of the group, and we all worried about her. She was timid and too sweet for her own good. She was also drop-dead gorgeous, but she didn't know it, which made her even more desirable. Luke had ended up in so much trouble when he'd punched Kyle Derby for talking about Taylor at a party one night. When Uncle Jeff had found out why Luke had punched Kyle, he'd pulled Luke to the side and told him he was proud of him, but Aunt Ari was never to know he'd said that. Taylor had dreams of living in Italy, which scared the piss out of all of us.

"Dude, I think that's an amazing idea. We need to start that tradition this summer," Luke said.

Will nodded his head. "I agree. We've all grown up together, and just because some of us are going to be taking different paths doesn't mean we can't stay friends. Look at our parents. Their friendships grow stronger all the time."

"So, what are we going to do to start this new tradition?" Libby asked.

Lauren stood up and said, "The beach. We've always talked about going to the beach without our parents. Remember we couldn't wait until we were old enough to go down without them? Let's plan on it this summer."

Colt walked up to Lauren, picked her up in a hug, and spun her around. Lauren was completely taken off guard, and the flush on her cheeks showed her true feelings for Colt.

"That is a great idea, Lauren," Colt said as he set her down. "Hell, our parents all own a few houses right next to each other on the beach in Port Aransas. We can stay at one of the houses."

"Perfect! I think we should ask the folks now. Lauren, don't your parents rent their place out sometimes?" Maegan asked.

"Yeah, they do. I say we head back and start making the plans," Lauren said.

Her smile was so big that I couldn't help but laugh.

As we all started making our way to the parking lot, Will held me back. I turned to look at him and smiled. "What's wrong?"

He shook his head and pushed my hair behind my ear.

I love when he does that.

"I love you, Lex. I'm so sorry I didn't let you explain everything. I feel like all this heartache was my fault."

My heart instantly hurt, and I felt the tears building in my eyes. "No, Will. It's not all your fault. I'm to blame just as much. I came to A&M that day, and when I saw you with that girl, I let my imagination run wild."

The look on Will's face dropped. Then it appeared as if he remembered something.

Oh God. Did something happen between him and the blonde?

"Callie? You're talking about Callie. Alex, nothing at all happened between us. She's engaged to another guy, and they do all this mission work. I had just told her I would help them over Christmas break. I swear to you—"

I put my finger up to his lips. "I know. I think I knew then, but I was scared, confused, and angry with myself. It was easier to hide than to face everything."

"Will? Alex? Are y'all coming or what?" Libby called out.

I giggled. "Come on. If Lib's forced to ride with Luke, Lord knows what will happen."

Will laughed and put his arm over my shoulders as we made our way to Libby.

Finally, things felt like they were going to be okay.

WILL

Three Months Later

The door to my dorm room sprang open, and Luke came barreling in. He looked pissed, beyond pissed.

"What in the hell is wrong with you?"

He spun around and looked at me. "What?"

"You just came storming in here. You look like you're about to rip someone's head off."

Luke glanced around the room. He walked over to his bookshelf and moved a book before pulling out a bottle of whiskey.

"Where in the hell did you get that from?"

He shrugged and opened it up as he looked for a glass. The moment he found one, he poured some whiskey into the glass and downed it. He held the bottle out for me. "Want some?"

I shook my head. "Luke, dude, you have to talk to me. I've never seen you like this before. What in the hell is going on with you?"

"Nothing. I just need to release some steam. Too much fucking bullshit on my mind."

"Want to talk about it?" I asked.

Luke walked up to the window and stared out. His phone rang, and he pulled it out of his pocket. "Hey, Abigail. Are you free?"

I closed my eyes and let out a sigh.

"I'll be there in a few minutes." Luke shoved his phone into his back pocket and walked over to the shelf. He put the whiskey back and then walked into the bathroom.

"Why are you doing this, Luke?"

He poked his head out of the bathroom and asked, "Doing what?"

"Going to Abigail."

He walked out and looked at me like I had two heads. "I'm going to Abigail because I want to get laid. What's wrong with that?"

"What about Libby?"

He turned and looked at me. "What about Libby?"

I instantly got pissed off. Lex had talked to Libby over Christmas break, and Libby had finally told Lex what had happened last summer between her and Luke. The only problem was that Luke didn't remember what he'd said to Libby, and it was tearing Libby apart.

"Do you have feelings for my sister?"

Luke swallowed hard. He shook his head and looked away. "Luke?"

He snapped his head back and looked at me. "I can't. I mean, I won't do that to her. She means everything to me, and I'll fuck it up, Will. I already broke her heart with the dick move I made on her before I left for college. What if I can't...I mean, I don't think I can...I'm not good enough for her, Will. She deserves someone better, and she found him."

My eyes widened as I stood there, shocked. "Wait—what do you mean, she found him?"

He let out a gruff laugh. "I mean, she's dating someone. I saw them just now. I was going to ask her if she wanted to see a movie when I saw her leaning against a building. Then, some dick fucking kissed her." He turned away and whispered, "She looked happy."

My head was spinning. I knew for a fact that Libby was in love with Luke, but even Lex had said that Libby wasn't going to wait around for Luke to stop acting like a jerk. Even Grace had tried to talk to Luke.

"So, because you see Lib kissing a guy, you run to Abigail?"

Luke reached down for his jacket and grabbed his truck keys. "I haven't been with a girl in months. I need to get fucked."

I grabbed his arm. "Don't do this, Luke. If you want to be with someone..." I closed my eyes and couldn't believe what I was about to say. "If you want to be with someone, be with the person you love. Luke, Libby loves you."

His eyes widened in horror as he took a step away from me. He began shaking his head. "No...she doesn't love me, Will."

"Luke, for Christ's sake, will you just admit you love her? Libby was already your best friend once. Stop pushing her away. She cares about you, and you—"

He held up his hand. "I've gotta go. Abigail is waiting on me."

"Don't do this, Luke. I swear to God, you'll regret it."

He turned away from me and headed out the door. I took in a deep breath as I took my phone out and sent Libby a text.

Me: Lib, are you dating someone?

Libby: Why?

Me: Luke said he saw you kissing someone, and he is out of control right now, Lib. He really cares about you, but he thinks he's not good enough for you.

Libby: Luke only cares about himself and his fuck buddy, Abigail. She made sure to tell me how much they hook up. I seriously doubt he cares about me when he has her. I'm heading into a movie.

What in the hell? Libby talked to Abigail? How do they know each other?

> *Me: Wait. Lib, when did you talk to Abigail?*

> *Libby: Two weeks ago. She came up to me in the library and started talking about her and Luke.*

None of this was making any sense. Luke hadn't seen Abigail in months.

> *Me: Libby, this doesn't make sense. Luke hasn't seen Abigail in months.*

> *Libby: Will, I'm tired of this. I don't care anymore. I've moved on. Please let it go. I have to go. I love you.*

I pulled up Luke's number and hit it. It rang two times and then went to voice mail. I called again. After two more rings, I got voice mail again. I tried a third time, and it was obvious he wasn't going to answer his phone, so I left a message.

"Dude, I just talked to Libby. She thinks you and Abigail have been hooking up all this time. Abigail talked to Libby in the library a couple of weeks ago. She made it seem like y'all were together. Luke, please don't do this. Call Libby."

I hit End and stared at my phone, but nothing happened. I tried to call Libby, and her phone went directly to voice mail. I sat down on my bed and let out a frustrated moan.

My phone pinged.

> *Lex: I miss you. <3*

> *Me: God, I miss you.*

> *Lex: Guess what?*

> *Me: You're naked and touching yourself, and you want to FaceTime?*

> *Lex: Nope. Better.*

> *Me: What in the hell could be better than you naked?*

> *Lex: Me standing in the hallway outside your dorm room and somewhat naked.*

I stared at her reply for a few seconds. I got up, walked to the door, and opened it.

"Surprise!" Lex smiled at me.

"Lex? You didn't tell me…" I looked her body up and down.

She was dressed in a long coat and had a large purse over her shoulder.

"Why in the hell are you wearing that coat? It's not that cold out."

She looked both ways down the hall before she untied it and held it open.

Motherfucker.

She was completely naked under the coat.

I grabbed her by the hand and pulled her into my room before shutting the door. "Holy hell. Tell me you didn't drive like that?"

She giggled. "Nope. I met a girl outside your hall, and I told her I was here to surprise you. She let me use her bathroom to change."

I couldn't help the smile that spread across my face. "You sneaky thing. What if Luke had been here?"

She shrugged her shoulders as she took off the coat and let it fall to the floor. I licked my lips as I took in her perfect body. I reached behind her and locked the door. Then, I picked her up and carried her to my bed.

"I missed you, Will. I can stay until Sunday."

I gently kissed her lips. I began kissing down her neck and made my way to her breasts. She let out a soft moan.

"God, I missed you, too, Lex."

I began sucking on her nipple as she ran her fingers through my hair. "Yes…Will."

"Oh, Lex, you feel so good."

"Touch me, Will. Please touch me."

I moved my hand down her body and between her legs as she spread them open for me. I slipped my fingers in and let out a moan as I moved my fingers in and out of her wetness.

"You're so ready, Lex."

I began kissing her neck as I worked my fingers. I moved down to her breasts and sucked on one nipple and then the other.

Her breathing increased, and she pushed her hips up to me. "I need you, Will."

I quickly stood up and stripped out of my clothes. I reached into my side drawer, took out a condom, and rolled it on. I couldn't wait to bury myself inside her. I crawled over her, and her smile made my stomach take a fast dip. I placed my tip at her entrance and teased her for a bit while I kissed her lips tenderly.

"I love you, Lex," I whispered as I pushed my dick into her.

She let out a gasp and whispered back, "I love you, too, Will. I love you so much."

I moved in and out of her slowly and gently as we kissed passionately. Nothing felt better than making love to Lex. If I could crawl into her body, I would.

We hadn't seen each other in two weeks, and I had missed her touch more than I'd thought. We could now only go two weeks max without seeing each other. I had three tests coming up this week, and I was planning on driving to Austin to see her this weekend, but her coming here on Thursday gave us more time to spend together and gave me time to study.

"Lex, you feel so good, baby."

Her fingertips lightly moved up and down my body, leaving a trail of fire in their wake. With each stroke, I felt my love for her. I didn't think I could love her any more, but every time I saw her, made love to her, or talked to her, my love would grow stronger and stronger.

"Will…" she whispered as she arched her body. She began saying my name over and over.

"Talk to me, Lex."

"Will, oh God…"

I pushed in more and tried to hit the spot that would send her over the edge. My own desire was beginning to bubble up, and I didn't want to come before her.

She snapped her eyes open and looked into mine. I pressed my lips to hers, and I took in her moans of pleasure. It wasn't long before I was releasing myself and moaning back into her mouth.

As I slowed down and came to stop above her, I saw a tear beginning to roll down her face. I leaned down and kissed it away. I whispered, "Is that a happy tear, Lex?"

She nodded her head and whispered back, "Very happy tear. You make me feel so loved and so wanted, Will."

I swallowed and closed my eyes briefly before opening them again. "Lex, I'll love and want you until the day I die."

"Will…" She placed her hand on my neck and brought me in for another kiss.

Our kiss was filled with so much love that I could feel it moving between our bodies.

I got an idea. "Can I take you somewhere, Lex?"

She smiled. "Are you going to take me to heaven and back again?"

I grinned. "How about later? I don't think my guy can recharge that fast."

She pushed my chest and laughed. "You can take me anywhere. First, will you hand me my bag, please?"

I got up, reached for it, and handed it to her.

She began taking her jeans and T-shirt out. "Where are we going?"

"Somewhere special," I said with a wink.

"Will, it's so beautiful here," Lex said as she looked around.

It was a bit chilly, so Lex was wearing one of my A&M sweatshirts. She looked beautiful, all swallowed up in it. Her shoulder-length brown hair was swept up and piled on top of her head with a few strands hanging down. Her blue eyes looked like diamonds sparkling when the light hit them in just the right way.

I took her hand and walked us over to a bench overlooking the pond. The sun would be setting soon, and the sky was turning an orange-pink color. I sat down, and she sat next to me.

"The time we were apart, I would come here every day, sometimes twice a day, while I was running."

She squeezed my hand as she looked at me.

I looked at her. "I did a lot of thinking during that time, and I know you did, too."

She nodded her head and smiled. I began playing with her promise ring. When I had come home for Christmas, I had never been so happy when I looked down and saw it on her finger. Since then, I'd wanted to ask her if she'd ever taken it off.

"Did you ever take this off, Lex?"

She glanced down to her ring and then back up to my eyes. "Never. Not once."

I smiled and placed my finger on her chin. I pulled her closer to me to kiss her. My lips were still touching hers when I whispered, "I love you so much."

She smiled. "I love you more."

I laughed and looked out over the water. The sun was sinking farther in the sky. I took a deep breath and got ready to do the one thing I'd been dreaming of since I was ten years old.

I turned my body and faced her, and she did the same. I took both her hands in mine and began rubbing my thumbs back and forth across the backs of her hands.

"Lex, I remember the first time you looked at me and smiled. Right then, I felt something happen. I swear, I was only ten. In that moment, I knew that I wanted you to be mine. The way you smiled at me used to literally take my breath away." I chuckled. "Hell, it still does."

Lex sniffled, and I saw a tear rolling down her face. I reached up and wiped it away. She smiled at me, and my heart soared.

"I know your daddy loves you, and I want to do this proper and all, but I also want this moment to be just you and me. I want it to be a moment that is only ours and no one else's."

She let a sob escape her throat.

"Lex, I love you so much. I never want to be apart from you again. I can't breathe without you. When I think of my future, I only see you in it. I want to make love to you every day. I want to take long walks on the ranch with you and watch you fuss over Banjo. I want to see you coming toward me in a beautiful white dress before I take you somewhere amazing for our honeymoon. I dream of holding children of our own in my arms and watching them grow up to love the ranch as much as we do. I have so many dreams for us, Lex."

She started crying, and my voice cracked. I had already bought her engagement ring a few weeks ago. Originally, I had planned on asking Gunner for her hand in marriage and then formally asking her when we all went to the coast this summer.

"Lex, will you marry me and be my secret fiancée?"

She started crying harder, but then she started laughing. She threw herself into my body. "Yes! Oh God, Will, yes, a thousand times."

She pulled back, and I placed my hands on the sides of her face.

I whispered, "You're mine," and then I kissed her.

She smiled. "Always."

"Promise me," I whispered.

A tear slid down her face as she whispered, "I promise you, Will."

Will pulled up to the hotel where Grace and I were staying this weekend and parked his car. I smiled, and I couldn't wait to tell him that I had a separate room from Grace. His face had fallen when I told him Grace had come along so that we could check out A&M. I had a sneaky feeling that Grace was hoping to run into Noah again, but she'd told me I was nuts for even thinking that.

"Maybe you should go back to your dorm and pack up some clothes and your books."

Will pulled his head back and looked at me. "I'm not sure Grace wants me bunking with y'all."

I bit down on my lip and grinned. "We have our own rooms."

The smile that spread across Will's face caused me to giggle.

"No shit?"

"No shit. When she said she wanted to come, I told her she had to get her own room, and she agreed. She didn't want to spoil our weekend."

"God, I love Grace," Will said as he lifted his eyebrows.

"Me, too!"

Will reached over and quickly kissed me. "Give me a few minutes to go back to my room and grab some stuff. When I come back, we can get some dinner."

I nodded my head. "Sounds good. Be careful, but hurry!"

"I will, baby."

I jumped out and headed into the Hilton Hotel. When I got up to my room, my phone pinged, and I pulled it out of my purse. Grace had dropped me off earlier at Will's dorm, so I figured she was texting me. Instead, I saw it was from Libby.

> Libby: OMG! Grace told me y'all are in town all weekend!

> Me: Yep! What are you doing?

> Libby: About to go to dinner at Saltgrass Steakhouse.

> Me: With who?

> Libby: A guy named Zack. We went out to a movie and will be heading to dinner soon.

My heart dropped to my stomach. Libby was out on a date.

Damn it, Luke.

> Me: *A date, huh? What about Luke, Lib?*

> Libby: *I can't wait for someone who clearly doesn't want the same thing I want. Besides, he's been hooking up with that Abigail girl the last few months.*

> Me: *What about what he said to you, Libby?*

> Libby: *He was drunk. Alex, I'm done waiting. Want to meet us for dinner?*

> Me: *Okay. Will went back to his dorm to get some clothes, so he could stay with me at the hotel for the weekend. Can we meet you there in half an hour?*

> Libby: *Sure! We're just talking at Starbucks.*

> Me: *Okay. See you soon, sweetie!*

I sucked in a breath and let it out as I got up. I changed my clothes and fixed my makeup and hair. I had texted Will and told him a key was waiting for him at the front desk. I also texted Grace and told her we were meeting Libby at Saltgrass for dinner in about thirty minutes.

I heard the door open and close, and I instantly felt my lower stomach clench with anticipation. Will walked in and leaned against the doorframe.

My breath caught for a moment. He was so handsome. His brown hair had just been cut, but it was still long enough for me to run my fingers through and grab while we made love. He hadn't shaved in probably two days, and he had that perfect scruff look. Will had an amazing body, and I could see his muscles through his tight blue T-shirt. With all that working on the ranch, he didn't even need to go to the gym, but he did every single day, and his body showed it. His blue eyes made my stomach do crazy flips. I licked my lips as I practically undressed him with my eyes.

"You like what you see?"

I blushed, knowing I had probably been eye-fucking the hell out of him. "I do very, very much. It's a shame we have to meet Libby and Zack for dinner because I really want to be—"

My phone began ringing. I held up my finger for Will to hold my thoughts. He laughed as he went to sit on the sofa.

I looked at Will with a shocked expression on my face.

Why is Luke calling me?

"Hello? Luke?"

"Hey there, baby girl. Grace told me y'all were in town."

I smiled. "We sure are. We wanted to come check out the campus. Plus, we both have appointments tomorrow."

Luke laughed. "Uh-huh. I'm sure that's the only reason y'all are here. I see Will has already been to our room and packed up his shit."

I felt my face blush as I looked over at Will.

"Why, I don't know what you mean."

"You never could pull off a lie, Alex. Hey, Grace told me about dinner. Gonna jump in the shower. I'll see y'all there."

"Okay. See ya." Then, it hit me. *Shit!* "Wait! Luke?"

He had already hung up, and I looked at Will with a look of horror.

"What? What's wrong?"

"Oh God, Will. Libby invited us to dinner, and I sent Grace a text to invite her as well."

He looked at me, confused. "Okay. And what's the problem?"

"The problem is that Grace invited Luke to come along, and Libby is with her date, Zack."

Will's face dropped. "Oh shit, this is not good, not good at all, Lex."

"What are we going to do? Tell Luke he can't come?"

He pushed his hand through his hair, and I couldn't help but be turned-on. I loved when he did that. Hell, anything he did turned me on.

"Maybe we should just tell Luke that Lib is going to be there with a date."

I shook my head. "You know Luke. That will just make him want to come even more. Has he said anything to you about Libby?"

He nodded his head. "Yeah, today. He admitted to having feelings for her, but he's afraid of hurting her. Thinks he is not good enough for her. Honestly, I think he's just scared of how strong his feelings are for her. He saw her kissing this guy, and he took off for Abigail. He thinks Abigail helps him forget about Libby."

I rolled my eyes. "Yuck. That turns my stomach, Will."

He nodded his head. "How do you think I feel? It's my sister."

Thirty minutes later, Grace, Will, and I were sitting down at a table at Saltgrass. Libby had sent a text saying that Zack had to run back to his dorm and change, so they would be a few minutes late.

I looked up to see Luke walking in.

Grace jumped up and stopped him. "Hey, do you want to go see a movie?"

Luke looked at her funny. "After dinner?"

"No, now. Let's you and me grab something fast and go catch a movie." Grace tried to take Luke's arm and pull him back toward the door.

Luke laughed. "Damn, girl. I don't want to see a movie. I want to visit with you and Alex. What's wrong with you?"

Grace's mouth dropped open. "Brother, sister"—she pointed between herself and Luke—"togetherness. Don't you miss me?"

Luke leaned down and kissed Grace on the cheek. "I miss you more than you'll ever know, sweet pea."

He stepped around her and made his way to the table. I looked at Grace, and she shrugged. I smiled and stood up when Luke walked up to me.

He kissed me on the cheek and hugged me. "I've sure missed you, Alex."

Luke truly was a sweetheart. He was going to make someone very happy one day—if he could just learn to open his heart and not be so afraid. He'd never really had a serious girlfriend. Every time he'd tried to date, the girl would get jealous of his friendship with Libby. When the girl forced him to pick, he would always choose Libby.

If Libby were in the same situation with a guy she was dating, she would do the same and choose Luke.

We chatted for a few minutes when Grace kicked me under the table. I looked up, and Libby and Zack were walking up. Libby's smile dropped the moment she saw Luke.

She quickly looked at me.

I mouthed, *Sorry*.

Will stood up, which caused Luke to look.

His smile instantly vanished, and he muttered, "Son of a bitch."

Libby and Luke both stared at each other.

Libby forced a smile. "Hey, y'all. Um…Zack, this is my brother, Will."

Zack stuck his hand out for Will to shake. "It's a pleasure to meet you, Will."

Will smiled and nodded.

"This is Alex," Libby said.

Zack reached over and shook my hand. I smiled as I looked into his light blue eyes. He was about five feet ten with dark blond hair, and he had a smile that would melt a girl's heart.

"Alex, it's a pleasure. I've heard a lot about you."

I smiled. "Nice to meet you, Zack."

Libby turned to Grace. "This is Grace."

Zack smiled. "Grace, pleasure to finally meet you. Lib's been talking about you and Alex a lot."

Oh God, he called her Lib.

Luke was the one who had started calling her Lib.

Libby swallowed hard and turned to face Luke, who looked like it was taking everything for him to stay calm.

"Um…Zack, this is, um…this is Luke. Luke and Grace are brother and sister."

Poor Zack. I felt so sorry for him.

Luke reached out his hand and shook Zack's. He didn't give Zack a chance to talk first. "Hey there, Zack. So, how long have y'all been dating?"

Libby's mouth dropped open as she glared at Luke.

Zack looked back at Libby, and she quickly smiled.

"What? About two weeks now?"

"Yes, almost three," Libby said.

Zack pulled out her chair. Libby sat down, and Luke, Will, and Zack followed.

"What year are you, Zack?" Luke asked.

Will gave Luke a look. Luke peeked at Will and smirked. The boys were always overprotective, but I could hear it in Luke's voice. He was beyond jealous.

"I'm in my sophomore year," Zack said.

"Where are you from?" Luke asked.

Will cleared his voice.

"With the twenty questions, I'd think Luke was the brother," Zack said with a laugh.

Both Will and Luke snapped their heads at Zack, and Grace chuckled nervously.

Libby attempted to laugh. "Zack, one thing you need to know is we are all very close. We grew up together. Will, Luke, and Alex's brother, Colt, have always been a bit…overprotective. Let's chill out on the questions, Luke. Okay?"

Luke glared at Zack and then looked at Libby. "Fine," he said between gritted teeth.

"Well, to answer your question, I'm from Colorado Springs."

"I love Colorado," I said with a smile.

Zack turned to me and smiled.

"So, what? No good schools in Colorado? You had to come to Texas?" Luke asked.

Zack's smile lessened just a bit. "No. We have plenty of good schools. My father lives in Austin. I wanted to be close to him while I attended school. My mother passed away during my senior year of high school."

Grace and I both sucked in a breath of air. "I'm so sorry," we both said at the same time.

Luke looked down and then back up at him. "I'm really sorry to hear that."

"I'm sorry to hear that, Zack," Will said.

"No worries. Thank you though. It's much appreciated."

For the rest of dinner, Luke didn't utter a word to Libby or Zack. He never even so much as looked at them. He mostly talked to Grace about UT and us coming to A&M next year. He asked about her plans for the weekend, and then he made arrangements to show her around tomorrow and Saturday.

My heart hurt as I watched the whole thing play out. I couldn't help but notice Libby looking at Luke. I could understand her wanting to move on since Luke hadn't made a move.

Dinner ended, and we all made our way out to the parking lot. Luke kissed Grace and me good-bye.

He turned to shake Zack's hand. "It was nice meeting you, Zack."

"Same here, Luke."

Luke turned to Libby. His whole body seemed to slump over, and his eyes looked so sad. "Lib, I'll see you around."

I saw the light from the streetlamp catch Libby's eyes. They filled with tears as she nodded her head without uttering a word back to Luke.

"Right. See y'all later." Luke turned and headed to his truck.

When he pulled out his phone, I knew what he was doing—texting Abigail. I looked back at Libby, and I knew she was thinking the same thing.

She turned to Zack. "I'm not ready to end the night. Let's go dancing." Will and I shook our heads.

"I'm tired, so I'm going to have to pass," I said.

"I'll go with y'all!" Grace said.

"Y'all have fun," Will and I both said.

We made our way to Will's truck. After we got in, we both let out a sigh. Will looked back at Libby and Zack as they walked to what I guessed was Zack's car.

"Shit. Why do I have a feeling Libby is going to do something she will regret?"

My heart literally hurt. I prayed that Libby wouldn't do the one thing I had a feeling she was going to do—give herself to Zack to push Luke out of her heart.

I glanced up from my notes to see Lex reading on the bed. She was swinging her legs around as she lay on her stomach. She was so beautiful. This weekend had been amazing. We had made love earlier, and the glow on her face was still present. When she had whispered in my ear that she was mine and I was hers, I'd come so hard and had such an intense orgasm that I had to look away from her. I had felt the tears building in my eyes.

She looked up and smiled when she saw me staring at her. "You taking a break?"

I nodded my head. "I'm distracted."

"By what?" she asked with a crooked smile.

"Those legs."

She sat up and crossed her legs. "Oh, yeah? What about my legs?"

I decided we'd had enough of sweet lovemaking. It was time to get a little dirty. "I want them wrapped around my body…while I fuck you."

Her eyes widened, and she licked her lips. My dick jumped as I watched her body react to what I had just said.

"Can we try something different?" she asked.

Oh hell, I think I just came.

"Lex, I'll try whatever you want."

She got up on her knees and pulled her T-shirt up and over her head. Then, she took off her bra. She held it in her hands and bit down on her lip. "I want you to tie me up and take me from behind."

I swallowed hard. "Wha-what?"

Her face dropped. "Do you not want to try something like that? I mean…" Her face turned a deep shade of red, like she was embarrassed.

I jumped up. "Fuck, no…I mean, yes! I want to do that…all of that."

She smiled bigger and began unbuttoning her shorts. "I want you so much, Will."

I quickly stripped out of my clothes as Lex moved to the edge of the bed before standing up.

"Turn around, Lex."

I had no fucking clue what I was doing. I took Lex's hands and tied them behind her back with her bra. My dick was throbbing with anticipation. I walked her over to the chair and gently pushed the front of her over the back of it while I used my foot to spread her legs open.

I reached between her legs and moaned when I stuck my fingers inside her. "So damn wet."

She dropped her head. "Mmm...again."

I pushed my fingers in again as I began priming her body for my dick. The moans she was letting out were driving me crazy. I was about to push myself into her when I remembered something.

Condom.

"Fuck," I hissed. I quickly got a condom and rolled it on.

"Will, please. I need it."

"What do you need, baby?"

"You. Now. Hard and fast, Will."

I teased her entrance with my tip. I wanted to hear her say it. "Tell me what you want, Lex," I whispered as I pulled on her tied hands.

"God, Will, don't tease me." She pushed her ass back toward me, causing me to smile.

I pushed into her just a bit and pulled back out.

"Will!"

"Tell me, Lex."

"Fuck me, goddamn it! I want you to fuck me!"

Holy shit.

I pushed myself so fast and hard into her that she let out a scream.

"Did I hurt you?"

She shook her head. "No...more. Will, more!" She sounded frantic.

I used my hand to pull her arms back as my other hand grabbed her hip. I moved in and out of her, hard and fast.

"Jesus, Lex. This feels so damn good."

"Oh God, yes! I'm going to come. I'm going to come!"

I began to thrust deeper into her as she called out my name.

"Lex, oh, baby, I'm coming."

Three more hard thrusts, and we both called out in pleasure. I untied her hands and removed the condom. I was attempting to catch my breath when Lex pulled me over to the bed and crawled on top of me. She began touching her breasts as she moved against my exhausted dick.

"Jesus, Lex. I can't...even...breathe."

"Oh God, Will. I'm still so turned-on. It's unreal. That was the hottest and most amazing thing ever, but it was way too fast."

I smiled. "Yeah, it was."

"I need more."

I placed my hands on her hips and moaned as she rubbed against me. She was moving her hips as she touched her breasts. When she began playing with her nipple, I couldn't believe my dick was coming up again.

"Damn, Lex. You're driving me mad."

She looked down at me and licked her lips. "My turn to fuck you."

My heart began to pound faster in my chest as she moved up and slowly sank down onto my dick. We both let out a moan as I felt her warm body sucking me in deeper. My eyes about rolled to the back of my head.

"Ride me, Lex. Ride me fast and hard."

She grinned and began doing just that. The way her breasts were bouncing up and down as she moved was bringing me closer and closer to the edge. She reached up and grabbed both breasts as she rode me faster.

"Jesus, Lex, you're the sexiest woman on earth," I panted out.

She looked at me and smiled. "This feels so damn good. I'm going to come. Oh God, yes…Will. Oh, yeah…yes, that's it! I'm coming, Will. Yes! Oh God! Yes!"

She threw her head back and began calling out my name as my orgasm hit me like never before. My whole body experienced the most incredible feeling, and I began calling out her name.

"Lex, oh God, Lex. I'm coming, baby. Feels. So. Amazing."

It felt like I was never going to stop coming as I poured myself into her body.

"Oh God, I'm coming again!" Lex screamed out as she placed her hands on my chest and moved faster and harder.

The next thing I knew, she was draped over me, gasping for air.

"Motherfucker. Lex, that was fucking incredible. I could feel you squeezing my dick." I wrapped my arms around her.

We stayed like that for at least five minutes until our breathing slowed and steadied out.

She leaned up and kissed me so passionately. "If I knew you had such stamina, Mr. Hayes, we would have been doing *that* all weekend."

I laughed as she moved up and off of me. The second she was off of me, I knew I had made the one mistake I never wanted to make. Lex stopped moving and looked at me with an expression of horror. I looked down and saw cum on my dick.

"Oh my God," Lex whispered.

I looked up into her eyes. "Lex, I'm so sorry. I totally got so caught up in the moment, baby, that I forgot. Fuck!"

Lex just stood there, cum slowly making its way down her leg. She seemed stunned. Then, she smiled, and I looked at her like she was nuts.

"Is that why it felt so amazing?"

What?

I looked down at my dick again and then at Lex. It had felt incredible. I had thought it was from Lex being on top.

"It did feel fucking amazing," I said.

Lex giggled. She quickly turned, walked into the bathroom, and turned on the shower.

I fell back on the bed, and my one moment of ecstasy turned into panic.

What if Lex gets pregnant? Gunner is going to kill me. I'll never live to see the light of day. I'll have to take over my father's business and make furniture. No ranch for me. What about Lex and her dreams?

"What did I just do?"

"Hayes, what in the hell has been wrong with you?" Luke asked.

I looked up at him. "What do you mean?"

He shook his head as he sat down at the table where I was sitting at the cafe. "You haven't eaten in days, you've been sleeping maybe three hours a night, and you look stressed as hell."

I swallowed hard. If I told Luke what I had done, he would want to beat the hell out of me.

I shook my head. "Jesus Christ, Luke. I had sex with Lex and forgot to use a condom. I'm going crazy. What if she's pregnant? I mean, I can't believe I put both of our futures—"

Luke held up his hands. "Hold up. Is she on the pill? God, please tell me she is on the pill."

I nodded my head. "Yeah, she's on birth control."

Luke laughed. "Then, what in the hell are you worried about?"

My mouth dropped open. "Did you hear me? Sex. No condom. Only takes one time!"

Luke sat back in his chair and looked at me as he shook his head. "Is Alex worried?"

"No! She kept going on and on about how amazing it felt, and—"

"Oh, hell no, dude. That is way too much information right there. Too. Much. Jesus H. Christ. I just threw up in my mouth some."

I rolled my eyes and let out a laugh. "Luke, I'm being serious."

"So am I. I don't want that visual in my head. Yuck."

I let out a sigh. "Have you ever forgotten to wear a condom?"

"Nope. I will wear one until the night of my wedding. No way in hell a girl will ever get me not to wear one. Hell no. I don't care if she's on twenty different pills. I will always wear one. Always."

I let out a gruff laugh. "Wait until you're with the one girl who changes everything."

Luke stared at me and then smirked. "I gotta ask. Did it feel different?"

I smiled and nodded my head. "Felt fucking amazing. Makes me never want to wear one of those damn things again. But I have to, and I will even though Lex has begged me not to."

"Again, too much information." Luke was smiling as he shook his head. He glanced up, and his smile instantly vanished.

I turned around and saw Libby and Zack. They were holding hands as they walked by, and Libby was laughing. I turned back to look at Luke. He watched them go by. I couldn't help but notice how Lib glanced at Luke and quickly looked away. I peeked over to Luke, and he looked down at his book and began reading.

My phone vibrated, and I took it out of my pocket. I smiled when I saw Lex's name.

> *Lex: You can stop stressing out. I started my period.*
>
> *Me: Thank the Lord above.*
>
> *Lex: I am on birth control, Will.*
>
> *Me: I don't care. That scared the piss out of me.*
>
> *Lex: Are you still coming this weekend?*
>
> *Me: I plan on doing a lot of coming this weekend.*

"Dude, that's not cool." Luke kicked me under the table.

"Ouch, you bastard. Why in the hell did you kick me?"

Luke tilted his head and gave me a look. "The smile on your face screams, *I'm sexting*. Knock it off."

I laughed. "We're in the clear."

The relief that washed over Luke's face showed that he must have been worried, too, even though he hadn't let on that he was.

> *Lex: I'll see you in less than twenty-four hours. I love you. Gotta run.*
>
> *Me: I love you, too, baby. Bye!*

I pushed my phone into my pocket and stood up. "I'm heading back to pack for this weekend."

Luke nodded his head as he began to pack up his books. He looked around quickly, and I knew he was looking for Libby.

Our parents—Jeff and Ari, Gunner and Ellie, Scott and Jessie, and my dad and mom—had all chipped in to buy a house in College Station since Lex, Grace, Colt, and Lauren would all be here next year. Luke and I had moved out of the dorm and into the house this past weekend, but Libby was still in her dorm. I knew she didn't want to move in because of the whole Zack thing.

"I'll see ya later," I said to Luke.

"Yeah. I've just got one class left, and then I think I'm heading home for the weekend."

I looked at him. "Home? As in Mason?"

"No, home as in Timbuktu. Yes, Mason."

"Why?" I asked.

He shrugged his shoulders. "Just want to go home."

"Spring break is in a week, so we'll see everyone then."

He stood up and looked at me. "Jesus, Will. I just want to go home. I didn't realize I had to fucking clear it with you."

He stormed off as I stood there and watched him retreat away. He glanced over to look at something, and I followed his gaze. Libby and Zack were sitting at a table, completely engrossed with each other. After one quick look back at Luke, I knew exactly why he was going home. It was either home or Abigail.

Grace skipped by me and dropped something into her suitcase as she smiled. "Bikini, check. Sunscreen, check. Romance book to read on the beach, check. Hell, I'm all set and ready to go."

I laughed and shut my suitcase. "I can't believe we're heading to the beach!"

"I know. There had better be some hot guys at the beach, that's all I can say. I've been waiting weeks for spring break!"

"I thought you were through with guys? Have you had a change of heart?"

She motioned with her hand like I was crazy. "Pesh, I've given up *dating* guys. I'm totally open for a fling over spring break."

My mouth dropped open. "You wouldn't, Grace Johnson."

"Why wouldn't I? Why is it okay for guys to have one-night stands, but girls can't? I'm going to pull out my inner Maegan and slut it up."

I put my hand over my mouth and giggled. "You do know Maegan is all talk, right?"

She rolled her eyes. "She's not all talk."

I let out a gasp. "What do you know? And why haven't you told me?"

Grace sat down and gave me an evil smile. "I just happened to walk up on Maegan and Josh Philips."

I sat down on my bed and stared at her. "And?"

"And what?"

My whole body dropped as I looked at her. "And…what were Maegan and Josh doing?"

She tilted her head and looked at me like I had grown six heads. "Really, Alex? They were screwing. You know, having sex, getting it on, bumping uglies."

"I know what screwing means, Grace! When did you see this?"

"New Year's Eve party. I left my phone charger in Meg's car, and she had parked it behind Grams and Gramps's barn. I walked up and heard little Miss Meg crying out, and she wasn't saying, 'Oh God,' 'cause she was praying."

I slammed my hands over my mouth. "No way. Her parents were there. Everyone was there! She could have gotten caught."

Grace rolled her eyes. "Please, I think Meg likes the thrill of having sex right under everyone's nose."

I shook my head. "Wow. Do you think Meg's had sex with a lot of guys?" I stood back up and put my suitcase on the floor near the door.

"Nah. She told me she's only been with three guys."

"Only three guys? Gesh, that's a lot if you ask me."

Grace got up and put her suitcase next to mine. Then, she stopped and looked up, like she was thinking hard. "Considering we've only been with one guy each, I guess three probably seems like a lot, but it's not. I knew some girls from Mason who slept with almost the whole football team."

"That's true."

"Hey, Lex. Can I ask you something?"

The look on her face told me she was about to ask me something she had thought long and hard about. Grace wasn't impulsive by any means. When she turned serious, it would usually be because she was about to talk about something serious.

"Of course you can, Grace. Always."

She began chewing on her bottom lip. "Are you…I mean, do you think you'll be happy with just being with Will?"

I gave Grace a small smile. "Yes. I can't really imagine being with anyone else."

"What about when y'all were apart? Or when you were going through that whole crazy thing with Blake? Did you ever once want to be with someone else?"

I didn't answer right away as I thought about her questions. "I can honestly say, Grace, I've never wanted to be with another man besides Will."

"When did you really know Will was the one?"

I smiled, and my heart started beating faster. "I think I knew for sure the moment he picked up Emma after I'd dropped her while I was swinging. He dusted her off and smiled at me as he handed her back to me. I couldn't have been more than ten years old, but I remember thinking to myself that I was going to marry him. Then, when I got Banjo and Will began helping me train him, he touched me one day, and something happened. It was so weird, like my body just said, *Oh, yeah, he is the one.* I'll never forget it. In that moment, I think he stole a piece of my heart with just his touch."

Grace smiled. "That's beautiful, Alex." She looked down at her hand. "Just a touch," she whispered.

"Just a touch," I said.

She looked back at me and shook her head. Her eyes changed. I wanted to ask her why she was asking me all this, but something told me that Grace might have experienced something with someone, and she wasn't really sure what to think of it.

"You still gonna have a fling this week?" I asked.

The left corner of her mouth rose up, and she smirked. "Hell yeah, I am."

I shook my head and laughed.

I sat in the beach chair, reading, as Grace sat on one side of me and Libby sat on the other. Lauren and Taylor were playing football with the guys as Maegan stood off in the distance, talking to some girl from Baylor she'd run into.

"Odd to see Maegan talking to a girl," Grace said.

I glanced up. "Why?"

"I don't know. She just always seems to gravitate toward men. Maybe being at Baylor is a good thing for her."

"She said she loves it there," Libby said as she looked at her magazine.

"Break time. Damn, I need to cool off!" Luke shouted as he took off toward the water.

Colt followed, but then Maegan walked by, and he stopped and said something that made her laugh. She was smiling as she made her way to her chair next to Grace.

"God, I need to get laid," Meg said as she plopped down.

"Me, too," Grace mumbled.

Libby shot her head around me and looked at Grace. "What did you say, Grace?"

Grace smiled and winked at her.

I laughed as I watched Will, Lauren, and Taylor all walk to the edge of the water. Will dove in as Lauren and Taylor just stood there and talked. I looked back down at my book and smiled as I attempted to get lost again in the story.

A few minutes later, I heard Meg start laughing.

She called out, "Holy shit! It's like a wet T-shirt contest, but better! Mr. Johnson, you, my dear, are packing some serious heat."

I looked up and saw Luke standing there, drinking a Coke.

He looked confused as hell as he stopped drinking and looked at Maegan. "What?"

Meg laughed her ass off. She looked over at Libby. "Too bad you have a boyfriend, Lib. You could be getting some of that!" She threw her head back and laughed harder.

I looked down at Luke's swim trunks. They were mostly white with a light-tan band running around it. My mouth dropped open when I noticed what Meg was laughing about.

Grace busted out laughing as she pointed to Luke. "Dude, I can totally see your dick!"

Luke looked down and then back up. He quickly looked at Libby, which caused me to look at her. She was blushing as she stared, and she was staring hard. She finally snapped out of it and then glanced back down at her magazine.

Luke grabbed a towel and wrapped it around his waist as he looked at Grace and Maegan. They were both still laughing their asses off.

"Fuck off, both of you." Luke started off toward his truck.

I couldn't help but giggle as I watched him walking away. I turned back and looked at Libby. I leaned over and bumped her arm. "Don't let Maegan get to you, Libby."

She raised her hand like she couldn't care less, but I could see it all over her face. She might be dating Zack, but her heart belonged to Luke.

WILL

As we walked down the street, making our way to Desserted Island Ice Cream, I listened to Luke and Libby arguing about where to have dinner. I rolled my eyes and looked down at Lex.

"I don't want to go where our parents are all going, Lib," Luke said.

"Then, don't, Luke. I haven't seen my parents since New Year's, and I want to spend time with them."

"I have to agree. I'd like to have dinner with my mom and dad," I said.

Lex nodded her head. "Me, too, Luke."

"I'm with Luke. I say ditch the parents," Colt said as he and Luke slapped hands.

"We can just go pick up a few girls then," Luke said as he winked at Colt.

"Nice. Don't you have a girlfriend, jerk-off?" Lauren asked as she pushed Colt.

Colt smiled. "Why, no, Lauren, I do not. I happened to walk in on her and some dick football player from Fredericksburg getting it on at a party a few weeks ago."

Lauren frowned. "Oh...I'm really sorry, Colt."

Colt shrugged his shoulders and looked straight ahead. "Doesn't matter. I'm done with the whole bullshit thing called relationships. All women do is fuck with your head...and heart."

"Amen," Luke said.

Libby peeked over to him and then looked straight ahead. Lauren peeked up at Colt and then looked down and away with a sad expression on her face.

After we walked into the ice cream parlor, I held Lex back. I kissed her sweetly on the lips. "I love you, Lex."

She smiled. "I love you more, Will."

I smiled bigger, and my heart melted.

"I'm so blessed to have you in my life. I just wanted you to know that. Thank you for loving me."

My stomach did a weird little flop, and I looked down at my thumb rubbing across her promise ring on her left ring finger. We hadn't told anyone we were secretly engaged. For now, we were using the promise ring as an engagement ring.

She placed her hand on the side of my face. "I'm just as blessed, Will."

I leaned down and kissed her again.

"Dude, that's my sister you're sucking face with, and it kind of grosses me out. Stop, please," Colt called out from across the room.

I pulled back just a bit and smiled.

She smiled back and whispered, "He's just jealous."

I laughed and shook my head. "Probably."

I took her hand as we walked up and ordered.

Libby and Luke each ordered the espresso-soaked brownie sundae. For the last five years, they'd been ordering it to share with one another after declaring it to be the best sundae they had ever eaten. This was the first time they hadn't split it.

I sat down next to Libby and smiled as I took a drink from my chocolate milkshake.

"I say we camp on the beach tonight. Throw up two tents and build a fire," Luke said.

"Oh my gosh, yes!" Lauren hopped up and down.

"Totally sounds like a good time," Meg said with a smile.

"We can make s'mores," Colt said as he looked at Lex and winked.

"We have to have s'mores!" Lex said with a giggle before turning to me.

I looked at her and gave her my panty-melting smile. She gave me a sexy smirk as she bit her bottom lip. I already knew what she was thinking because I was thinking the same thing.

"Taylor, you in?" Colt asked.

She nodded her head. "I'm in. Sounds like fun."

Luke looked at Libby. "Lib? You down for some camping?"

She smiled weakly and nodded her head. "Why not? Sounds like fun."

"Grace? You down?" Luke asked as he gently hit her on the side of the arm.

"Hell yes, I'm down for that!" Grace said with a laugh.

"Then, it's a plan. We're camping on the beach tonight," Luke said as he glanced around the table and smiled.

Colt, Luke, and I all sat on the sofa while our fathers just stared at us.

"Camping on the beach, huh?" Jeff asked.

I glanced over to Gunner. He was looking at me. It was almost as if he had read my thoughts from earlier.

"Yes, sir. We have two tents. One for the guys, and one for the girls."

My father nodded his head. "Where at on the beach?"

"We can pitch them right out front, if y'all want," Luke said.

I wanted to look at him like he had lost his damn mind, but I kept my eyes forward and my mouth shut.

"You boys will make sure the girls stay with you. No one outside of your group is allowed to hang with y'all," Scott said as he looked at each of us.

"Of course," Luke said.

Brad took in a deep breath and slowly let it out. "Boys, we're trusting you. Don't make us regret this."

"No, sir. We would never," Colt said with that damn smile of his.

Anytime he was ever in trouble, that smile would work on everyone.

"You can camp a bit farther down the beach, if y'all want. Just know we can walk down the beach and check on y'all at any moment. No alcohol or any other…fun type of activities." Gunner looked directly to me.

I swallowed hard and nodded my head.

"Yes, sir. We understand, sir," Luke and I both said at the same time. We quickly looked at each other and then back to Gunner.

My father stood up and clapped his hands. "All right then. I guess since y'all will all be sharing a house this fall it's time to let the trusting begin. Let's get all the stuff y'all will need."

I couldn't help but smile. I had a feeling our parents wanted us gone tonight as much as we wanted to be gone.

The tents were set up, and the fire was going. Lex was driving me mad with the way she kept looking at me.

"Grab a stick and roast some marshmallows, y'all." Luke passed out the sticks.

He sat down next to Libby and said something to her, but I couldn't hear what it was. She nodded her head and stared straight into the fire.

Lex and Grace were giggling about something as they roasted their marshmallows. Colt started talking to me about school next year. He was going to be playing football for A&M, and Gunner couldn't have been prouder of him. I glanced back at Luke and Libby, and they were talking—not arguing, but talking for once.

As I looked around our group of friends, everything felt right. No one was fighting. They were all just talking and laughing. It felt like…home.

I wasn't sure how long we sat around the fire and just talked. We talked about school and the ranch. That led to Maegan mentioning how she never wanted to live in the country. Then, Taylor talked about her desire to study for a year in Italy, but her dad had said absolutely no way.

"Tay, you can't blame him. If you were my daughter, there would be no way in hell I'd let you go to another country by yourself for a year." Luke pushed a marshmallow in his mouth.

Taylor sighed. "I don't see why."

Luke looked at her and tilted his head. "Taylor, you're a beautiful young woman. The problem is, you don't know it, and that makes you even more beautiful. Those Italian bastards would stop at nothing to get in your pants. No. No way are you going to Italy for a year."

We all started laughing.

Taylor stared at Luke. "You're not my dad, Luke."

He looked back over at her and smiled. "No, but I say one comment about you in front of your dad, and he'll lock your ass away for the next five years."

Maegan and Grace busted out laughing as the rest of us chuckled. Even Taylor giggled. When I looked over to Libby, she was staring at Luke until her phone went off. She pulled it out and smiled.

Must be Zack.

Luke was laughing, but when he glanced over to look at Libby, his smile instantly faded. Libby stood up and began walking off toward the water as Luke watched her.

"Do you want to sneak away?" Lex whispered.

I looked at her and grinned. "Do you even have to ask?"

She bit down on her lower lip and looked around. "When?"

"Once everyone starts heading to bed, we can go for a walk along the beach. I have a bag packed behind the guys' tent."

Her smile grew bigger. "Look at you thinking ahead."

I winked. "Hell yeah."

"Wow, I'm exhausted. Must be all the sun from today. I'm turning in, y'all. Isn't that one girl we met today having a big beach party tomorrow at her place? What was her name? Cassidy? I'm down for a good beach party," Grace said as she stood up and stretched.

"Oh yeah, I forgot that she mentioned having a big party." Lauren jumped up. "I saw some really good-looking guys hanging around her place today."

Grace made a little fist-pump action. "Good, I need to get laid."

Luke jumped up. "What? What the hell did you just say, Grace?"

Grace rolled her eyes. "Please, don't even go there. How many girls have you hooked up with during the two days we've been here?"

Luke looked back to where Libby was standing. She was now talking on the phone to someone and laughing.

"None," Luke said.

Grace shrugged her shoulders. "Well, look at you. I'm impressed. Wear those shorts again tomorrow, big brother, and I bet they'll be lining up for ya."

She walked past Luke as he glared at her.

Everyone but Lex and me started getting up and heading to the tents. I watched Libby.

"I'll stay out here and make sure Libby is okay, Will," Colt said.

"Nah, that's okay, Colt. I wanted to spend some time with Lex."

Colt shook his head and said, "Remember, my dad could come at any moment. Keep your hands off my sister."

"Colt, knock it off!" Lex said.

Colt smiled and headed toward the tent. I glanced over and saw Luke standing there, looking at Libby. She was now off the phone, but she was staring off into the black night sky.

"I'm, uh…going to say good night to Libby," Luke said, barely above a whisper.

I stood up, held out my hand, and helped Lex up. "Let's go for a walk, Lex."

She quickly nodded her head. As we walked by the tent, I headed to the back and grabbed the backpack I had packed earlier. We started off down the beach, and I looked back over my shoulder to see Luke and Libby talking. They didn't appear to be arguing, and that was a good sign.

At least I hoped it was a good sign.

33

Will and I walked in silence for a bit.

Finally, I asked, "What is weighing so heavily on your mind, Will?"

He sighed. "Libby and Luke."

I nodded my head. "Yeah, what about Colt and Lauren? Did you happen to notice how the two of them look at each other?"

Will chuckled. "I have. What is wrong with the four of them?"

I shrugged my shoulders. "I'm not sure. I do know though that Libby is really starting to like Zack."

Will looked at me. "Really? What has she said?"

"I don't know. Normal stuff. He treats her really good and showers her with attention."

"That's good. I wouldn't want to kick his ass."

I giggled. "She said things are moving along…in their relationship."

Will rolled his eyes. "Ugh, Lex. I don't want to hear that."

I stopped walking, and so did Will.

"Will, I don't want Libby to do something she would regret. I asked her about her feelings for Luke."

"What did she say?"

I shook my head. "She won't answer me. She dances around the subject by saying things like, 'He has Abigail,' or, 'He doesn't feel that way about me.' It is so frustrating."

Will looked down at the ground and then back at me. "Maybe Libby's moved on."

I just looked at him. "Do you really believe that? Do you not see the way they look at each other? Will, you and I both know they are in love with one another. One of them is going to make a mistake and possibly push the other away for good."

Will placed his hands on my shoulders. "Do you remember when your father said if our love was a true love, it would find a way?"

I nodded my head. "Yes, I do remember that."

"The same thing holds true for Lib and Luke, and for Colt and Lauren. We need to let them work it out for themselves, Lex. We can't force any of them to be with someone unless they feel it in their own heart. Love always finds a way, baby."

My heart did a little skip as I smiled. I looked down at the backpack and then back up into Will's eyes. "Make love to me, Will," I whispered. I leaned up on my tippy toes and kissed him.

Will dropped the backpack, pulled me into his body, and deepened the kiss. When he pulled away, he said, "With pleasure."

I watched as he opened the backpack and pulled out the blanket. He spread it out, and then he took out two bottles of water and set them to the side. He pulled his phone out of his pocket and swiped across the screen. He hit a few buttons, and music began playing. When I heard Dan + Shay's "19 You + Me," I couldn't help but smile.

I pulled my T-shirt up and over my head as Will pushed his shorts down. I swallowed as I looked when his dick sprang out, clearly showing how much he wanted me. I wanted him so much, but every time, I would get nervous as hell. I wasn't sure why. He walked up to me as he pulled his shirt off and tossed it to the ground. All I could hear were the waves crashing against the shore and my heart pounding in my chest. I pushed my shorts and panties down in one movement and stepped out of them. Will looked my body up and down as if he couldn't get enough of me.

"Lie down, Lex," he said in a husky voice.

My libido came to full attention as I lay down on the blanket. My insides were clenching with anticipation as I watched Will move over my body. He gently began kissing my neck, and then he moved his lips up to mine. The way he kissed me so tenderly caused me to let out a small moan, and I pushed my fingers through his hair.

"Oh, Lex, I love you so much," he whispered against my lips.

I was so overcome with emotion that I wanted to cry out.

"I love you, Will. I love you so much."

He began moving his lips down my neck. "I can't wait to make you my wife someday."

I let out a moan as I felt the wetness between my legs. I needed him to touch me.

"I want to make love to you every morning and every night."

"Will, please touch me." The need in my voice surprised me.

The way he could make my body come to attention with just his words was unreal to me. He placed his hand on my thigh, and I gasped.

"Yes. Please…" I said.

He moved his fingertips gently across my leg, and then he finally brushed his fingers across my lips. He slipped his fingers inside me and let out a long, deep moan. "Lex, you're so damn wet. Baby, do you want me?"

I nodded my head frantically. I wanted to go slow, to enjoy him inside me. "I always want you, Will. Always."

He began kissing my nipple as he slowly worked his fingers in and out of me. He was building me up, and I loved every second of it.

"Feels…so…good. Will, I'm so close," I whispered as I tugged gently on his hair.

The next thing I knew, Will's lips were taking me to heaven and back, and I softly called out his name. He moved his lips up my body and to my neck.

"Lex…" Will quickly pulled back and looked at me. "Oh God. Lex, baby, I don't have a condom. They are in my other bag in the tent. We can't do this."

I placed my hand on the side of his face. "Will, I'm on birth control. Please, please make love to me. I want to feel you inside me. I want it to just be you and me."

He closed his eyes and then opened them. "I never want—"

"Will, it's okay."

He leaned down and gently kissed me. He moved over me and slowly began to push himself inside me. We continued to kiss, and after he pushed all the way in, he pulled back and moaned.

"You feel amazing, Lex. You mean so much to me, and I'll always love you."

Feeling how our bodies were one caused tears to build in my eyes.

"Will…" My voice cracked.

He stopped moving.

I wrapped my legs around him and pulled him closer to me. "I love you so much. I need you."

I had never felt so wanted in my entire life. The way he was making love to me was beyond anything I could ever describe. It was more than magical. The love between us felt as if it had grown even more. Will made love to me slowly, lovingly, and passionately. It was one of the most amazing moments of my life.

Will whispered in my ear, "Lex, I never want tonight to end."

I ran my fingertips up and down his back. "Neither do I."

I began to feel the familiar buildup my body craved so much. "Will, oh God…I'm going to come." I looked into his eyes.

"Lex…" He pushed in deeper.

I let my release go as I grabbed his arms and quietly called out his name. Our eyes never faltered as he continued to work my orgasm.

He briefly closed his eyes and then opened them. "Baby, I'm going to come. Lex…my God…"

I moaned when I felt his warm liquid spilling into my body. I knew that I would never be able to breathe without Will in my life.

He slowed down and hovered over my body. The moment was so intense for both of us that I thought we just needed to…be…just for a few seconds.

Will slowly pulled out of me as he looked into my eyes. "Alexandra Eryn, my life would be nothing without you. You are my entire world, the reason I breathe."

A small sob escaped my mouth as we wrapped our bodies together. We held each other for a while as we whispered back and forth how much we loved each other. I didn't want to break our connection.

"Lex, we should get back. It's getting late."

I pulled back to look into his eyes. "Thank you. That was another amazing moment in my life."

He smiled, and my heart melted all over again.

Will he always have such an effect on me?

"It was for me, too, Lex. I can't even put it into words right now. Being able to give myself into you like that…it was beyond words."

I smiled back and started to stand up. Will pulled me into his arms and kissed me again. The love poured between our bodies and mixed together as the sounds of the waves crashed on the shore.

I'll never forget this night for as long as I live.

WILL

I heard the front door open and then slam shut. I was studying for my last final exam. I also had to get the house ready to close up for a few months since we'd be heading home in a week. I headed downstairs and saw Luke pacing back and forth with his hands in his hair.

"Fuck. Son of a bitch. Fucker. Fucking bastard!"

I stopped at the bottom of the stairs. "Luke, what the hell is wrong?"

He snapped his head over and looked at me. "She slept with him. She…she gave herself to him."

"What? Who?"

He looked like he was about to be sick. I had been worried about him ever since we had come back from spring break. He never went out. He stayed home almost every weekend, only leaving to go study or go to the gym.

"Oh my God. Oh God, what have I done?" Luke dropped his hands to his knees and leaned over. He was sucking in one deep breath after another. "That was why she didn't move in here. That was why. She knew she was gonna sleep with him."

Libby? Is he talking about Libby? My fists balled up.

I walked over to him and grabbed him. "Luke, look at me and calm the hell down. Are you talking about Libby? What's going on?"

He dropped his head back and let out a long, drawn-out breath before looking back at me. "I went to Libby's dorm room. I needed to talk to her because seeing her with him was too much. I couldn't take it anymore. It turned out that she wasn't alone. Zack was there, and…and…"

"And what?" I asked him even though I knew the answer.

"She was in a robe and kept telling me that now wasn't a good time to talk. She said if I wanted to talk, we should have talked months ago. I pushed my way into her room and saw…"

I closed my eyes. *Dear God, no.*

"I saw Zack in her bed. I took one look at him, and I just turned and left."

I needed to calm myself down before I attempted to calm Luke down. I knew my sister was a grown woman, but all I wanted to do was beat the shit out of Zack.

"Ah shit. Damn, Luke. You had to know she was going to move on. I mean, they've been dating for a few months, and I'm sure that wasn't the first time—"

"Stop! I don't even want to think about any of this." He started to head up the stairs.

"Where are you going?"

"Out."

I closed my eyes and pulled out my phone. I quickly sent Libby a text message.

> Me: *Libby, you're a grown woman, so I won't tell you what you can and can't do, but I sure hope you know what you're doing…with Zack, I mean.*
>
> Libby: *I need to get out of here. Please come get me.*

My heart started pounding. *What if that fucker forced her to have sex with him?*

> Me: *Libby…did Zack hurt you? I'll fucking kill him.*
>
> Libby: *No.*
>
> Me: *What's wrong then?*
>
> Libby: *I just made the biggest mistake of my life, Will. I slept with Zack. I thought it would help me forget Luke. I need you, Will.*
>
> Me: *I'm on my way.*

Luke came down the stairs with a duffel bag.

I grabbed his arm to stop him. "Don't go to Abigail."

He looked at me, shocked. He slowly shook his head. "I haven't seen Abigail in weeks. I took my last final today. I'm going home."

He pulled his arm from mine and headed out the door. I let out a deep breath and hit Lex's number.

"Hey, handsome. I'm about to take my last final, and then I'll be packing up the rest of my stuff and saying good-bye to UT!"

I smiled, and if I wasn't so worried about Libby and Luke, I would be turned-on. Just the sound of her voice had my body craving her.

"Awesome. Baby, I've got a problem."

"What? Are you okay? Is everything okay?"

"I'm fine. It's Libby and Luke."

She sighed. "Grace just showed me a text from Luke. He said he is on his way home and that he ruined everything with Libby. Is he okay?"

"No, he stopped by Libby's dorm room to talk to her. About Libby and Zack. The only problem is, he walked in on Libby and Zack together. I texted Libby, and she is really upset and asked me to come get her."

"Oh God. She slept with Zack? He didn't force her, did he?"

"No. I asked her, and she said she just made the biggest mistake of her life. Lex, can you call her? I'm on my way, but talking to you and Grace might help."

"Of course. Yes. Grace will call her right now, and we'll talk to her."

"Thank you, baby. I'll call you in a little bit."

"Will?"

I grabbed my truck keys and started heading out of the house. "Yeah?"

"I love you so much."

My stomach did that funny little flip thing, and my heart felt like it skipped a beat. I realized how damn lucky Lex and I were.

"I love you, too, Lex, more than you will ever know."

I knocked on Libby's dorm room door and slowly started opening it. I walked into the room and saw my sister sitting on her bed. She had her legs pulled up to her chest as she rocked back and forth. The moment her eyes met mine, my heart broke, and I wanted to kick someone's ass.

"Libby...Jesus, honey, what's wrong?" I quickly walked over and sat on the bed.

She threw herself into my arms. "I should have moved into the house with y'all. What did I do? Oh God. Oh God."

Her body was shaking, and she was crying so hard that I could hardly understand her. I pulled back to look at her and used my finger to make her look at me.

"Libby, you're scaring the hell out of me right now. Honey, please tell me what happened. *Please*, Libby."

She shook her head. "His face. I'll never forget the look on his face."

"Whose face? Did Zack do something to you?"

She shook her head. "No, I thought I was ready. I thought it would help me move on and forget...forget..."

I was so confused. "Libby, I need you to calm down. You're not making any sense, and honestly, I'm ready to go find Zack and pound the shit out of him."

She smiled slightly, and she started to take in a few deep breaths before letting them out. I waited patiently as she calmed herself down enough to talk.

"I thought I was ready to...to..." Her voice cracked. She closed her eyes and slowly opened them. "I thought I was ready to sleep with Zack. I mean, I like him. I really do. Well, we..."

I grabbed her hand and held it in mine. It was harder than hell to sit here and listen to my sister talk about having sex with someone.

"We had sex. It wasn't great or life-changing, and it was not at all like how Lex talks about her first time with you."

She smiled slightly as I grinned back at her. My heart was already breaking for her.

"I thought I wanted it, Will. I thought this might be the final thing that would connect Zack and me…and make me forget about—" A sob escaped her mouth. "Make me forget about Luke." She began crying but quickly regained her composure.

My heart was pounding so hard in my chest. I wasn't sure if I wanted to beat the hell out of Zack for touching my sister or fight Luke for pushing her away like this.

"When someone started knocking on the door, I quickly jumped up and put on a robe. I wasn't even thinking that it could be Luke. He hasn't even looked my way since…"

I tilted my head. "Since when?"

She swallowed hard. "Since spring break." She shook her head as if trying to erase a bad memory. "I opened the door, and he was standing there. He asked to talk to me, and I said it wasn't a good time, but he…he just wouldn't take no for an answer. Then, he pushed his way in and saw Zack in my bed. He turned and looked at me, and the look in his eyes…" She dropped her head, and tears began falling. "He looked devastated, broken. He didn't say a word. He just stared at me, and then he left."

"Libby, shit. You and Luke need to sit down and talk." I wiped her tears away.

She nodded her head. "In that very moment, I knew I had made a mistake. I knew Luke and I pushing each other away was the cause of all of this."

She looked into my eyes. Her eyes were so sad.

"But he's slept with other people, Will. He's been with Abigail this whole year, and he comes in and makes me feel like I'm the bad person."

"Libby, sweetheart, Luke hasn't been with Abigail in months. I don't even remember the last time Luke went to a party."

Her mouth dropped open. Then, she turned her head and stared out the window. "But…Abigail told me…I thought…"

"Libby, listen, it's not your fault, okay? You can't feel guilty. You and Zack are dating. Luke had plenty of chances to tell you how he felt about you. If he wasn't so afraid of his feelings for you, y'all would have talked it through and stopped playing this cat-and-mouse game."

She quickly looked back at me and shook her head. "No, it's my fault. This is all my fault."

I didn't know why she was saying that. "Libby, Luke has never given you any real reason to think he has feelings for you. This is not your fault."

She quickly wiped away her tears. "Where is he? I need to talk to him."

I pushed my hand through my hair and stood up. "He, um…he's gone."

She jumped up. "Gone? What do you mean, gone?"

"He came home, and he was really upset. He said he was heading home. He took his last final earlier today, and…well, he left."

Her hands came up to her mouth, and she began crying again.

I pulled her to me. "Shh…it's okay, Libby. Let's just get you all packed up and out of here, and we'll be home in a few days. You and Luke can talk then."

She nodded her head. "Let me splash some cold water on my face, and we can start taking some stuff to your truck. I'm all packed up, except for a few things."

I watched my sister slowly make her way to her bathroom. I let out a sigh and sent Lex a text message.

> Me: With Libby. Packing up her stuff. She's moving into the house. She's a mess. She and Luke need to have their damn heads smashed together.
>
> Lex: I know! This summer will be different. Things will get better. I can feel it in my bones!
>
> Me: I hope you're right. Talk to ya later, baby.
>
> Lex: Okay. I love you! Hey, don't forget that Grace and I are going to a party here. It's the last party of the year, and we want to say good-bye to a few friends.
>
> Me: Right. Just be careful.
>
> Lex: Always! I'll text you or call you later.

Libby smiled. "That's the last of it. My dorm is cleared out. I guess I get first pick of the other rooms!"

I laughed. "You and Lauren are bunking up, right?"

She nodded her head. "Yep. I can't wait. Grace is going to be pissed 'cause I'm picking the room with the balcony!"

I laughed and sat down on the sofa.

Libby fell into a chair and let out a sigh. She looked at me and said, "Thank you."

I smiled. "Libby, I'll always be here for you, no matter what. You're my sister, my life. You and Lex will always be first and foremost in my mind."

She went to say something when the front door opened. I looked over and saw Luke walking in.

He didn't even bother to look at us. "I fucking forgot my laptop and everything else in my rush earlier. I made it all the way to Austin and had to turn around, and—" He stopped talking when Libby stood up.

"Luke," she whispered.

He stopped walking and looked at her. "What are you doing here?"

She swallowed hard. "Will helped me move all my stuff in, and I…well, I want to talk to you."

For one brief second, it seemed like Luke was relieved.

Then, he frowned. "We don't have anything to talk about, Libby."

"I think we do, and if—"

Luke shook his head. "Listen, it was wrong of me to stop by there. It was a mistake. I know you're happy with Zack, and—"

Libby took a few steps toward Luke. "If you'll just let me—"

Luke held up his hand. "No, Libby. I'm happy for you that you found someone." He quickly made his way upstairs.

Libby stood there. I was just about to tell her to go after him when she bolted up the stairs.

I got up, made my way to the kitchen, and grabbed a root beer. Not two minutes later, Luke was coming down the stairs. He looked at me, and the sadness in his eyes surprised me. I figured Libby had gone up there to talk to him, but here he was, leaving.

"Luke…dude, where are you going?"

He stopped and looked at me. "Home. I have no idea after that." He opened the front door and left.

I stood there, stunned. I wanted to run upstairs and ask Libby what had happened, but my phone rang. I looked down to see Grace was calling me.

"Hello?" All I could hear was commotion. "Hello? Grace! Can you hear me?"

"Will!" she screamed.

I dropped the root beer and held on to the counter. *Something happened. Lex is hurt. Oh God, please let her be okay.*

"Grace…"

The front door flew open, and Luke looked at me.

"Get in my fucking truck now. Libby!" Luke yelled out.

Libby came running down the stairs. "I just got a text from Grace. Something about Lex being taken away in an ambulance?"

Luke grabbed her and said, "Go get in my truck. We're going to Austin."

I stood there, still on the phone with Grace. All I could hear was Grace's muffled voice.

"Grace! Tell me what the fuck is going on."

Grace was crying. "I found her, Will. I found her, but he was hitting her. I screamed, and…oh God, Will. Blake was about to…he had Alex. Oh God! He was trying to…when we walked into the room, he was hitting her while she was trying to fight him off. I think he might have given her something. Will…I'm so sorry I didn't keep an eye on her. We're on the way to Brackenridge Hospital."

"I'm on my way." I ran out the door and jumped into Luke's truck.

He took off like a bolt of lightning. The only things I could hear were Libby crying in the backseat and Lex's voice repeating over and over in my head.

I love you, Will.

35

A Few Hours Earlier

Chrissie walked up and handed me a bottle of Bud Light. "I'm going to miss you, Alex!" she yelled over the music.

Chrissie and I had been lab partners in chemistry class. She was a sweet girl, but she was hell-bent on getting into some sorority. She still was crushing on Blake pretty hard as well.

"I'm going to miss you, too!" I yelled back.

We were at Chrissie's brother's house. The party was mostly frat guys and sorority girls, but Chrissie had begged Grace and me to come since we wouldn't be back next year.

I took a drink of the beer and looked around. Grace was talking to some guy who was attempting to make a move on her. She gave him that smile of hers, and I swore he was eating out of the palm of her hand.

"So, are you excited about A&M next year?" Chrissie asked.

I took another drink of my beer. I smiled and nodded my head. "I'm really excited. The fact that I get to be with Will just makes it all the more sweeter."

Chrissie's smile faded for a brief second as she looked around, and then she looked back at me. We talked for a bit more about our plans for this summer. I took another sip of beer, and then some guy ran smack into me, causing me to drop the bottle.

"Shit," I mumbled.

"Damn it!" Chrissie said.

We both bent down and started to clean it up.

I stood up and felt a little dizzy. I put my hand up to my head. "Shit, I must have stood up too fast."

Chrissie smiled slightly at me. "Let me go throw this away. I'll be right back."

I nodded as I glanced back over to Grace. She was still talking to the same guy. She looked my way and winked at me. I giggled and shook my head.

"So, do you want another beer, Alex?"

I turned back to look at Chrissie. I was beginning to feel dizzy and a little groggy.

"Um…no. I guess I drank more than I thought." I placed my hand to my head. "I'm not feeling very well. I feel a bit dizzy."

Chrissie looked around and grabbed my arm. "Let me show you to the bathroom."

She pulled me so fast and hard that I almost tripped twice while trying to keep up with her. I looked back to see Grace, but every time my head moved, I got dizzier. Chrissie stopped, and I looked up to see Blake standing there.

"Blake?" I asked.

He smiled and looked at Chrissie. I glanced back at her, but the room started spinning.

"I gave it to her. Now, will you put in a good word for me?" Chrissie asked Blake.

I looked at Blake as he smiled. The room was spinning faster.

"I don't feel right. What's going on?"

Blake smiled at me as he picked me up. "Let me take you somewhere private, angel."

I attempted to look for Grace, but I began to feel nauseous. "Blake, I think I'm going to be sick."

"I'll make you feel better, angel. Just hold on."

I closed my eyes to try to stop the spinning of the room. When I opened my eyes, Chrissie was following us up the stairs.

"The second bedroom on the right. Blake, are you sure about this? She only had a couple of—"

Blake stopped and turned to Chrissie. "She belongs to me. Get the hell out of here, Chrissie, if you want me to put in a good word for you with that sorority."

She belongs to me? What?

"Wait…put me down, Blake."

Oh God. I feel like I'm going to be sick.

"Chrissie, please get Grace. I'm not feeling well."

Chrissie looked at Blake and then at me.

"Chrissie, walk away if you want to be in the sorority," Blake said with anger in his voice.

I could smell the alcohol on his breath, and it turned my stomach even more.

Will…

I shouldn't have come to this party.

Will…

Blake turned, walked through the door, and then shut it. He gently lay me down on the bed and looked at me. I tried to stand up, but I was so dizzy and felt so sick.

"What? Wh-why am I…I feel sick."

Blake began taking his pants off.

My heartbeat picked up. I swallowed hard and put my hand to my stomach. "Why? What are you doing? I want to leave. I need—"

I leaned over when I felt like I was going to throw up.

I feel so tired. I just need to leave.

"Alex…"

I closed my eyes in an attempt to gain some control of the situation.

Will, I need you.

I took in a few deep breaths. I felt so groggy. *What is wrong with me?*

"Alex…"

Blake's voice pulled me back into the moment. I turned and looked at him. He wasn't wearing any pants.

"No. God, please no. Blake, don't do this. I don't want this."

"Just calm down, Alex. The drug will set in soon, and you won't remember a thing, angel."

I shook my head and then moaned. The room was still spinning. I pushed myself further away from him as he smiled.

"That's it, baby. Let's get those shorts off now, shall we?"

I began kicking my legs the best I could. They felt so heavy though.

I can't breathe. I need air.

Will!

I began crying as I whispered, "Please don't do this, Blake."

He pushed my legs down and held them as he began to unbutton my shorts.

I closed my eyes.

Will!

Oh God, Will, I need you…please.

I began thinking about the last time Will and I had been together. I was his and only his. Our love was a perfect, untouched love.

I snapped my eyes open. I was *not* going to let this happen. I relaxed, which caused Blake to relax his grip on my legs. Blake was saying something about waiting too long to have me.

I said, "Let me…let me take my own…shorts off." I could barely talk.

"That's what I'm talking about, angel."

My head was beginning to hurt more. I lifted my leg and gathered all my strength. Then, I kicked him as hard as I could.

Blake let out a loud moan and then yelled, "You fucking bitch!"

I attempted to quickly move and run away, but I was so dizzy and felt so insanely sick.

Blake grabbed me and threw me back on the bed. The moment his hand came across my face, I let out a scream.

I closed my eyes. *This is not happening to me.*

Will…

I love you. Our love is forever.

I opened my eyes again and looked into Blake's eyes. They were filled with anger.

"Why the fuck are you not passing the fuck out, you bitch?"

I was going to fight him with everything I had left in my body. I began hitting him as hard as I could.

I took a deep breath and screamed out, "Grace!"

"Shut. The. Fuck. Up." Blake ripped my shorts open and stuck his hand down my panties.

I began slapping him, but I felt my energy slowly slipping away.

"Alex, fucking stop fighting me, you bitch."

I was feeling groggier.

I can't stop fighting. I won't stop fighting.

I won't let him do this to us, Will.

I began pushing Blake away from me. His fingers were inside me, and I felt like I wanted to puke. When I pushed him with all my might, he pulled his hand out. Then, I saw Blake balling up his fist, and I braced myself for what was about to happen.

The bedroom door flew open as Grace screamed out my name.

I turned to look at her. "Grace…help…me," I slurred.

Then, everything went black.

36
WILL

"Will, slow the hell down, man," Luke said as he and Libby attempted to keep up with me.

I walked into the emergency room and frantically looked around. I didn't see Grace. "Where's Grace?"

Luke walked up to the nurses' station. "Excuse me, ma'am? My cousin, Alex Mathews, was brought in a little bit ago."

She looked at a chart and back up at Luke. She glanced over to Libby and me. "Are you all family?"

Luke nodded his head. "I'm her cousin."

She nodded her head. "Your name?"

"Luke Johnson."

"Mr. Johnson, you can go back there. Your sister, Grace, should be there. I believe the doctor will be talking to her shortly."

I stepped forward. "What about me?"

The nurse looked at me with sympathetic eyes. "You are?"

"Her fiancé, Will Hayes."

Libby gasped, and Luke turned and looked at me.

"Mr. Hayes, I can't allow you to go back there yet. Give me just a few minutes. Mr. Johnson, please follow me."

Luke said, "Fuck, if I had known, I would have had you—"

I slowly shook my head. "Go. Just find out how she is."

I watched as Luke followed the nurse through the double doors. My legs felt like they were going to give out.

"Will, let's go sit down, okay?" Libby guided me over to the waiting room. She pulled out her phone. "Colt is almost here. He can't get a hold of his parents or Mom or Dad. They all went to some ranch in west Texas. They must not have a signal out there. Jeff and Ari are on their way."

I nodded my head. "What in the fuck happened, Libby? Grace could hardly talk on the phone."

She shook her head. "I don't know. Grace was in a state of panic when she called. She kept saying it was all her fault. I don't know, Will."

We sat in silence until Luke cleared his throat. He was about to start talking when Colt, Lauren, and Taylor ran up. Meagan had sent a text saying she was on her way from Baylor.

"Where's Alex? What's going on?" Colt looked around to each of us.

Luke put his hand on Colt's shoulder. "She's okay, Colt. Take a deep breath, dude, and sit down. I was just with Grace, and the doctor came to talk to us."

Colt sat down, and Lauren sat next to him. I couldn't help but notice that Colt reached for Lauren's hand when Luke started talking. She held it and wiped a tear away with her other hand.

"They were at a party. Someone must have given Alex something to drink with Rohypnol in it."

"Oh God, no," Libby whispered.

Taylor and Lauren both started crying. My heart was beating so hard and fast in my chest that it almost drowned out Luke's words.

Luke cleared his throat. "She wasn't raped."

Libby let out a sigh and said, "Thank you, God."

I shook my head. "Raped? Someone tried to rape her?" I felt sick to my stomach.

"They were at some girl named Chrissie's brother's house. Grace said she noticed that Alex had disappeared, so Grace began looking for her. Grace walked up to Chrissie and asked her where Alex was. She said Chrissie started acting funny and started frantically looking around. Then, she just blurted out that Blake had promised to get her into some sorority if she slipped something in Alex's drink. Chrissie admitted that she did it, and then she told Grace where Blake had taken Alex. I guess Chrissie's brother was standing there, and he and Grace ran upstairs. Grace said she heard Alex screaming out her name, and Chrissie's brother kicked open the door. Right as it opened…um…"

I looked at Luke. Anger along with tears filled his eyes. I looked at Colt, who had already been crying.

I slowly glanced back to Luke. "What? Just tell us."

Luke looked down. "Grace said Alex asked her to help her, and then Blake punched Alex. She hasn't woken up yet."

Colt and I stood up.

"That motherfucker. I'm going to kill him," I said.

"What about Alex?" Colt asked.

"The doctor said they drew blood and pumped Alex's stomach. After Grace explained to them what happened, they're certain that Alex was drugged."

"Has anyone called the police?" Libby asked.

"Yes, they were called. I'm going to be honest with you, Will and Colt. I know where the fucker is. He's still at the party, and Grace gave me the address and said the brother wasn't letting Blake go until the police get there."

Libby jumped up. "No! Luke…" She turned to Colt and me. "Will, Colt, don't do this. Do *not* do this, please."

I looked at my sister. "I love you, Libby." I kissed her on the forehead. "Where is he?" I asked Luke.

Libby began crying as she turned to Luke and put her hands on his chest. "Please. Please don't do this, Luke. I know you're angry, but please don't go. I can't bear the thought of you getting hurt." She turned to look at Colt and me. "Or any of you getting hurt. Don't do this."

Lauren walked up and said, "I disagree. Go teach that asshole a lesson."

"No! Oh my God, Lauren!" Libby stepped in front of me. "Don't. Do. This. I understand you're angry, Will. I am, too. Let the police take care of it. What would Dad tell you to do, Will?"

I looked at Luke and then Colt. They both nodded their heads.

"I'm coming with you," Grace said in a weak voice from behind me.

"No…" Libby whispered.

"Let's go," I said.

Luke and Colt turned and started to head out of the emergency room.

"Will! Luke! Colt! Please don't do this!" Libby shouted.

I closed my eyes quickly to blink away my tears. When I opened them, I knew what I had to do.

We walked into the house, and Grace immediately pointed to Blake.

Most everyone was gone, and Blake was sitting down, talking to two guys. I recognized him the minute I saw him. I started to head over to him.

Grace stepped in front of me. "Will, Alex is going to need you when she wakes up. I'm not sure how much she'll remember, but she'll need you. You won't be able to be there for her if you're in jail. I told the police everything I knew, and I'm sure they will be here any minute to arrest Blake."

"She's right, Will. Let Colt and me take care of this ass before the police get here," Luke said.

I shook my head. "No, he hurt Lex, and now, he's going to hurt."

I walked up to Blake and stopped right in front of him.

He jumped up. "Will? What are you—"

"How far did you get?" I asked.

Blake looked at me. "What? Is Alex awake?"

I grabbed him by the shirt and pulled his face close to mine. "What the fuck did you do to her? I'll fucking kill you if you touched her."

Blake pushed me, and I stumbled back, but Colt grabbed me. The way Blake was smiling at me turned my stomach.

"What's wrong? Your girlfriend doesn't remember how fucking turned-on she was for me? Her pussy sure was wet enough when I slipped my fingers inside her."

The flood of anger moved through my body like I'd never felt before. One of the guys standing nearby called Blake an asshole. I took two steps toward Blake and pulled my fist back. Blake was saying something to the guy, and when he turned around, he didn't see my fist coming straight to his face. The moment I made contact, he fell backward and hit the chair.

I started for him when I felt someone grab my arms. "Let me go!" I shouted.

"Dude, the cops just got here. I want to hurt him as much as you do, but calm the hell down," Luke said.

Colt walked up to Blake and kicked him in the side as hard as he could. "That's for my sister, you motherfucker!"

Some guy walked up to Colt and said something to him as he backed Colt away.

Lying on the floor, Blake moaned like the pussy he was. I wanted nothing more than to beat the shit out of him. When the cops walked up, they asked for Blake Turner, and one of his friends bent down and helped him up.

"Who hit him?" the cop asked as he looked around.

No one said a word. I watched as Blake's friends all shook their heads.

"Fine," the cop said as he proceeded to put handcuffs on Blake.

"I didn't do anything wrong. Let me the fuck go!" he slurred.

It was then I noticed how drunk he was. I turned and watched as the cop began reading Blake his rights while walking him out of the house.

Luke walked up to me and put his hand on my shoulder. "Come on, let's get back to the hospital. My dad sent me a text. My parents are at the hospital, and Gunner and Ellie will be there shortly."

I began following Luke and Colt out. I glanced over and saw some girl crying hysterically, and one of the guys who had been talking to Blake when we'd walked in had his arm around her as she talked to a cop. I turned and looked for Grace. She was watching the same scene play out as she walked slightly behind Luke.

She looked up at me and said, "That's Chrissie and her brother."

I nodded my head. "I'd like to slap the shit out of her."

"You'd have to get behind me," Grace said.

I shook my head as I looked back at Chrissie. She looked at me, and her face said it all. She was racked with guilt.

Good. Serves her ass right.

We piled back into Luke's truck, and my phone went off. I pulled it out to see a text from Libby.

*Libby: Will, the nurse said Alex is sleeping, but she's calling out
your name. Please come back.*

Me: We're on our way now.

"Luke, I need something from our room. Please, it's for Alex," Grace
said.

Luke nodded his head. "Okay, but be quick, Grace."

When we got to Duren Hall, Grace jumped out of the truck and ran
into the building. I continued to stare out the window. I couldn't drown out
Blake's words, no matter how hard I tried to block them.

Her pussy sure was wet enough when I slipped my fingers inside her.

I felt the bile building up, and I opened the truck door. I jumped out
and began throwing up.

Colt was out and standing there within seconds. "Jesus, Will, are you all
right?"

I shook my head and threw up again.

Luke walked up and put his hand on my back. "It's gonna be okay,
Will. I promise you."

I stood up and wiped my mouth as I looked at him with tears rolling
down my face. "You don't know that, Luke. He touched her. God knows
how far he went. I pray to God she doesn't remember. Oh God, I hope she
doesn't remember." I felt my knees give out as I began crying harder.

Colt and Luke both grabbed me as my legs buckled from underneath
me. Colt pulled me into his arms as I let out every emotion I had been
holding in. They helped me back over to the truck, and I slowly got into the
back seat where I attempted to get control again.

Grace got back into the truck and asked Luke what happened. When he
told her what happened, she wrapped her arms around me.

"I swear to you, he didn't get that far. Her pants were still on, Will, I
swear to God."

I pulled back and saw Colt quickly wiping away his tears. I nodded my
head and looked down at what Grace was holding. She had Lex's doll.

"Emma," I whispered as I looked up into Grace's eyes.

She smiled and nodded her head. "Come on, let's get back before she
wakes up."

We weren't that far from the hospital, but it felt like an eternity before I
was walking back through the emergency room doors. I overheard as the
nurse told Lauren, Libby, and Taylor that Alex had been moved to a room.

As everyone walked to the elevator to head up to the floor where
Alex's room was, Libby grabbed my hand. I peeked down at her, and she
smiled at me. My heart instantly felt better from just having Lib here with

me. I closed my eyes and waited until the elevator door opened, and we exited.

We walked up to the nurses' station. A nurse told us that only two people could visit at a time. Colt and I looked at each other.

He nodded his head. "Let's go," he whispered.

I looked back at Libby.

She nodded her head and mouthed, *It's okay*.

Colt and I stopped at Lex's door and looked at each other. I glanced back at the door, pushed it in, and walked inside. Colt followed, and he walked directly up to Lex as I held back.

He started crying. "Oh God. Oh, Alex. I'm so sorry…oh God, I'm so sorry." His body was shaking as he cried harder.

I closed my eyes and opened them again before I walked around the bed, still not looking directly at Lex. When I got to the other side of her, I took a deep breath and looked at her. My heart slammed against my chest, and a feeling I'd never experienced before washed over my body. I bit down on the inside of my cheek to keep from crying. I was afraid she could hear us. My heart had never beat so fast and so hard in my life.

I looked at her swollen face and swallowed hard. Her right eye was black and blue and three times the normal size. Her lips were busted open. The whole right side of her face was bruised. I put my hand up to my mouth and attempted to hold back the sobs wanting to come out.

Colt looked at me and shook his head. He turned and walked out of the room as I tried to regain some sort of composure.

Thirty seconds later, Libby walked in. She looked at Alex and started crying as she made her way over to me. She turned me to face her, and she wiped away her tears.

Taking in a deep breath, she whispered, "Be strong for her right now. Do you hear me, William Gregory Hayes?"

I quickly nodded my head. I somehow reached deep down inside me and pulled out the strength I needed to settle down. I would be here for Lex.

I'll be the strength she needs right now.

Taking in a deep breath, I turned back to face Lex.

I took her hand in mine. "Lex, baby, I'm here now. I promise you, Lex, you're safe. I love you so much. Please wake up for me, baby."

I needed her to hear the love in my voice. I needed her to come back to me.

37

"Lex, I love you so much. It's time to wake up now, baby."
Will...

"Alex? Baby, please wake up now. Grace brought you Emma. Oh, Alex. Please, honey, wake up."
Mom...

"Hey, baby girl. Daddy's here now, Little Bear. You're all right."
Daddy...

My face hurt. My body hurt. I just wanted to sleep, but everyone was talking to me.

Will...

I need you, Will.

Someone took my hand.

"Lex, I'm right here."

Will...

I forced my eyes to open, and the first things I saw were his beautiful blue eyes. I attempted to smile, but my entire face hurt like hell.

"Will..." I said in a raspy voice. "I hurt so bad."

He nodded his head. "I know, baby. I know." He leaned over and did something.

"Yes?" a voice answered from what sounded like an intercom right next to my ear.

"She's awake," Will said.

"Thank you, Mr. Hayes. I'll let the doctor on duty and her parents know."

I looked around. *Where am I? What happened?*

"Where am I, Will? I just remember needing you. I was so scared, and I needed you."

His eyes filled with tears. He looked away and then turned back to look at me. "You're in the hospital, Lex, and I'm here. I'll always be here for you."

The nurse came in, took all my vitals, and gave me some medicine.

"The doctor will be in shortly, Ms. Mathews." She smiled sweetly at me before turning and leaving.

I was about to ask Will something when I heard a door open, and I slowly turned my head to see my mother and father walking in. They both had fake smiles on their faces to hide their fear.

"Oh, Alex…baby, I'm so glad you're awake." My mother walked to the side of the bed and took my hand in hers.

I looked over to my father, who was standing next to my mother. "Hey, Little Bear. There's my girl. I love you, sweetheart, so very much."

Something was terribly wrong. My father only called me Little Bear when something was wrong or when he was very emotional about something.

"What happened?" I looked at them and then back to Will.

Will peeked over at my father.

"Will?" I asked.

He kept his eyes on my father. Looking back at my father, I saw he was staring at Will. They both had looks of terror on their faces. I glanced over to look at my mother.

My mother swallowed and tried to smile. "Alex, honey, don't worry. You're okay. You're just a little banged up, and they…well, you…" She turned away.

"Excuse me, Mr. and Mrs. Mathews?"

My parents turned to face a beautiful lady, probably in her mid-twenties, with shoulder-length blonde hair. She stood there, holding a file folder, and I noticed that I was having a hard time seeing. It was almost like I was looking out of only one eye. I reached up, touched my right eye, and let out an inner cry.

Holy shit. That hurts like hell.

"Hello, Janet." My mother looked back at me. "Alex, Janet is here to talk to you, sweetheart."

The blonde turned her attention to Will. "How are you doing this morning, Will?"

He smiled slightly and said, "I'm good."

Janet cleared her throat and pointed to the police officer standing next her. "This is Officer Franks."

My mother quickly nodded her head and took a step back. My father held her in his arms.

Why is a police officer here?

I attempted to smile as Janet walked closer to me. Something about her made me feel...safe and comfortable. It was like she recognized this strange feeling inside me.

"Alex, my name is Janet. I'm a counselor, and I work for the hospital. I'm here to ask you a few questions. Is that okay?"

"Hi, Janet. Um...sure," I said.

She smiled back. "Alex, do you remember anything about last night? Anything at all?"

"Um...not really. I was at a party with Grace." I closed my eyes and tried to remember.

Damn, maybe I drank too much. I must have fallen and hit my eye—

My eyes snapped open. I frantically looked around the room.

Oh God. Oh God. No...Blake.

"Blake," I whispered.

A warm sensation filled my body as Janet touched my hand.

"Alex, you're safe, sweetheart. He's not here."

I felt the tears burning my eyes, and my head began pounding. "He...he tried to...I think he gave me something...he...Oh God. He slapped me because I was fighting him back."

Janet held my hand. "Alex, sweetheart, Officer Franks would like to ask you some questions."

I nodded my head and looked back to where Will was standing.

Officer Franks cleared her throat and took a step closer to me. "Alex, I'm going to ask you some personal questions. If you prefer, I can ask everyone to leave the room."

I shook my head and whispered, "No, they can stay."

"I need to ask you something important," Officer Franks said.

I looked back at Janet. I began crying harder as the memories of last night started to come together.

"O-okay," I whispered.

"How much do you remember about last night? Specifically, about your time with Blake Turner?"

I closed my eyes.

Chrissie...

The room was spinning.

She told Blake she gave something to me.

I felt sick.

Blake carried me up the stairs.

Get Grace, Chrissie...

"I asked Chrissie to get Grace. Blake wasn't acting right, and he said…he said…"

"It's okay, Alex. Take your time," the officer said.

I opened my eyes. "He was mad about me not passing out. He ripped my shorts open and put…"

I looked at Will. I slowly turned to my parents and then to Officer Franks. Then, I looked into Janet's eyes.

"I can't…" I shook my head.

Janet looked up at Will and then back at me. She nodded her head.

Officer Franks took my hand. "It's okay, Alex. You did great. I want you to know that Blake has been arrested. Chrissie spoke to the police and confessed that she gave you a drug called Rohypnol. Blake had given it to her. You must not have had very much to drink because you were able to stay awake and fight him off."

I took in a deep breath as I remembered that I'd dropped the beer Chrissie had given me. "I only took a few drinks of it. Someone bumped into me, and I dropped it."

Janet turned around to look at my parents. I noticed my mom wiping a tear away.

"I don't want to talk about it anymore," I said as panic began to set in.

Janet walked up to my parents and said something to them. She then turned, moved next to Will, and whispered something to him. He nodded his head before turning and smiling at me.

"Lex, I'm going to go sit in the waiting room with your mom and dad." He leaned down and gently kissed me on my lips. "I love you," he whispered.

"I love you, too."

He smiled at me and walked toward my mom and dad.

My mother moved next to the bed. She leaned down and kissed me on the forehead, followed by my father.

"We love you, sweetheart. We'll just be right outside," my father said with a smile.

I tried to smile, but every time I moved, my face hurt.

The moment they walked out the door and shut it, I looked at Janet and began crying.

She sat down and took my hand. "Alex, it's okay. It's just us now, sweetheart. Whenever you're ready…you tell us."

I swallowed as I looked at Officer Franks. She smiled sweetly and nodded her head.

I took a deep breath. "Blake told Chrissie that I belonged to him, and then he told her to leave. I begged her to get Grace. Then, he put me on the bed, and he took his pants—" A sob escaped my mouth.

"Take your time, Alex. Just take in a deep breath," Janet said in a soft voice.

Somehow, I pulled out my inner strength to tell Janet and Officer Franks what had happened to me in that bedroom last night. When Officer Franks told me that Blake had punched me right as Grace walked in, my sore face made sense.

"I don't remember anything after that."

I looked down and saw Emma—the doll Grams had made for me—lying next to me. I smiled as I picked her up and held her tightly.

"Alex, you might want to talk to someone once you're out of the hospital," Officer Franks said.

"What do you mean...talk to someone?" I asked.

"About what happened. Janet can help you with that." Officer Franks looked at Janet. "Janet, I've got enough for now." She looked back at me. "Alex, if we need any additional information, we will be in touch with you, okay? For now, I think we've gotten a good statement from you."

I nodded my head and looked out the window. "What will happen to him?"

Officer Franks cleared her throat. "With your statement, Chrissie Weaver's confession, and what Grace Johnson and Mr. Weaver witnessed, Blake will be charged with aggravated sexual assault."

I snapped my head back to her. "But he didn't...he didn't..."

She nodded her head. "I know he didn't. But Texas laws can move it up it from attempted to aggravated because he used Rohypnol, and it was thought out ahead of time."

Deep down inside, I was glad. I wanted to see Blake rot in jail. "Oh...okay," I whispered as I looked back out the window.

Janet and Officer Franks talked for a couple of minutes. After Officer Franks left, Janet sat down in a nearby chair.

"Alex, you were sexually assaulted. He touched you without your consent. You should talk to someone about it. You can't deal with this on your own."

I didn't look at her as I said, "Can I talk to you?"

She reached for my hand. "If that's what you want."

I slowly nodded as I felt a tear moving down my face. "Yes," I whispered as I closed my eyes.

I felt sleep beginning to take over. I hadn't realized how tired I was. *Will...I'm so sorry. I didn't fight hard enough.*

38
WILL

I glanced over to Lex as she stared out the passenger window. The whole way from Austin to Mason, she didn't utter a single word.

I thought back to my conversation with Janet.

"What do I need to do for Lex?"

Janet smiled. "Just be there for her, Will. She's most likely going to withdraw a bit. Even though Blake didn't rape her, he still violated her in more than one way. Be patient with her, love her, and don't push her, but don't let her push you away either."

I nodded my head. "I love her so much. I just want to take away her pain."

Janet grinned. "I know you do. I've talked to Mr. and Mrs. Mathews. Alex has seemed to develop a trust with me. Will, I've been in Alex's shoes, except I was raped. I think she feels that I know what she is going through. I'll do whatever I can to help her and her family."

My heart instantly hurt for Janet. "I'm so sorry, Janet."

She smiled back and shook her head. "I will help Alex through this, Will. I promise you."

I pulled up and parked behind Gunner's truck. Grace and Luke were heading to Austin today to pick up all of Grace's and Lex's things. Then, Luke was going to drive Lex's car back to Mason.

I reached over and touched Lex's arm, and she jumped. I quickly pulled my hand away as I felt the pain piercing my heart.

"I'm sorry. I didn't mean to scare you, Lex."

She turned and gave me a weak smile. "It's okay."

I returned her smile. "Let me get your door."

I jumped out of the truck and jogged to her side. I opened the door and held my hand out for her. She was gripping her doll, Emma, tightly. She got out of the truck and began walking toward the back of the house.

"Um…Lex? Where are you going?"

Gunner and Ellie both walked out onto the front porch.

"Alex? Honey, where are you headed off to?" Ellie asked.

Lex didn't bother to look over at her parents. "I'm going to see Banjo. I just need some time alone, if y'all don't mind."

I just stood there. I felt hopelessly lost as to what to do for Lex. Janet's words kept playing over and over in my mind.

Don't push her.

I watched as Lex made her way down to the barn. When I felt a hand on my shoulder, I turned to see Gunner.

"I don't know what to do. I feel like…like she doesn't want me around. She didn't talk to me at all the whole way here, and when I touched her arm, she…she pulled away from me." I could feel the tears in my eyes building, and the last thing I wanted to do was cry in front of Gunner.

He gripped my shoulder tightly as he nodded his head. "Come on, I've got some work to do on a fence. You can help me." Gunner turned to Ellie. "Give her some time and then check on her."

Ellie wiped a tear away and nodded her head.

Gunner slapped my back and headed toward his truck. I looked back toward the barn one more time, but Lex was gone. I walked to the truck and got in. Neither one of us said a word as we drove to the east pasture of the ranch. I leaned my head back and closed my eyes.

I wanted to scream. I wanted to hurt someone.

Blake.

I wanted to hurt Blake. I let out a long sigh.

Gunner cleared his throat. "When we were younger, Ellie was in a car accident, and it was during a time when we weren't together."

I snapped my head over to Gunner. "Did y'all break up or something?"

He smiled and nodded his head. "It was a misunderstanding, but yes, we were broken up for a bit. Anyway, she was trying to get to me when she had the accident. I remember sitting by her bedside for hours and hours, just praying she would be okay. I'd never felt so helpless in my life."

That was how I was feeling right now. I looked out the front window.

"I know you feel the same way, Will. I know you want to take the pain away. Hell, the whole thing away. I'm feeling the same way. The restraint it is taking for me not to beat the fuck out of that little asshole is something I'm working on every day."

I smiled as I turned to look at Gunner.

He glanced at me and winked. "You're lucky. At least you and Colt got to get a hit in on the little prick."

I nodded my head and chuckled sarcastically. "It wasn't enough, sir. I wanted to kill him. I still want to, but…but I'm more worried about Lex. I can almost feel her pulling away from me, if that makes sense."

Gunner parked his truck behind Jeff's truck. "It makes sense."

We both jumped out of the truck, and that was when I noticed my father, Jeff, Colt, and Luke standing against Colt's truck.

I walked up to Jeff and shook his hand and then my father's. Colt and Luke both walked up and gave me what the girls would call our bro hug.

"Boys, we wanted to talk to you about Alex—especially you, Will." My father gave me a weak smile.

"What about, sir?" I asked.

Jeff cleared his throat as he looked at Luke. "Before you were born, Luke, your mother and I were expecting a baby. I know we've told you this along with the meaning behind your sister's name before."

Luke nodded his head. "Yes, sir, I remember."

"What you don't know is, that day, I walked away from your mother to go to another woman. It's not what you think. It's a long story, and honestly, it's not one worth repeating. The point is, I left your mother…alone. I didn't even know she was pregnant. She was upset, and she got on a horse to go riding with Ellie and Heather. Ari's horse got spooked and threw her."

Luke looked down and shook his head.

"By the time I found out what had happened, I rushed to the hospital. I still didn't know your mother was pregnant. For all of about two minutes, I was happy as hell because she was okay. Then, she told me she lost the baby, and I was living in hell. I hadn't been there for her, and to this day, I've never really forgiven myself for the pain and hurt I caused her."

Jeff turned and looked at me. "You didn't cause Alex's pain, but I see on your face how you blame yourself. Will, you couldn't have helped her any faster than you did."

I nodded my head and wiped away a tear.

"Ari slowly began pulling away from me…from everyone. I let it happen because I didn't know what else to do. I figured she needed time…maybe she needed to hate me for a bit…to blame me. I just didn't know. Boys, Alex is going to pull away. I know how the three of you fiercely look after each of these girls. You'll have to give Alex space though, but *don't* let her push any of you away."

"Dad, how do we know if we are pushing her or not?" Luke asked.

Jeff shook his head. "Son, I don't know how to answer that."

Colt kicked a rock. "How did you and Ari come back together?"

Jeff smiled as he looked at Gunner and then my father. "One day, I just decided I wanted my girl back. I was tired of just sitting back, so I didn't let her push anymore, and she pushed like hell for me to leave her alone, but I stood my ground." He smiled and looked at Luke. "Your mother and I firmly believe that on the day she came back to me, we made another life."

Luke smiled as his face blushed.

"You see, boys, I know y'all look at us and think you want the perfect relationship that you see with your own parents. I've overheard y'all talking about it. Just know that some beautiful sunsets have had rainstorms that came before it, but the rain only makes the sunset that more beautiful."

"Dad?" Colt asked.

"Yes, son?" Gunner said.

"My heart hurts so bad for Alex." Colt was beginning to get choked up.

I had to fight to hold back my tears. I was pretty sure Luke was feeling the same, but there was no way I was going to look at him.

"I know, son, I know. As do all of our hearts. Just watch over her this summer, boys. Show her how much you love and care about her. Just be there for her if she needs you. And know that none of you could have protected her from this. Don't let guilt play a hand in this, boys. You can't be with the girls twenty-four/seven."

Each of us nodded. My father walked up to me, pulled me into his arms, and held me. I couldn't hold it in any longer. I let go of the anger, fear, and guilt that had been building the last couple of days.

"I love her, Dad. I love her so much," I cried out.

He held me tighter. "I know you do, Will."

"Oh God, Dad...why? Why did this happen to her? Why?" I no longer cared what Luke or Colt might think. I cried out as my father held me.

The next thing I knew, Gunner had his arms around me. I wasn't sure how long the three of us stood there, but I finally regained some composure. When I pulled away, I saw both my father and Gunner wiping their tears away.

I knew what I had to do, and I needed to do it right now. "Gunner, sir, may I speak with you alone?"

Gunner looked at me, surprised, but he nodded his head. I looked back at Luke and Colt, and they both smiled. Luke and Libby had both asked me why I said I was Lex's fiancé. I'd told them that Lex and I were secretly engaged. Then, I'd told Colt, Lauren, Meagan, Grace, and Taylor. I was sure Colt and Luke knew what I was about to do now.

Gunner walked a ways away and leaned up against a fence. He looked at me as I gathered up the courage to ask him the one thing I'd been dreaming of asking for a few years now.

I cleared my throat, took a deep breath, and looked Gunner in the eyes. "I'd like to ask Lex to marry me, sir. It wouldn't be anytime soon. I know she has a lot to deal with, but I want nothing more than to make her my wife. I'd like your blessing, sir."

Gunner didn't do anything at first. I silently prayed to God that my life wouldn't end here, in the east pasture, at the hands of Gunner Mathews. I held my gaze and didn't back down. I loved Lex, and I wasn't going to walk away from her—not now, not ever.

Gunner slowly let a smile move across his face. Finally, his full crooked smile appeared, and he let out a small chuckle. "William Gregory Hayes, do you have any idea that you just proved what type of man you are?"

My mouth dropped open. Anytime my parents used my full name, my ass would be in trouble, so I wasn't sure how to read this situation.

"Um...no, sir, I guess I don't. Truth be told, your smile used along with my full name has me all kinds of confused."

Gunner threw his head back and laughed. When he looked back at me, he shook his head. "Will, after what happened to Alex, not very many guys would stick around—let alone, ask her father for her hand in marriage. I'm proud of you, Will. I'm proud that you never once backed down when I pushed you and Alex for a break, that you never gave up on the one thing you loved. It shows the man you've become. Your daddy and mama have done a fine job in raising you, Will."

Gunner smiled as he reached his hand out for mine and shook it. "Will, I'd be honored to have you ask Alex to marry you, and I'd be even more honored to call you my son-in-law—after y'all graduate from college and Alex starts her career, and not a second before then."

I smiled, and the sense of relief washing over my body was unreal.

"When are you planning on asking her?" Gunner's face became a bit more serious.

"I wanted to ask her this summer, but I know she has so much going through her head right now. Even though we've talked about it, I think it is best if I wait for a bit."

Gunner nodded his head. "I agree. Thank you for taking her feelings into account, Will."

"Always, sir. I love Lex more than anything. I'll spend every day of my life loving her and protecting her the best I can, sir."

Gunner pushed off the fence, grabbed me, and pulled me in for a hug. "Jesus, it was just yesterday when you were riding on top of my shoulders, telling me you wanted to be a rancher."

He slapped my back hard—probably harder than he needed to—before he pushed back and winked at me. "Now, was that so hard, Will?" He turned and walked toward Jeff and my father.

I stood there, stunned. "I'll never understand that man—ever," I whispered.

I walked up to Luke and Colt, who both held out their hands to shake mine. I felt happy for a few minutes until we all began working on repairing the fence.

My mind kept going back to Lex and how sad she had sounded while walking toward the barn.

I just need some time alone.

I closed my eyes. *God, please don't let her slip away from me. Please.*

39

My phone buzzed in my back pocket, and I pulled it out. My heart skipped a beat when I saw it was a text from Will.

> *Will: Hey, sweetheart. Would you like to go to dinner and a movie tonight?*

Yesterday, I had gone to talk with Janet about my fear of giving myself to Will. I felt dirty, thinking what I shared with Will had been tarnished, and I was so afraid Will would look at me differently now.

It had been three weeks since I came home from the hospital. I'd managed to keep myself surrounded with a lot of people, or I'd spend time alone with Banjo. Will and I had been alone only twice. Both times, I'd panicked for some reason. I wasn't sure why. When I'd asked Janet, she'd helped me to understand my thoughts. I was so afraid of what Will thought of me now that I kept pushing our relationship aside. She told me how important it was for me to talk to Will about my feelings. I just couldn't. Not yet.

Will had been so patient, but last night, he'd told me he was ready to have some alone time to reconnect. It hurt my heart so much to know I was hurting him. I closed my eyes and decided I was ready to be with Will again. I needed him even though I was just so afraid.

> *Me: How about a picnic at the clubhouse with just you and me?*

> *Will: I'd love that, Lex. I'll take care of everything. Pick you up at seven?*

> *Me: Perfect. Will, I love you.*

> *Will: I love you more, Lex.*

I smiled as I tucked my phone away.

"That smile must mean you were talking to my brother?" Libby raised her eyebrows and smiled at me.

"Yep. He wanted to go to dinner and a movie, but I mentioned a picnic at the clubhouse with just us."

Libby's smile faded one second before she smiled again. "That sounds amazing, Alex. Y'all deserve some time together."

Grace walked back into her room and sat down on the bed.

"What's wrong, Grace? You look like someone just shot your horse," Libby said with a giggle.

Grace let out a gasp. "Bite your tongue, bitch. How could you say such a thing?"

I laughed as I went back to flipping through a book I had picked up from the library.

"So, what's bugging you, Grace?" I asked.

"Nothing."

Libby tossed a pillow at Grace. "Bitch, please. You haven't been yourself ever since that night you came back from your fling during spring break."

I sat up as my mouth dropped to the floor. "What? What fling? You had a fling? Oh. My. God. You had a fling, and you didn't tell me. What the hell, Grace? We're best friends."

Grace glared at Libby.

Libby shrugged her shoulders. "Sorry. I thought for sure that Alex knew about it."

I shook my head. "No, *Alex* didn't know anything about it. Grace Johnson, spill the beans right now."

Grace looked at me, then Libby, and then back to me. "It's not a big deal. It was nothing, and I haven't been acting differently since spring break. You've only been around me three weeks, Libby! Have you noticed a difference, Alex?"

"Um…no, not really. Well, you do stare off into space a lot, like you're thinking hard. But I want to know about the fling!" I moved to my knees and started hopping. I was just glad the conversation was not about me.

Grace laughed and pushed me over.

"Come on, Grace. Tell her about hot Noah," Libby said with a wink.

I stopped jumping. "Noah? Isn't that the name of the guy who bumped into you at A&M? It was Noah, right?"

"Yes!" Libby said as Grace answered at the same time, "No!"

Libby looked confused. "Grace, you two did so know each other. He said he was glad he didn't knock you down this time."

Again, my mouth was hanging open. "You had sex…with the hot A&M guy? How in the hell did you manage that?"

Libby giggled.

Grace began moving about nervously. "It's not a big deal. I don't want to rehash it. It's over."

Libby's smile faded.

I reached for Grace's arm. "Grace, did he hurt you or something?"

Grace rolled her eyes. "No! God, no. He was actually a great fuck. That's all he was though." She got up, headed over to her desk, and sat down. She opened up the laptop and began searching on the Internet.

Libby and I looked at each other.

I wasn't sure if I should push for more info or not. "Well, can I ask if you knew he was going to be there?"

Without turning to face me, she said, "Nope, I had no clue."

"So, y'all just bumped into each other again and decided to, as you call it, fuck?"

She turned and looked at me, and I swore she had tears in her eyes.

"Yes, Alex. We exchanged numbers on the beach. I wanted to get laid, and he wanted to get laid, so it all worked out perfectly. We fucked, and when we were done, I got up and left. End of story." She turned back and began typing an email.

There was more to the story than Grace was letting on.

Libby stood up and walked over to Grace. "Grace, do you want to talk about it?"

Grace spun around in her chair and smiled at us. "No. Really, y'all, it's not a big deal. Please, can we move on?"

Libby and I both said, "Okay," as we looked at each other.

I glanced back up to Grace and made a mental note to talk to her alone later.

I pulled up and parked behind Will's truck. Instead of having Will pick me up, I had decided to just meet him at the clubhouse. I took a deep breath as I opened the car door and got out. I walked up to the clubhouse door.

Right before I reached it, Will opened it. "Hey, beautiful."

My heart skipped a beat, and my stomach dropped at the sight of him. I loved him so much, but I knew I had been pushing him away. I couldn't deal with the fact that he knew Blake had touched me. Lying in bed at night, I would wonder if Will thought any different of me.

He reached for my hand, and I began to panic. We were going to be alone in the clubhouse. Will would surely want to make love.

Am I ready?

Yes.

No.

I closed my eyes, and I took in a slow deep breath. I gently blew it out as I opened my eyes and took a step toward Will. He took my hand and led me through the door. When I walked in, I sucked in a breath of air. White lights were draped across the ceiling, and a few candles were lit. On the floor, a picnic basket and a bucket with a huge bottle of water were sitting on a blanket.

I giggled as I looked at Will. "Water?"

He smiled the smile that took my breath away as he nodded. "Yep. Since we're both driving this evening, I thought it would be best to play it safe."

I shook my head and walked over to the blanket.

"Sit down, Lex."

I sank down to the floor as I watched Will move about, taking care of a few other things. He finally sat down and picked up a remote. He pressed a button, and Colbie Caillat's "Stay with Me" began playing. I smiled as Will gave me his panty-melting smile back.

My heart started beating faster, and I began chewing on my lower lip to calm my nerves.

What if he goes to kiss me and then thinks of Blake's hands on my body?

"My mom made her famous hummus that you love so much," Will said as he began taking food out of the basket.

We're just eating. That's all. Just eating.

Will and I ate and talked about simple things—what Will was helping my father with on the ranch this summer and how him and his dad were making some office furniture for a lawyer in Austin.

"So, your dad said you've been riding Banjo a lot," Will said with a smile.

I grinned back. Something about my horse always kept me calm. I would feel safe when I was with Banjo.

"Yeah, I've missed him a lot this past year. I'm thinking of taking him to A&M next year."

"That would be awesome, Lex."

I smiled and nodded my head as Will began cleaning up.

Once he finished, he reached down for my hand. "Dance with me, Lex?"

"Still Fallin'" by Hunter Hayes began playing. I stood up and let Will pull me into his arms. We danced for a few minutes, and I felt so safe in his arms.

"I love you, Lex," he whispered before kissing my neck.

His hot breath did things to my body, and I let out a small moan.

I need him. I need his touch.

"Lex, I want you."

My mind was going in a million different directions. As much as I wanted to be with him, I was afraid of what he would think of me. I knew that he knew what Blake had done to me.

"Will…" I whispered.

He reached down and picked me up. He carried me to the bed, and he gently laid me down on it as I attempted to push my fears away.

"Lex, I'm going to make love to you."

I closed my eyes as I felt him unbutton my shorts. I lifted my hips as he began to pull my shorts and panties off.

"So perfect and beautiful," he said.

My eyes snapped open, and I looked at him admiring my body.

I'm not perfect. I'm tainted. He touched me. He violated me.

Will gently spread my legs apart.

The moment he touched me, I screamed out, "Stop! I can't! I can't!" I instantly began crying.

Will jumped off the bed and away from me. I frantically began searching for my shorts and panties. I slipped them on as Will just stood there.

"Lex, I didn't mean to push you into…I mean, I thought you wanted me to…I thought that's why you wanted to come here."

I wiped my tears away and grabbed my keys. "I just need time."

I turned to open the door when Will grabbed my arm.

"Lex, stop pushing me away. Why are you pushing me away?"

My head was spinning, and all I could see was Blake's body over mine as he reached his hand inside my pants.

Oh God, make it go away.

I swallowed hard. "I'm…I'm no good for you, Will."

His mouth dropped open. "What? Lex, what in the hell do you mean? You're my everything. You mean the world to me."

I shook my head and pushed him away from me. "No, he ruined it."

Will used his hand to shut the door. "He ruined what, Lex? Please talk to me, baby. Please tell me what you're thinking."

I knew the only way Will would let me go was if I told him he was scaring me. In my heart, I knew Will would never hurt me, but I wasn't ready to talk about this with him.

I looked him in the eyes. "You're scaring me."

Will immediately dropped his hand from the door and took a few steps back. The look in his eyes and on his face gutted me. I never wanted him to think I was afraid of him.

"Lex, I would never…" His eyes began to fill with tears.

I wanted to tell him that I didn't mean what I'd just said. I went to say something, but he turned and picked up his truck keys. He came back to the door and reached around me to leave the clubhouse. I stood there, not knowing what to do. I'd just hurt the only person I ever loved.

He began walking to his truck.

Say something, Alex.

"Will! Will, please wait," I said as I began running to him.

He jumped into his truck. "The last thing I'd ever want to do is scare you."

I shook my head. "No, no, Will. I just didn't want—"

"I get it, Lex. You need time. I'll leave you alone for a bit."

I started crying harder. "Will…I didn't mean that."

"I saw it in your eyes." He threw his truck into drive and started driving off.

I stood there, alone.

I'm all alone.

I don't like being alone.

"Will…"

WILL

"Motherfucker!" I shouted.

Luke and Colt laughed.

Colt said, "Don't take it out on the fence, dude."

I threw the fence pullers and cursed again. "Fuck this shit."

"Y'all want to call it a day? The barn dance is tonight. I'd like to head home to shower and get ready," Colt said with a smile.

"Why are you so happy?" Luke asked.

Colt shrugged his shoulders. "I don't know. I just want to dance and have a little bit of fun."

Luke turned to me. "Have you talked to Alex yet?"

I shook my head.

Colt let out a sigh. "Will, Alex cried her eyes out the other day when she came home. What happened? My parents tried to get her to talk to them, but she wouldn't."

"She pushed me away again. I tried to get her to talk to me, and she told me…she told me…" My voice cracked.

Colt and Luke both stood there, waiting for me to finish.

"She told you what?" Luke asked.

I looked down to the ground. "She told me I was scaring her."

"What?" Colt and Luke both said.

"What in the hell were you doing?" Colt asked.

I looked into his eyes. "I put my hand on the door, so she couldn't open it and leave. I was asking her to please talk to me, and that was when she…she, um…she said I was scaring her."

"Will, you need to understand that she probably didn't mean it like that," Luke said.

I snapped my head over to look at Luke. "How in the hell could I have misread that? She said I was scaring her, Luke. Her eyes were filled with something I'd never seen before. She was afraid I was going to hurt her. She said that he ruined it. I asked her what she meant, and she just freaked."

Colt pushed his hands through his hair and then sighed. "She must have been talking about Blake. Do you think maybe she just said you were scaring her because she didn't want to talk about Blake?"

"I don't know. I don't know anything anymore. All I know is, the girl I love is afraid to be touched by me."

Colt shook his head. "No, Will, I don't think that's it. Listen, I went and talked to Janet. I wanted to talk to someone who had been through something like what Alex had. Janet told me she felt dirty for months, like she was unworthy of anyone's love. Just because Blake didn't rape Alex doesn't mean she doesn't feel the same way. He touched her, and by the comment he made to us…" Colt balled up his fists and took a deep breath. "By the comment he made, I'm going to guess he managed to get his hands down her pants. If he touched her, that could make Alex feel the same way."

Luke said, "That makes sense, Will. She said he ruined it. You and Lex have only been with each other. You have a perfect and, for lack of a better word, clean relationship. You've only been with each other. By another guy touching her, she's probably worried about how that makes you feel."

I stared at Luke and then looked at Colt. "Do you think that's what it is?"

They both nodded.

"I mean, I'm no expert by any means, but after talking to Janet, I really learned a lot. Alex's control was taken away. Blake tried to take something that, in Alex's mind, only belongs to you, Will. Blake tainted that."

"Do you know if she'll be at the barn dance?" I asked.

"You haven't talked to her?" Luke asked.

I felt the guilt instantly overtake my body. "No, not in three days. I told her I would leave her alone for a bit."

"That's the last thing she needs, Will," Colt said.

I nodded my head. "Yeah, I fucked up big time."

Luke started laughing. "Yes, you did, and that means a visit to Gramps. He'll tell you how to fix it."

I started heading toward my truck.

"Where are you going?" Colt called out.

"To see Gramps. Just make sure Lex is there tonight, Colt!" I yelled as I started running.

I sat down as Grams handed me a sweet tea. Gramps sat across from me as he smiled at me. Grams sat down next to him and took his hand.

I inhaled in a deep breath through my nose and blew it out through my mouth. "I'm just going to say it. I messed up with Lex. I don't know what to do. I acted like an idiot, and I thought she was pushing me away, but I think I'm the one who pushed her away. I don't know how to make it right." Once I'd gotten it all out, I felt a little better.

"Sounds to me like you need a song," Gramps said.

I looked at him as Grams started chuckling.

"Excuse me, boys, I need to get ready for my walk," Grams said.

Gramps and I both stood up as Grams stood and walked out of the room.

When we sat down, Gramps said, "Mr. Nat King Cole."

I smiled. "The same song my dad plays when my mother is mad at him? That old song?"

"Son, that song might be old, but I promise you, it is magic. It's called 'Send for Me.'"

"So, do I sing it to her or something while we dance?"

Gramps just looked at me. "Let me hear you sing a couple of bars of something."

"Uh…okay." I started to sing a country song.

Gramps held up his hand. "Oh, hell no. Don't sing, boy. Let Nat do all the swooning."

I let out a chuckle. "I take it that you don't think I sing very good."

Gramps dropped his hand. "I wouldn't call that singing—at all."

I held up my hands. "Fine, fine. I never claimed to be a singer."

The front door opened, and I heard her sweet voice.

"Grams? Gramps?"

I looked back at Gramps. My heart started racing at an unbelievable pace.

Lex came walking around the corner and stopped dead in her tracks. "Will? What are you doing here?"

"The boy came to talk to me. I take it you and Emma are going on a walk?" Gramps asked.

Lex pulled her eyes from me to look at Gramps. "Um…yes."

Grams walked up and put her arm around Lex. "Shall we go, sweetheart?"

Lex smiled at Grams and then looked at me. When I smiled and winked at her, her face seemed to instantly relax.

"I'll see you at the dance tonight, Lex?"

Her smile grew bigger on her face. "I'll be there."

I glanced down and saw her rubbing the promise ring. I looked back up into her eyes. Her spark still wasn't there, but I was going to do everything in my power to get it back.

Grams and Lex headed out the door. I turned and looked back to Gramps.

"She loves you. Don't give up on her," Gramps said as he stood up and walked over to me.

"I love her, too, Gramps, more than anything. Life without Lex is not an option."

Gramps laughed. "That's my boy. Now, come on. Let's go play a game of dominos."

I chuckled and followed him. We sat down at the kitchen table, and as he took out a deck of playing cards, he looked me in the eyes and grinned. His blue eyes had fire in them as he tilted his head.

"I thought we were playing dominos," I said.

Gramps smiled and winked. "William, be prepared to get your ass kicked in poker. How much money do you have on you?"

"Um…what happened to dominos?"

Gramps started shuffling the deck of cards. "Oh, that was just in case Emma was still outside. Come on, son, put your money down."

I laughed as I reached for my wallet, and I threw a twenty down. Gramps looked up at me and frowned. I pulled another twenty out.

He winked. "Let's do this."

The moment he won the first hand, I knew I had just lost my forty bucks.

alex

As we walked up to Mr. Banks's barn, Grace and Maegan wouldn't stop arguing. Mr. Banks had been letting us use his barn for barn dances since I could remember.

I finally stopped and spun around to face them. "Shut the fuck up. I can't take it anymore. Maegan, stop acting like such a bitch. If you wanted to wear something different, you should have put the damn thing on in the first place. Grace, stop egging her on. My God, the two of you are acting like you're in middle school."

Maegan's mouth dropped open, and Grace smiled at me.

"It's about damn time Alex Mathews showed back up." Grace blew me a kiss and walked by me.

Maegan continued to just stare at me before she finally said, "Fine, I'll be happy with what I'm wearing. There's no one in this damn town I want to impress anyway. Nothing but a bunch of country bumpkins are here."

Maegan walked by me as Lauren, Libby, and Taylor all started laughing.

"Ten bucks says she walks out with a guy," Taylor said to Libby.

"Taylor, that's your sister," Libby said with a giggle.

"Please, you just don't want to take the bet 'cause you know I'm right."

We all started laughing as we walked in. Libby stopped and stared out onto the dance floor. I followed her gaze to see Luke dancing with Claire.

Ugh, that girl is a pain in the ass.

I glanced around and saw Will. He was dancing with some girl I'd never seen before. It wasn't a slow song, so they were just two-stepping. As he kept spinning her around to Dustin Lynch's "Where It's At," she was laughing. It seemed like they knew each other well.

"Who is Will dancing with?" I asked Libby.

She pulled her eyes from Luke and looked at Will. She smiled and said, "That's our second cousin, Trish. She is my mom's cousin's daughter. This is her first time in Texas. Will spent all day yesterday teaching her how to two-step. Her dad is in the military. She's been in Alaska for the last five years."

Will and Libby had gone to Alaska once to visit someone on their mom's side of the family.

"Don't worry, Lex. That boy only has eyes for you." Libby bumped my shoulder.

Will looked over and saw us watching him. He stopped dancing and whispered something into Trish's ear. She smiled and nodded, and then they began walking toward us.

Will stopped in front of me, and his smile melted my heart. For the first time in a month, my body craved something more.

"Lex, this is my cousin, Trish. Trish, this is Lex," Will said.

She held her hand out and smiled big. "I've heard nothing but wonderful things about you. Will hasn't stopped talking about you since we got here two days ago."

I reached out for her hand and shook it. "It's a pleasure to meet you."

Trish looked back at Will and hit him in the stomach. "You didn't tell me she was drop-dead gorgeous."

I felt my cheeks blush as Will grinned bigger.

"You want something to drink, Lex?" Will asked.

Panic set in.

Stop this, Alex. It's Will.

"Bottle of water if they have it."

Will frowned, but then he smiled. "You got it, sweetheart."

Grace walked up and started talking with Libby and Trish. I watched as Will walked over to a bunch of coolers. He opened each cooler, looking for water.

Claire walked up to Will and put her hand on his arm. She leaned in close and said something to him. Will shook his head as he dug through the cooler. She leaned in further and whispered into his ear. He stopped what he was doing and looked at her. I couldn't tell what he said to her, but she put her finger in mouth and pouted.

Oh no, she didn't! That little tramp.

Will shook his head again and went back to digging in the cooler. Claire shrugged her shoulders and began walking away.

"I'll be right back!" I shouted to Grace.

"Where are you going?"

I turned and looked at her as I smiled. "To set Claire straight once and for all."

Grace gave me a big smile and winked. "Go get her."

I made my way across the makeshift dance floor. Claire was now trying to put the moves on Luke, and he was pushing her away from him. I placed my hand on her shoulder and spun her around.

"What the—" Claire looked at me and gave me a fake smile. "Alex, gesh, I thought you were someone else."

"Who, Claire? Another girl whose boyfriend you've either slept with or hit on tonight?"

Her mouth dropped open. "Excuse me?"

I took a few steps closer to her and began poking my index finger in her chest. "Listen to me, and listen good. Will. Is. Mine. You so much as look his way again, and I'll beat your ass from here to China. Luke is taken, too. So, bitch, just back the fuck off."

Claire swallowed hard and looked at Luke. I peeked over to him, and he smiled and nodded.

"Um…sorry, Alex. I was just asking Will to dance, that's all."

"Why don't you focus on the guys who don't have girlfriends?"

She pushed my hand away. "I'm leaving. I don't need this shit."

I picked up my hand and waved my fingers good-bye in her face. "See ya."

She pushed past me and headed out of the barn to leave.

"Damn, little cousin. Where in the hell did that come from?" Luke grabbed me and pulled me in for a hug.

"I guess I got tired of hiding inside my own body."

Luke looked at me and grinned. "Welcome back, Alex."

"It feels good to be back. Hey, Luke?"

"Yeah?"

"Did Will tell you that Libby left Zack?"

Luke's smile vanished. "Um…yeah, he did."

"Stop hiding inside yourself, Luke. She's not going to wait forever."

He looked up and across the barn to Libby. "I know."

I turned and made my way back over to Grace and Libby. Grace was laughing, and Libby was smiling.

Libby looked over at me and laughed. "What in the world did you say to Claire? She stormed out of here."

"I told her to stay away from Will and Luke."

Grace shook her head. "That's it?"

"I might have hinted at her being a whore in a roundabout way."

Libby and Grace both started laughing. Grace handed me a bottle of water.

I looked around for Will. "Where did Will go?"

"He said he had to go take care of something," Libby said with a sly smile.

The moment he walked up behind me, I felt him. I turned to see Will standing there with the most gorgeous smile on his face. My heart skipped a beat.

I never want to live my life without Will in it.

Before the next song, the DJ got everyone's attention. I pulled my eyes off of Will and looked over to the DJ.

"Hey, y'all. This next song goes out to one very special girl. Lex, this song is dedicated to you from Will."

I looked back at Will and tilted my head as I raised my eyebrow. The moment I heard those familiar notes play, I started laughing. Will reached for my hand and led me to the dance floor. He pulled me into his arms, and we instantly became one. He moved me across the makeshift dance floor, and I felt like I was floating on air.

"Gramps?" I asked.

Will through his head back and laughed. He looked back at me. "I'm learning from the best."

"Damn straight you are!" I said with a laugh.

Will and I danced to Nat King Cole's "Send for Me."

"You know, this is the song my dad plays for my mother after he has messed up," I said.

Will pulled me closer. "Oh, I know. My dad plays the same song, and my mother melts. Is it working?"

I giggled. "Am I melting? Or is it working?"

"Both!"

"You don't have anything to apologize for. I do. I didn't mean to push you away, Will. I love you, and I just wasn't ready to talk yet."

Will spun me around, and everyone started to shout out our names as we continued to dance it up on the dance floor.

The song ended, and One Direction's "You & I" began playing.

Will smiled. "Something hit me so hard these last few days. It was the same feeling that I had last fall when we were apart."

"What was it?" I asked.

Will shook his head slightly. "I never, for the rest of my life, Lex, want to be without you."

The tears began building in my eyes. I bit down on my lower lip in an attempt to hold my emotions back. A small sob escaped my lips as I whispered, "That's not even an option."

Gently placing his hands on the sides of my face, Will wiped my tears away with his thumbs. "I love you, Alexandra Eryn Mathews. I love you so much."

I placed my hands on his arms as I looked into his sea-blue eyes. "I love you, William Gregory Hayes, more."

He chuckled, and then he leaned down and began kissing me. This kiss was the one thing I needed to help me see that our love was stronger than anything Blake had done to me.

Will loved me, and I loved him. Our love was and would always be…perfect.

WILL

Lex and I stood at the bow of the ferry as we made our way over to Port Aransas. I was surprised all our parents had been open to the idea of us coming down for our own celebration. Colt, Lauren, and Taylor had graduated, and this was how we all wanted to spend our last summer together. While the rest of us were heading to A&M, Maegan would be going back to Baylor, and Taylor would be attending UT.

"I can't believe how fast this summer is going," Lex said.

I watched her beautiful brown hair whip around from the wind. She finally got tired of it and reached for my baseball cap. She pulled her hair through the hole in the back and made a ponytail as she pulled the cap down over her eyes.

God, I can't believe she's mine.

"I know. It is going by fast."

I looked back to the cars—or trucks really. Luke, Colt, and I had all brought our trucks, and the girls had ridden down with us. I had been shocked that Libby ended up riding with Luke. Luke had intended on leaving for the whole summer, but after Lex's incident, he'd stayed. He'd avoided Libby pretty much the first month of summer, but that had changed after the barn dance a few weeks ago. At least now, they could be in the same room and apparently the same car together.

I looked back at Lex. "Have you talked to Libby about Luke?"

She turned and looked at Luke's truck. Luke, Lauren, and Libby were all laughing about something.

"She said they're talking, but it's nothing like what Libby wants. Luke is keeping a safe distance from her. I'm hoping things will change for them this week." She smiled and wiggled her eyebrows up and down. "If you know what I mean."

I scrunched my nose up and made a face. "Oh shit, too much, Lex. Yuck. That's my sister, ya know."

Lex started laughing as we headed back to my truck since the ferry was about to dock.

After getting in the truck, I grabbed Lex's hand. "You ready to have an amazing week?"

Lex smiled so sweetly that I almost had to catch my breath.

"Yes! I have a feeling this week is going to change a lot of things. It's going to be beyond amazing."

A few minutes later, we were pulling up to the beach house. The sea-blue color of the house always made me smile. Even as a kid, when we would come to the beach, I loved the color of the house. I stood there and stared at it until I felt someone slap me on the back.

"A lot of damn good memories in this house." Luke looked at the house.

"Sure is."

He turned and smiled. "Hell of a lot more will be made in the following week, no doubt."

I glanced at him and smiled before looking at Lex. She was talking to Grace about what to do first.

"Beach or pool?" Grace asked.

"Beach!" Lex said.

They both darted toward the front door.

I glanced back at Luke. "Do you think she knows? I mean, everyone else does, and I'm surprised Grace has kept it a secret."

Luke laughed.

Lauren walked up. "She's clueless. Grace has actually done a very good job at making it seem like nothing special is going on. I don't think Alex has any idea."

"Good." I kissed Lauren on the cheek. "Keep her distracted."

Lauren smiled. "Oh, I will. Now, my ass is going to get some sun on the beach."

Luke and I smiled as we watched Lauren skip away.

"Do you think she has any clue how damn adorable she is?" Luke asked.

"Nope," Colt and I both said at once.

Colt was walking by, carrying four pieces of luggage.

"Why the hell do these girls pack so much shit?" Colt said.

"Dude, that is one of many questions about women I'd like to have answered." Luke picked up three suitcases and followed Colt.

We walked into the beach house that my parents had bought when Libby and I were about four. Gunner and Ellie had built the house on our right, and Jeff and Ari had built the house on the other side.

I smiled as I looked around. My mother had the house decorated in what she called a beach-shabby chic style. It was mostly whites and blues. The walls were large pieces of plank wood that had been painted white. The floors were all stained, and the furniture was either mostly blues or leather.

The two-story house had four bedrooms and four bathrooms along with a small poolside house that could sleep two people.

The girls had already decided who was bunking with whom. Lex and I would get one room. Grace and Libby were in another room. Lauren, Taylor, and Maegan were sharing a room. Luke and Colt had fought like hell on who was going to get the poolside house, and Luke had won out after three rounds of arm wrestling.

Maegan grabbed two suitcases and started toward the stairs. "I'm gonna unpack and head to the beach. My white skin needs some sun, and my eyes need to look at some di—"

"Stop!" Grace and Lex said at the same time.

Libby laughed as she went to grab her suitcase.

Luke took it for her and smiled. "I'll get it for you, Lib."

Libby smiled back and nodded her head. I was glad to see the two of them were slowly getting back to somewhat of a normal relationship. Now, if they would just talk to each other about their feelings, everything would be even better.

"Things are looking good," Lex whispered as she watched Luke follow Libby upstairs.

"Yeah, I think so. Do you mind if I meet y'all down at the beach? I'll just be a couple of minutes. I want to work on something your dad wanted me to do."

Lex looked at me funny. "What did he want you to do?"

"Expense spreadsheets. I think he's starting to test me."

Lex laughed as she reached up on her tiptoes and gave me a kiss on the lips. "Of course I don't mind. I'm gonna go change into my new bathing suit. I think you will be very happy with it."

I instantly felt my dick getting hard. "Really? Well, I can't wait to see this new bathing suit. The quicker, the better."

I grabbed our luggage as Lex grabbed her backpack. We headed to the only bedroom on the first floor.

When we walked into the master bedroom, I set everything down and looked around. "Oh God."

Lex turned and looked at me. "What? What's wrong, Will?"

Lex had already begun to strip out of her clothes. I looked at her and then looked at the king-sized bed.

I shook my head. "I can't. I mean...I don't think I can."

Lex narrowed her eyes at me as a confused expression crossed her face. "What are you talking about, Will?"

I looked back at the bed. "Sex. I don't think I can have sex in this bed or even in this room."

Lex started laughing as she jumped on the bed. "Why? 'Cause your mom and dad have?"

"Gross. Yuck. Oh my God, that turns my stomach just from thinking about it."

Lex reached behind her, unsnapped her bra, and dropped it to the bed.

I had to control myself. I wanted to take her in my arms and make love to her. "You're. Killing. Me."

She slowly started to unbutton her shorts, and then she shimmied them down. The moment I saw the bright yellow boy shorts, I knew I was done for.

"Will, I don't want to make love on this bed," she said in a seductive voice.

"You don't?" I asked.

She began slowly pushing her panties down, further and further. She bit down on her lower lip as she shook her head. "Nope. I want to fu—"

Lex and I both jumped when someone started banging on the bedroom door.

Grace called out from the other side of the door. "Come on, Alex! It doesn't take that long to change into a swimsuit...unless you're giving Will a—"

"Give me two minutes," Lex said with a laugh. She quickly jumped up and skipped to her suitcase.

"So wrong of you to do that right now," I said.

She looked back at me and shimmied her chest. My poor dick was already aching, and now, it was aching even more.

"You don't play fair, Lex."

She looked over her shoulder as she held up a teal bathing suit. "I didn't realize you wanted me to play fair, Mr. Hayes."

I laughed as I walked over to my bag. I took my laptop out and set it down on the desk. I pulled up a bunch of spreadsheets in an attempt to look like I was going to work.

Lex cleared her throat behind me.

When I turned to look at her, my mouth dropped open. "Holy shit, you look beautiful."

Lex blushed as she moved around like she was embarrassed. I looked her perfect body up and down. Lex had the most amazing body. I'd heard her and Grace talk about how they both had hourglass shapes. Neither one of them had ever really worried about their weight, and I loved that. Really, none of the girls were fixated on their bodies, unlike how some of the girls in high school had seemed to be.

I looked at Lex's breasts. She seemed to be showing much more cleavage than normal.

She must have noticed. "It's a push-up top."

"Well, it's pushing 'em up, that's for damn sure."

She giggled. She put her finger in her mouth and gently bit down on it. It was a nervous habit she would do, and I didn't think she realized that it was sexy as hell. I looked her body up and down again. I wanted her more than anything, but I needed to remember what I needed to take care of. I could have Lex all night long.

"Lex, you're so beautiful."

"Thank you," she whispered as she walked over to me. She pushed her hand through my hair and kissed me. "I think you're beautiful, too."

I laughed and shook my head. "Go, before Grace has a heart attack, and I die from blue balls."

She walked over to her suitcase and pulled out a sundress. She slipped it over her head and blew me a kiss before leaving. "Don't work too hard. Daddy needs to understand that we're on our vacation!"

"I won't. I promise."

The moment she shut the door, I walked over to the window overlooking the deck and pool. I watched as everyone started making their way down to the beach. Luke and Colt were both carrying towels and a cooler.

I pulled out my cell phone, looked up the number to Mr. Shelton, and hit the button to call him.

"Hello?"

"Mr. Shelton, this is Will Hayes. Gunner Mathews talked to you about us using your house on St. Joseph Island this week."

"Yes, Will. How are you?"

"I'm doing well. Thank you. How are you, sir?"

"I have no complaints at all. So, I hear you're going to ask Gunner's little girl to marry you?"

I smiled. "Yes, sir, I am."

"You couldn't have picked a better spot, son. I've already talked to my ranch hand, Kip. He knows what day to expect you, and he has taken care of the ride over to my place and the dinner."

"That's wonderful, sir. I can't even begin to thank you for letting me use your yacht and house for this."

"Well, when Gunner called me and told me what you had in mind, I couldn't help but feel déjà vu. I asked my wife to marry me in a similar manner."

"Really?"

He laughed. "Yes, I did. We've been happily married now for eighteen years with three kids."

"I'll take that as a good sign then."

"Damn straight. After sunset, I suggest taking a stroll along the beach with a blanket, but I'll deny I said that to you if Gunner ever finds out."

I laughed and said, "I understand."

"So, Jonathon will be the one taking you over to the island on the yacht. I'll have him give you a call the morning of, so he can explain where y'all need to go."

"Perfect. I've already planned to tell Lex that we are going on a private cruise to see the dolphins and the sunset."

"That sounds reasonable. Now, if you need anything before then, don't hesitate to give me or Jonathon a call. You have his number, right?"

"Yes, sir, I do."

"Good luck, Will."

"Thank you, sir. Again, thank you for all your help on this."

"Anything for Gunner's little girl. Enjoy your stay at the beach."

"Will do for sure. Have a great day."

"You, too, Will."

I hung up and sent Gunner a text message.

> *Me: Talked to Mr. Shelton. Everything is set to go.*
>
> *Gunner: Are you nervous?*
>
> *Me: Why do I picture you laughing right now?*
>
> *Gunner: Probably because I am!*
>
> *Me: Yes. I'm very nervous. I've already checked six times to make sure I still have the ring.*
>
> *Gunner: Now, I'm really laughing.*

I rolled my eyes and sighed. He was going to torture me for years to come. I could already see it.

> *Me: Remember who will be taking care of you when you're old. It won't be Colt.*
>
> *Gunner: You have a point. Don't worry, son. It will be perfect, Will. You know you could ask her anywhere, and she would be beyond happy.*

No one but our friends knew that I had already asked Lex to marry me months ago. This engagement was just making it more official with a ring, and then we could go public afterward. As far as I was concerned, Lex had been mine since the day I put that promise ring on her finger.

> *Me: Thanks, Gunner. I promise to make it special for her.*

Gunner: I know you will.

I quickly changed and started to make my way down to the beach. As I walked down the boardwalk, I couldn't help but smile. Everyone was playing volleyball in the sand. Libby jumped and spiked the ball, and it landed right in front of Colt. Luke screamed out as he ran up to her, and he picked her up and spun her around a few times before setting her back down. Taylor high-fived Lex, and Grace was yelling that Libby couldn't play because she was too good.

My mind was taken back to the days when we'd all played football. I looked at each of my friends. Because of our parents' bond with each other, our bond had grown over the years. There wasn't anything any of us wouldn't do for the other.

Grace screamed, "Hayes! Get down here. Your damn sister is kicking our ass!"

I was snapped out of my daydream. I laughed and started jogging. I ran up and picked Libby up before throwing her over my shoulder as she screamed.

"Put our star player down!" Luke yelled as he took off after me.

Yep, this is going to be the best week ever.

alex

43

"Have you had a chance to talk to Luke?" I asked Libby as we walked along the beach.

Libby let out a sigh. "No. He is treating me like his best friend again. I mean, we went running on the beach together last night, and I tried so many different times to talk to him."

"Did he seem like he wanted to talk to you?"

Libby stopped and looked at me. "I think so. He started to say something, but then he ended up laughing. He brought up a time when we were in high school and pulled a stupid prank."

I giggled and shook my head. "Why is he so afraid?"

She looked down and slowly shook her head. She looked back up and into my eyes. "I told him that I can't wait any longer."

"What? Wait, Libby. You love him."

"Alex, I walked away from Zack."

"Did you love Zack?" I asked.

Libby looked away before turning back at me. "I cared about him—a lot."

I nodded my head. "Do you love Luke?"

Libby was about to answer me when we heard Colt calling out for us.

"Libby! Alex! Come on, we're all waiting on y'all."

Libby gave me a weak smile. "I tried, Alex. I really tried. How long am I supposed to wait? If Luke truly cared about me, he wouldn't be doing this to me." She quickly spun around and began walking toward Colt.

"Libby?"

She held up her hand as if she didn't want to talk anymore. I let out a sigh and began following her.

As we made our way back into the beach house, Luke and Grace were arguing about where to eat.

Libby walked by and headed upstairs. "I need a minute to grab my cell phone."

"I don't want Moby Dick's. We always go to Moby Dick's, Luke," Grace said.

Luke let out a gruff laugh. "Well, princess, I'm sick of Seafood and Spaghetti Works."

"I vote for clubbing in Corpus Christi, so I can feel a nice firm ass in my hands while I dance slow with a handsome guy."

Everyone looked at Máegan.

"You're such a slut," Grace said with a laugh.

Maegan winked. "I try."

Colt stood up and clapped his hands together. "Clubbing it is."

Libby walked into the living room.

Grace jumped up, grabbed her hand, and pulled her back toward the stairs. "We're changing. It's time to put our club clothes on."

Lauren, Taylor, and Maegan all let out a small scream and followed Grace and Libby.

I watched as Luke walked out the back door and headed to the pool house. I wanted to follow him, but when I felt Will's arms around my waist, I froze in place.

Will's lips moved gently against my neck, leaving a trail of fire where his lips had just touched. "I'm going to make mad, passionate love to you tonight."

"Mmm…" I lost myself in his touch.

"Do you like the sound of that, Lex?"

"Very much."

"I'm going to get you so turned-on tonight that by the time we get back here, all you will need is my touch to make you come."

I let out a small moan and attempted to talk. The clenching feeling in the pit of my stomach had me wanting to slip my own hand down my panties.

I turned and wrapped my arms around his neck. "Can we skip clubbing? I just want to stay here with you."

Will raised his eyebrows and seemed to be thinking hard about staying home and not going out.

Someone cleared her throat, and Will and I both looked over to see Grace standing there.

"Hell no. You are not skipping out on us tonight. This whole trip was all about us hanging together. And that's what we're doing. You two can do your *thing* later! Alex, get your ass upstairs. I'm going to make you up, so Will won't be able to keep his eyes off of you all night."

I giggled as I looked at Will. "I guess the anticipation will just build all night." I kissed him, and then I spun around and walked toward Grace.

She grabbed my hand, and we began heading upstairs. I looked over my shoulder and winked at Will. The smile on his face made my knees weak, and my insides craved his touch again.

"I love you, Lex."

I loved how my mother and father would always tell each other how they loved the other more. Will and I had picked it up, and every time I said it to him, he would smile bigger.

"I love you more."

Will chuckled.

Grace pulled my arm harder to get me to speed it up. "Jesus, y'all can go a few minutes without each other."

An hour later, I looked at all five of us.

"Holy shit. We look good!" Lauren said with a giggle.

Lauren was probably the sweetest one of the bunch. Hearing her swear always made me chuckle. Taylor was just as sweet but far more innocent.

"Hell yeah, we do. We are five hot bitches," Grace said, walking up to Libby and messing with her hair.

I looked Libby up and down. She had on one of Grace's dresses. It was a silver cocktail dress with a scooped back that stopped just shy of her ass. I was sure just a few more inches, and we'd be able to see the string of her thong. Her blonde hair was piled on top of her head with curls hanging down to frame her face. Taylor had done Libby's makeup, and her dark smoky eyes and red lipstick had even me catching my breath. I knew what Grace and Taylor were up to. They had made Libby look so incredibly hot that Luke was gonna shit his pants when he laid his eyes on her.

"Damn, baby sister. You. Look. Hot." Maegan smiled and looked at Taylor.

Taylor was dressed in a simple black cocktail dress with silver accents and a high slit on the side. Her push-up bra showed more cleavage than I'd ever seen Taylor display, and it made her look about three years older than she was.

Taylor blushed and smiled.

"You do look beautiful," Lauren said with a smile.

I glanced over and looked at Lauren. She had on a teal dress that hugged her curves in all the right ways. Her blonde hair was done so that half was up with the other half hanging down. The color of the dress brought out the color of her blue eyes even more. Taylor had also done Lauren's makeup, and she looked breathtaking. My poor baby brother was gonna be whimpering all night while watching Lauren dance in that dress.

Grace, of course, looked like a knockout. She had on a beige cocktail dress. If it were longer, she would look like she'd stepped out of *The Great Gatsby*. Her light-brown hair was done in a French twist, and her makeup had been done to look very natural.

I stared at my best friend. She was so beautiful, yet she had no clue how beautiful she was. She not only looked like Aunt Ari, but she also had her mother's spit and fire as well.

Grace glanced over and winked at me. "Shall we, ladies?"

Maegan did a little jump, and she was the first one down the stairs. Of course she looked like a knockout in a pair of black sheer pants and an almost see-through white blouse. Only Maegan could make wearing dress pants look hotter than hell.

As we made our way down the stairs, I could hear Will, Luke, and Colt talking. I didn't know whose face I wanted to see more.

I walked down second, and when Will saw me, his mouth dropped open. I loved that I had such an effect on him. I knew he was now regretting the decision not to stay here tonight.

Libby was right behind me, so I quickly looked at Luke.

I couldn't help but giggle when I saw my cousin's mouth about drop to the ground.

He swallowed hard and said, "Jesus, Libby, you look beautiful."

I glanced over my shoulder to see Libby smiling slightly at Luke.

She said, "Thank you, Luke."

Then, Colt said, "Holy hell."

I looked and watched Lauren making her way down the stairs, followed by Taylor, and Grace.

"Okay, we're ready to go." Grace made her way to the front door.

Libby turned to follow.

Luke let out a gasp. "Oh. Hell. No."

Grace and Libby turned and looked at Luke.

"Excuse me?" Grace attempted to hold back her smile.

"Libby, you're not wearing that. It...it goes down...I mean, it's..."

Libby tilted her head and looked at Luke. "What's wrong with this dress?"

Will walked over to Libby. "What's wrong with it? Libby, one more inch, and your damn ass is going to be showing. You need to change."

"Yes! You totally need to change. No way you're going out in that dress," Luke said.

Grace crossed her arms, and Libby's mouth dropped open as she looked at Will, then Luke, and back to Will. I couldn't help but giggle. Not only did she have her brother being overprotective, but she also had Luke.

"It's just like high school all over again. The big brother and the best friend being overprotective of Libby," Maegan said, walking by Grace and Libby. She opened the door to the garage. "Last I checked, she was over eighteen, Will, and she isn't your girlfriend, Luke." Maegan looked over her shoulder at Luke and made a face. "So, she's free to dress however she sees fit."

I glanced over at Libby as she looked at Will and Luke.

"That's right. I'm a"—she glared at Luke—"single woman, who is ready to have some fun."

She turned and followed Grace, Maegan, Taylor, and Lauren out the door.

Colt walked up to me and took me by the arm. "Alex, you can't let Lauren go out, looking like that. And did you see how Taylor was dressed? And what in the hell are you wearing?"

I smiled at Colt and gently removed his hand. I took a few steps back and smiled at three of the most important men in my life.

"I love all three of you, so I'm gonna keep it real. Two of you have your heads up your ass." I looked at Colt. "Stop letting Lauren push you away." I turned to Luke. "Stop pushing Libby away, you ass. Now, pull out the romantic shit that I know both of you have and do something about it. Frankly, I'm sick and tired of seeing the two of you mope around because you're both too damn afraid."

Will was smiling from ear to ear. "God, I love you." He walked up and took me in his arms.

He kissed me as Colt walked by.

"She's still my sister, you prick. Get your hand off her ass," Colt said.

When Will pulled his lips from mine, he smiled. "You have no idea how turned-on I am right now."

"Oh, Jesus H. Christ. Get a room," Luke said as he pulled Will away from me.

Luke took my arm and led me outside. I giggled as I looked back at Will.

This is going to be one very long evening.

WILL

After eating dinner at an Italian restaurant in Corpus, we headed to a dance club. I glanced over to the dance floor and saw all the girls dancing. They had pretty much been just dancing together in their little group since we got here.

Luke and Colt were talking about an idea Colt had for logging in the vaccinations for the cattle. I was just about to give my input when Luke quickly stood up.

"What is she doing?"

I looked out at the dance floor and scanned for the girls. I saw them all dancing…except for Libby. I quickly looked around for her and saw her dancing with some guy. He was about five-eleven and built like a son of a bitch, and he had my sister a little too close to him as they danced.

I stood up almost immediately. "Why is she…what in the hell is she…he needs to get his hands off my sister."

Luke went to walk out the dance floor when Colt jumped up and stopped him.

"You're just going to get her pissed at you. She's not your girlfriend, Luke. Will, she's an adult woman. We can't keep beating up every guy who looks at her wrong."

Luke's whole body sank. I turned and looked back out at my sister dancing. She was clearly dancing with the guy on her own free will, and I knew Colt was right. I sat back down and glanced over to where Lex was. She was still dancing but looking directly at me. She gave me a thumbs-up and smiled. I shook my head and smiled back as I got up and walked up to her. I pulled her body close to mine and began moving my hands up and down her body.

"God, I want you right now," I whispered as I moved my lips to her ear.

"Yes," she whispered back. "Now, Will. Please take me now."

I quickly looked around. If I didn't sink my dick into her soon, I was going to explode. I grabbed her hand and began walking us to the door.

"Where are we going?" Lex shouted over the music.

"To the truck," I shouted back.

The bouncer asked if we were coming back into the club, and I nodded my head. He stamped our hands, and as soon as we hit the cool night air, I reached down and picked her up. She let out a small scream.

"Will, everyone is going to wonder where we went," Lex said with a giggle.

I walked up to the truck and looked around as I put her down. My dick was literally throbbing. I needed her that much. Luke's truck was pretty much hiding us.

"I don't care, Lex. The only thing I care about right now is getting your panties off and fucking you against my truck."

She let out a gasp and then licked her lips. "Here? Right now?"

I smiled. "Does that turn you on more, Lex?"

She looked around before looking back at me. "You don't have to worry about getting my panties off. I'm not wearing any."

I let out a moan. "You have no idea what you do to me." I began unzipping my jeans, and I let myself spring free.

"Yes. Will, please hurry. I need relief."

I looked around once more before pushing her dress up and spreading her legs apart. One touch of her lips, and I knew how turned-on she was.

"I want you, Lex."

"Oh God, Will. I want you, too."

I trailed my fingers along her lips as she let out a moan and pushed her hips toward me. I slowly slipped two fingers in as I used my other hand to grab her breast. Lex dropped her head back against my truck and whimpered as she began moving her hips against my hand to gain more friction. I slowly pulled my fingers out, and Lex snapped her head forward and looked at me.

"Will, goddamn it."

I smiled. I loved seeing Lex like this. I looked around the parking lot one more time before I lifted her up and slowly sank my dick inside her.

"Yes," she hissed as we both began moving. "Faster. I don't want to get arrested."

I stopped moving, and she looked at me.

"Don't stop! Oh God, I'm so close."

I began going faster as Lex placed her hands on my shoulders and started moving along with me. It didn't take long for her to start moaning as she dropped her head back.

"I'm coming," she panted.

I felt her pulsing around my dick. I pulled out and slammed back into her, causing her to let out a gasp.

"Oh God, Lex. I'm coming. Baby, I love you." I buried my face into her neck as I poured everything I had into her.

I stood there for a few seconds and just held her while I caught my breath.

"Are you done?" she whispered.

"May I enjoy this hotter-than-hot moment for just a second?" I asked as I kept my face buried in her neck.

She hit me and said, "No! Put me down."

I let out a giggle as I pulled out of her. I opened the back door of my truck. I got a paper towel out and quickly cleaned her off. I pulled her dress down, and she slammed her lips to mine. I pulled her body closer to mine, and if I didn't know any better, I would swear my dick was coming up again.

She slowly pulled her lips from mine. "That. Was. Amazing."

I grinned and wiggled my eyebrows up and down. "Luke was right. Public sex is hot as hell."

Lex frowned but then smiled again. "I thought you were bringing me out to your truck. I wasn't expecting that. I was waiting to get caught."

I placed my hand on the side of her face. "You make me mad for you, Lex. My body is taken over by you, and I just can't control myself, especially when you look so incredibly hot."

Even though it was dark, I could see her face blush slightly.

I zipped up my pants and grabbed her hand. "We'd better get back before they go searching for us."

We walked back into the dance club and made our way over to the table. Luke was talking to Colt, and it seemed like a heated conversation.

"Oh Lord," Lex said.

I turned and followed her gaze. Lauren was dancing with someone. I rolled my eyes.

"Maybe this wasn't such a great idea," I said as we made our way to the table.

"It's like a soap opera—*The Days of Colt and Lauren and Luke and Libby.*"

I laughed as I grabbed Lex's hand. I thanked God for her.

Now, all I had to do was get through tomorrow evening.

45 alex

"You are an asshole, Colt Mathews. I will hate you for the rest of my life." Lauren had tears streaming down her face as she pushed Colt and then ran up the stairs.

"Lauren, wait," Taylor called out as she rushed after her.

Will and Luke thought they had calmed Colt down at the dance club, but they had been mistaken. Colt had been asking Lauren to dance all night, and she'd turned him down each time. When he had seen her dancing with another guy, he had wanted to chase the guy away, but Luke and Will had talked him out of it. But when he had seen Lauren dancing a little too sexy while moving her hand down to *the guy's dick and beyond*—Colt's words— Colt had gone out to the dance floor. He'd given the guy a push and then proceeded to tell Lauren that he never pictured her to be that kind of girl.

I walked up to my brother and looked at him. "Why did you say that to her?"

He pushed his hands through his hair and let out a frustrated moan. "Damn it, Alex. Last summer, she made it seem like she had the same feelings for me, and then she just dropped me. It was like she didn't remember everything she'd said to me. Then, she went off with that fucker, but she got pissed when I got back together with Rachel." Colt was raising his voice louder and louder. He pointed toward the stairs and yelled, "I left Rachel for her! I fucking dropped everything!"

I grabbed his arm and pulled him outside. When I shut the door, I punched him in the chest.

"What the hell, Alex? Why are you hitting me?"

I shook my head. "Colt, I don't know what Lauren said to you or why she all of sudden decided that she didn't want to be with you, but that gives you no right, none, to walk up to her and basically call her a slut."

Colt swallowed hard. "I didn't call her that."

I placed my hands on my hips and tilted my head. "Colt Hunter Mathews, you told her she was grabbing a guy's dick and that you never pictured her to be that kind of girl. What, in your mind, does that sound like you're saying?"

Colt sat down on the chair and dropped his head into his hands. He sat that way for a few minutes before he finally looked up at me. He closed his eyes and slowly shook his head. "I can't do this, Alex. It is obvious Lauren doesn't want the same thing I want."

"You don't know that," I whispered as I sat down and took his hands in mine.

"If she wanted to be with me, she wouldn't have been with him tonight."

My heart hurt for my brother because I knew he was right. I dropped my head in a silent acknowledgment. "Colt, I'm so sorry."

He let out a gruff laugh. "It's not your fault, Alex. I'm just not the guy for her."

I slowly shook my head, and I was about to talk when he pulled his hands from mine. He stood up and reached for me to help me stand.

"I guess this is a new beginning for me, huh, sis? I'll be heading to school and meeting new people." He nodded his head as if he was thinking of something and agreeing with it. "Football will occupy so much of my time. Dad's right. It's a whole new world." He smiled slightly. "Who knows? I might get lucky enough and meet someone who loves me the way you love Will."

"Oh no, Colt. I know Lauren has—"

He held up his hand to stop me. "I'm tired, Alex. I love you, sweetheart. I'm gonna go to bed."

He kissed me on the forehead. Then, he turned and walked back inside. I wiped the tear from my face and closed my eyes.

"Why does love have to be so hard for some?" I whispered.

The feel of Will's arms coming around me as he pulled me closer to him instantly warmed me. We stood in silence as we listened to the waves hit the shore.

"Is Colt okay?" Will finally asked.

I slowly shook my head. "I don't think so. He will pretend he is, and he'll move on, but I don't think things will be the same anymore."

Will rested his chin on top of my head. "How about you and I go on a sunset cruise tomorrow? Just us."

I smiled and turned to face him. "Yeah? But it's our last night. You don't think everyone will want to go out to dinner together?"

Will shrugged his shoulders. "All I know is I want one evening with you before we have to head back. I'm sure the others will understand."

I began to chew on my lower lip. It felt like our friendships were changing but growing stronger also. I wasn't sure where Luke and Libby were heading, and honestly, I was tired of worrying about it. Now, I had to worry about Colt and Lauren.

Ugh.

I attempted to give Will a sexy smile, and he raised his one eyebrow and narrowed his eyes at me.

"Are you thinking yes?"

"I think tomorrow night with just you and me is exactly the thing I need."

Will picked me up and spun me around. "Perfect. Leave all the details to me, and I'll plan it all."

I laughed and said, "Okay, you don't have to tell me twice."

He moved his lips to mine. "I'm going to make love to you now, Lex."

My stomach fluttered as Will walked us both back inside. I looked around, and no one was downstairs.

I hadn't seen Luke come outside, so I asked Will, "Where is Luke?"

"No clue."

I started to say we should find him, but then I decided to push everyone else's problems out of my mind and enjoy the rest of this trip.

Will pulled into a private parking lot and parked.

"I thought we were going on a sunset cruise?"

He turned off the truck and looked at me and said, "We are. You ready?"

He jumped out of the truck and walked to my side. When he opened the door and reached for my hand, I smiled.

"Um…are we taking out someone's boat? Do you know how to take out someone's boat?"

He winked at me, and we made our way down the ramp and onto the deck. An older gentleman with blond hair and a deep dark tan smiled as we approached him.

He stuck out his hand. "Will?"

Will shook his hand and smiled. "I take it you're Jonathon."

He grinned and nodded his head. "You're right on that one. Come on board."

Will helped me climb on the yacht.

Jonathon said, "I've got a nice little trip planned for y'all. I hope you like dolphins, Miss Mathews."

I was taken aback at how he'd known my name, but I figured Will must have told him when he'd made the arrangements.

I nodded my head. "Yes, I love them, and I'm super excited."

Jonathon looked up at the sky and grinned. "The weather couldn't be more perfect. The sunset is going to be amazing."

I looked at Will, who was grinning from ear to ear, but he also looked like he was about to be sick.

"Please head on down into the cabin. I've got some trays out for y'all to snack on while I get us going."

Will placed his hand on the small of my back to lead me down into the cabin. My heart skipped a beat, and goose bumps covered my body. I wasn't sure why, but I loved when he did that. It felt like such a romantic yet manly gesture.

When we got down in the cabin, my hands came up to my mouth, and I sucked in a breath of air. The whole cabin was filled with every kind of flower I could imagine.

Will and I both said at the same time, "Wow."

I looked at Will. "Did you plan all of this?"

He swallowed hard and dropped his mouth open just a bit. "Um…I, um…"

I threw myself into his arms. "Will, this is the most romantic gesture ever!" I lowered my voice. "I wish we were alone because I'd love to make love on a boat in the water."

Will's eyebrows lifted as he smiled. "Really? I'm going to have to remember that."

It wasn't long before we headed out. Will must have been feeling seasick because he looked like he wanted to lean over and throw up.

"Will, are you okay?" I asked as I rubbed his back.

He nodded his head and smiled. He jumped when I let out a small scream and pointed.

"Dolphin!"

Jonathon and Will both laughed. I couldn't believe how they were swimming and jumping at the bow of the ship as we sailed along.

"How far are we going?" I asked as I looked at my watch.

The sun wasn't setting for another two hours.

Will and Jonathon looked at each other, and then Will slowly looked at me.

Will smiled and took my hands in his. "I have a surprise for you, sweetheart."

Will

I watched as Lex's face lit up. She loved surprises, and I knew the moment I said it, she would get excited.

"Oh, yeah? Are we swimming with the dolphins? I thought that was illegal!" She began clapping her hands.

I wasn't sure if she was excited at the idea of swimming with dolphins or doing something illegal.

I stared at her for a moment and chuckled. "No, Jonathon is taking us to a private island—St. Joseph's."

Recognition hit Lex's face. "Mr. Shelton's ranch?"

I nodded. "Yep. We're gonna watch the sunset from there."

Lex slowly smiled. "I used to love going over there when I was little. Do you know how many sand dollars Colt and I used to find there?"

Jonathon laughed. "The untouched beaches of the island make it beautiful."

Lex looked around. "Well, darn it. Let me use the restroom before we get there, or I'll be peeing in the ocean!"

I watched as Lex retreated down into the cabin.

I spun around and looked at Jonathon. "Did you do all of that with the flowers?"

He smiled and nodded his head. "She was hoping y'all were alone, wasn't she?"

"Yes, and so in the hell was I."

Jonathon threw his head back and laughed hysterically. "Her daddy wouldn't like that response. He was the one who told me to do it."

My mouth dropped open. "Gunner did?"

Jonathon nodded his head. "Yes, sir, he did. Told me to fill the cabin with flowers. Stupid romantic bastard."

I chuckled and shook my head. "That he is, but he sure does teach me the right way to treat his daughter."

Jonathon rubbed his thumb and index finger back and forth across his chin like he was thinking. "I can imagine. The key is to always put them first, son. I've been married for almost thirty years. My wife comes first and foremost. She is my life."

Nodding my head, I said, "Yes, sir."

"Oh my gosh, there it is!" Lex shouted as she popped up out of the cabin. "I haven't been on that island in so long. Oh, Will, I wish you could see Mr. Shelton's home. It's breathtaking. I haven't seen it since I was eleven, I think. The last hurricane did some damage to it, but that thing was built to last."

I just grinned and pulled her next to me.

Jonathon gave me a wink as he made his way over to the private dock. "That's Kip, Mr. Shelton's ranch hand. He'll be taking care of y'all while I hang out here."

Reaching out to shake Jonathon's hand, I said, "Sounds good. Thank you so much, Jonathon."

Lex shook his hand next and said, "Thank you so much. I'm looking forward to the trip back at night."

"Will and Alex? I'm Kip," he said as he helped Lex out off the yacht.

"Hello, it's a pleasure to meet you." Lex looked around.

Reaching out and shaking Kip's hand, I introduced myself and said, "Thank you so much for taking the time to do all of this."

Lex had already begun walking off down the beach. I smiled as I watched her.

"She is totally clueless, isn't she?" Kip asked.

I rocked back and forth on my feet. I was proud of the fact that I had been able to keep this surprise from her. "Totally clueless."

"If you want to take advantage of asking her at sunset, I suggest we head up to the house and start with dinner. My wife, Cassie, did all the decorations. Mr. Shelton is thinking of having weddings at the house, and when he saw how Cassie had done up the place for y'all, he said he was one step closer to that." Kip had a huge smile on his face.

"Does she do party-planning?" I asked.

"Nah, she's just a rancher's wife stuck on an island and bored out of her mind. If Mr. Shelton did this, it would make her so happy and give her something to do."

I let out a sigh. "So, tonight's like a test run?"

Kip chuckled. "No pressure, but yes. I hope y'all like what Cassie has done."

"We're going to love it." I looked back at Lex as she stood with her feet at the edge of the water. "Lex!" I called out.

When she looked at me, I waved for her to come back. She picked up her flip-flops and headed back over to the dock.

Alex

When Will called me back over to the dock, I had a feeling something was going down. "I thought we were gonna walk along the beach?"

The smile that spread across Will's face caused my heart to drop to the ground. I wanted to push my legs together or have him take me off somewhere to have his wicked way with me.

"Alex, we're heading up to the house," Kip said.

I jumped up and down. "Really? Is Mr. Shelton here?"

Kip didn't answer as he walked over to his truck and opened the passenger door for me. I slipped my flip-flops on and made my way over to the truck. Will got in and slid in next to me. Kip started off toward the house.

"Oh, Will, wait to you see this house. It sits on the highest point of the island, and the view is amazing. I can remember being little and dreaming of a house like this one. It's rustic—or at least, it was when I was here last."

Kip nodded his head. "You have a good memory, Alex. The log cabin was built back in the early nineteen hundreds for hunting. A few presidents have graced the island with their presence."

"LBJ stayed there. Colt stayed in the room he stayed in," I said.

Will grabbed my hand. He began rubbing his thumb back and forth quickly as we drove to the house. I'd peek over every once in a while, and he was just staring out the window.

"Will? Are you okay? You just don't seem like yourself."

Will turned quickly and looked at me. "What? Baby, I'm totally fine. I think I might have just gotten a little seasick, that's all."

I gave him a gentle kiss on the lips. He placed his hand behind my neck and deepened the kiss a little too much. I pulled back and motioned for Will to remember that Kip was in the truck.

"Here we are," Kip said as he parked the truck.

Will jumped out, and I slid over and took his hand. We followed Kip up the stairs.

A beautiful older woman with red hair greeted us at the door. "Will, Alex, it's such a pleasure to meet you."

I smiled and nodded my head. *Okay, this is getting weird.*

I peeked up at Will, and he was smiling at the lady.

He is up to something.

"I'm Cassie, Kip's wife. Let me show you where you're going to have dinner."

Will started following her, but I grabbed his arm.

"Dinner?" I shook my head. "Will, did you plan this or something?"

He gave me that panty-melting smile of his as he winked at me. He took my hand and pulled me along as he followed Cassie up a flight of stairs.

The house was just as I remembered it. The log beams through the house gave it such a rustic feeling. The deer, moose, turkeys, and ducks mounted all over the walls screamed hunting lodge.

"This place is amazing," Will whispered.

I giggled. *I knew he would love it!*

Cassie walked up to a set of double doors and pushed them open. I let out a gasp as I walked into a grand ballroom.

"It's more beautiful than I remembered." I turned and looked at Will. "Grace and I used to pretend we were princesses, and that our Prince Charming was going to scale the castle walls and set us free…but not before he danced with us." I let out a sigh as I shook my head. "Silly romantic dreams."

Cassie walked past us and pushed a button. Classical music began playing as she walked up to another sent of French doors. She turned and gave me the sweetest smile before turning back and opening the door.

The lodge house had a wraparound porch on the first floor and the second floor. My mouth dropped open when I saw the white lights hanging down with a round table in the middle of the deck. It had a white linen tablecloth on it, and the table was set for two. In the middle of the table was a beautiful arrangement of flowers, and two tall candles were lit. It was stunning.

I walked up to the table and then turned to Will. "Will…" I whispered.

Will

Lex's eyes looked amazing against the backdrop of the blue ocean. When she turned and looked at me, I thought it was the first time it really hit her that I had planned all of this.

"Will…" she whispered.

I walked up to the table and pulled out one of the chairs. "Lex, will you do me the honor and have dinner with me this evening?"

She sucked her lower lip between her teeth and nodded her head. "Yes," she barely said.

I pushed her chair in and then handed her the napkin. When our hands touched, the bolt of lightning shot through my body. Lex's eyes widened, and she began breathing slightly harder. She'd felt it, too.

I sat down opposite of her and placed my napkin on my lap. I glanced out and looked at the amazing view. When I peeked back over to Lex, she was looking out over the ocean as well.

"The sunset is going to be breathtaking," she said with a smile.

"That's not the only thing that is breathtaking this evening."

Lex's chest began moving up down faster and heavier. "I love you, Will. This is all so beautiful"

"I love you more, Lex."

The evening progressed along as Cassie brought us out salads first, then soup, and finally grilled salmon and steamed veggies. I hardly ate any of my food because my stomach was in knots. I hadn't made up my mind if I wanted to ask her on the beach or up here. I was leaning more to staying here and then taking her to the beach with a blanket like Mr. Shelton had suggested.

The sun was slowly starting to sink further down. Lex kept looking over and watching it. We had a perfect view of the west sky.

Cassie cleared the plates. Then, she came back and placed two glasses of champagne down on the table. Lex was so focused on the sunset that she didn't even see the glasses.

"Oh, Will, look at how the sun is reflecting off the water." She stood up and moved to the rail.

Perfect.

I stood up and pulled the ring from my pocket. I walked up behind her.

I got down on one knee and took in a deep breath. "Lex, baby, I need to ask you something."

When she turned to look at me, she was surprised to see me kneeling down. Her mouth dropped open, and her hands slowly moved to cover her mouth.

I saw the tears beginning to build in her beautiful blue eyes.

Alex

My heart had never beat this fast or this hard in my life—not even that day next to the small pond when Will had asked me to marry him.

"Lex, I know we've already told each other how we feel when we were at the pond. I want you to know that everything I said that day holds true today, if not more. You are my life. You are my world. And I love you fiercely. Alexandra Eryn Mathews, will you do me the honor of becoming my wife—but not until you're finished with college and well on your way to being an independent woman?"

I pulled my head back and looked at him. "What?"

Will chuckled as he looked at Cassie and then back to me. "Your dad. When I asked him if I could have your hand in marriage, he said I had to make it very clear that you were to finish college first before I could officially make you mine."

I couldn't help it. I let out a sob and a laugh at the same time.

Will swallowed hard and looked away and then back at me.

"Um…I mean, I know you already said yes once, but you're kind of freaking me out here, Lex."

I nodded my head and dropped to my knees. I placed my hands on the sides of his face and brought his lips to mine. "Yes. I'll marry you. A million times yes, Will."

I pushed my lips to his as I wrapped my arms around his body. We deepened the kiss and soon got lost in each other.

When I heard Kip clear his throat, I pulled back some.

"I love you, Will."

Will smiled, and for the umpteenth time this evening, my heart melted again as I waited for his response.

"I love you more, Lex."

He removed my promise ring and placed it on my right index finger and then slipped the solitaire oval diamond onto my finger as I began crying harder.

It is perfect.

The ring was simple, nothing extravagant, just like I'd asked of him. A beautiful oval diamond ring was flanked by four smaller diamonds on each side, all placed on a white gold band. Another sob escaped my mouth as he leaned in and gently kissed me.

He pulled back and smiled as his eyes searched my face. "This was the first ring I saw. I knew the moment I saw it, it had to be yours."

"Oh, Will, it's so beautiful. It's perfect, beyond perfect."

Will's eyes filled with tears. I began to see the reds and purples of the sunset reflecting in his eyes. We both stood up as the sun slipped below the horizon, ending one of the most amazing days of my entire life. Will placed his hands on the sides of my face and gently wiped the tears away.

Raising his eyebrow, Will asked, "Would you do me the honor of taking a walk with me on the beach?"

I giggled and nodded my head. "It would be my pleasure."

Will

Lex and I headed down to the beach.

Cassie came running after us, calling out my name. "Will! Wait!"

Lex and I both turned to face her.

"You forgot this."

I looked down at the blanket in Cassie's hands and let out a nervous laugh. "Thank you so much."

I turned back to see Lex blushing. I placed my hand on the small of her back and led her down to the beach. The west sky was still filled with the most incredible colors, yet the stars were beginning to make their presence known as well.

We walked up about ten feet from the shore.

"How's this?" I asked Lex.

"Perfect."

I laid the blanket down, only to find out Cassie had given me two blankets. I set the other blanket to the side and sat down as I held my hand out for Lex. She slowly sank down. I placed my arm around her, and she snuggled up next to me. She fit perfectly as I pulled her closer to my body. She shivered, and I reached for the other blanket and covered us both up.

"Thank you," Lex said as she turned and looked up at me.

I grinned and asked, "For what?"

"For loving me always."

My heart began to beat harder in my chest. I had to close my eyes and open them again quickly to make sure this wasn't a dream. The waves crashing against the shoreline along with Lex's body slowly moving with each breath reminded me that this was far from a dream. Not even a dream could be this perfect.

I gently kissed her. Pulling back only slightly, I spoke against her lips, "I'll love you for the rest of my life."

"Never leave me, Will."

"Never, Lex."

"Do you promise?"

"I promise you, baby. Never."

libby

I stood on the beach and looked out over the dark blue waters. The sun had already begun to sink beneath the horizon, and I smiled, knowing Will was probably asking Alex to marry him right now.

I slowly inhaled the salt air through my nose and then blew it out. I loved it down here. Something about the wind and the sound of the waves hitting the shore calmed my nerves and helped me forget.

I knew the moment he walked up behind me. I could feel his energy. I closed my eyes.

I can't do this anymore.

My heart cannot take the pain any longer. I needed to tell him I had decided to go back to Zack. I'd already sent Zack a text message saying I needed to talk to him. I didn't love him like I loved Luke. I'd never love anyone like I loved Luke.

He stepped closer, and my breathing increased. I longed for his touch, for his lips to softly brush against mine, and for him to whisper he loved me.

"Hey, Lib."

His voice made my heart drop and my stomach flip.

I took a deep breath and turned to face him. "Hey, Luke."

His smile was forced. Something was on his mind, like something was on mine.

"Do you think Will's popped the question yet?"

I gave him a weak smile in return. "Yeah, probably."

I started walking along the beach, and Luke followed. My phone beeped in my pocket, and I pulled it out. It was Zack.

Luke let out a laugh, and I looked over at him. He was walking next to me but looking ahead.

"Do you remember the time we put salt in your mom's sugar container and Alex put three huge scoops in her oatmeal?"

Luke somehow always talked me into doing his crazy pranks with him.

I smiled and nodded my head as I said, "Yeah, I remember."

Luke started talking about how he'd gotten grounded for that prank as I opened up Zack's text.

> *Zack: Libby, I'm so glad to hear from you. Baby, I understand you were confused, but I'm here. I'm waiting for you if you want to make this work.*

I quickly hit the Home button on my phone and pushed it back into my back pocket. My heart was pounding.

Shit. I shouldn't have texted Zack.

No, I did the right thing. Didn't I?

My head was spinning, and Luke was talking about damn pranks.

I stopped walking and turned to him. I shook my head. "I really need to be alone right now, Luke. I have to think, and I can't think with you living in the past."

His smile dropped, and he nodded his head. I turned and started walking again.

The moment his hand touched my arm, I felt the most amazing rush sweep through my body. I almost wanted to whimper with the way his touch affected me. Zack's touch never did this to me.

I looked up into Luke's eyes. He had the most beautiful green eyes. I could see why women melted when he looked at them. I quickly looked away.

I can't do this anymore. I can't.

"Luke, I can't stand here and pretend like nothing is wrong. Everything is wrong, and I...I need to move on with my life, and I can't with—"

He held up his hand and shook his head. I stopped talking. His eyes searched my face and then moved to my lips. I instinctively licked them, and he snapped his eyes back up to mine where he searched them intently.

I held my breath and waited for what he was about to say.

"Libby, I have something I need to tell you."

thank you

First and foremost, I have to thank God. If it weren't for his blessings, none of this would even be possible.

Darrin and Lauren—I think you both know how much I love you. Thank you for being so supportive. It means more to me than you will ever know.

To my readers/friends—Without you, none of this would be possible. I wake up every day, and I'm stunned that I have such incredible people in my life. Thank you for the words of encouragement. Thank you for buying and sharing my books. Thank you for leaving reviews. Thank you for telling your friends and family about my books. Thank you for lifting me up when I need it most. I'm so blessed to be able to follow a dream that I've had since I was sixteen. To be able to share the crazy stories floating around in my head is just amazing. I love you all, and from the bottom of my heart, I thank you for your support.

Mom—I miss you.

playlist

Kip Moore "Young Love"—Will and Alex in the Prologue.

Kris Allen "Out Alive"—Gunner talks to Will.

Love and Theft "She's Amazing"—Will tells Gunner about his feelings for Alex.

Gloriana "Best Night Ever"—Will and Alex dance at a party.

Dan + Shay "First Time Feeling"— Will and Alex make love for the first time.

Hunter Hayes "Still Fallin'"—Will and Alex dance at the river party.

Sam Hunt "Raised on It"—Everyone is dancing at the field party.

Miranda Lambert "Automatic"—Alex and Gunner ride horses together.

DJ Snake and Lil Jon "Turn Down for What"—Grace dances at Blake's birthday party.

Jason Derulo "Wiggle"—Grace and Blake dance at Blake's birthday party.

Jason Derulo "Stupid Love"—Alex and Blake dance at Blake's birthday party.

Lean Turner "Pull Me Back"—Alex pushes Will away.

Brad Paisley "Then"—At the pond, Will tells Alex he wants to marry her.

Dan + Shay "19 You + Me"—Will and Alex make love on the beach.

Colbie Cailliat "Stay with Me"—Will has a picnic at the clubhouse.

Hunter Hayes "Still Fallin'"—Will and Alex dance before he tries to make love to her, and she panics.

Dustin Lynch "Where It's At"—Will dances with his cousin at the barn dance.

Nat King Cole "Send for Me"—Will and Alex dance at the barn dance.

One Direction "You & I"—Will and Alex are at the barn dance.

Keith Urban "Without You"—Will asks Alex to marry him.

Cascada "What Hurts the Most"—Libby and Luke in the Epilogue.